My Internet Dating

Nightmare

- A Cowboy's Wildest Ride -

a novel by
David G. Brown

REMINGTON GALLERIES
A Publishing House

2

ISBN 978-0-692-75164-0
ISBN – 10: 0692751645

Cover art and design by Peggy L. Stivers

Published by Remington Galleries, May, 2016 www.Remington.Gallery

Dedication

This book is dedicated to Yvette Nall,
Without whose "inspiration" this story
Would not have been possible.
I am sincerely grateful for all you taught me,
But more importantly, I thank you for
Bringing me back to God.
Sometimes, to find Heaven,
You must first walk through Hell.

Special Thanks!

There are so many people who gave me ideas and inspiration, I cannot possibly list them all. The top of the list is Yvette, for inspiring me to get back on the computer to write again! And, my dear friends Rick & Teri Miller for giving me a "dungeon" to lock myself away, while I wrote most of this. And for so much more...

I would also like to thank my sister, Debbie, Connie Keeler, and others, who helped with proof-reading, and for sharing their impressions. And finally, my friend and partner, Peggy Stivers, for her creative artwork and editorial help!

And I wish to thank all of my family, including my grandson, Tyler, my daughters, Danielle and Lindsey, and my step-son Marc. Your support and confidence in "Papa," makes all the difference, every day of my life!

Prologue

There are three kinds of people in this world: those people who do everything "by the book;" those who *refuse* to go by the book, and then, there are people like David Remington, who *write* their own book.

David was always curious about everything new and exciting that he encountered, even as a youngster. He always wanted to know how things worked, and *why*. He was always looking for a "better way" to get to the same destination, but by a different route, perhaps?

David had an amazingly high IQ, and breezed through schoolwork like a child possessed. And unlike most "intellectually gifted" children, David was also an athlete. He was the youngest of four children, his brother the eldest child, with two sisters in between. David used to tell people he had to get strong and tough, just to fight his way to the feed-trough!

In his school days, he had lettered in nearly every sport the school offered, and he was usually team captain. The Remington home soon began to fill with trophies and medals, for each sport he played.

David was fast and strong, but he was never one of the "big kids." In basketball, for instance, he was the shortest member of the school team. Yet, he became the starting point guard, and ultimately captain of the team. In football, David began playing in the Pop Warner program, at eight years of age. It was his first "organized" team sport, which may be why it was his favorite childhood sport. He became a running back, then a quarterback, as his teammates kept getting bigger, and he leveled-off at 5'8".

Athletics was not the only thing Remington excelled at, he was also an exceptional student. He was always placed in the "gifted" or advanced classes, and by the time he reached high school, he was able to skip a year, and he graduated at the age of 16.

Two weeks after his 17th birthday, his father reluctantly signed the papers to allow David to join the United States Navy. Vietnam was just winding down, in 1974, and David's father, an Air Force colonel, did *not* want his son to go to war. What father would? But David was afraid he might miss it!

When Vietnam ended, the military began reducing numbers as quickly as possible. When Remington applied to become a pilot, like his father, brother and uncle, doctors found a glitch in his esophagus, which prevented him from passing a flight physical. Remington was given an Honorable Discharge, under medical conditions.

The whole process occurred so quickly, that David had no idea what he was going to do next with his life. So, he decided to just drive from the East Coast, through Texas and Arizona, where his father was now stationed, as Logistics General for the 12th Air Division.

David stopped many times, along the way, to visit friends and family, and after seeing his parents, in Tucson, he decided to pop up to Las Vegas, Nevada to visit his former best friend, from high school, Keith Wolman. Jobs were plentiful, at that time, in the growing metropolis of Las Vegas, and Keith convinced David to get a job and stick around.

David applied for an apprenticeship through the local Carpenter's Union, and since Vegas was the fastest growing city in the U.S., at that time, he was accepted into the program, and started work on a casino resort hotel, almost immediately. David was still sleeping on Keith's sofa, and he knew after he received a paycheck or two, he would need to find his own place.

Remington made friends easily, and found another apprentice, "Rob" Robinski, a rodeo cowboy, who was also looking for a place he could afford on apprentice pay. So, the two of them rented a house together in the Las Vegas suburb of Henderson.

While they were still moving into the house, Rob asked David if he had any plans for the upcoming Sunday?

"Not really," David replied. "Why?"

"Well, I thought we might go to a rodeo," Rob responded.

"A rodeo?" David asked with a smile. "Cool! I've never been to a rodeo!"

"Really?" Rob said with a sly grin. "Well, I entered us both in the bareback riding."

"I don't know anything about rodeo," David replied nervously.

"We're about the same size, so you can use my equipment," Rob explained. "Just listen to what I tell you, and you'll be fine.

David wasn't entirely convinced, so Rob added, "David, once you ride bucking horses and bulls, you are gonna *love it!*"

So, the very first rodeo he ever *saw*, he was a contestant! Remington's ride lasted about 4 seconds, and when he was unceremoniously dumped onto the arena dirt, he rolled onto his knees, with a huge Cheshire Cat grin on his face! He was *hooked* on the sport immediately, probably because it was the first sport he had ever tried, that he did not immediately master!

It took him two years, and dozens of rodeo-wrecks, before David finally made it to the 8-second whistle. And a year after that, he finally won his first rodeo, and the buckle that goes with it. But, it was just a little, small-time, amateur rodeo, with a little tin buckle—and David wanted more!

Remington knew that, before he could call himself a real bareback rider, he'd have to win in *professional* competition. And thus began a 17-year run for Remington, riding bucking horses, and the occasional bull, in the ProRodeo Cowboy's Assn. David carved his initials on the wooden fences of Cheyenne, Calgary, Pendleton, Houston and San Antonio, as many generations of cowboys had done before him.

He may not have grown up as a cowboy, but he certainly was one now.

Rodeo became just a hobby, when David met, and married Dana, a pretty little redhead who had grown up in Henderson. They had three children, and David knew that rodeo was not a dependable full-time occupation for a family-man. It was just too risky, to pin his family's financial future on "the luck of the draw."

So, he found a great job, working as an air traffic controller for the Federal Aviation Administration, and rodeo became only a "weekend" adventure. He figured, if he couldn't *be* a pilot, he would make a career out of telling pilots where to go!

It is said that "Rodeo is a young man's crusade," and at the age of 42, he rode his last bucking horse. At the age of 50, he retired with full pension from the FAA, and he took his retirement savings, more than $100,000, and invested it *all* in a new business.

This is a man who seldom failed at anything. And, if he failed at something, he would examine his mistakes, make improvements, and try, try again, until victory was his. David was extremely competitive, in all areas of his life. But he was not prepared for the business he founded, nor the economic downturn in America, around 2010.

Slowly, the savings account was being drained, and Remington began working 16-18 hours a day, seven days a week. His frustration and disappointment mounted, and soon he began to take it out on his family. The children were all grown, and David had seven adorable grandchildren, and the love of his beautiful wife, Dana. But it wasn't enough.

Dana finally had enough neglect, and watching their hard-earned savings dwindle, with no say in the matter, so she filed for divorce. It was an amicable split, and they always remained friends thereafter, but at the age of 55, he was suddenly single, for the first time in 35 years. And two years later, he was also bankrupt and had to close his business.

Of course, he still had his pension, although Dana got half of the money, through the divorce. So, David decided then, that perhaps, he was finally *ready* for retirement. He had always dreamed of owning a small "hobby ranch," just 10-20 acres of grass, where he could build an arena, and have a small herd of cattle, a few good horses, and a lot of cowboy and cowgirl friends to share it with.

Of course, that dream always included a woman sitting beside him, so they could grow old together, and never be a burden on their children. However, as David began his search, for the woman he would grow old with, what he found was that the *dating world* had undergone some radical changes, during the 35 years he had been married.

"In this day and age, computers and Smart-phones were the way to meet women," he was told.

So, he decided to take his search to the internet, hoping to find just the right girl, build that little hobby ranch, and live happily ever after. At least, that was the dream.

This story is how the dream of David Remington, was turned into a nightmare… the *wildest ride* that old cowboy had ever seen!

Chapter 1
"The Booty Buffet"

"Bullshit," David Remington said. "On a computer web site? Real girls?"

"That's what I am telling you, man," Chance said, with a wide smile. "I've had a profile on a couple of sites… girls just send *me* flirts! I don't have to do nothing, but pick and choose."

Chance Corbin was David's best buddy, in Las Vegas, and he had been a widower for half-a-dozen years. They frequently got together on the Remington back patio to drink coffee, swap lies, and talk about grandchildren. Usually. But sometimes, like today, the discussion was about how two "suddenly-single old guys," could find romance, or even love, in today's techno-savvy world. "How much do they charge?" David asked.

"They're not hookers! I told you, just regular girls!" Chance was still smiling.

"No, no. I meant for the web site? How much does it cost to sign up?"

Chance rolled back in his chair with an easy belly-laugh. That's what David loved about his buddy… always quick to laugh, and always happy. They were both, technically, Vietnam veterans, but while David's military service had been in a submarine, Chance actually got to see the jungles that David had hoped also to see. But, in David's service time, all he saw was miles and miles of open sea. Chance, on the other hand, saw more time in-country than he should have.

Chance had been Army Special Forces, a Ranger. Seldom did Chance ever talk about his time in the jungles of Southeast Asia, but when two veterans become friends, it slowly comes out… the terrifying stories.

And, after his first tour, he volunteered for a second. After all, what good is a trained "killing-machine," outside of combat? But, during a HALO jump (High Altitude, Low Opening) somewhere along the Ho Chi Minh Trail, his luck changed for the worst. Ordinarily, during a HALO jump, soldiers parachute from 20,000 ft. altitude, or higher. And they free-fall all the way down to just 1,000 feet, where an altimeter in their parachute rigging automatically opens the chute. At that low altitude, the chute barely has time to fill with air, before the soldier lands. That gives the soldier less time to be seen by the enemy, and less time to be a helpless, floating target.

During his last jump, Chance's altimeter malfunctioned, opening just seconds late. The chute never had time to fully deploy, and his comrades in the jump told him later that, he bounced at least six feet, after he hit. Chance didn't remember that part.

Chance spent the next 20-something years in a wheelchair. But his "cowboy heart," would never let him quit trying to get out of it. And finally, in spite of what doctors had told him repeatedly, Chance stood up! He walked with a walker, at first, then a cane, then nothing at all, to support him. That's about the time Chance met David Remington, and they became lifelong friends.

David admired Chance for his winning, "never say never," attitude. He was forever an optimist, always smiling, and even on David's worst days, Chance would bring a smile to his face.

"Some of them dating sites are free," Chance said, "and some just charge like five bucks, or so."

"Wait a minute," David objected, "I heard some of them, like E-Melody dot com, cost like $200 a month?"

"Well, yeah," Chance scoffed. "But you can get the same thing for a lot less, if you look around.

David was not convinced.

"So, have you actually met any of these 'real women,' who have contacted you?"

"Well, not exactly," Chance admitted. But I am flying down to L.A. next weekend to meet this pretty little redhead I've been talking to…"

"Actually *talking*, or is it all email and stuff?" David asked. "Yeah, no…" Chance stammered. "We talk. I mean it starts out just *chatting* on the dating site. To keep your real identity secret, ya know? If you guys like each other, you can swap email addresses and phone numbers. That's what we did."

David was curious. After 35-years of marriage, the dating scene had changed considerably, and David wasn't entirely sold on the whole "internet dating" thing. But, only because it was new to him, and he knew very little about it, except what others had told him.

"Aren't you a little nervous? I mean, flying to L.A. to meet someone you've only seen pictures of?"

"That's what it's all about, man. Meeting people," Chance explained. "You ain't gonna fall in love, until you actually meet in-person… you can fall in *lust*, maybe. But this whole internet dating thing is about *meeting* people, that's all." David looked confused.

"See, what I do, is look at the pictures. If she's cute, we start chatting a little, and if we like each other, I try to *meet* them as soon as I can. That way, you know if there's a spark." "And if there is?" David asked.

"Well, then… you know. You've met someone new, and you can get to know each other better… just like if you met in a bar, or at a church social. The internet thing is just a new way to meet girls, that's all."

"And what if there isn't a spark? When you meet?"

"Well, then, at the very least, you've made a new friend. You visit with your new friend for a while, then go your separate ways."

"Do you have to keep in touch with her? I mean, the whole idea is to find a new *girlfriend*, not just a friend. If this one ain't gonna work? Why keep going with it?"

"That's the beauty of it," Chance said smiling confidently. "You just *delete* them."

"Delete them?"

"Yeah, you know, delete their phone number and email address," Chance explained. "And, on the dating site, you remove her from your list of favorites, and put a 'block' on her, so she can't contact you anymore. Simple!"

"So, no real downside?" David contemplated. "You meet, and if you don't like her, just delete her, eh?"

"Yeah. But I don't think that's gonna happen with me and Darlene," Chance said confidently. "She's 35 years-old, a gorgeous redhead, built like a brick shithouse, no kids…"

"Seriously? If she looks like that, what the heck is she doing on a dating web site?"

"She told me that she was really shy…"

"Oh, please!"

"No, really. She said she has to get to know someone a little, before she can relax and be herself. The dating site lets her look guys over, pictures and profile, and she can get to know them a little, before she ever meets them."

"And if he's a jerk?"

"Then she just deletes *him*, and moves on!" Chance explained. "Everybody does it that way."

Oddly, it made a little sense, to David. He just rubbed his chin, contemplatively.

"Hmmm," he grunted. "Okay, so maybe I will give it a try." "Just sign up with E-Date dot com," Chance said authoritatively. "It costs five bucks a month, but on the free-sites, you get too much spam… people sign up, just to try to sell you crap. You get some of that on E-Date, but not nearly as much."

Chance patted himself on the chest, with a smile, as if, "My work here is done."

"Well, okay then," David agreed. "I'll give it a try. What have I got to lose?"

"You're gonna love it, Cowboy," Chance said as he stood up and stretched. "I've gotta get moving… lots to do today."

"No worries. Thanks for telling me about that E-Date thing. I'll take a look online, today, and maybe give it a whirl."

Chance patted David on the shoulder with a smile.

"You're gonna love it. Good lookin' guy like you? Them gals will be all over you."

Picturing a harem of gorgeous women surrounding him, David smiled.

"We'll see," he said skeptically. "Same time tomorrow?"

"Absolutely," Chance replied, heading toward the back door, to leave. "Right after I drop off my grandson at school."

"I'll have the coffee on," David replied, standing to walk Chance out.

After Chance left, David raced to his computer, and started searching for "E-Date.com" online.

"Well, this looks pretty easy," David said to himself, after locating the site. The web site made it fairly simple by having sort of a "questionnaire" for new members to fill out. It asked about your physical description, height, weight, hair color, eye color, etc., as well as questions like, "What traits are you looking for in a new mate?" and "Write a paragraph describing *yourself* to potential mates." Simple!

After David built his profile, he finally got to see pictures of the ladies, who were also members. The site had a "search profile," where you could be as specific as you wanted, right down to looking for women of a specific age range, specific religion, specific height or weight, or just general body-type ("athletic" to "a little overweight"), or you could be more general, and just mark one or two categories, in the search parameters. One thing David was not interested in, was a *long-distance relationship*. Flying off to L.A., or Cleveland, just to meet someone, seemed like a lot more trouble, and expense, than it was worth.

All the dating web sites had an option of choosing how far away you want to "search," so you could be sure to see only women within, for example, a 50-mile radius. This is the choice David checked.

Age was also an interesting choice. David was 55 years-old, and he had heard that "age appropriate" was plus or minus five-years. But then, Chance was 62, and he was flying off to meet a gorgeous 35-yearold woman, so David decided to go a little younger, on his search parameter, just in case some cute young gal had a thing for older men. What could it hurt? So David listed the age-range he was looking for as 40-60 years.

"That ought to cover it," he thought.

David had been fairly general in his selection of search parameters, leaving most items unchecked. He was mainly concerned with distance, and making sure the girls he saw were not too old, or too heavy. So, he clicked the "search" button, and was rewarded with a few dozen prospective mates, all within 50-miles of Las Vegas, and all between 40 to 60 years of age.

"Man, this is quite a booty-buffet," David thought, looking at the ladies who fit his search parameters.

The way most dating sites work is, when you "search," it brings up potential mates, within your parameters, one at a time, and it lists their age and "home town," or distance from you. At the bottom of their photo, there are two buttons, "Interested," and "Not Interested." If you click on "Not Interested," it moves to the next person.

Members also have an option of reading the lady's full profile, and more photos, if she has more posted (some people don't have any photos at all). If, after seeing what photos are available, and reading her profile, you decide to go further, you click the "Interested" button, and the system automatically sends the lady a note, with your photo, telling her that someone is interested. If someone really strikes your fancy, in addition to the "interested" note, you can also send them a private message, or a "flirt."

"Flirts" are preset little sayings, just a few words or a single sentence, like "You had me at Hello," or you can "send a bouquet," which is just a photo of flowers, but it gets the point across. Whether you send just the "interested" message, a personal message, or just a flirt, the lady will see your photo and profile, and she'll be able to decide if she wants to contact you, or just delete you.

David spent the next two hours "shopping" through the web site, sending out several "flirts," (his favorite was, "Do you wanna go for a horseback ride?") and messages to potential mates in his search parameters. He felt the reference to horses would let the ladies know that he was a *real* cowboy.

David had taken a lot of time, while building his profile, to be as honest and truthful as he could be. He assumed everyone did. He posted several recent photos, so the girls could see him in his boots, jeans and cowboy hat, in a variety of places, like family picnics, rodeos, and just a studio portrait, to show the best possible images of himself.

What David had not considered initially, is that, when he selected his search parameters and he very specifically requested "local girls," he didn't realize that *his* photo and profile were coming up on the Women's pages, according to *their* search parameters. The women might not be so specific, in their search parameters, as David was, as far as *distance*, body-type, age, etc.

This was to be his first "lesson" in Internet Dating. Before he finished his initial "search" of the local ladies, David got his first "flirt." It was a girl from New York... not exactly cowboy-country, but when David looked at the girl's photo, and read her profile, he started to get a little excited.

The girl, sending him his first flirt, was 32 years-old, blonde haired, blue eyed, and so pretty, and well built, that she could have been a model! Remember the old saying, "When things seem too good to be true, they usually are?" Well, David had forgotten that saying, as the blood rushed from his head to, well, you know. As he looked at her pictures, he felt a stirring in his Wranglers that he hadn't felt in quite some time—and all common sense drained out of his head, too.

But, David didn't care about any of that, just then, as lust for this gorgeous lady overtook him. He just couldn't imagine why such a young, beautiful, well-built woman was interested in *him*? But, he desperately wanted to find out why, so he returned her flirt, along with a brief personal message, and his first "internet romance" was already starting.

David suddenly understood why Chance was so enthusiastic about this internet dating! It truly was like a smorgasbord of lovely ladies, just waiting to be picked.

David was also about to find out that, every buffet might have just a little rotten food in it. But he was so hungry, he just dived right in, without bothering to check. He was about to get a case of botulism, so to speak, from the little delicacy he'd found in New York.

Chapter 2
"Who are you? And, where is Darlene?"

Due to all the new TSA regulations, non-passengers were not allowed past the security check-point. So, Chance and Darlene had agreed to meet in the baggage claim area, even though he hadn't checked a suitcase. He carried a small gym-bag, with toiletries and a change of clothes. He was scheduled to return the following afternoon, so he didn't need much for an overnight trip.

Besides, based on what Darlene had told him, that she intended to do to him, once he got to L.A., he probably wouldn't need clothes for very long, anyway. As he approached the baggage claim carousel, he was looking for a 35-year-old redheaded woman, cute as a button, and alone. She said she would be holding a Mylar balloon, with little hearts on it.

At 6'2", Chance had a little height advantage over most of the other passengers, also making their way to baggage claim, from his flight. He saw the balloon right in front of his carousel, but he was still too far away to see who was holding it. His heart skipped a beat, as he had cautioned himself several times on the plane, that she might not even show up.

Once he saw the balloon, his trepidation turned to himself. He was afraid that, when they met, she might run screaming away from the terminal in horror. But he knew that his pictures were fairly recent, and he was in pretty darned good shape, for an old guy. So, he reassured himself, that everything would be fine. His characteristic smile flashed across his face, as he quickened his pace.

"Naw, this can't be right," Chance said to himself, as he saw the woman holding the balloon. She was still looking through all the faces of the passengers, trying to find her man.

The lady with the balloon was, indeed, a redhead, but she appeared to be in her late 40's, and she weighed close to 300 lbs.!! As Chance drew closer, he started looking for another balloon, perhaps Darlene was somewhere else... he just knew this could not be her. Besides, she was supposed to be alone, and this lady had two small children circling her legs, and tugging on her skirt. Unfortunately, there were no other balloons in the area, with or without decorations. His heart began to sink.

"Maybe Darlene couldn't make it, and sent her older sister, instead," he thought to himself. The woman still had not recognized Chance, from where he stood about 20 feet away, off to the side, making himself as *small* as possible. He quickly grabbed his smart phone, and pulled up her pictures. He studied the face in the photo, and the woman's face, and he could definitely see a resemblance.

"It *has* to be her sister," he thought hopefully. So he drummed up the courage, and approached her.

"Darlene?" he said cautiously.

The woman turned, saw Chance, and a huge smile ran across her face.

"Chance," she shouted exuberantly, as she turned her massive frame to him, and clutched him in a bear-hug. One of the children clutching her skirt said, "Mommy, is this our new Daddy?"

The Army Ranger in Chance came out, and he got tough quick, as he struggled to escape her clutches.

"Hey, hold on there, lady," he stammered. "This ain't right."

He still had her picture on his phone, and he turned it, so she could see. She blinked, but kept on smiling.

"Well, yes, that's me," she explained. "It was a few years ago, but I am still the same person you fell in love with, on the internet."

"And a few kids ago, too, I see," he said.

"Aren't they beautiful?" she said brushing her nearest waif's her with her fingers. "I was saving them, to surprise you!"

"Surprise? Ambush is more like it," he said. "Look, this just ain't right…"

"I know I lost my figure, but I am dieting really hard, and in six-months, I'll be back in swim suit shape," she explained. "You'll see." "No. No, Darlene, I *won't* see," he said, as he turned and headed toward the ticket counter, to exchange his return ticket for a flight leaving immediately.

Darlene began to wail, tears instantly rolling down her chubby cheeks. Her children, seeing their mother in tears, also began to cry.

"But Chance… I love you! Where are you going?" she yelled after him.

"Home" he snarled over his shoulder.

Darlene didn't try to follow. She just stood there sobbing loudly, trying to calm her children.

"I've seen some scary shit, in my lifetime," Chance said to himself. "But, that was the most frightening thing I ever saw!"

Chapter 3

"Where the heck is Ghana?"

"Charlene Horton," David said to himself, as he looked over pictures of his New York girl. They had been corresponding for several days, and had just switched from the dating site's communication protocol, to regular email. He had tried also to get her phone number, but she claimed that she had accidentally dropped her phone in the sink, while washing dishes, and he'd have to wait to talk to her, until she got it replaced.

When he inquired about how long that might take, she said she just didn't have the money right now, and as soon as she could afford it, she'd get a new one. For now, she said, the internet would have to do.

"How much could a cell phone cost?" he asked her in an "instant message," or IM, which had a potential to be even "better than a cell phone, anyway," David thought. Computers had web cams, so you could actually *see* the person you were talking to—and *that* had some interesting possibilities!

"About $100," she replied. "That's a lot of money."

David had heard of girls doing stripteases, and even masturbating in front of the camera, for their boyfriends. His imagination took hold, for a few seconds, then, he brought himself back to reality. But, since she didn't have a phone, he figured it was at least worth asking about… not the striptease, not yet anyway, but at least while they were IM'ing each other on the computer. "Do you have a web cam?" he typed.

"No," she replied. "I have an old computer, and it didn't come with one."

"You can buy one, and just attach it to your old computer," he said. "They're even more expensive than a new cell phone," she replied.

"Heck, I just bought one at Wally World for $60," he typed.

"Not in New York," she typed-back.

"How much there?"

"I think I can get one for about $150," she responded quickly. "But that will *really* have to wait. I can live without a web cam, but I am dying without my phone! Once I get enough money together for the phone, I'll start working on a web cam, for you."

"Darn," David typed back. "I was hoping to at least be able to see you, live and in-person. You're so gorgeous and sexy!"

"And, you're so darned handsome, I just can't wait to be lying naked in your arms."

"What's this?" he thought. She had never used the word "naked" before. Maybe they were moving to "the next level," whatever that was? It was a term he had seen used on the dating web site, a few times, on girl's profiles, and such.

"Yes, I have imagined it many times. But at least, with a web cam we could *see* each other naked?" he typed hopefully.

"Oh, YES," she responded. "If I had a web cam, I could show you *all* my special places."

The idea of seeing this delicious young, beautiful woman *naked* was almost overwhelming to David. And here she was, offering to show him *all* her special places. The man had not had sex with a woman in nearly six-months! His sex-drive, which had lain quietly for so long, was now gripping him tightly by the balls. He did a quick calculation in his mind.

"You know, I could just send you the $150 for a web cam," he offered.

"That's sweet of you," she replied. "But, as I said, I really need a phone first. And that's another $100."

"Okay, so I'll send you $250," he typed in quickly.

"Really? You would do that for me?"

"For US," he replied. "It would be well worth it, just so we could see each other naked! ;)"

"Oh, my gosh," she replied. "That would be so amazing. Thank you... but there's something I have to tell you, first." "What's that? You're not married are you?" He added, sort of as a joke, but also nervous about what she had to tell him. "Well, I had to leave New York... about six months ago." "Had to?" David asked.

"It's my grandmother," she replied. "She got very sick. Grandpa died about two years ago, and she was all alone. She was in and out of hospitals, for six months before I got here, and her insurance money was nearly gone. She used almost all she had left to buy me a one-way plane ticket, so I could come and care for her. She's a wonderful lady, and I love her so much. But now, I haven't a job, and we're struggling month-to-month, just to get food and pay our rent."

"Have you applied for food stamps, or public assistance? Surely you qualify for that?"

"That would be nice, but I am not in America any longer. My family emigrated to America when I was just a little girl. My grandmother lives in Ghana. That's where I am now."

"Ghana?" he responded. "Where the heck is Ghana?"

"It's a small African country near the Ivory Coast."

"But you've got blonde hair and blue eyes? I thought Africa was mostly Black people?" "It is, silly, but there are White families here, too," she typed back. "My great-great grandfather came here from England, when it was still under the British Empire rule, and he had a huge cocoa plantation."

"What happened to that?"

"Wars, followed by independence from England. All our land was taken away when the new government of Ghana was formed. My grandpa could have moved away, but Ghana was the only home he had ever known, so he went to work in the shipyards, and they did very well. But my father and mother hated it there, so when I was very young, they emigrated to New York. That's where I grew up. And now, with only Grandmother left, and a few of my cousins, I had to come here to take care of her. It's quite simple, actually."

"Heartbreaking, is more like it," David responded.

"Oh, it's not so bad, really. Except now, that we are so broke. Things are very difficult for us."

"So, the price of the web cam, and the phone? Are those your local prices? Can you even get that stuff in Africa?" David asked.

"LOL. That's so funny! Yes, not everyone in Africa runs through the jungle in loincloths," she typed back.

David pictured her for a moment in just a loincloth. He shook his head again, to clear it.

"My cousin has a verification number with Western Union. I've used it before."

"I've never used Western Union. How do I go about it?"

"I'll email you all the information you need. They must have cash, of course…"

Charlene finished explaining the process to David, and he took notes, just to be sure he remembered all the details. Later, she emailed him the name and address of her cousin, and his verification number.

David thought it all quite strange, but he figured, she would have the money by tomorrow, and it would take maybe a day or two to get the new web cam, and get it installed. And then… naked-city!! Once he saw that luscious body, it would all be worth it.

Chapter 4

"Wake up and smell the coffee"

The smell of freshly brewed coffee, wafted gently through the kitchen window, where David and Chance were sitting on the patio enjoying the cool, early morning air of the Nevada desert, as they often did. Chance wore a look of humility, and David was grinning like a kid at Christmas.

Chance had told David the whole story, about meeting Darlene in Los Angeles. And like a puppy with a pillow, David ripped into him, and quickly tore him to shreds, albeit with sarcastic humor. It had always been the Cowboy-Way, to go straight to the humor of any tragedy, personal misfortunes or even surviving acts of nature, like tornados and earthquakes. But, once a cowboy took his good-natured ribbing from his buddies, they would usually let the poor fellow off the hook. "Well, Amigo," David said patting Chance on the shoulder. "You learned a valuable lesson about making sure, whoever's picture you are looking at, better be recent. Get her to send you a 'selfie,' from her cell phone, next time."

"You got that right," Chance said humbly. "I was just thinking with the wrong 'head,' that's all. Her picture was just so cute! I couldn't believe someone that young... well, you know."

"Well, at least your fat girl, was actually a girl, and not out to get your money," David said, pushing back from the table, and practicing his look of humility.

Chance had taken his razzing well, and now, David knew, it was his turn! Chance leaned in closer, a smile beginning to play on his face.

"What's this? You mean Charlene?"

"Actually, 'Charlie' is closer to the truth," David admitted.

Chance's face lit up, as he crossed his arms, and bellowed with laughter, waiting to hear more.

"Well, you remember, I sent her money to buy a new phone and a web cam?" David asked.

"Oh, yeah," Chance replied. "I told you that all sounded kinda funny."

"Yeah, well talk about thinking with the wrong head!" David confessed. "After I sent the money, I sent her a message, to make sure she got it, you know?"

Chance was nodding his head, and rubbing his chin thoughtfully. "Anyway," David continued, "She tells me that her grandmother had a small stroke, and had to be taken to the hospital…. And she had to use all the money to pay for the hospital admission. She said Granny was still in there, and they won't release her until they get another $250, to pay her bill."

Chance could see what was coming, and his face showed it. "So, Daddy Warbucks," Chance chided, "what did you do?"

"Well, I told her I wasn't about to send any more money! I told her I had already sent twice as much as I intended… I just wanted to buy her a web cam, that's all."

"Ah, the 'Little Head," again," Chance remarked humorously.

"Yeah… that's right," David replied. "Anyway, I started looking on the internet for information, and I found this web site…" David pulled a piece of paper out of his shirt pocket, and slid it over toward Chance.

"What's this?" Chance asked, unfolding the paper. On it was printed http://ghana.usembassy.gov/romance_scam.html.

"It's the U.S. Embassy, in Ghana, warning people about the scammers who live there. Apparently, diamonds are the top revenue source, for Ghana, and internet scams run a close second!" David might have been stretching the truth, just a bit, but it made a better point.

"So, what'd you find out?"

"Well, the article I read on the Embassy web page said that they have these 'internet cafes,' where the locals skip around, to avoid getting caught, and they often work in teams on these scams." "How they do that?" Chance asked curiously.

"Well, they go online, to these sexy cam-girls' web sites," David explained. "They download pictures of the girl, and sometimes even video. Then, they make up a new name, post the pictures, and a make-believe profile, on dating web sites… like those pictures was actually them!"

"Well, at least Darlene's pictures were really her… just really old pictures!" Chance said.

"Anyway," David continued, "they had a bunch of pictures posted there, on the embassy web site, and sure enough, there was Charlene!" "You're kidding?"

"And, I recognized two or three of the other girls' pictures from the dating web site! They had links to the real cam-girl web sites, and I found out that 'Charlene's' real name is Autumn something. College kid in upstate New York, paying for her schoolin' with her web cam. It's a pretty sophisticated business, actually."

David continued his story, telling Chance how he paid for, and downloaded, a few nude photos of Autumn, or "Charlene," from her web page. "Always glad to help a kid pay for college," he'd said. Then, when he had gotten back online with "Charlene," later yesterday evening, she was continuing to cry about "Granny's" poor, miserable plight, being held prisoner in a hospital, until she could pay enough to get out. "Look, I sent you $250, so I could see you on the web cam," David had told her, the night before. "Or at least, you could use the cell phone I paid for, to take a few photos of yourself."

"I told you, I had to use all the money, to pay for Granny's hospital," Charlene replied. "And it is still not enough."

"Look, here's what I'll do," David had offered. "You send me a few pictures of you naked, and I'll send you the money for your grandmother."

"But, I have no such pictures," she said, registering shock and dismay that he could even be thinking such things!

"Well, here," David said, as he attached a few of the nude photos he had downloaded from Autumn's web site. "Use some of mine."

He clicked "send," then added, "You know, for a few extra bucks, you can download the nude shots, when you go there to steal the girl's freebies. You might want to try that, next time."

David told Chance the whole story, from the previous day's conversation with "Charlene." He said, she/he/they initially tried to deny it, but caught red-handed is caught red-handed.

"The guy actually had a pretty good sense of humor," David concluded the story. "He already had a web cam, and he turned it on to give me a salute, for figuring out the scam!"

"Seriously?" Chance asked.

"Yeah, no shit. He was a very dark-skinned African, and all around him, I could see the internet café, and a half dozen other Black scammers, working the computers. After he saluted, he clicked off, and vanished forever into cyberspace."

"No shit? That is freaking amazing!" Chance said, too stunned to give David the razzing he had coming.

"Oh, it gets better," David said. "I went back onto the dating site… to report 'Charlene' to the web administrators as a scammer. Then, I went to the girls' pictures I had recognized from the embassy web page, and turned them in, too. But, before I did, I had a little fun with them! Hell, I was up until two in the morning!"

"Whatcha talkin' about? '…had a little fun with them?'"

Chance leaned in, to listen more attentively. He didn't want to miss a single detail.

"I'd find one of the fake profiles, and send an IM," David explained. "If they didn't answer right away, I just reported the profile to the web master of the dating site, with a link to that embassy mug-shot page."

Chance leaned back, with a big grin. "And, if the girl did answer right away?"

"Ah, that's when it really got fun," David laughed. "It was a pure battle of wits. I'd come on like a guy with a broken heart, and let them love-up to me." "Yeah, then what?" Chance asked trying to hurry Dave along. "I always told them I was a rich cattleman," David explained. "Instead of them hooking me on sex appeal, I was hooking them on greed. It turned the scam around." "Did it work?" Chance asked.

"About half the time," David continued. "Once I figured out that the reverse-scam had played out, and I knew they weren't going to beg me for money until later, I'd just ask them, 'Oh, how's the weather in Ghana? Is it as hot as they say?'" David laughed. "Usually, they just deleted the IM's, and vanished. So, I reported them to the web administrator. One of them actually told me that "he-she-they," were actually in Nigeria, not Ghana… and yes, it was hot!"

"And what if they did ask for money?" Chance asked, totally enjoying the story.

"Oh, then it was easy," David responded. "If they took the bait, I'd just tell them I would not send a dime until I had seen them naked, either on a web cam, or at least photos. Then, I'd just do to them, what I did to Charlene…offer to let them have some of the ones I had of 'them.'"

Chance sat back and laughed. "That's
unbelievable," Chance remarked.

"Hey, some of them even had some nude photos, so I'd wait until they sent them before I called their 'game,' and reported them. But, one African-scammer even had a video of the cam-girl, they must have recorded the screen when they had paid her to do it."

"Did they play it for you? I mean, how could they do that?" Chance asked.

"I'm not sure how they did it, but it really looked like it was 'live.'" David said. "It was pretty cool."

"Yeah, but was it worth two-hundred-fifty bucks? You could've gotten a hooker for that much!" Chance said, getting in his first "digs," at David's misfortune with Charlene.

"Yeah…no," David admitted. "It dang sure made me feel better, though. Especially, getting half-a-dozen of them scammers off the dating web site… but NOT worth $250."

"You know, all them scammers you reported, they'll just change pictures, and start all over again tomorrow," Chance said, factually.

"Yeah, I know," David admitted. "But it sure made me feel good last night! One other thing I read on the embassy web page was that, most of the scammers really are broke… it's a desperately poor country… so they said most of the scams occur on the cheaper dating sites, or the free ones."

"Ah, that makes sense," Chance said. "So what about the more expensive ones, like E-Melody?"

"Well, I checked into it a little," David replied. "And, E-Melody does 'identity verification,' so there's no chance of the scammers getting in. Some of the other dating sites do, too. But, a lot of them don't check at all, so you just got to be careful."

"Man, I had no idea shit like that was going on," Chance said rubbing his head.

"Me neither," David agreed. "But, I'll tell you what… that's the last time I'll go on one of those 'cheapie,' dating sites. Tonight, I'm going to do some 'comparison shopping,' and see if I can find something a little better… even if I have to pay more for it."

"Now that makes a lot of good sense, Cowboy," Chance agreed. "Let me know what you find out."

"Yeah, Buddy," David said confidently. "No more scammers for me!"

"Me, neither," Chance added.

"No, sirree, Amigo… No more scammers for me!"

Chapter 5
"It's all about the sex!"

David logged onto his computer that evening, fairly early, so he could start "comparison shopping," between the dating sites. He hoped, with a little more expensive site, that he could avoid the "Ghana Girls," and the "Cam-Girls," like Autumn, who made a lot of money with their web cams. When he typed "Dating web sites," into the Google Search, it came back with well over 100 sites. David just rubbed his eyes and blinked.

"Dang," he said aloud. "I might be here all night!"

But he wasn't. Did you ever wonder why men can't get anything done, when they set out with a good, solid plan? Sex. The minute a man gets even a whiff of a woman in the neighborhood, all rational thinking stops!

"Hold on here," David said scanning yet another page of Dating Sites. With so many to choose from, David had decided to just scan through, and write down the names of those he thought looked promising.

"BeNasty dot com? Hmmmm…"

He clicked on the link that took him to the Home Page, of BeNasty.com. After reading a few disclaimers, and verifying that he was over 18 years of age, he filled out a quick profile, and took a look at what the site had to offer!

Boy, was he tickled! Like most sites, it allowed him to "join" for free, and fill out a profile. But, like most, for new members to actually flirt, chat, message, or contact, any of the women on the site, a person had to sign up for a full-paid membership. So, this time, he decided to see what kind of women, and pictures, were being presented, before paying for a membership.

"Wowwee!" he exclaimed, as the pictures started loading on the "Search" page. "This site is only $25 a month," he said to himself. "And half the girls are naked! Or at least topless. Dang, dang, dang! This is where I should have been all along! It is all about sex!"

David had typed in the same parameters he had used on his other site: the girls had to be within 50 miles, and between the ages of 45 to 60. Almost immediately, he began to get IM's from young, pretty girls from all across the country, and even around the world! He patted himself on the back, realizing that the only reason a pretty, young thing from Copenhagen would want to flirt with him, was that she was a cam-girl, or a Ghana Girl. So he just deleted all those, and sent messages out to a few of the "normal-looking" women, who fit his search profile.

Then, he got a message from a gal who looked like a normal lady. She was 40-years-old, and lived in the Dallas area. David had family around Ft. Worth, and north of Dallas, so he decided, if she was for real, he could just combine a trip to meet her, with a visit to see his family.

Kim had dirty-blonde hair, hazel eyes, and a very nice figure for a gal her age. She didn't have any topless or nude pictures, which was another reason David figured she was a legitimate member of the web site, and not just farming for cash. But, she did have a picture of herself in a very sexy teddy, with a lacy top and sheer panties, which left little to the imagination.

After looking over her profile, and a few more "regular" pictures, he was convinced that she was real, so, he decided to respond to her message. Then, she replied to him, and said she had found his profile to be "fascinating." Thus began David's newest "riding" adventure in internet dating!

One thing David learned, right off the bat, was that, while dialogue on most dating sites, between interested members, was almost overly polite and stilted, not so on BeNasty. It seemed, right from his first contact with Kim, they were on "advanced" level (David still wasn't sure about all these "levels" but he was trying to catch on), because the very first time they IM'd, on the dating site, they talked about sex. While it was not the only topic of conversation, sex was the center of interest for both parties. But, David also knew that a good, healthy sex-life was a critical part of any new relationship, and he figured, this site just made it the top priority!

Actually, except for open talk about sex, and a lot of naughty photos, it wasn't much different than other dating sites. David learned that Kim was involved in a "difficult" situation where she lived. Her "boyfriend" and herself had, essentially, broken up, but were still living together, as many former "couples" do, because of the high cost of moving, and living alone.

David was immediately suspicious that she might be reaching for his wallet. However, the subject was lightly touched upon, and they moved on.

Over the next several days, they "chatted" online, sometimes two or three times a day, for hours each time. As with other Dating Sites, prospective matches need to get to know one another. They talked about their families, and hobbies, and such. With Kim living in Dallas, which has more New Yorkers living in it today than Native-Texans, and with her being born and raised in Arkansas before moving to Dallas, Kim had never even met a real rodeo-cowboy.

"Shoot," David typed into an IM message to Kim, "You don't even know what Texas is about. You've got to get out to the small towns, like Boyd and Decatur, where my Mom and sister live. THAT'S Texas! People will smile, and say 'Howdy,' just passing on the street."

David learned that Kim owned a ski-boat and trailer, which were currently parked in the yard where she lived. Which, she explained, was one of the reasons she was still living there. Finding a place to store the boat was going to be a little more expensive than she had thought.

Kim had explained that, since it takes at least two people to ski – one to drive the boat, and one to ski – that pastime is what drew her, and her current ex-boyfriend together. So, rather than doing the "tourist thing" in small-town Texas, if they had any free time, they were off to one of the numerous lakes, in the area. Which was another reason she'd never met any real cowboys locally, because her ex had always been with her on those days.

David had learned to water ski when he was just 4-years-old, at his grandfather's cabin on Lake Otsego, in Michigan. And, since he was retired from rodeo, and he knew that swimming was a great way to stay in shape, becoming involved with a gal who owned a boat might be both interesting, and good for his health. Especially with a gal like Kim, who had a terrific figure, and said she preferred sunbathing in the nude, when she could find an isolated beach, or island, to park her boat.

David and Kim decided to move "to the next level," whereupon they traded real email addresses and phone numbers, to get away from the Dating Site's communications protocol. David was proud that he had been looking for all the signs of a rip-off, and hadn't seen anything yet. But he was leery about Kim not having enough money to move, which may or may not be a real issue, as far as his wallet was concerned.

Remembering Chance's misfortune, with Darlene, and her 15year-old photos, David wanted to be sure that he was not looking at old pictures of Kim! But he wasn't real worried, because he had shared Chance's LA story with Kim, and they both had a good laugh.

"Well, you don't need to be worried about that with me," she had said. "What you see, is what you get."

"Well, what I have seen, I really like!" David had replied.

Now, since they were talking, or texting, on cell-phones with cameras, he thought he would just ask her to send something.

"Would you mind sending me a new "selfie," just so I can be sure that, you are you?"

He didn't want to mention his "romance" with "Charlene," who turned out to be a Black man! But, he still felt the sting, when he thought about it.

"I'd love to," Kim purred. "I'll show you mine, if you'll show me yours…"

"That sounds like a challenge," David laughed. "I accept!"

They agreed to hang-up, and switch to texting. Neither of them was really savvy about the new phones, so rather than take a chance of disconnecting the call, it was easier to just text, when pictures were involved.

A few minutes later, her photo began to load onto his phone… adding a few centimeters at a time to the downloading photo, like a curtain slowly being lowered to uncover a beautiful statue or piece of art. First, the top of her head, then her face, then her bare shoulders…

"Holy shit," David said to himself, as he realized, not only was she as cute today as she had been in her Profile Pictures, but the photo was a medium shot, from her waist-up… and she was topless! "Yippee kay yeah!!" he exclaimed.

He took a deep breath, his mind racing at the possibilities…

"WOW!! Well, okay then," he typed. "You showed me yours, so I guess I'll show you mine."

"I'm counting on it," she purred in her reply.

"And let me just say, OMG! What gorgeous boobs you have!" David gulped.

Very quickly, he took off his shirt, put on his best cowboy hat, and made sure he was wearing a nice buckle with his Wranglers. Then, he took a quick look in the bathroom mirror. It had been more than a decade, since he had ridden his last bucking horse, but he still looked pretty darned good, for a man of 55, he thought. His belly was still tight, and his chest was still well-defined, but he had lost a lot of muscle, through neglect, and spending most of his time, since his last ride, sitting in front of a computer.

He held his camera-phone up, and took a picture of himself in the mirror. After a few attempts, he finally felt he had the right "look" on his face, so he sent the photo. "MY topless shot," he typed into the message.

Apparently, while he was taking his "topless shot," she had been busy also…

"Nice! ;-)," she typed in response.

But, before he could begin another text, his phone "binged," and another photo of Kim began to download. As the photo slowly began to unveil itself, the first thing he saw, at the top of the photo, was her belly button, with a diamond belly ring. He gulped.

"Now we're talkin'," he said to himself.

As the picture finished loading, it was framed from her belly button to the top of her knees. She was wearing some incredibly sexy red panties, fairly sheer, giving just a hint of the treasure that lie beneath.

"Your turn," she typed with a smiley face.

"So, underwear, it is," David said, rushing off to his full-length bathroom mirror.

He was almost giggling, as he pulled off his Wranglers. David had never done anything like this… taken "sexy" pictures of himself. He found that it was very fun, and somehow, exhilarating, and yet, also quite liberating. He decided to ramp it up a notch, and instead of just a picture of himself standing in his underwear, he hooked his thumb in the waistband of his boxers, and pulled them down a little, so that he looked like some sexy, young GQ model.

"Oh, Baby," Kim typed in quickly. "That is making me SO hot!"

Her next photo began to download very soon, and it was a close-up of just her exposed genitals. Her fingers were visible, sliding through her wispy blonde pubic hair. David sucked in his breath… "Wow," he said to himself. "That is the sexiest picture I ever saw!"

By the time they finished sending photos back and forth, they had both achieved orgasm, and David had been introduced to modern "phone-sex." Afterwards, David called her up, and they talked for a little while.

"We just had our first sexual experience," David had told her, "And we haven't even met in person, yet. That's freaking amazing!"

"Oh, just wait until we do actually meet," she purred. "I don't know if I'll be able to wait until we leave the airport!"

"You know, I have always had this little fantasy," David said hesitantly. "About airports,"

"Ooooh, it sounds fun already!" Kim replied.

"The girl meeting me at the airport is wearing a cotton, summer dress, that buttons all the way down the front... and nothing underneath."

"It gets awfully windy here, sometimes," she objected playfully. "That's the whole point," David smiled. "And you can unbutton a few top buttons, and a few bottom buttons, so that you are dangerously close to being over-exposed!"

"If I did that," Kim said, matter-of-factly, "there would be no way I could wait until after we left the airport parking garage, before I jumped all over you!"

"If I knew you would wear that," David replied, "I would order my plane ticket, today!"

"So, when do you get here?" she asked erotically.

"Well, when is a good time for you?" he asked nervously. "Wow, this is so fast," he added, to himself.

"Let me check my schedule, and make sure we're not going water skiing next weekend," she said. "Is that too soon?"

"Maybe, just a little... I have to make reservations, and get someone to hold down the fort, here, while I am gone." He said, going over all the details in his mind. "How about the weekend after?"

"Sounds good," Kim replied. "I'll tell my ex that I am going away to Tyler, for the weekend, to visit my sister. He'll buy that."

David was a little nervous about the pretension with her ex-boyfriend. He figured, if they were really on the splits, she wouldn't need to make up an excuse like that. But he didn't care, at this point, because he had a girl here, who was going to make his "airport fantasy" come true. Then, she was going to spend the entire weekend with him, having crazy-wild sex!

"Mama...Sis... I got some good news and some bad news," he said to himself. "I'm coming to Dallas in a few weeks... that's the good news. Bad news is, you're never going to know I was there!"

41

Chapter 6

"Welcome to Dallas, Cowboy!"

David walked briskly from the jet way, heading toward baggage claim. He had already sent a text to Kim, and she responded that she was already waiting for him near his baggage carousel... in a button-down cotton dress. He didn't ask what she wore underneath, but he suspected that it was nothing at all!

As David came through the double-glass doors that separated the secure gate areas, from the unsecure baggage claim area, he saw her immediately. She was standing beside a concrete support column near the carousel, which had not yet begun running. Kim saw him a moment later, as he approached her, and she fairly leapt into his arms. They kissed, a long, deep, passionate kiss, as David pushed her gently back into the concrete pillar.

There was a method to his madness, as it were. With his arms wrapped around her, none of the other passengers could see that his hands had slipped down to her bottom, and he was erotically rubbing her cute tush. And, he noticed immediately, she was not wearing any panties. She responded to him, by pressing herself more tightly against him, and wrapping one of her legs around his.

"Ummm," she groaned passionately.

Suddenly, with beeps and flashing lights, the carousel came to life, and bags began to come up the conveyer. It snapped the lovers from their sexual reverie, as David pulled away, stepped back, and just admired this very lovely woman.

During her wait for David's plane, she had buttoned her dress up, a little more conservatively than described in David's "airport fantasy," but as she pulled him in for another gentle kiss, she discreetly unbuttoned two more top buttons. When they pulled away, so David could go search for his suitcase, he noticed that it was now fastened just below her sternum. Her C-cup breasts were barely held under the dress, and any sudden movement threatened to expose them to the world. He was delighted!

"I'll grab my bag," he sighed, breathing deeply. As he moved toward the carousel, Kim turned toward the column, and unbuttoned two more buttons, from the bottom of the dress. David was busy watching the bags come up the conveyer, and didn't notice until he turned around. Then, he saw that the dress was open, up to a point just inches below her crotch. The dress itself fell below her knee, and it was free-flowing, so only a hint of her thigh showed, as she walked.

"Where are we parked?" he asked, bag in hand.

She nodded toward the door leading to the parking garage, then looped her arm through his, snuggling against him as they walked.

"I can't wait to get those jeans off of you," she whispered seductively, as the doors to the outside opened automatically, allowing a gust of wind to blow her dress open in the front... just enough that David caught a quick glimpse of Heaven, before she reacted quickly to hold it closed.

"That was perfect," he smiled.

She gave him a knowing look, and she released the dress again. As they walked across the sky bridge to the parking garage, there were no people coming the opposite direction, so each time the wind opened the skirt just a little, she allowed it to flutter in the gust, displaying for David, brief glimpses of what he had seen, only in pictures, up until now.

"There," she said pointing. "The red Ford dually." "Nice truck," he said as they approached.

He stopped behind the truck to bend over and grab his suitcase, while Kim walked toward the driver's door, digging in her purse for her keys. David tossed his bag into the back of the truck, and eased up behind Kim, as she was unlocking her door.

From behind, he wrapped his arms around her torso, and gently kissed her neck and ear. She leaned back into his arms, enjoying every touch of his lips. He glanced around, and saw no one who could see anything more than their heads, from a good distance, so he slipped one hand into the lower opening of the skirt, and gently stroked her fine public hair... and then some. His other hand found its way into the opening up top, and he caressed one of her gorgeous breasts.

Kim moaned again, then turned around to face him, her lips seeking his, in another deeply passionate kiss. His displaced hands quickly found their way to her bottom, and he pulled her dress up, so he could squeeze her bare cheeks, with both hands. After a moment, Kim kissed David on the nose.

"The motel isn't too far, is it?" she asked climbing up into the driver's seat.

"Actually, it is a bit of a drive," he replied honestly.

Dallas Love Field was basically in downtown Dallas. Boyd was 35 miles north of Ft. Worth, some 60 miles away. But, David had a buddy in Boyd, who had several hundred acres of ranchland, and he had said he might let Kim park her boat there for free. The rancher had several 18-wheelers, and various pieces of heavy equipment parked out near the barn, as well as a camping trailer, a motor home, a horse trailer, and a long stock trailer. David knew his friend would not mind the boat being there, so he figured, if he and Kim stayed in a motel close by, he would be able to take Kim over there, introduce her to him, and get his permission.

Besides, Boyd had a nice motel, which featured a "Honeymoon Suite," with a hot tub in the room, a round bed, with a huge mirror over it, and romantic furnishings to boot.

"How long of a drive is it?" she asked skeptically. "You've got my motor running now, Cowboy. I'm not sure how long I can wait!"

"Boyd," is all he said, as he leaned in for another long, deep kiss.

45

The dress, which had barely covered Kim's lady-parts when she was standing, rose up a few inches while she was seated, and it covered nothing, now. David's hands worked their magic on her body, and she began breathing deeply in anticipation.

As David continued his firm, rhythmic foreplay, their tongues plunged deeply and passionately inside each other's mouths. Her breathing became so erratic and intense, she was soon panting, like a puppy after a long run! Finally, she gripped the steering wheel like a NASCAR driver, and released a loud, intense moan of ecstasy.

While she slumped down, trying to catch her breath, David stepped back, closed her door, and walked around to the passenger side to get in. He was grinning like a cat who had just eaten a canary! Kim let out a soft breath of air, as he closed his door.

"Well, that ought to hold me, for a while," she said wistfully, finally catching her breath, and letting a playful smile play across her face. "At least until we get to the room."

"Well, I'm glad you enjoyed it," David responded, proud of the pleasure he had brought to her.

"Now, it's your turn, Cowboy," Kim said, leaning over in the seat, as she reached for his belt buckle.

Within just a few seconds, Kim skillfully, yet teasingly, took him into her mouth. It didn't take very long before it was *his turn* to push back and moan loudly, with his eyes closed tightly.

When it was over, he sat perfectly still, his eyes still clenched tightly. The sound of the truck firing up startled him out of his reverie, and his eyes popped open.

"So… Boyd, huh?" Kim said putting the truck in reverse and heading for the exit.

"Ah, yeah," David responded. "Super-Eight on highway 114," he sighed. To himself, he added, "I can't believe I just got a blow-job in the parking garage at Love Field! And, oh, my God, this was so much *better* than any fantasy I *ever* had about airports!"

That was the beginning of a non-stop, "Honeymoon" weekend of sexual activity, unequalled by any in David's lifetime, including *his own* honeymoon, which had been fairly intense! The room he had found was, appropriately enough, the Honeymoon Suite, which featured a hot-tub in the room, a circular bed with a mirror mounted on the ceiling, and a walk-in shower, for two. The ambiance was all very romantic, and Kim had brought along a half a dozen pieces of lingerie, none of which was worn for more than a few minutes, before it lay crumpled on the floor.

The only time the lovers left their room, it was to get a bite to eat, or run to the store for more wine, or munchies. David became a little concerned, however, when they were out of the room, and able to talk just a little about the status of their "relationship." Kim usually steered the conversation away from her and David, and she would bring up other issues.

David told her about his friend, whose ranch was just a few miles up the road, and that if she wanted, they could go meet him, and possibly have a place to park her boat. According to Kim, that was the only thing keeping her from moving out from her boyfriend's house. And, since David was starting to have *more* than just sexual feelings for this little blonde bombshell, the *last thing* he wanted was to have her living with another man, even if they were, technically no-longer a couple. "Oh, I think I have the boat taken care of," she said. "Why don't we just jump in the hot tub, instead?"

It was an offer David could not refuse, and going to meet his rancher-friend was never going to happen. He felt badly for being so close to friends and family, and not even telling them he was here. But he also knew that, if they never knew, no one could be offended by his decision to remain locked in the Honeymoon Suite for a weekend. As far as anyone here knew, he was still in Las Vegas!

By late Sunday morning, they checked out of the hotel, and Kim began the drive back to Love Field. David sat quietly for a few minutes, realizing that, while they had spent an incredible, romantic weekend together, he actually had learned *very little* about this sexy lady. He knew that he was not "in-love" with her, but also felt he could wake up every single day, for the rest of his life, sleeping next to her. He hoped that she felt the same way.

"You know, as much fun as all this has been… and, wow, has it been fun," David began. "We never really got a chance to talk much, you know, about _us_."

"What about us?" Kim replied, shifting nervously in her seat. "Do you want to plan another trip like this, soon?" she asked with a coy smile.

"No, goofy-girl," David said. "I was talking about us moving our relationship forward. We did meet on a dating web site, you know?"

"David," she said placing a hand on his thigh, "we met on a sex site, not a dating site." He was confused.
"What's the difference? I mean, it _says_ it's a dating site. I don't get it."

"Honey, most of the people who are on that BeNasty web site are just looking for a 'hook-up,' or a wild weekend, if they're lucky, like we just had. It was great."

"Well, it was amazing," he agreed, thinking of the airport fantasy, now checked off on his 'bucket-list.' "So, this is it?" he asked sincerely, finally getting the picture.

"Unless you want to start planning another weekend? My husband is going…"

"Husband?" David nearly shouted. "I thought you and, ah, what's his name, were just living together?"

"We are living together," she said, "But, we're also married." She saw the downcast look of hurt on David's face.

"I'm sorry. I really thought you knew," she added tenderly. "He really _is_ a jerk. And, I'm pretty sure he has a girlfriend, on the side. If I'm lucky, we might have sex once a month… or every other month. He never touches me unless he's wasted. So, I signed up for BeNasty dot com, and decided to just take a walk on the wild side. You're not my first weekend lover, you know?"

David finally, and fully, understood. He just sighed deeply. Not another word was spoken until they got to the airport. She parked the truck, and walked around to the other side, as David pulled his suitcase out of the back. He set the suitcase down beside him, as Kim walked up and they embraced.

"You might not have been my first," Kim said sincerely, "but you were definitely the best. Ever."

David smiled, recalling the wild weekend. "It *was*

fun, wasn't it?" he replied with a sly smile.

"Yes, it was," she purred softly, stroking his cheek. "And, that's *all* it was… an amazing, sexual, weekend."

David nodded his head, gave her one last, long kiss, then turned and walked toward the ticket counter with his suitcase. He never looked back.

"Well, at least she didn't weigh 300 pounds… and she surely wasn't after my money," he thought to himself. "And, I guess if I had to take a wrong turn *looking for love*, finding wild-monkey sex, instead, ain't a bad way to go!!"

When he returned to Las Vegas, he cancelled his membership in the "sex" site and determined to get back onto his list of dating sites, and try, try again. He was *still* in the market for a new wife!

Plus, David recorded yet another sink-hole in his book of internet dating perils… you've got to make sure they are not *married*!

Chapter 7
"Getting to know you."

David and Chance finished their usual "morning coffee," which allowed David to tell Chance every detail about his "sexual-weekend" with Kim—with even a few twists he made up, just to make it a better story. After Chance left, David got right back to his "research" on various web sites.

It never occurred to David to look, even one-time, for *a book* about internet dating. Most of those books clearly give warnings, which may have kept David from banging his head against the wall, so many times! But, that just wasn't the "Cowboy-way!"

Some dating sites, like Match.com, actually have their own books, or booklets, on common scams and stumbling blocks most "newbies" encounter. Even bestselling novels, such as *"Men are from Mars, Women are from Venus,"* would have given David *some* insight into the changes in dating, since the 1970's, when he was last "on the market." Also, many celebrities, especially talk show hosts like Steve Harvey and Dr. Phil, have their own "self-help" finding-love books. And, there are dozens of other dating books by bestselling authors, too.

But, that all just seemed like too much work for David. He was only looking for *one* girl! How tough could that be? He was certain that he would not need to read a book, just to find one girl?

David was a cowboy, and no matter how tough the bronc, he always just put his rigging on, and nodded his head, taking whatever the bronc had to throw at him. Sometimes, he'd have the winning ride! And sometimes, they'd haul him out of the arena on a stretcher. That was rodeo, of course, but it was how David approached *life!*

When a young cowboy is first learning to ride, he gets thrown off a lot. But, the "cowboy-way" is to get right back on again, even if you have to get a few stitches and bandages, first.

So it was, for David, in the Internet Dating arena, too! He felt that he was just *learning to ride* in a *new event*, internet dating, and he was getting thrown, a lot! But, he was determined to dust himself off, and get right back on!

"Well, this looks interesting," David said to himself, after typing "dating web sites" into his search engine.

It was a "consumer" comparison of web sites, and listed the top-five, ranked by experts, and complete with user-reviews. He typed http://www.consumer-rankings.com/dating/ into his address bar, and gave the site a look. The #1 site listed was "Zoobie.com," for matchmaking. David looked no further…

"Now that's what I'm looking for," David mumbled aloud, as he clicked on the link that would take him to Zoobie.com, the top-rated dating web site, on the internet.

As with most dating sites, David was learning, Zoobie allows people to "join" for free. In fact, most *require* you to fill out, at least a basic profile, before allowing you to browse their offerings. And, it is only after doing all of that, does a new member find out what it is *really* going to cost.

Yes, the initial membership is free, but if you want to *communicate* with anyone you might find on there, you must first purchase an "upgraded membership." So, David filled out all the initial "free" membership forms, uploaded a picture, and filled out a basic profile, then he put in his usual search-parameters of age (45-60), and location (within 50 miles) and began to look.

"Hey, these are some good choices," he thought looking at the first few "potential local matches."

He was very much interested in a particular girl, so he clicked the "flirt" button beneath her picture. The Zoobie web site responded with a pop-up page that indicated that, if David wished to actually *contact* any of these girls, he would have to pay *just* $29.95 for a month.

"What the heck," he thought. "For thirty bucks, I'll play in this sandbox for a month!"

So, he pulled out his credit card and filled in the information. Soon, he was searching and flirting to his heart's desire. As with his previous attempts at "finding true-love," David was looking for someone nearby, but again, *his profile* was coming up on the ladies' pages, all around the world. He felt perfectly comfortable deleting the "hits" he was getting from the young and beautiful girls, because he figured, "What cute, young girl is gonna flirt with a broken down old rodeo cowboy, unless they are up to no good?"

But, Tina McNabb was much different, although he wouldn't learn her real name for a few days, yet. She sent him a flirt, from Louisville, Kentucky, and there was something about her photo and profile that piqued David's interest. The profile stated that she was 41-years-old, obviously not a cam-girl or a Ghana-girl, but still quite young. Her photo looked more like she was in her early 30's. She worked for her county government in a clerk's job, and had been single for several years. On the surface, she looked fairly "normal," so David contacted her via the dating site's message option. She responded back.

After a few days of general questions and answers, between them, they decided to "move to the next level," and exchange personal email addresses and phone numbers. Tina had one grown daughter, she said, from her first marriage, but the girl was an adult, and living a few miles away from her mother. Tina told David that Brianna, her daughter, was more like her best friend. She told him that the two of them became very close, when her most recent husband fell into a whiskey bottle, and came out an abusive and potentially violent monster.

Tina said, she didn't mind getting knocked around a little, it was *her man*, after all. But, when he gave *Brianna* a black eye, Tina drew the line, and had him arrested for assault. David's heart swelled. There were few things he hated more than a woman-beater.

He had raised two daughters, and when they each got married, and to both new husbands, David had "the talk." In it, David explained that he was old, and had lived a terrific life, with a lot of wonderful memories.

"If God should take me right now, I would die a happy man," he explained to both sons-in-law, on their wedding day. "And, you know, every father, who loves his children, will tell you, that he would give his life, in a second, if it would save one of his children from harm. It sounds quite touching. But, I'll take that one step further.

"Here is *my* _promise_ to you – if you ever raise a hand to my daughter… if you harm her in any way at all… I will kill you. It's not an idle threat, it's a promise. You'll never see me coming, and you'll never have a chance to try to talk me out of it. Hit her one time, and you'll get a bullet in the back of the head. That's my promise. Now, go build a wonderful life, with my little girl."

That is how much David hated men who get physical with their women. So, when Tina told her story, David was very sympathetic and compassionate, and he congratulated Tina for having the courage to call in the police. "A mother's got to protect her baby," Tina had said.

"A mother also has to protect *herself*," David had added. "You should have called the cops the very first time he hit you. It might have stopped him from getting into the *habit* of turning to his fists!"

Tina agreed, and promised if anything like that ever happened to her again, the police would be her first option. David was glad to hear that, and he also said that physical violence was something that she would never have to worry about with him.

Since they were in the very early stages of just getting to know each other, David found it tough to ask the really hard questions, like "Can you show me your divorce papers?" so he could be sure she was single. But he was convinced that she was not a Cam-girl, or Ghana-girl, so he relaxed a little on that one. But there was one thing that bothered him… she only had a few pictures up, and every time he asked her about getting some new ones, just for him, she had a ready excuse.

Her favorite line was, "When Brianna and me escaped from that monster, we just packed our clothes, and ran away. I have a great little instamatic camera, but it is in a box somewhere in the house. And the

54

since I have a restraining order against him, well, it works *both ways…* I can't just pop over and get it. It's all very complicated."

"But Tina, what about the camera on your cell phone?" he asked her one day.

"That bastard threw it at me one day, when I was walking out the door," she replied, choking back tears.

A cowboy is always susceptible to a woman crying, so he bought the story, even before she finished telling it! Sex and tears, are both sure ways to motivate a cowboy. "Oh, my gosh," David replied sympathetically.

"Yeah, it shattered the screen, but I can still make out texts, and obviously the phone part works, because here we are talking on it. But the camera function won't come on at all."

She went on to explain that, it had been a very nice, and rather expensive, phone called a "Caramel," which she had gotten for free by signing a new three-year agreement with her service company. That part was good, but there was still a year remaining on the contract, and she was not eligible for a new, free, "upgraded phone," until the current contract expired.

"And I can't afford to just buy a new one, because, dang, they cost like $350," she finished.

"It's a Caramel?" David asked, to be sure.

"Yes, that's right. You heard of them?"

"Heard of them?" David responded. "Heck, I have two of those things somewhere around here in boxes."

He told her that, when his business was running, he bought two of the Caramel phones, and issued them to his employees. When the business shut down, and he had to let his workers go, they returned the phones. They were disconnected, and he just shoved them into a box for storage.

"Shoot, these things are already paid for," he continued. "I can just put one in the mail to you, and you take it down to your service provider… bingo, bango, they'll swap phones, and you'll be back in business, with a brand new phone."

"Really? Do you think that would work?" she asked.

"Of course it will," he confirmed. "I've done that a few times myself... swapped phones. It's simple. And once you get the new phone, you can send me some new 'selfies' that you'll be able to take with it." "Oooh, Baby," she purred. "If I had a new phone, I could send you some really *sexy* pictures! But you've got to promise not to show them to anyone!"

David gulped, feeling the stirring in his jeans.

"Well, ya know," he stammered, trying not to let his libido take control of his brain. "That would be completely up to you... but, shoo-howdy, it would sure tickle this old cowboy, plumb to death!"

In that instant, even without actually *seeing* her sexy pictures, his "big-head" went to sleep, and his "little head" took over! He told her that he would find the phones, and put one in the mail to her the very next day. She giggled again.

"I have a pink one and a purple one," he offered. Which would you like?

"Yes, yes, the pink one!" she exclaimed excitedly. "I would love to have a pink phone! It'll make the other girls so jealous!" "Then, pink, it is," David replied.

"And when that phone gets here," she promised, "I am gonna go to Vicky's Secret and buy a brand new lace teddy, just for you. And, when I take new pictures, I'll be wearing my new lingerie... at least for a little while!"

He gulped again.

"Oh, Sweetheart, that would be amazing!" David gulped. "So, where do you want me to send it? I don't know exactly where you live, just Louisville."

"Hmmm. Well, first off, I don't actually live in Louisville," she said.

All David could think of, when she said that, was his "Ghana girl," who had claimed to live in New York. But Tina hadn't asked for the phone, he had offered it, so he felt a little better about it. "Then, where do you live?" he asked reluctantly.

"Well, it's a little town called Paoli, across the border in Indiana," she explained.

David breathed a sigh of relief.

"It's only 50 miles to Louisville, and when people come visit, they have to fly in to Louisville."

"Okay, well, that's not so bad," David remarked. "So, where do you want me to send your phone?"

"Well, the apartment where I live, see, when packages come in, they just leave them by the door," she explained. "And I'm afraid some kids might run off with it, or something."

"Okay, so what are you thinking?" David asked.

"I think you should send it to me, here at work," she replied. "All the county offices are in the Orange County Courthouse, and once it gets to the courthouse, nothing ever gets stolen! I work in the county business license department."

She gave him the full address, which he typed into his phone's "notes." That way, he figured he could just bring it up, after the new phone was boxed and ready-to-ship, and write down the correct address.

"Perfect," he said. "Like I said, it'll be in the mail tomorrow."

"Oh, Baby, I can't believe you are doing this for me," she purred again, like a little sex kitten. "Just wait... you'll see... when you get those pictures I am gonna send you, you are gonna be *so* happy!"

"I might even send some sexy pictures of myself, right back to you," he offered.

"You better," she admonished. "If I'm going to let you see, well, *all of me*, then I darned sure expect to see all of you, too!"

David was intensely excited at the prospect of seeing *all of* Tina. And he figured, if she wanted to see "all of him," then perhaps she'd even take it up a notch, and maybe they could have *phone sex*... in living color! Or, he was thinking quickly, he might consider something even better.

"Tina?" David asked. "I know that I am just getting to know you, but so far, I really like you a lot."

"David, I feel exactly the same way! You know, it's like we've known each other forever. I just feel like I can talk to you about *anything*."

"I know what you mean," David replied more confidently. "I feel exactly the same way, but…" "But?" Tina asked.

"But, we've never even met in-person, yet," David concluded.

"I know… and I can't wait," she said breathlessly. "What did you have in mind?"

"Well, I have some frequent-flier miles left over, from my business trips last year," he explained. "So, I could fly to Louisville for free. I could rent a car, or something, and drive up to Paoli to meet you."

"Oh, my," she exclaimed excitedly. "There's really nothing here in Paoli, so why don't I meet you in Louisville?"

"That would be terrific," David chimed-in. "We could get a really nice hotel, go out to dinner at a fantastic restaurant…I'm sure there's a few in Louisville?"

"Oh, yes," she agreed. "A romantic weekend in Louisville, with you, would be amazing!"

"Well…" David interjected. "You see, there's the catch. They won't let you use frequent flier miles for weekend travel. So you'd have to arrange to take some time off work, and we could meet during the week. What do you think?"

"Well, I work for the county, so we get plenty of vacation time," she replied thoughtfully. "How soon were you planning to come visit?" David's brain was quickly calculating. He knew that, to cash in his free-miles, he had to make the reservation at least a week in advance. And since Tuesday was the slowest air-travel day of the week, chances are he wouldn't get bumped. So, he quickly brought up the calendar on his phone, and looked at the dates.

"How about… eleven days?" he said, finally. "I can fly in on Tuesday, the third. You can pick me up at the airport, and we'll go to the hotel…"

"Have you ever stayed at the Sheraton?" she asked excitedly.

"I've stayed at a few different Sheraton's, but I've never been to

Louisville."

David also remembered how *expensive* those stays had been. But what the heck?

"Oh, please, please, can we stay at the Sheraton in Louisville? I promise, I will do things for you, in bed, that will make your head spin, if we stay there!"

"Yeah, yeah, sure," he stammered, wondering about those "head-spinning moves."

"Oh, it is so beautiful!" she continued. "It's really close to the airport, and every time I go pick someone up, I look at that beautiful hotel and wish I could afford to stay there, just for one night, even."

"Well, how about two nights?"

"I'd better get more than one teddy at Vicky's Secret," she said. "Okay, so here's the plan," David continued. "You'll need to put in for three days off, the 3rd, 4th and 5th. Once you are sure you have the time off, I'll book my reservations to fly in on Tuesday, the 3rd, and fly home on the 5th. Then, we'll have all day on Wednesday to do the 'tourist-thing,' in Louisville, and see all the sights. What do you think?"

"Oh, David, I wish I could hug you, right now!" She exclaimed breathlessly, "That sounds like the most romantic thing, ever!"

"I know, I'm getting really excited, too," David confessed. "And it's not *just* about the sex!" he lied.

"Oh, I don't know about that," she countered. "I can't think of anything else, *but* the sex! Oh, the rest will be fun, too. I just can't wait to wrap my legs around your naked body!"

David noticed that it was not just a little tingling in his jeans, it was a full-fledged <u>salute</u>! And, a man with an erection has *absolutely* <u>no</u> *blood* flowing to his brain!

"Okay, when you go in tomorrow, put in for those days-off, and as soon as you know you've got them, I'll make the reservations."

"Oh, you bet, Honey. I'll go in early tomorrow, just so I'll have time to fill out the paperwork, before I even clock-in!"

"How long does it usually take to find out?"

"Oh, they always get back to us the very next business day," Tina replied. "But since tomorrow is Friday, I won't find out until Monday."

David knew that he had to make the reservations on Monday, if he was to use the free miles. But he *all day*, and since Louisville was on Eastern time, and Las Vegas was on Pacific Time, Tina would be at work for hours, before he even got out of bed.

"That'll work," he said. "Just text me, the second you find out for sure."

"I really don't think it will be a problem," she said. "But, you're right to wait… just in case."

"Okay, Doll… dang, it's one o'clock in the morning, your time! You'd best get to bed, so you can get up in time to get to work early!" David said.

"Oh, you're right! Boy, I was enjoying our conversation so much, I just forgot what time it was. I need to get going… but David?"

"Yeah, Hon?"

"Tonight, I am going to sleep naked. And, I'll be thinking of you, sleeping naked beside me." David gulped.

"Well, now, Darlin'," David replied throatily. "If'n you do that, there's a good chance you won't get a wink of sleep."

"Who needs sleep, as long as we're naked together?" she replied in her sexiest voice yet.

"Well, we're not together yet," he admonished. "So, get your little bottom to bed, and get that vacation-time put in for, you hear?"

"Ooooo, I love it when you take command, Cowboy!" she said sweetly. "And, don't forget my phone… or the Sheraton?"

"The phone will be in the mail, first thing in the morning," he said, "and I'll call the Sheraton as soon as my airline reservations are confirmed."

After they disconnected, David just sat there, humming a playful little song to himself.

"Oh, my, my…" he said to himself. "This cute little lady might be *just the one* I've been looking for! Oh, my, my, my!"

Chapter 8

"Welcome to Louisville"

There are no direct flights from Las Vegas to Louisville, and by the time a passenger changes planes in Detroit, it makes for a very long trip. Plus, flying West to East, you lose an additional three hours, so David decided to take the "Redeye," leaving Las Vegas at 1:00 a.m. He figured that, once Tina picked him up, at 10 a.m. local time, they would be going straight to the hotel, and he could catch a nap... after their first romp in the hay, of course!

David had arranged, as with his previous encounter, to meet at baggage claim. He said he'd be easy to spot, because he'd have on a purple cowboy shirt, and a black cowboy hat, which he thought would be fairly unique in Louisville. And it was.

He had spoken to Tina the night before, and she sounded totally excited about their romantic get-away. She vowed to be at the airport early, in case she had trouble finding a parking space. David was happy that she was so excited... almost as much as he was, it sounded like. Since David didn't know what Tina would be wearing, as he approached the baggage claim area, he made himself very visible, by walking to the side of the main flow of travelers. Meanwhile, he was straining to see every woman, who was alone, had blonde hair, and was about his height.

David saw no one who even closely resembled Tina, as the carousel came to life, and began disgorging passenger bags. Of course, he was still looking at the older pictures of her, which Tina posted on her dating profile. For some reason, the phone he had mailed to her more than a week ago, had still not arrived. He thought it very odd, but packages sometimes take a lot longer to deliver, so he didn't give it much thought. He knew he'd be able to take his own pictures of her, once they met up.

"Where are you?" he texted to Tina. "I'm at baggage carousel #3." There was no response.

His signal strength was very weak, as was common inside airport terminals, due to all the electronics, so, after grabbing his suitcase, he headed outside to wait for her, and he would try to call her, if the signal improved.

Outside, on the passenger pick-up sidewalk, his signal strength was four-bars of 4G, so he placed the call. Tina's voice came almost immediately on the phone.

"Tina, where the…" he said quickly, before he realized that he was listening to her voicemail greeting. "Damn."

David knew something was definitely wrong, but he was certain it must be something simple like, car trouble in an area with no cell service available. It couldn't be anything else, except something as simple as that, he was sure. He looked at his watch.

"I was on the phone with her just twelve hours ago," he mused.

"And, she was as excited about this trip as I was."

He even recalled her saying that, if anything happened to her car, she would *walk* to Louisville to meet him, if she had to. Surely, she was on her way? Surely, she could get to a phone, by now? Surely…

David waited curbside for nearly two hours, before he caught the Sheraton's "airport shuttle" bus, to his hotel. In order to get the "discounted rate" of a mere $350 per night (a 25% discount), he had to pay *in advance*, on a non-refundable reservation. He rationalized the cost of the expensive room, because his plane ticket had been free, and also, with his libido racing wildly out of control, he was imagining all the ways Tina would "thank him" for the incredible room.

After sitting on his suitcase for two hours, and calling or texting Tina every ten minutes, or so, with the same result; his libido had shut down completely, and he realized, she wasn't coming. That's when he decided to go check in at his hotel, and get some sleep. He was exhausted after spending the whole night on a plane, or in airport terminals.

"Welcome to Louisville," the hotel clerk said with a deep Southern drawl, and a cheery smile. "Is this your first time to visit our lovely city?"

David was in no mood for pleasantries. He was tired, cranky, and he'd seen about all he cared to, of Louisville.

"Remington, David," he said, ignoring the clerk's questions. "I've got a pre-paid reservation, and I am exhausted. I just want to check in, and go to my room."

The smile vanished from the clerk's face, as he began typing quickly into his computer. It was only one o'clock in the afternoon, and David knew check-in time wasn't until three. But his icy stare was just *daring* the clerk to tell him he would have to wait! If he did, David would give him both barrels!

David knew it was Tuesday, a slow hotel day anyway, and the nearly empty parking lot confirmed that the place should have many unused rooms ready for occupancy. The clerk got the silent message.

"Here are your keys, Sir," he said with an efficient smile. "The elevator is to the right, and you'll be on the eleventh floor with a beautiful view of the city. Would you like some help with your baggage?"

David took the keys, and his copies of the registration paperwork the clerk had offered him.

"Thanks. No." David said, as he walked toward the elevators.

He tried calling her one more time, before he went to sleep, and it, again, went straight to voicemail. He hung up, again, without leaving a message. What was the point? He'd already left several. He finally faced the fact that she wasn't coming.

"Why?" he kept asking himself. He reasoned that, well, Charlene was clearly after money, and Kim was clearly after sex... but why would Tina do this to him? For a used cell phone? It just didn't add up.

By the time he woke up, from a very fitful sleep, it was nearly 8:00 p.m. He wandered down to the coffee shop, the least expensive place to eat in that hotel, and by the time he ordered a hot turkey sandwich, a plan was beginning to take shape, in his mind.

He went up to his room, grabbed his laptop, and decided right then and there, since the hotel's WiFi was free, he'd just spend the next few hours, signing up for yet another dating site. This time, however, he decided to go straight to the top... the most sophisticated and elite dating site on the internet – E-Melody. It was also the most expensive.

David had seen the commercials on television, and knew that, not only did they have a very extensive questionnaire, to begin a new membership, but they also verified whatever information they could, which was much more than any other site. It was nearly midnight, before he finished all the forms and questionnaires, but when he looked at his profile, it really looked nice. As always, he had been very, very honest and straightforward, and didn't "fudge" on a single item. He actually thought everyone did this, but he was having his suspicions.

In the morning, he caught the hotel's airport shuttle back to the terminal. His flight didn't leave until the next day, but he knew it was the best place to rent a car, for him, so he could just turn it back in, at the airport, the following day.

Today was supposed to be the day that he and Tina went sightseeing in Louisville. But, he figured, he'd already seen enough of the city. He was wearing his blue jeans, hat and cowboy shirt, but he also added a Western suit-jacket. It made him look like a cattle baron, or something, but definitely, he could pass for a businessman.

After he climbed into his mid-sized sedan, he pulled out his phone, and looked at his "notes" section. The address was still there. He quickly typed it into his GPS navigation system, and headed down the road.

"Well, I think maybe I'd like to do a little sightseeing, on my own..." he said aloud. "...starting with Paoli, Indiana, and the Orange

County Courthouse."

He dialed up a Country radio station, which was easy to find, being so close to Nashville, and in just over an hour, he was sitting in the parking lot of the courthouse. It was an ancient building, very stately and beautiful, with a curved dome and a spire. The cornerstone had "1886" inscribed on it. But, next to the courthouse, attached by a breezeway, was a more modern, two-story office complex, with a sign in front that said, "Orange County Administration Building." David took a deep breath, and exhaled slowly. "Alright, boys and girls, it's *show time!*"

David stepped out of the car, with his small leather briefcase in his hand. He left his hat in the car, and smoothed his jacket, as he headed toward the doors. When he stepped into the breezeway, there was a directory listing all of the major departments, the floor, and room number, as well as a small arrow to point the way. "Well, this ought to be easy," he thought.

The sign pointed the way to the business license department, in room 211, second floor. David climbed the first set of stairs, then easily located the business license department. A pair of businessmen were approaching from the opposite end of the hallway, deeply engrossed in conversation, and oblivious to David's presence. The men turned, and entered the licensing office, so David just followed them inside.

The office was laid out, in typical government fashion. There was a counter to his right, with a dozen blank forms displayed, and signs explaining which forms needed to be filled out, for which purpose. Directly ahead was where the line formed, to speak to an administrator, and along the left, was a long counter that stretched the entire length of the room. Part of the counter was a hinged "gate," that could be lifted, to allow the office staff to come and go.

The two men David had entered with, apparently, already had their forms, so they kept walking past the forms-counter, to the hanging sign, which indicated "Line Forms Here." There was one woman ahead of them.

Directly behind the long counter were two small desks and computer stations, where one county employee was handling all the

"Walk-in" customers. Further back, were a half dozen other desks, arranged so that three were along the window, and three were closer to the long counter.

David stopped at the forms-counter and pretended to be looking over the document offerings, so he could find the right forms. He was actually studying the people working there. He observed that the girl serving the customers appeared to be in her early twenties, with dark hair and eyes, and a distinctly Hispanic accent. So David turned to look at the desks behind the counter.

Two of the desks were unoccupied, two had male employees seated at them, both busily working on their computers. Then, at the two remaining desks. there was a Black lady, and a rather obese White woman. The black woman was talking loudly on the phone, to someone who "just didn't get it." The large White woman had a man, who was wearing a suit, seated at her desk, and they were talking quietly, while going over his paperwork.

"This may not be as easy as I thought," David mumbled to himself.

Since he had actually *spoken* to Tina, he immediately dismissed the male employees, leaving just the Black woman, and the White woman. He rationalized that he had been fooled by a Black *man* before, although he never actually *spoke* to the person pretending to be Charlene. Of course, there were two empty desks, and since neither of the female employees looked even remotely like Tina, he began to think that, perhaps, Tina had actually taken the day off, even if it wasn't to go to Louisville.

But, since he had come this far, he figured he would just play out the hand. He could easily hear the Black woman talking on the phone. She talked slowly, with a deep Southern drawl, and very poor grammar. "That is definitely not the voice I heard," David surmised, and he dismissed the Black woman, as a suspect. "Well, that leaves one White woman, and two empty desks. Now, what am I gonna do?"

David tried to hear the woman's voice, as she was still talking to the man in the suit, but with all the office chatter, ringing of phones, and so forth, it was impossible to hear. He studied the woman, without trying to seem like he was staring at her.

The lady's face resembled that of a Bulldog, with hanging jowls, but her eyes were clear and bright, and when she smiled, he could see that, perhaps, once, she might have been pretty. But, it was hard to tell. She was built like a linebacker for the Dallas Cowboys, with very broad shoulders, and the fat on her upper arms rolled like the tide, every time she moved her hands. David had always had difficulty guessing women's ages, especially fat women, but he figured this lady to be in her early 50's.

"That is certainly not Tina," he thought.

But he still had his doubts, so he continued watching her. Then, an idea popped into his head. He pulled his cell phone out, and hit "redial." It took a few seconds to connect, but at the very first ring, the fat lady began shuffling papers around, looking for something underneath. She came up with a cell phone... a pink one. David recognized it immediately, as his.

The lady looked at the caller I.D., silenced the ringer, and put the phone away. David listened in stunned silence, as Tina's voicemail greeting played in his ear.

"Well, I'll be damned," he whispered softly.

David continued to watch, in fascination. The man at the desk was now gathering his paperwork, and the large woman stood to bid him farewell, and shake hands. David still refused to believe that it was Tina. But, as the gentleman began to walk away, the lady called out to him.

"Bill," she said in a loud, clear voice, "...don't forget your coffee cup."

It was the same voice. It *was* her!

David felt the anger beginning to well up inside of himself, as he contemplated just rushing back there and taking his phone away from her. But, looking around at all the warning signs, he knew the instant he lifted the gate, at least four people would call security. And he had no way to prove the phone was his. He just stood and glared at her, as she sat back down.

Then, as he watched, something strange happened. The big smile melted off of her face, and a look of sadness overcame her countenance.

She glanced around, to see if any of her co-workers were watching, as David pretended to be filling-out a form. She picked up her pink cell phone and looked at it. David knew *his* was the last call, and it would still show his number as a "missed call."

"Well, I'll be damned," he said, as Tina stared at the phone, and began to wipe away tears. She stood quickly, and rushed to the gate, heading for, David assumed, the ladies' restroom. He heard her sob, as she brushed past him, not even giving him a second look.

When she had left the room, David eased over to the gate, as if to get a better look at an instruction sheet, which was taped to the counter there. He looked at Tina's desk, and he saw a framed photograph… it was obviously a family picture, of "Fat-Tina" and a slender, blonde woman. They had their arms around each other, and huge smiles on their faces. The blonde woman, he recognized immediately as a picture of the woman *he thought* he was meeting in Louisville.

"Her own daughter," David said with disgust. "She used pictures of her own daughter!"

He turned and walked back to his car.

It was a long drive back to Louisville. At least, long enough to give David time to put all the pieces together. His anger turned to pity.

From what David could gather, Tina was not satisfied by only living vicariously, *through* her daughter, so she moved it up a notch, and had actually taken *her identity,* and posted it on the dating page. Using her daughter's looks and charm, that old bulldog of a woman found herself, for the first time in her life, *wanted* by men. She could be sexy, and flirty, and men desired her. David knew that it was probably the only time in her life that she could know the joy of being a desirable, vivacious and sexy, young woman.

But, if that were the case, why hadn't she told him *before* he flew to Louisville? Why had she continued the pretense, right up until the time he left his home, for the airport?

Then, he figured it out! She continued the pretense, because, a part of her really was planning to go there, to meet him. Like Chance's "cute little redhead," who turned out to be part water-buffalo, Tina must have argued with herself that, if she went and actually met this guy, he might just love her, for *who she really was.*

But, in the end, she lacked the courage to go through with it, canceled her vacation time, and just went back to work. The pink cell phone was her only reminder of how special she had once been, to some cowboy in Nevada.

"She can keep the danged phone," David said out loud., as he pulled into the parking lot of the Louisville Sheraton.

"I think this whole thing hurt *her* a lot more than it did me…"

David knew he should have learned his lesson about seeing recent pictures, especially selfies taken with a cell phone, from his buddy Chance's experience with the redhead in L.A.

"Well, if it's true you learn lessons from your mistakes," David thought to himself as he boarded his plane back to Las Vegas, "…then, I'm dang-sure gonna have a college degree in online dating, before this is through!"

Chapter 9

"Checklist Rule #1 – Keep it close to home!"

During the long flight home, David had a lot of time to think, mostly about his dating experiences up to this point. His father had been a pilot, and when David worked for the FAA, he had spent countless hours flying "jump-seat" in the cockpits of commercial airliners.

He had made the observation then, that "flying is simple. Just follow the checklist." Commercial pilots had checklists for every different phase of flight, from push-back to shut-down, and for every step in between, there was a checklist.

"That's what I need," David realized, "…a checklist! And, if so much as *one item* is _not_ checked off, the relationship goes into a holding pattern, until the item is resolved.

"And I'll start my checklist with a set of *rules…*"

He pulled out his laptop, and placed it on his tray table. He opened a new document, and titled it, "Dating Rules," then, the very first item, in bold letters was, "Rule #1 – Keep it close to home!"

Despite the fact that he had, ultimately, felt only pity for Tina, and he honestly bore her no ill-feelings, the fact remained that, even with him having a free airline ticket, he had spent quite a bit of money on this trip. Worse, David was no closer to finding a new wife, than he had been before. His bank account was very low, and his credit cards were all nearly maxed-out.

After a few basic rules, including one rule, stating that David would actually *study* the lady's profile before attempting contact, to make certain they had things in common, he began listing "checklist" items. His final "deal-breaker" rule was, "No alcoholics!"

The "rules" stood alone, and a separate "checklist" sheet would be made up for *each* potential match, once the prospective couple had made contact. "Communication," he had learned, is what they call the "first-level," whatever that was?

The top item on his checklist, for each new girl, was to get her to send a cell-phone "selfie." It didn't have to be a sexy picture, or even a good photo... just something she snapped _now_, and texted to him immediately, so he could be certain of exactly *who* was on the receiving end of his romancing.

After adding a few more items to the list, he reflected on his own, "run-n-gun" approach to the ladies. As soon as a girl showed him even the slightest interest, David realized, he was going right from the starting gate, directly to the finish line, without taking the time to actually *run the race*. With Tina, for example, he had only been communicating with her for two weeks, when they were already planning to have a romantic get-away. That was just way too fast!

He added this to his rules: "Slow down! Take time to develop a friendship, ensure you have things in common, before moving forward."

David was still a bit confused about the whole online dating scenario, and he had been rushing through it like a bull in a china shop. He tried to draw a comparison between meeting someone in person, like in a bar or bowling alley, or even a church social; and "meeting" them online. David felt that the whole point of online dating was simply to _meet_ people.

He reasoned that, if you see a cute girl in a bar, buy her a drink, and she smiles an invitation to you, well, you walk over and introduce yourself. You would know *absolutely nothing* about this girl, shoot, she could be a serial killer on the run from the law. Who knows? The only thing that brought you together was a physical attraction. That's it.

David also knew that, when meeting a stranger in person, the one very positive thing is, you can look into each other's eyes. David believed that "the eyes are the key to the soul, and the soul resides in the *heart*."

Over the years, he had developed a keen instinct about people he met, and, if he could feel that hair rising on the back of his neck, he knew it spelled trouble. He had learned to *trust* his instincts about people. He also knew that, the only way to get that feeling, was for him to look into their eyes.

With women he met in-person, he was looking for what he termed, "magic." There had to be, sort of, a cosmic-connection between them, if they were truly to, first, become friends, then lovers. So meeting people in-person was *all about* attraction, and zero about information…until you actually start talking. Then, you can look into her eyes, as the questions are asked, and the information flows. Oh, sure, she could be lying, but David realized most of the women online "fudged" just a bit, on age, weight, and so forth, so what was the difference?

The difference, he knew, was in the *eyes*. In person, he could look into her eyes, and his instincts would kick in, about whether she was right for him, or not. Another bonus, he reasoned, is that, while talking on the phone, you can *hear* some reaction, perhaps, to what he was telling her, but in-person, he could watch her body language, to see if a smile jumped onto her face, or a frown. He'd see the sparkle in her eyes when she laughed, so he would know that it was not pretentious or fake.

Online dating, on the other hand, was exactly the opposite. Oh, sure, you can look at posted photos, but people of all genders and descriptions, will generally post the photos that, *they feel*, make them look their *very best*. (if it's a real photo of her!) That's human nature.

Can you imagine anyone, male or female, staggering into the bathroom, immediately after arising from bed, and snapping a selfie of that "morning face?" Perhaps they could take it, but they would never *show it* to anyone

So, David concluded, online there was a *very basic* opportunity for physical attraction, if the posted photos are accurate (see checklist). But there is absolutely <u>no chance</u> to feel "the magic."

On the positive side, however, people can read data on height and weight, and David had learned to add a "plus or minus" factor, depending upon the woman's (or man's) vanity. Men can also read what the woman was looking for, in a man, or vice versa. Most sites list people's hobbies, the types of movies and television they watch, and even what a "perfect" romantic evening would be, for them.

Yet, despite the mass of information available on a person's profile, especially with sites like E-Melody which have extensive questionnaires, David had found, that most of the women he "met" online, wanted even *more* information! Most women, he discovered, had very, very extensive checklists of their own, and many pushed their information gathering almost to the point of neurosis.

"To summarize," he concluded silently, "…meeting in person, equals "magic" with no information, and dating online equals information, with no magic."

And without magic, there can be no romance. But, without information, there can be no long-term relationship. Both were necessary ingredients, he surmised, in a search for a new wife.

The result of his thoughts were a decision, on his part, that he would study all of the information a potential mate posted on her profile, and look over her posted photos, to see if he could imagine himself in those pictures with her. If a basic, but general, attraction existed, David vowed that, after making sure all of the items on his new checklist were marked, he would suggest that he and his potential love-interest should meet as soon as possible. He felt, there was no sense going through reams of information, if there was no magic. And, the only way to discover if there *is* magic between a couple, David reasoned, is to *meet in person*. If the magic exists, he thought, then the information will flow a lot more freely, anyway.

He reflected back, on the night before when, in his hotel room, he had perused the "offerings" of his new dating site, E-Melody. Yes, it was the most expensive dating site going, but David rationalized the expense by figuring, people like Tina would be screened-out, and he would not have spent more than $1,000 for three lonely days in Louisville.

His heart was never really into "dating" last night, but he looked over profiles, and pictures, on the new web site, and he'd found a few "local girls" who held some promise. He sent out a couple of "flirts," half-heartedly, before calling it a night and going to bed.

After getting a rough start on his new rules and his dating checklist, David tapped into the airline's WiFi system, and took a second look at the girls he had sent "flirts" to the previous night. Of the five girls he had initiated contact with, by sending "flirts," one of the girls, a real doll, lived in the L.A. area. Reluctantly, David deleted her from his "favorites" list. She was too far away.

"I'm going to have to get tough about this," he reasoned with himself. "The rules are there for a reason, and I have to stick with them. And, I have *got* to keep the *Little Outlaw* chained up in shackles, when I am looking for new girls."

"The Little Outlaw" is the nickname David gave to his sexual libido, or his "little head." He knew that much about himself, anyway… if he let the Little Outlaw run loose, trouble always followed.

David went back to the four remaining women on his "favorites list," who all lived in Las Vegas, or one its many suburbs. Mentally, he checked off "Must be locals," on his checklist for them all. Then, he began, not only to re-read their profiles, but to *study* them.

One by one, as he applied his new rules to those remaining women, he wound up deleting three more of them from his favorites. When he finished, only one girl remained on the list. As much as he had hated to "let the others go," David was proud of himself for following his own rules.

"Now, all I have to do is wait for her to respond," he reasoned. "And, when she does, we'll set up our first meeting, to see if there is any magic."

David knew that it would be a "tough-sell," to try to convince any of the girls to go straight from "Hello," to "Let's go on a date." But, he recalled a technique he had used in his young and single days, when meeting someone in-person was the *only* option. Even back then, women were reluctant to go out with a fellow they had only just met in a bar. So, David came up with a way to get around that… he called it, "a safe-date."

Instead of asking a new acquaintance out for a romantic evening, David would suggest an afternoon picnic at a park, or going hiking up at nearby Mt. Charleston. He would suggest they take wine and cheese, or lunch, to eat outdoors. And, if the girl was still reluctant, he would even suggest that she could bring along a friend, or relative, as sort-of a chaperone. He would also tell them that, he had to be back in town by six p.m., because he had a dinner date that evening (whether he did or not). And, because he did not want to miss that date, he could *guarantee* his newfound friend, that she would be home before dark. That usually did the trick.

David also knew that, because he had met those girls in person, back then, he had already established that there existed "magic," or sexual attraction, between them. So the "safe-date" was purely for information sharing, and getting to know one another better. The *Little Outlaw* was always locked away, and sex was never mentioned…not by David, anyway.

Internet Dating, David surmised, was exactly the opposite, since plenty of information had already been exchanged. The purpose of an "Internet Safe-Date" would be to establish if there was any "magic" between them. David knew, all that it would take is a few minutes, and one deep look into her eyes.

"Short, sweet, safe," David thought. "Especially 'safe.'"

One of the things most people like about internet dating, or what they hate, depending on which end of the action you are on, is that, when you reach a "deal-breaker," with a prospective love-interest. The protocol seemed to be, just to delete them from your favorites list, and not to respond to any further attempts they might make to re-establish contact. Their anonymity was protected, and they didn't have to worry about stalkers, or the like.

The plan David came up with, for his "Internet Safe-Date," was to simply invite them out for coffee at any one of the dozens of coffee houses scattered around the city. They could meet at the chosen establishment, so no addresses were exchanged. They would have a single cup of java, and by the time it was gone, David would know if there was any magic between them.

This plan also included an "escape clause," which David was always quick to point out.

"If you walk in and see some rowdy in a cowboy hat, and you get a bad feeling, just turn around and walk away. I'll never even know you were there. It's totally safe."

The "safe-date" would become his best tool, with locals, for meeting new potential mates on the internet. As the P.A. announced that the plane was beginning its descent into Las Vegas, and that passengers needed to stow their gear and lock their tray-tables, David took one last look at his work, and he was proud. He also sneaked a last look at the one remaining girl on his "favorites list."

"Now all I've got to do is wait for her to contact me," he said to himself, as he closed the computer. "Then, I'll invite her on a "Safe-Date," and we'll be on our way!"

The only problem with David waiting for this particular girl to respond was, apparently she *also* had a list of rules, and David didn't make the cut.

She never called...

Chapter 10

"Can we just meet for a cup of coffee?"

"Oh, my God," Chance exclaimed, as he took a sip of coffee on David's patio. "That poor woman!"

David had just finished telling Chance about his trip to Louisville. At first, Chance'd had a good laugh, but when David told him about his "detective work," in going to the courthouse, Chance's attitude changed to one of pity, for the girl.

"Chance, the only difference between Tina, and your L.A. redhead, is that, your redhead had the guts to go to the airport to meet you, mine didn't."

"I never thought of it, that way," Chance admitted, reconsidering his own experience.

"But, I came up with an idea, on the flight home," David said reaching for some papers he had placed on the table. He slid the papers to Chance. "What's this?" Chance asked.

"A set of rules, and a checklist!" David exclaimed proudly. "I am tired of getting burned!"

Chance looked over the rules and the checklist. "Can I keep these?" he asked. "That's why I printed them out for you," David smiled. "Two old farts like us, gotta stick together!"

David went on to explain to Chance, the whole process he had devised on the flight. The crown jewel, David felt, was the quick and efficient, "Safe-Date." He further explained how he had gone back in, and applied those rules to the five gals he had "flirted" with, his last night in Louisville.

"Yeah, out of the five girls, only one made the cut!" David explained. "So, I guess I'm just gonna have to wait for her to contact me!"

"Wait a minute, wait a minute. What?" Chance asked. "You're waiting for *one girl*?"

"Well, yeah," David answered hesitantly. "I think this girl might be 'the one,' so…"

"Oh, bullshit," Chance guffawed. "You got your whole life on hold, just hoping this one gal will send you a note?"

"Uh huh," David nodded. "I always just work one girl at a time. I'm a one-girl kind of man."

"You idiot," Chance teased. "You gotta work this like an assembly line, man. You send out ten flirts, maybe, just maybe, you'll get one response. Just because she seems right for you, don't mean you're right for her… in her eyes, anyway."

Chance went on to explain the "process" he used to "work" the dating sites. He said that he sent out dozens of "flirts" at a time… nearly every night.

"Of course, that was before the list of rules, and the checklist."

He concluded that, by using the rules, it would slow down the process, but the result would be the same.

"Then, when someone responds, I move her onto my 'favorites' list, and we'll start to chat," Chance finished. "I might be chatting with five girls at the same time."

"I dunno. I really don't like chatting with more than one girl at a time," David responded. "It gets too confusing, remembering what I talked to this one about, what that one told me she did for a living, kid's names, that kind of thing…"

"Hey, Einstein," Chance mocked, "…you've got a checklist sheet made out for *every girl* on your 'favorites list,' right?"

"Yeah…"

"And the idea is to keep the checklist handy, as we talk to these gals, so we can check shit off, right?"

"Well, yeah…"

"Turn it over and take notes, Dumbass!"

David just smiled and shook his head, admiring the simplicity of it.

"Checklist on one side, 'talking' notes on the other," David clarified. "Damn, that's a great idea, Chief."

Chance was part American Indian, and his grandmother had been a shaman, or medicine woman, passing much of her knowledge on to Chance. So, David frequently called him, "Chief."

"Well, Boss, I gotta get goin'," Chance said draining his cup and standing to leave. "Lot's of crap to do today." David stood and hugged him around the shoulder. "Thanks, Chance," he said.

"Are you kidding? You're the one came up with this whole checklist thing. That's gonna be great!"

David always enjoyed Chance's company, but he was glad to see him go, today. David was eager to get back on the dating site, and start his "search" anew. He had already decided that, even though Chance had said that *everyone* flirted with numerous people, David felt that six new girls per day would be enough… at least until he found "the one." Plus, he knew he could take his time that way, and make sure each one he *did* flirt with, was up to standards, according to his rules and checklist.

"This is gonna be a whole new ballgame," he said as he sat down at the computer.

It took David two days, of sending out a half a dozen flirts per day, to finally get a single response. He placed the girl in his favorites list, and they began to chat. At first, when he had suggested they meet for coffee, she was reluctant. She explained that she preferred the anonymity of the dating site, until she started feeling comfortable enough with someone to exchange phone numbers, and arrange a meeting.

They "chatted" for nearly an hour. David learned her real name was Grace, and that she was a Keno runner at a small casino, but she wouldn't reveal which one. Because she worked the swing shift, usually 4 p.m. to midnight, she was available during the days, to chat, but by the time she got home from work, she'd usually sleep until 10 or 11 a.m. Finally, Grace had to take off, to go grocery shopping, so they made arrangements to meet online again the next day.

After hanging up, David felt a little disappointed that she hadn't jumped at the chance to meet for coffee. He knew that if, when they met, there was no "magic," then all this chatting was a waste of time. But, she was very nice, and he had enjoyed the "conversation."

Even though he now had one lady in his "favorites" list, he got right back into his search, until he had sent out a half a dozen "flirts" for the day.

"Just like an assembly line!"

The next day, when he and Grace connected, after the initial pleasantries, Grace brought up the "coffee-date." She'd been thinking about it, after they had chatted the day before, she said, and by the way David had explained it, it sounded perfectly safe.

"And don't forget the 'escape clause,'" David reminded her. "I'm one of those people who is always 15 minutes early for everything, so I'll probably already be there. I'll be the guy in the black cowboy hat. If you don't like what you see, you can just leave. Nothing to it."

So, they made arrangements to meet the next day for coffee. David allowed her to pick a place close to her home, so she wouldn't have far to drive. When they finished chatting, David went back to his search, and made certain that he got his six-flirts in for the day!

"Hot dang," he said. "Gonna meet my first local gal, tomorrow… and she just might be 'the one.'"

He smiled, and found himself going back to look at her profile, and pictures, at least once an hour! He felt that she was awfully pretty, with brown hair and green eyes. She was almost as tall as he was, 5'7" to his 5'8", and listed her body type as "athletic." He was a little concerned that, at 45-years-of-age, a full ten-years younger than David, that she might not be interested in an older guy. But she's the one who responded to the flirt, and she has agreed to meet up, he reasoned, so he felt that age was not going to be an issue.

David arrived at the coffee shop 15 minutes early, as planned, and he assumed Grace would not be there yet. So, he scanned the room, saw several empty tables, then got in line for a large coffee. As he was talking to the clerk, he didn't notice the woman walk in behind him. She touched him on the shoulder.

"David?" she asked coyly.

David turned around and looked into the most beautiful green eyes he had ever seen. They held him in a trance, for just a moment, then he took in the rest of her face, and knew instantly it was Grace.

"Hello, Grace," David said, extending his hand.

"Hi," she said shaking his hand.

"I've got to warn you," he said, "…that'll probably be the last handshake from me. I'm from a very 'huggy' family, and it's tough for me just to shake hands with a gal, once we get to know each other a little."

"Oh, that's perfectly alright," she said. "My family is the same way." "What can I get you?" he asked, as the clerk set his coffee in front of him.

"Umm… how about a café mocha, non-fat, no-whip, extra hot?"

David looked to be certain the clerk heard the order. She had, and she added the mocha to David's total. He paid the bill as Grace walked down the counter to wait for her drink to be prepared. He watched her walk away…

"Maybe… a *little* athletic," he surmised looking at her bottom, waist and legs.

David figured that she was 15 to 20 lbs. overweight, especially for an athlete, but that was about average, for most women, he thought. Besides, she carried those extra few pounds, without any loss to her curvy figure, and David was delighted.

"Man! Talk about magic!" he said to himself. "I'd like to throw her on the table right now and take her *right here*!"

She turned and smiled at him, after grabbing her mocha.

"Where do you want to sit?" she asked.

David pointed to a table in the corner, which was not in the direct sunlight, and was removed a bit from any other customers.

"This okay? He asked.

"Perfect!"

She sat down, and David sat across from her. They talked for more than an hour, and each had a refill on their coffees. They talked about work, family, friends, hobbies, and even spent some time looking at phone-pictures of grandkids! She laughed easily, and had such a beautiful smile, David was ecstatic. Finally, Grace finished her second mocha, then looked at her watch.

"Speaking of grandkids," she said. "I have to get going... I have to pick Melissa up at school in 15 minutes. But it's not far."

David was sorry she had to leave, but in his book, family was always the number-one priority.

"I totally understand," he agreed. "I need to be going, too," he said, although he really didn't have any place else to be.

As they stood to leave, Grace leaned in and gave David a quick hug. And, he loved the feel of her against his chest. They bid each other farewell, and promised to touch bases with each other later that night, on the dating site.

David was stunned and amazed by how well the whole thing went! Here it was, David was thinking, just three days since he had sent her a "flirt," they'd already met, and David was ready to fall in love.

"Beat's the Hell out of flying halfway across the country, to spend the night alone!" he thought. "I should have been using this checklist system from the very beginning!"

David was smiling, at finally getting it right! He decided right then and there that the more expensive dating site had proved to be a very good investment. He drove home, singing a George Strait song, from the radio.

He had been worried that, once he saw the lady, she would look nothing like her pictures, and he'd be disappointed again. But, that was just not the case, he thought. She had looked just like the pictures, well, except for a few extra pounds, but they looked good on her, and David was as happy as a tick in a dog's ear.

"I thought I might have to delete her," he said to himself. "But there is no chance of that. Quite possibly, this one is going all the way to the alter!"

He was so proud of himself, it never occurred to him, that she might delete *him*! And a few hours later, when he tried to contact her on the E-Melody communications network, he found out that, she had done exactly that!

Grace deleted David, and the wedding bells, in his head, rang a very sour note. He was crushed... again!

"Well, I guess the age difference might have been a factor, after all," he deduced, after replaying every moment of their "coffee-date," in his mind.

He remembered her reaction, when he had mentioned that he graduated high school in '74, and that he was a Vietnam-era Naval veteran. He didn't mention that he was only 16 when he graduated, and had just turned 17, when he had enlisted in the Navy. Grace had graduated in 1985, and really, it was two different generations. Plus, talking about grandchildren, she had pictures of her two, Melissa had just started second-grade, and the other was an infant. David had six grandsons, the eldest of whom was eighteen years old... and that shocked her. And again, he failed to mention that he had only been 39 when his first grandson had been born.

He hadn't thought anything of it, at the time, because they were having such a pleasant afternoon. He made a mental note to pay more attention to body-language, in the future. He also decided to change his "search" parameters, from 45-60 to 48-62. It might not make *much* of a difference, but perhaps?

Even though David was unable to chat with Grace any longer, he had two new potential "future Mrs. Remington's" who had sent him messages. He knew that they had both been through the checklist, and had passed, so all that remained was to meet in person, and see if there was any real attraction between them.

During the course of the next two weeks, he had five "coffee dates," with five different women, and one lady who canceled beforehand. Of the gals he met, three did not make any bells or whistles go off for David, *no magic*, so he deleted them. The other two ladies, David was very much attracted to, but like Grace, they had deleted *him*.

The one who canceled *before* the coffee-date, had great potential, and they had been IM'ing frequently. She had dark hair and eyes, and stood 5'6" tall.

"How tall are you?" she had asked, on their second or third time "talking."

His height was plainly (and honestly) listed on his profile, anyway. He wondered why she hadn't just looked?

"I'm 5'8"," he said. "Is that a deal-killer," he added jokingly.

"I'm afraid so," she said quite seriously. "I never date men under 5'10"."

"Are you kidding?" he responded.

It was too late, as she had already deleted him!

"She must have been raised in California," David surmised, still in shock about what had just happened. He had made an observation that, to California girls, horses and cowboys were just fashion accessories.

"This is going to be a whole lot more difficult than I thought," he said with a sigh. "But I paid for a month, and by golly, I'm not giving up yet!"

He might just as well have given up then. The rest of the month, his results mirrored the beginning of the month. By the time he had only a day remaining on E-Melody, the "expensive" site, he took down his profile and shook his head.

"I am only looking for *one* girl," he said to himself. "Someone to grow old with, but have a lot of fun along the way." How tough could that possibly be?

Chapter 11

"Wait a minute, Cowboy, we're not exclusive!"

At their usual morning coffee session, David and Chance talked about the success of the "rules and checklist," and how terrific the "safe-dates" were working out. But, they both had failed to make a single romantic connection. Chance, at least, had moved to a real date, with two of his "favorites," but just one date per lady. He deleted one girl, the other deleted him.

"You know," Chance said, "…I seen a commercial on TV last night, for "senior folks, like us…"

"Yeah, yeah, ah… 'Old Timers R Us," right?" David joked.

"No, Butthead. It's called 'SeniorFolksMeet.com,'" Chance admonished.

"I don't recall seeing that one on my list of dating sites,"

"That's because, it's what they call a "specialty site," Chance replied. "Instead of typing 'Dating Sites,' into Google, try, 'Specialty Dating Sites.' There's a bunch of them…"

Chance went on the explain that there were "specialty sites" for senior people, for "Christians," for several specific races and ethnicities, and so forth.

"Heck they even got a few for Gays," Chance remarked.

"So, how many responses are you getting on that gay-site?" David teased.

Chance flipped him off.

"Bite me," he added.

"Hey, you know, you might just be onto something though," David replied thoughtfully. "My membership is up, on E-Melody, and I was thinking I might just give-up on the whole notion of finding love online. But, maybe, a site for old folks, might be just the ticket…"

"Hey, you can't give up now, Man. You're just figuring it all out… besides, look at all the fun you're having." David laughed at the sarcastic remark.

"Both of us," David agreed. "What the heck, I might as well give 'SeniorFolksMeet.com' a run. What's another month of this torture, right Chief?"

"Hey, you might just find that gal you're looking for!"

"Well, one thing," David observed, "…there won't be any 'cougars' on that site. I've found a bunch of them on those other sites."

"Hey, guys are always looking for, 'young and pretty,' why not the old gals?" Chance offered. "But, I know what you mean, Hoss. I flirted with gals my same age, and they send back, 'You're too old for me.'"

"Me too!" David agreed enthusiastically. "That's why I'm thinking, a dating site for people who are all over fifty, might be just the ticket."

"Yeah, you'd be one of the *young* guys," Chance agreed.

"SeniorFolksMeet dot com," David wrote down on his notepad. "Let's just see what another month might bring!"

After coffee, David headed right up to his computer, and brought up the "Old-Timers" web site. After filling out the usual questionnaires, and establishing a "free" membership, just so he could see what the site had to "offer," he finally entered his search parameters.

Since the site was only for people "over 50," he just went with 50-62 as the age limits, and within 50 miles of his home. Then, he clicked "search," and he was ready to begin window-shopping. And, on the very first page, he found two nice looking ladies that fit his rules, so he absently clicked on "Send Flirt," for one of them.

The web site responded by bringing up the usual pop-up window telling him that, in order to actually "communicate" with any of these people, he would first have to purchase an upgraded membership.

"Well, here goes another $29," he said to himself.

He punched in the credit card number, and was soon involved in his search protocol, with his rules and checklist right beside his monitor. He usually flirted with just six women per day, but he was brand new on the site, and it was much easier, since he had gotten the hang of following his own rules, so he did ten.

"That ought to do it," he said proudly.

A lot of dating sites offer to send you a notification when someone "new" signs up, so all the veterans on the site can look at the "fresh meat." Apparently, David's profile rang a few bells, around the country, and he immediately got a flirt, then another. He went to look.

One of the gals was from upstate New York…too far away, so David deleted her. The other was from Denver, and he deleted another.

"Well, at least the site is active," he thought.

Another trick he had learned was, most dating sites let you see the people who have looked at your profile. David found that, if he sent a "flirt" or a message to a gal, and later saw that she had read his profile, but did *not* respond to him, he knew she never would. They had seen him, and deleted him, he knew, so, that way he knew to delete her, and move on.

Over the next few weeks, David went on several "safe-dates," and he noticed that many of the gals he met looked a lot older, in person, than they had in their photos. That's when he realized that it was pretty common, especially from women over-50, to fudge a little on their ages. That wasn't a problem, young or old, it was all about the "magic."

One gal he met for coffee, had a cute face, and a delightful figure, but when the gal smiled at him, her teeth were brown and quite rotten. It was an immediate deal-killer!

"How could I have missed that?" he thought.

He went back and looked at her profile, and the three photos she posted all had closed-mouth smiles.

"Ahhh," he whispered aloud.

David added a new rule. He had to make sure that the photos showed teeth!

But, still, in six-weeks of using his new "system," while he had met a lot of ladies, he never got to a "second date," with any of them. He was starting to get discouraged, when he got a message from a lady who lived in Dolan Springs, Arizona. He knew Dolan Springs, because he had won his first rodeo there, many years ago, and it was only about 70 miles away.

"This might work," he said, looking over her profile.

She was 55, slender figure, and had a great smile. Her name was Rachel, and she had blue eyes and light brown hair. And, she had a lot of pictures, mostly of her and her two horses, which she listed in her profile, as co-residents of her place in Dolan Springs.

"By golly, a cowgirl," David said with admiration. "And a dang nice looking little gal, at that."

He made contact, not sure how he would pull off the "coffee date," from so far away, but he figured, worst case, he would drive 70 miles for a cup of coffee, then drive home again. But, as it turned out, when he mentioned that, usually, he met new matches at a local coffee shop, she said she was coming to Las Vegas in a few days. She had an appointment with her dentist, for a routine checkup, and she had to buy groceries and supplies. David was delighted that she took good care of her teeth!

"I'd love to stop by for coffee," she said.

So they made a date at a coffee house located close to the highway. She was familiar with it, the exit anyway, so they were all set for their "safe-date."

They exchanged phone numbers, just in case she ran into delays at the dentist. So, they had the opportunity to actually talk on the phone, before they met, which was also a bonus. David thought she had a sweet voice, and a slight southern drawl, which was a delight to the native Texan.

Rachel's profile indicated that she was 5'9", an inch taller than David, but when she walked into the coffee shop, with her slender build, she looked even taller to him. But, they had talked about it, and she said it didn't bother her a bit, if it didn't bother him? She said, she normally wore tennis shoes or "Ropers," a brand of boots with a very low heel. So, he made sure to wear his dress boots, with pointy toes and tall heels.

After talking on the phone a few times, they both felt as if they had already met, and were friends, so David felt hesitant about sticking out his hand, as she smiled and headed toward him. His Texas family *really was* a bunch of huggers, and it just didn't feel right. He needn't have worried.

She swept right up to him and hugged him, like a family member, not romantically, but that was all he had in mind anyway. For the moment.

"David," she said, slightly out of breath. "I have been running around like a crazy-woman, trying to get everything done. It's awful when you drive 70 miles to get home, just to realize you forgot something important! I try to drive to Nevada just once a month, but sometimes I have to make several trips…

"And, hello to you, too," David said teasingly.

Rachel laughed and put her hand to her cheek, slightly embarrassed.

"Oh, my gosh! How rude of me!" she mumbled. "I forgot this was our first time meeting. In just these past few days, I've felt like we've known each other forever!"

"I know, me too," David said, letting her off the hook. "What would you like me to get you?"

"Just black coffee," she said. "Those fancy things are okay once in a while, but wow, like $4 for a cup of flavored coffee is ridiculous."

He was beginning to like her more and more, with each word she spoke. He felt the same way about those fancy coffees. They sure tasted good, but in his mind, anything more than six-bits for a cup of coffee was overpriced!

Even though they had already talked a couple of times on the phone, their visit at the coffee house lasted for more than two hours. She told him all about her "place," near Dolan Springs. It was a new double-wide mobile home, set on a five-acre desert lot.

"I'm a few miles outside Dolan, so there is no city-water available,' she said.

"Do you have a well, then?"

"Oh, God, no," she chuckled. "It's more than 2,000 feet to water, through granite bedrock, caliche, and lava beds. Who can afford that?"

"Dang! So, what do you do for water?"

I have a 10,000-gallon water tank, and they come once a month, with a truck, and fill it up."

"I guess you don't do a lot of irrigating, do you?" he smiled.

"I even hate watering my flower beds around the house," she replied, "But I love my roses! Problem is, it has a small pump-house, just like folks do with wells, to get the water into the house under pressure. But there's a danged leak in the pump, somewhere. It's not a lot, I guess, but the ground inside the pump-house is always wet. That's why I've got to stop at Home Depot... a friend of mine told me to get some plumbing tape? I'm not even sure what that is."

David could smell a "damsel in distress," and his Knight in Shining Armor Suit was quickly donned!

"You don't know much about plumbing?"

"Nothing at all," she said. "But, I'm going to look it up on the internet, and see what I can do. How tough could it be?"

During their conversation, she had previously mentioned that, when she bought the lot, it was empty desert. She had the mobile home and water tank set up professionally, then she had invited her 25-yearold son to come visit for a week, from Phoenix.

Rachel bought steel fence posts and a dozen rolls of "horse wire" fencing. With her son doing most of the work, they got an acre or two, near the house, fenced in, so she could bring her horses there.

"I went to Wally World and bought one of those "beach" things… you know, a tent-top, but the sides are open? Anyway, I put it up next to the house, so the horses will have, at least, *some* shade," she had said.

She had also mentioned that, a carpenter friend of hers had given her a list of material, to build a proper loafing shed. She had purchased the material, and she borrowed a post-hole digger and tractor one day, to get the holes dug for the supports, where he had marked. But, she was still waiting for her carpenter to show up to build it.

"Did you know," David volunteered, "…I'm a journeyman carpenter? I haven't made a living at it since I was a teenager, but I still have all my tools, and I always love building stuff. I built a two-story room addition on my house, and drove every nail myself."

She leaned forward, with a very provocative look on her face.

"And?" she said softly.

"And if you've got the holes dug already, I could throw that thing up in an afternoon. I might could even take a look at your leaky pump."

"It's a date!" she said with a smile. "My gelding is in Kingman, at the trainers, so I only have one horse at the house… but I can show you the place. And I promise to help, all I can. Come early, and we'll make a day of it."

David couldn't believe his ears! For the first time, he was moving on to a *second date*! Well, okay, a *working* date, but they'd have a whole day together. Of course, he'd never expect anything more than just an afternoon, but there was always the possibility…

"I'll be sure to load all my carpenter tools… and I have plenty of plumber's tape. We'll get you all fixed up."

They agreed that she would email him the address, and he'd drive down in two days, with all his tools. Rachel was ecstatic, and gave him a bear-hug, when they parted.

On the drive home, David was singing along with the radio again. "Oh, happy days!"

When the appointed day rolled around, David packed all his tools, and an overnight bag, "just in case," and he was rolling an hour before sunrise. All the way there, his thoughts kept turning to Rachel, their warm, friendly conversations, and how she made him feel so "special," like he was the only man in her life. He knew that he was on the right track, with this one!

By the time he got to her place, the sun was just peering over the mountains. Even though David had little affection for the harsh and arid desert, it certainly was beautiful, sometimes. Especially on a day he was going on his "second date," with a lady he hoped might be "the one."

After Rachel gave David a quick tour of the place, which was exactly as she had described; a double-wide mobile home on some raw desert, with about a quarter of it fenced, and, not much else. She invited him in for coffee, before they got to work. He gladly accepted… coffee was like mother's milk for him, and always had been.

Inside, the home was actually quite nice, very comfortable, with a brick fireplace, sloping ceilings, with exposed beams, and nicely furnished. When they sat down to drink the coffee, any chance for small talk went right out the door… she had turned into a construction foreman!

Rachel started explaining what materials she had, and where it could be found, and so forth. Since that was the purpose of his visit, he turned his attention to the work at hand.

After he finished his coffee, they headed outside, and David started digging through the lumber pile. There were also two bags of redi-mix concrete, near the lumber, which he'd need to anchor the corner posts.

"We'll get the corner posts in," he announced, "…and while the concrete is setting up, I'll take a look at your water pump."

They labored all day, during which time, she had made an absent comment about, "Once you hit sixty, you get into a mad rush to get what you want out of life…"

"Wait…" David said looking closely at her. "You're only 55."
She waved her hand in the air to dismiss that notion.

"Oh, God, I just put that age on the dating site, because I really *do* look younger, don't you think."

David nodded his head in agreement. She really did look like she was in her early 50's.

"So, how old are you really?"

"65."

"Damn," he said to himself, then, "Well, you're right, you do look a lot younger."

"Age is all in how you feel," she said pleasantly. "And I feel like a kid, most days. I'll go get us some lemonade."

He went quietly back to work, as she went inside for the cold drinks. He had already fixed the leaky pump, which was dripping out of the valve stem, not just a joint he could seal with plumbing tape. He took the pump apart, and repacked the stem, then put it all back together. It worked perfectly, but instead of a quick-fix, he'd had to work on it for nearly two hours.

In the desert sun, two hours was more than enough time for the concrete to set firmly, so he then went to work in earnest, as a carpenter. By the time the sun was just beginning to touch the Western ridge, he stepped back to admire his work. Rachel was quickly beside him.

"Oh, my gosh, it's gorgeous," she said.

"Well, I wish we'd had a bunch of old railroad ties," he replied. "...for the side walls. Those things are awesome when you stack them up."

"Oh, my horses will love this!" she said in earnest. "C'mon inside, and you can wash up before you go…"

"Before I go?" he thought. "So much for a romantic supper!"

David was a little disappointed that she hadn't even offered to make supper for him, but at least she'd fed him a tuna sandwich for lunch, and she'd kept his lemonade glass full all day. And, this whole "date" was about him coming in and putting in a day of labor for her, so he'd done what he set out to do. There was plenty of time for romance, down the line, he reasoned.

When they got into the house, David headed straight for the bathroom and washed his arms, hands and face in the sink. When he finished, he went back out to the living room, and Rachel was on the phone with someone, and she was laughing a lot. David figured it must be her son, the one she'd mentioned who built the fences.

It wasn't.

"Okay, so what hotel are we meeting at?" She asked into the phone. "Oooh, that's one of the nicest hotels in Laughlin."

David was a little perplexed. He saw that there was still coffee in the pot, and he'd brought his own thermal travel mug in from the car, so he held it up and pointed, and she indicated that he could refill it. As he was pouring the coffee, she concluded her phone call.

"Okay," she said into the phone, "I'll meet you there around 7 p.m., in the lobby. Gosh this is going to be fun, Bill."

"Bill?" David said to himself. Her son's name was Josh…

Then, she hung up and turned to David with a warm smile on her face.

"So, who's Bill?" David asked curiously, but politely.

"Oh, just this guy I am seeing…"

"Wait," David responded, as if someone had just hit him over the head with a hammer. "We're just starting to date, and you're going away on a romantic weekend with some other guy?" Her expression turned very stern.

"Wait a minute," she exclaimed. "We're not exclusive! We haven't even been out on a *real* date, yet. Where do you come off thinking that I can only date one guy at a time?"

David had nothing to say. He just took his coffee and walked out the door. Perhaps he was wrong, he thought to himself on the way home, but he was a one-girl kind of man, and he expected the same thing of a girl he was seeing. It was just a courtesy.

He made a mental note to add that to his checklist – "Are you seeing anyone else, even casually?" But it was too late for this gal. She had already broken his heart.

On the long drive home, he recalled all her references to "my friend the carpenter, and my buddy has a tractor with a post-hole digger

I borrowed," and so forth and he realized that each of those "friends" was probably guys just like him… fellows she met online, who were handy with tools.

"Well, it worked," he said aloud. "For a tuna sandwich and a pitcher of lemonade, she turned a pile of lumber into a nice loafing shed for her horses. And the labor didn't cost her anything but a smile."

The minute he got home, he raced up to his computer and deleted Rachel… he just couldn't wait. Besides, once she had agreed to the "second date," he figure they were starting a relationship, so he stopped looking online for anyone else. Now, he'd have to go back in, and try, try, again.

"Well, that's one more lesson-learned," he told himself. "Dammit."

Chapter 12

"Specialty dating-sites, for every interest!"

"I'll bet the fella Rachel is meeting in Laughlin owns a construction company," Chance said laughing, the next morning at coffee. "Well, it's not exactly a scam," David observed. "It's just a woman using her charms to get what she wants. Women have been doing that since the caveman days!"

Chance had not been having much luck lately, either, on the "old timer" site, and he suggested that, perhaps it was just not the *right* specialty site.

"What is it you are really looking for?" Chance asked. "I mean, I know you want a lady, but where will you live? What will you do with your life?"

David thought about it for a few minutes. He knew what he wanted to do, but he hadn't been real clear on it, in his profiles.

"I guess, I just want a little hobby-ranch. Someplace where grass grows all by itself," David said, referring to the arid desert, and the water needed to irrigate just a few acres of grass.

"So, you wanna go back to the ranch, eh?" Chance was going somewhere with this. "Didja see that new site they been advertising on TV? It's called 'RanchersOnly.com.'"

David didn't watch much television, but he had seen the commercial for the dating-site, which was specifically designed for "cowboys and cowgirls," or just any Country people.

"I told ya, they've got specialty dating sites for every interest!" Chance chimed. "If you want a place in the country, with a few horses and cows, well, why not look at a site where everybody wants the same thing?"

"Dammit, Chance. You just aren't gonna let me quit this internet shit, are you?"

"Not until you've found your future ex-wife," he teased.

"So, RanchersOnly.com, eh?"

"Hey, that's not what I'm looking for, but the minute I saw their commercial, I thought it would be perfect for you."

"You just might have something there, old buddy," David said thoughtfully. "And maybe we can find a specialty site for you? Ya know, like 'RichOldBroads.com?' I'm sure you'd find a 'Sugar-Mama' on there!"

Chance bellowed with laughter, nodding his head in agreement. "And if things don't work out for you on RanchersOnly, I'm sure there's a site for guys who seem to love being scammed, burned and ripped-off, like 'Burn Me Baby.com!'"

"Kiss my ass," David scoffed.

They had a good laugh, and when Chance left, David again headed to his computer to look up yet another new dating site. There were parts of this online dating he enjoyed, but it just didn't seem to be getting him any closer to finding "the one."

"Wait a minute, wait a minute," David said, after he had filled out a brief profile, and began to look at the "offerings" of the new site. "I think I might have just fallen into some pretty tall cotton, here at RanchersOnly! Yup, I believe I am *home!*"

As he browsed the girls who appeared in the "general" search engine, he noticed that most of the girls had pictures of their horses, too! Many had "hunting" pictures, with the lady in cammo, holding a trophy deer or elk. And many were still living the ranch-life, and looking for someone to share it with!

There was only one small problem. When David typed in his usual search parameters, using 50 miles as his limit, there were no actual "country-girls," per se, since Las Vegas was a big city in the desert, and not at all rural. A few of the local girls had horses, but most were just city-girls "looking" for a cowboy to sweep her away.

"This might make it a little tougher," he thought to himself. "But you can't keep a squirrel on the ground in timber country!"

David was very careful about total honesty in his profile, and he even made sure he put a note in there about "looking for someone nearby," to discourage the gals from places like New York, sending him flirts. He could just delete them, of course, but it was easier if they didn't come in at all. He was just too soft-hearted sometimes.

The comment about distance actually did very little good, except now, the girls began their messages with, "I know you're looking for someone close, but..." He looked them all over first, and then deleted them! A few of them caused him a lot of hesitation before hitting that delete button... man, they looked good, on paper! But his equanimity took hold, and he "stayed the course" he had laid out. Besides, he knew that the lust he felt sometimes, was just the Little Outlaw, getting in a word!

"Follow the rules, keep a checklist handy!" he said to himself, when the decision was contrary to his heart... or the Little Outlaw, whichever one controlled his thinking, at that point!

As with the other sites, he had several "coffee-dates," with a few local gals, but either David or the lady, hit the "delete button" when it was all over. Except for one, and they never actually got to coffee!

Jenny Kendall was an Air Force doctor, stationed at Nellis Air Force Base, just outside of Las Vegas. She was only in her mid-forties, and did not come up in David's search, because his age parameters were set older, to what he thought was more age-appropriate. But she contacted him, and they began communicating.

David learned that Jenny was born in Texas, in a little town 30 miles from Austin. He knew the area well, and he had ridden not only at the Austin rodeo, but those in a half-dozen smaller towns in the area, too. David loved her Texas drawl… it made him a little homesick!

Like David, Jenny didn't care much for the dating site's email system, so immediately after their initial contact, they exchanged real email addresses and phone numbers.

David had called her right away, with the idea of setting up a coffee-date. They talked for more than an hour, and both really enjoyed it. However, as a doctor she was on 24-hour call about half the time, when she wasn't actually *scheduled* to work, and she had to remain on base during those times. So while she claimed to really want to meet, she'd have to figure out when she would next *be able* to leave the base… and she had suggested they meet for cocktails, instead of coffee.

David liked the sound of that, as well as the way they had hit it off, so he didn't mind if he had to wait a few days to meet her in-person. The way she had explained her "work-week," was that, she went into the hospital for two days, 48-straight hours, then she had three days being on-call, where she was off duty, but could not leave the base. Then, she had three days totally off-duty, before it started all over again.

When they had first talked on the phone, she was on her final day off, so it would be at least six days before they could meet in-person. "Something tells me it will be worth the wait," he said.

Meanwhile, during those next five days, they talked often, briefly sometimes, as she might have to rush off quickly at a moment's notice. And, he found that, during her on-call days, she usually spent at least 8-10 hours per day at the hospital.

"That P.A. system is not my friend," she had told him jokingly. "Every time there's an announcement, it usually starts with 'Doctor Kendall, please report to…'"

David soon learned that she was not kidding, either! But, they enjoyed the conversations, especially since David's father had been in the
Air Force, and he was quite familiar with "Air Force ways."

They made arrangements to meet on Tuesday, for cocktails, at a cozy little lounge called the Peppermill, just off the Las Vegas strip. David had been there once before, and knew it to be set up like someone's living room, almost. They had sofas and overstuffed chairs, coffee tables, lamps, and all gathered around a fire-pit that sat in the center of the main room. Except for weekends, it was very quiet, very intimate and *very* romantic. And, the best part, so far as David was concerned, is that *Jenny* is the one who had suggested it.

On Monday evening, her last day of on-call duty, she gave David a call.

"Have you been watching the news?" she asked him immediately.

"No, not at all," he said truthfully. "Why, what's going on?"

"There's been an accident at... well, let's just say, outside of Tonopah."

"Dreamland?" he asked.

"How do you know about Dreamland?" she asked in surprise.

"Retired air traffic controller, remember? Janet flies out of McCarran, where I spent most of my career," he responded.

"Janet" was the radio call-sign of a "secret" fleet of unmarked Air Force B737's, that ferried materials, and civilian workers to the nuclear test site, known as Area-51. All of the airspace that comes even close to Area-51 is restricted to military aircraft only, and it is a huge chunk of central Nevada. This "no-fly" zone was called "Dreamland," and while it referred to the airspace above, people who worked there often called the place by the same name.

His answer satisfied her... she forgot that FAA and the military worked very closely together, and all air traffic controllers had top-secret security clearances. They also received regular briefings from the military liaisons, whenever there were top secret operations in progress. "Well, the story the Air Force 'leaked' to the press was that there had been a small explosion, two fatalities, and dozens of workers injured," she explained. "The casualties are correct, but it wasn't exactly an explosion..."

"Nuclear spill?" David asked.

"I didn't say that, but I won't deny it," she said tactfully. "Anyway, we can't evacuate the people who have been exposed to radiation… they're in a small medical facility on-site, with only one doctor…

"And you're packing your B-4 bag for a little TDY?"[1] David finished.

"Yes," she admitted regretfully. "It'll be at least a week, maybe two…"

"So, we'll just carry-on as we have been," David offered. "Talk when we can, chat whatever."

"No, this is so hush-hush they've instructed us, no personal cell phones, no laptops… they don't want a word of what is happening there to get out."

"Damn," David whispered.

"David, I am so sorry…" she began.

"No, no. It's your job, I remember things like this with my Dad, too. You go, take care of those guys."

"I will call you the second I get out of Dreamland… sooner, if I can figure out a way to do it, without getting shot." She wasn't kidding about the "getting shot" part either.

"Look, just do the best you can… I'll still be here when you're through."

"Thank you, David. That means so much to me," she said sincerely. "But, I've got to go. We'll talk again in a week or so."

"Bye, Doll. I'll be thinking of you every minute of every day," he said.

"Me, too," she said, then the line went dead.

David stared at the phone for a few seconds, before pressing the disconnect. He found himself in a very odd dilemma! He was "working his plan," using the rules and the checklist, and normally, he kept right on working it, until *after* their first meeting. Six new flirts per day was

---

[1] a B-4 bag is a military suitcase, which opens for hanging clothes, and is designed to be the only bag needed on short trips. TDY is a "temporary" assignment, at least overnight.

his goal, and every other day, or so, he'd get a response. So, he'd begin to work on getting a coffee-date scheduled with that girl, too.

Only, *after* discovering if there existed any magic between them, and they both were interested in a second date, would he stop his search-routine. That had only happened once, and it hadn't turned out so well, with Rachel. But, he got right back on that bronc, and he returned to working the plan, almost immediately.

Jenny, however, was so different, that she de-railed his plan very quickly. David knew that he *should* still be looking for new matches, according to his plan. However, once Jenny had agreed to meet, not just for coffee, but a real honest-to-goodness date, in a very romantic setting, which *she* had suggested, David just granted her a "bye," as it were, in the tournament of dating. He felt so good talking to her, almost nightly, that he just didn't *want* to look for anyone else. So he checked off "magic" on his list, as if they'd already met for coffee, and he was moving on, in his own mind anyway, to the big second date!

David had stopped searching for new flirts, but his profile was still up, and girls were still sending *him* messages and flirts. And, since he hadn't even met Jenny yet, he didn't really want to blow off any potential matches, but he also didn't want to "cheat" on Jenny. So, he typed up a sort of "form letter," that he would send to any *local* girls who flirted with him, who also made the minimum grade on his list of "rules."

The "form letter," which he cut-n-pasted into a RanchersOnly message, told the local gal that David was *beginning* a relationship with a lady he'd just met on this site." He explained that, it was just a start, and it could be over in a week, or last a lifetime. But to be fair to his new love-interest, he would not be able to "connect" with them, unless things didn't work out with the new girl. Then, he'd save their "profile," and he would contact them, as soon as he was free again, if that ever happened.

And, David *did* save their messages, just in case things didn't work out with Jenny, he'd have a few flirts to send out right away. He usually read the long distance contacts, as well, but always just deleted them, according to his process.

Somewhere during the first week that Jenny was gone, David got a long-distance message from a gal in Chico, California. He was not a big fan of California-Cowgirls, who felt that their horses were just accessories, to make *them* look prettier, but he dutifully opened the message and read it. It was from a gal named Karen Goodwin.

"I know you are not looking for any long-distance relationships," it began. "But I read your profile and find you very interesting." "Standard bullshit," David was thinking.

"Unlike most women on here, I am not looking for romance," it continued. "Well, maybe someday, perhaps, with the right man, but I know it takes a long time to build a true, loving relationship, and it absolutely must be built on a foundation of solid friendship, first. So, I'd really just like to be friends, *just friends,* with no romantic involvement at all. I feel if we take romance off the table completely, it removes a lot of pressure, and we can just become better friends as time passes. I figure people can always use new friends! Are you interested in just making a new friend, even long-distance?"

David had never gotten any messages like *that* before. He clicked on her profile, just for fun, and took a look. She was a blue-eyed girl with long blonde hair, and she was only 5'2" tall. Short and petite, just the way, David had found, he preferred his women! Plus, she owned a horse! So he grabbed his "rules," and found that, except for being long-distance, she met every other criterion.

"What the heck," he said to himself, "...if she only wants a friend, and no romantic involvement, why not?"

So, he composed a response to her message, very similar in content to his "form letter" for local girls. David explained about his new, and budding relationship with a gal he'd met there on RanchersOnly (but he didn't mention that he'd never even *met* Jenny yet). He indicated that he was a "one-woman" kind of guy, but if all Karen wanted was to be friends, with no romantic involvement, then he welcomed the opportunity to make a new friend... even if she was a "California-Cowgirl," although he left that part out of the message.

Besides, he figured that, so long as Jenny was "off the grid," and they couldn't talk, he could kill time getting better acquainted with Karen. But, he also made a note to himself to tell Jenny about his new "friend," the very next time they talked... just so she'd know that David wasn't hiding anything.

By the time David next spoke to Jenny, he and Karen had exchanged phone numbers, and had had several lengthy conversations. True to their promise to each other, they did not talk about romance, or even meeting. Instead, they talked about horses mostly, and problems she was having with her Paint gelding. David had spent enough time breaking and training colts, in his early days of rodeo, that he was able to give her suggestions and ideas. He also learned that, Karen grew up in Oregon, not California, and she had spent a lot of time working on ranches in Oregon.

"So much for being a California-Cowgirl," he thought, at the time.

He was beginning to like this feisty little gal, but he kept reminding himself that, it was only about friendship! He still had Jenny. She might have a tough job, in the Air Force, but Jenny was close-by, and was very much interested in a romantic relationship. But, David still felt obliged to *tell* Jenny all about Karen, as soon as they spoke again. He never got the chance...

"David?" Jenny asked into the phone.

"Oh, Jenny," he responded. "God, it is so wonderful to hear your voice!"

"Same here," she replied. "I thought about you all the time while I was up there."

"I couldn't stop thinking about you, either." "But, David... I have some really bad news." He did not like the sound of that!

"I'm listening..."

"When I got back to Nellis, I had, *have*, orders for a PCS move. I leave in 30-days."

David knew that "PCS" was a Permanent Change of Station... she was being transferred!

"Oh, my God," David said, truly shocked at the news. "Where? Where are you going?"

David was thinking that, perhaps, he could just move with her? They still had a month, and plenty of good things could happen during that span of time. He had only known his first wife *for a week*, before they got married, and that one had lasted for 35 years!

"Afghanistan," she said. "A year there, then, wherever they send me."

So much for David accompanying her! "Damn,"
he gasped aloud.

"Look, I really like you… *a lot*, even though we've never even met," she began, with an emotional edge to her voice. "But, it just wouldn't be fair for me to ask you to wait a year, for me to return."

"I'd wait," he said. "My dad spent a year in 'Nam in '68, and Mom waited for *him*."

She chuckled.

"It's not the same, and you know it. No, I've thought about it a lot, and I think I just need to put this whole 'dating' business on hold, until I get back. And, who knows where I'll wind up, when I do get back to the States?"

"So this is 'good-bye,' then?"

"I'm afraid so," she said choking up.

David was also feeling a little overwhelmed with emotion, and he could hear Jenny beginning to sob, which made it even worse for him, too. As hard as it was for him, he realized that it was even *more* difficult for her. The Air Force had been *her* choice, and as with every choice in life, it has its consequences. This, was one of hers.

They just held on to the phones, listening, hoping for a better solution, but none was forthcoming.

"I've got to go," she sobbed, finally. "David, I'm so sorry…" "Me, too," was all he could say, before the line went dead. David laid his phone down, walked to the cupboard, and pulled out a bottle of Pendleton whiskey.

"I was saving this for a special occasion," he thought. "I figured it would be a happy occasion, but this one will have to do."

Before the night was through, it was only a half a bottle of whiskey. But, David slept like a baby.

The next morning, not terribly early, David was up, and looking forward to Chance coming by for coffee. He really needed a friend to talk to, if only to vent a little, and share his grief. But Chance called, and told David that he had a doctor's appointment that morning, and the VA hospital was on the opposite side of town, so he wouldn't be able to make it for coffee.

"Great," David said, after hanging up the phone. "The one day I really need a friend to talk to, and it's the one day Chance can't make it. That's just Jim Dandy..."

Then, he cocked his head to one side, as a thought ran through his mind. He looked at his phone for a second, then dialed a number from his directory.

"Hello, Karen?" he said when she answered. "You gotta few minutes to talk? I really need a friend, right now..."

Chapter 13
This is "The One," I just know it!

Over the next few weeks, David and Karen spoke more and more often. Jenny had left the picture, so, they no longer enforced the "friendship only" rule they had placed upon their conversations, in the beginning. They were, however, mainly focusing on their friendship, and building trust, but allowing detours in their chats, about what kind of "mate" they were hoping to find, eventually.

In all dating, those first few weeks, even months sometimes, of getting to know each other, is a period of "discovery," about the other person. You learn subtle things, like what makes them laugh, or what brings out anger or fear, or tears. You also learn things such as their history, upbringing, education, and the kinds of jobs they had held over the years. But, throughout all of this period, honesty in all revelations is absolutely essential.

If you say it, and they believe it, and it is a falsehood – then it is a train wreck in the making! This is especially true in long-distance Internet Dating, where couples can't even look into each other's eyes, or see body language, to affirm the sincerity of the of the facts.

David knew this, but he also felt that, Karen's voice was so sincere, so honest, that he could trust her, and he believed her every word. For instance, David knew that, during the last ten years of his marriage, he became so fixated on his own goals and ambitions, that he forgot what it was to show love, even to his family. He had become a cut-throat businessman, and there was no room, or time, for emotion or kindness. And, when he told Karen about this fault of his, he added,

"It's not that I don't care about other people's feelings. But, I often just say what's on my mind, directly, and without thinking about how it might affect others."

This was a trait often admired, or hated, by people, about most real cowboys. They always spoke their mind, and damn the consequences. The truth, or how they saw the truth, was always what they related. But, being hurtful was never their intention, it was only about being honest.

When most cowboys, including David, crossed the line with their frank and honest assessment, and they hurt someone's feelings, the cowboy was usually, genuinely sorry. It's not that they would have changed their opinion on the matter, but with a little thought, they could have voiced it more considerately, more gently.

When David admitted this personal observation he had made about himself, Karen responded by telling David that she completely understood, and that he would never have to worry about that, with her.

"If someone gets my dander up," she said, "I just let 'em have it with both barrels. I am real quick to tell anyone when they've crossed the line, or hurt my feelings. I learned that on the ranch in Oregon. The best way to handle a cowboy, is to be just as honest and direct as he is." These were words of comfort to David. He knew he had a way of "being too quick," with his opinions, sometimes, and he never wanted, or intended to hurt. But if the person he offended did not tell him about their hurt feelings, he might never know!

"Oh, if something is bothering me, I won't let it become a burr under my saddle," she had responded. "I'll bring it up right away, so we can talk about it, and come up with a better way to get there. That's a promise."

Again, words of comfort, to David. He told her that, if they ever became a true couple, he would depend upon her to keep that promise. He knew that those festering wounds, caused by problems not discussed, were the demise of so many good relationships. Deep, sincere and rational communication was the key to a successful love, he told her. And, she readily agreed.

Story after story they shared with each other, about their lives, loves and passions. Her stories were often about her horse, or adventures she had lived on the ranch on Oregon, and the lessons she learned there. David shared stories of life on the rodeo trail, as well as his business exploits, and failure. The good, bad and ugly were all laid bare, just so that they could see the trails they each had taken, to arrive at their present point in life.

Along the way, often, they discussed the physical distance between them, just over 600 miles separated them. It was not exactly a "day trip," David pointed out. But an idea was taking shape, in his mind. "How long does it take for you to get to Reno, from where you live?" he asked.

"About three hours," she replied hesitantly. "Why?"

"Well, it takes me six or seven hours," he explained, "We could stay at a hotel in Reno, go take a tour around Lake Tahoe, even..."

"David, I don't think our relationship..." she interrupted. "Well, I just don't think we are even close to the point where we should be planning a romantic weekend together!"

"Who is talking about a romantic weekend?" David replied happily. "We can get separate rooms at the Silver Legacy. It'd be just two good friends, meeting up for a weekend of getting to know each other better!"

"No sex?" she asked suspiciously.

"Heck no," he replied honestly, although the thought had crossed his mind. "What do they always say on these silly dating sites? 'We're not there yet.' Look, you can make your own room reservation... but I'll pay for it, of course. All you've gotta do is buy your truck a brand new tank of gas, to get there, and I'll take care of the rest." "And it's just sightseeing, and doing the 'tourist-thing?'"

She was still suspicious of his motives, but sounding more enthusiastic. And David really was sincere. He figured that he had kept the
"Little Outlaw" chained up for this long, he could keep the little guy under wraps for a while longer. At least, he aimed to try!

"We'll see the sights during the day… Saturday. But at night, we can go dancing, or see a show, or just drop some quarters in the poker machines."

"Or, just find a cozy little lounge, somewhere quiet, while we just talk, you know?" Karen added convincingly.

"Shoot, yeah," David thought, remembering his planned date with Jenny at the lounge in Las Vegas. "We could have a glass of wine, or two…"

"I'm not much of a wine drinker," she confessed. "I prefer whiskey. I guess that's the cowgirl in me!"

"Have you ever tried Pendleton?" he asked.

"Yes, I love that stuff."

"Me, too," he said. "I just tried it last year, and I switched brands instantly!"

He made a mental note to buy a new bottle, to take with him, "just in case." Over the past few weeks, they had discussed nearly every aspect of their lives, and of course, David had told her about his business failing, and having to file corporate bankruptcy.

"I should have filed personal bankruptcy then, too," he had told her, at the time. "Toward the end, I was paying company bills with my own credit cards, and a line of credit on my house."

He explained that, he still had money coming in, but it was not nearly enough to pay the first, and second, on his house. Plus, he had three credit cards with more than $20,000 charged on each, and a few smaller ones. His finances were ugly, he told her.

Karen was a meticulous bookkeeper, with excellent credit, and only one credit card, with a small limit. She was frugal and conservative, in matters-financial, she had explained, so he had better get his "act" cleaned up, if he ever wanted to marry her! But, she had said it lightheartedly, especially since they hadn't even talked about the possibility of getting married, yet.

"That's okay," he had responded, "If we get married, I'm just going to sign over my retirement check to you, and you can take care of all the bills!"

David had said it with a smile in his voice, but he was also very serious. He knew that he had become too accustomed to having a large income, and a wallet full of platinum credit cards. If he wanted something, even something frivolous, he just bought it. It was a bad habit to get into, especially after retirement had cut his income in half, and then the divorce lawyers cut it in half again.

Knowing of David's financial situation, and her own, when David suggested they meet on a Friday night, in Reno, Karen hesitated. She knew it would be very expensive for him to pay for two rooms, for two nights, especially at someplace as elegant as the Silver Legacy. So, she explained that, she couldn't leave work early, because of some project her boss had her working on. And, she went on to explain, she would just be too tired for a three-hour drive, after dark.

"Let's just meet around noon, on Saturday, at the Legacy," she suggested. "We can get a late checkout time, and leave early Sunday afternoon. What do you think?"

David liked the idea of only paying for one night, instead of two, especially since he volunteered to pay for both rooms. He quickly calculated his drive time, and knew he'd have to leave Las Vegas by four a.m., if he was to be in Reno at noon.

"That sounds like a terrific idea," he agreed.

They agreed on the date for their Reno trip, some ten days away. David was pushing for the very next weekend, but Karen refused.

"I am not going anywhere, until I get my hair and nails done," she explained. "And I already have an appointment for this Saturday, so we'll just have to wait another week."

David understood. After all, he'd been married for 35 years, and he knew that a woman's vanity was not a wall any man could, or should, take down. An old cowboy saying came to his mind, "Most women are about as pretty, as they can be."

So, they agreed to meet on the following weekend. Later, David realized that it was nearly the end of July, and he was almost broke. He didn't get paid again until the 1st, so he was very glad that she had that hair appointment. Now, by the time they met in Reno, he would have a brand new retirement check in his bank account.

They say that, "When you fall in love, the sigh you hear, is all the common sense leaving your body!"

David was actually happy to see that, at least one of them was using some common sense. In typical cowboy fashion, once David made his mind up to do something, he just did it. So, he was glad that Karen had a more level head. Especially in this instance!

Once the trip had been set, their conversation turned to other things. When David had filed corporate bankruptcy, he had told his attorney, back in December, that he was having trouble keeping up with his home mortgage, and wondered if there was a way to include it in his filing.

"Only if it is titled in the company name," he'd responded. "But, our firm has a department dedicated to getting mortgages refinanced, with lower payments." For a separate fee, of course.

The lawyer explained that there was a federal program, wherein the mortgage company would forgive all arrearages, then, combine any second-mortgages to come up with the new mortgage amount. After an appraisal had been done, due to the real estate crash in the 90's, if the homeowner was upside-down, the mortgage company would reduce the mortgage amount to 80% of the appraised value.

David knew that he was upside down, by a lot. He had taken out his second mortgage line of credit, when the market was at its highest, then the price of real estate fell like penny dropped from the Empire State Building. His home was now valued at half of what it had been when the loan was new.

"How can they do that?" David wondered. It just seemed too good to be true.

"It's a federal program," the lawyer explained. "Everything your mortgage company writes-off, is reimbursed by the fed, including any past-due amounts."

"Well, I'll be damned," David said. "I'm paying close to $2,500 a month right now, and it's killing me. If I could get that dropped to, say, $1,200, I could keep up with everything, no problem."

"So, how far behind are you, in your payments?"

"Oh, I'm not behind," he stated. "But I have been struggling a lot, to pay the mortgage, and my electric bill. I've had the power shut off a few times, but never missed a mortgage payment."

"David," the lawyer had told him, back in December, "...our average refinance client is six-months past due. The government will pay that for you, once the new loan is made. If you are not behind on your payments, the mortgage company may not feel that you need federal assistance."

"So, what are you saying?"

"I'm saying, you need to stop making your mortgage payments, to help you qualify for the federal mortgage reduction program."

That was like music to David's ears. He would suddenly have an extra $2,500 a month to spend, so he could get at least one of his credit cards caught up. Then, he'd have money to buy groceries, and pay the huge power bills, which often ran more than $500 per month.

A few months later, when he began his online quest for a new wife, it was this skipped mortgage payment that gave him enough cash to, well, send a few hundred to Ghana, or fly off to Louisville. Okay, he never said he was going to spend it wisely, but at least he had something to spend, now.

That had been seven months previously, and still, he did not have the new mortgage, or even any dialogue with the mortgage company, so far as he knew. And now, he was seven months behind in his mortgage payments. The law firm hadn't called him, and when he called them to learn of their progress, he was continually stonewalled, or just told that they were waiting to hear back from the mortgage company.

David told Karen the whole story, of course. And, while it was nice living in a beautiful home, "rent-free," as it were, he was worried something had gone wrong. Despite the repeated promises from his attorney to the contrary, he felt he might just lose the house.

After they talked about Reno, David told Karen that he had just received a note from his mortgage company that, since he was so far in arrears, they were starting foreclosure proceedings. Of course, David had immediately called the lawyer, who told him that it was a routine thing, and not to worry. "Are you sure that your lawyer has a valid license to practice law?" she asked incredulously.

"Shoot, it the biggest law firm in Las Vegas," he told her. "And, I'm dealing directly with one of the partners, George Haney, not some flunky right out of law school." "Well, I guess all you can do is hope he is right, then," she agreed. Karen only paid $400 per month, where she lived outside of Chico. It was a tiny, one-bedroom, single-wide mobile home in a trailer park.

But, since it was just her, she didn't mind. She said she had chosen it, because it was right next door to the stables where she kept her horse.

"I just walk over there, every day, to see my horse," she told him. "I'd really like to have a place where I could keep him at home, but dang, who can afford that?"

"Well, if there were two incomes, it might not be so tough," David replied with a smile. "Then, you could ride any time you wanted!" There was a slight hesitation, before she answered quietly. "I've been meaning to tell you about that," she began nervously. "I had a wreck last year, at the stables. I was helping one of the trainers sort horses, in the round-corral. There were about six horses, and I had the one she wanted separated, and was trying to hold him… the other five came around and just flattened me!" "Oh, my God!" David exclaimed.

"It was mostly just cuts and bruises," she continued. "But, one of them stepped on my hip, and, well sort of crushed it."

"What do you mean, 'sort of crushed it?'"

"Well, I have a very pronounced limp, and I haven't been able to ride my horse since the accident."

"Damn," David said sincerely. "Can they do anything about it?"

"Oh, yeah," she replied. "I've actually got a very good orthopedic surgeon… one of the top rated surgeons in the country, in fact. I'm scheduled for surgery, the first week in October." "Are they gonna be able to fix you up, good as new?" "Better," she said. "He's doing a total hip replacement." "How long is the recovery time?" David asked.

"Well, there's a lot of variables, of course," she explained. "But if all goes well in surgery, my doctor said I should be up and walking within two weeks, and it will be another six to eight weeks before I'll be back to normal."

"Well, that's not so bad," he admitted.

David had seen his share of rodeo-wrecks, and been through quite a few himself. He knew about recovery times, as it was always time off the rodeo circuit. Even though it had been years since he had ridden bucking horses, he still had surgeries that needed to be done.

But rodeo cowboys become so used to the pain, it becomes a way of life. The pinched nerve in his neck, and two torn rotator cuffs, still flared up occasionally, and he often thought of getting them fixed. But, he always found an excuse to put off surgery, yet again.

"You know, if your doc is really good, I might just have him fix my rotator cuff," he said.

"You have a bad rotator cuff?" she asked.

"Both of them, actually," he admitted. "The left one ain't so bad, but the right cuff is completely severed. Any time I hold my arm at shoulder height, or above, it tingles and starts going numb almost immediately."

"Well, that doesn't sound good."

"Aw, you get used to it… except at night," David stated. "I have to sleep with my hands folded on my belly, like a body in a casket! And, I can't sleep on my sides… which makes it really tough to cuddle up with someone."

"Yes," she stated flatly. "You'll definitely have to get that fixed. I love to cuddle! That's one of the things I miss most, by living alone!"

David liked the sound of that. He also loved to cuddle and spoon, he admitted, but he was just getting used to doing without.

"Well, we won't be doing any cuddling in Reno," she teased, "But, maybe, if we hit it off, well… maybe somewhere down the road?"

"I'd like that," David said sincerely. "Especially if it is with someone like you!"

They finished their conversation shortly thereafter, and hung up. David was ecstatic.

"Hot damn," he said out loud. "I'm going to Reno, to meet the future Mrs. Remington!"

So far, it was all roses and cream, for them. He was just praying that it wouldn't turn sour!

"This is 'the one,'" he said to himself. "I just know it!!"

Chapter 14

"Lake Tahoe casts its magical spell!"

The drive from Las Vegas to Reno was made in record time (for him anyway), as David played all his old Chris LeDoux, and Kyle Evans CD's. He sang nearly the whole trip, and was getting hoarse by the time he got there. The music by these great cowboy artists, took David back to his rodeo days, and for a while, he felt like he was in his 30's again. He was ecstatic about meeting the woman he hoped would be "the one," but, he was also concerned.

"Basically, this is just a coffee date," he thought. "Our first time meeting."

And, as he clicked through the ladies he had met during the past few months, since he began his "system" and the "coffee dates," his record of success hadn't been much to brag about. Not only was he concerned that he might not feel the "magic" for her, but, what if she didn't feel it for him?

Their conversations, during the past two weeks, since they had connected online, had moved to the point that he was certain that he had nothing to worry about, in any other regard, except for this very basic physical attraction. But, it was a critically important factor.

David knew that physical attraction alone was not a reason to fall in love... fall in lust, perhaps, but that was only for a night or two. But, sincere friendship, and genuine caring, without a physical attraction, is also not right. Physical attraction, or sex appeal, was a crucial ingredient in any successful romantic relationship. And, that's what both he and Karen wanted, right? A successful romantic relationship? David also realized, a relationship like that requires trust, honesty, and a true feeling of caring, that goes way beyond the bedroom, too.

He was content with the knowledge that, this was not supposed to be a romantic weekend, just two friends, staying in separate rooms, exploring Lake Tahoe by day, and the sites of Reno, by night. If he did not feel any "magic," when they met, he knew that they had already established a solid foundation of friendship. If romance was not in their future, it would still be a fun and memorable weekend, with a new friend.

Of course, that all sounded good, but in his heart, he still believed that Karen was "the one," and he desperately hoped for "magic," this weekend, so they could move on to the "next-level," whatever that might be?

When David topped the ridge near Sparks, and he first saw the city of Reno, his phone buzzed, telling him that he had an incoming text. It was from Karen, letting him know that she had just arrived at the hotel.

Since it was too early for check-in, David suggested she find a coffee shop, or something like that, inside the hotel, and they could meet there. He told Karen that he was less than a half an hour away, so she wouldn't have long to wait. Especially since his foot was now buried deeply into the gas-pedal!

Soon, David was in the parking garage, and found a place to park. He texted Karen and asked where she was.

"Well, I wasn't really hungry, and I've had more coffee this morning than I usually drink in a week, so I found a little Mexican Cantina. They have a full menu, if you're hungry, but I am having a drink, to settle my nerves!"

She chuckled at the last comment, but David's nerves were also a little on edge. He was also not hungry, and was glad that she had found a place where he could get a cold beer, instead.

"I'll be right there," he responded.

122

The Silver Legacy, like most major resort hotels, had a "shopping concourse," with fancy shops that sold every manner of expensive souvenirs, clothing ($100 for a glittery tee-shirt!), ski-wear and equipment, and even art galleries. Along this concourse were several restaurants, taverns, and fast-food chains, as well as the Mexican Cantina David was searching for.

When he first saw the sign for the Cantina, David noticed that it was basically a long bar in back, by the full-length windows, which showcased a view of the city. There were also tables and booths, which were filled with tourists eating lunch. The entire Cantina was "open" to the concourse, separated only by a wrought iron railing, which guided people to the hostess-podium, for seating. As he walked along the railing, headed for the entrance, the entire place was visible, including the long bar.

He scanned the tables and booths, looking for a diminutive lady, with long blonde hair. Then, he saw her… or at least, the back of her. Seated at the bar. Near one end of it, were a group of tourists, laughing and talking, but at the opposite end of the bar, seated quite alone, he saw a short woman with long blonde hair.

The girl was facing away from him, and sitting on the bar stool, her long blonde hair cascaded down the back of the chair, reaching nearly to the seat. She was wearing a fancy "Buckaroo-style" cowboy hat, jeans and a black leather jacket. He raced past the Hostess, pointing to the bar, and she acknowledged him with a nod. Approaching her from behind, David also noticed the woman-at-the-bar, had a nice, shapely figure, and he sucked-in his breath.

"Wow," he muttered out loud.

He slowed his pace, as much to catch his breath, as to be able to drink-in every detail of the lady he was about to meet. She was still looking outside, through the window, and he stepped up beside her. When she turned her head to face him, a smile lit up her face, and her beautiful blue eyes began to twinkle.

"Karen?" he asked.

"David?" she responded, as she swiveled her chair to face him.

David knew what he was feeling, at that exact moment, and from her expression, it seemed, she felt it, too. Magic!

David took her hands in his and kissed one of them lightly, but their eyes were locked. Neither spoke for, what seemed, an hour…although it was only a few seconds.

David thought that she looked an awful lot like her pictures, except her complexion was not as youthful as it had once been. But, he knew, people who spent a great deal of time in the sun, such as cowgirls, often suffered the consequences by showing age-lines, and wrinkles around the mouth and eyes. And, while it made her look more her age, a few years older than himself, it also added to her character, and proved that she was not just a "wanna-be" cowgirl, but the real thing.

David wasn't sure where the words came from, but as he gazed lovingly into her eyes, he said:

"As I stand here, seeing my own reflection in your eyes, for the very first time, I can say truthfully, and from the heart, I think I'm falling in love with you."

He almost expected her to say, "But David, we're not there yet," as was so common in internet dating. But, instead, she just beamed with joy, totally speechless. He wasn't sure who started it, but they found themselves locked in an embrace, that lasted for a full minute. When they pulled apart, slowly, neither wanting to let go, her smile turned coy.

"I think that's the sweetest thing anyone ever said to me," she responded, finally.

The bartender broke their trance when he asked David if he wanted a drink. David glanced at Karen's glass, which was still half-full of, what he guessed, was whiskey and water, and he ordered a beer. With the spell broken, he climbed onto the seat beside her, so they could talk.

"The desk clerk said it is way too early for check-in," she said, "So, I just left my bags at the bell desk. They told me I could leave them there for as long as I needed."

"I figured as much," David replied, "So, I just left mine in the truck."

He actually drove a huge SUV, a Nissan Armada, but it was his workhorse, so he referred to it as his "truck." Karen, on the other hand, had a ¾-ton Dodge pickup, which could haul her horse trailer up and down the mountains of central California, with no trouble at all.

"Want me to put these on the same tab?" the bartender asked, as he set the glass of beer in front of David.

"Absolutely," David replied.

David told Karen that he had once been an air traffic controller at the Reno airport, for close to three years, with an apartment in Sparks, before he transferred back to Las Vegas. Over the years, she explained, she had visited frequently, both Tahoe and Reno, since it was only a three-hour drive. And, for the next hour they spoke, mainly, about various adventures they had enjoyed while in the area. He told her that, in 1998, when he first moved to Reno, he took a tour of the Ponderosa Ranch, near the lake.

"I've never seen that," she said. "But I used to love watching Bonanza on TV!"

"Well," David said, as he glanced at his watch, "...we're burning daylight, Pilgrim. You want to take a drive up to Lake Tahoe?" "I'd love that," she said enthusiastically.

"When we get back, we can get checked in to our rooms, freshen up a bit, and head out for the evening. What do you say?"

"That sounds wonderful," she said with a very coy look on her face.

David didn't notice the look on her face, as he was signaling the bartender to bring him the bill. He would find out a few hours later, just what the look had been about, if he had seen it, that is.

What he did notice, however, was that, when she slipped down from the barstool, all five-foot two-inches of her, she had a fairly severe limp, and she had to walk with a cane.

"So, we're not going to be hiking up any trails at Tahoe, I see," David said jokingly.

Cowboys always dealt with tragedy through humor, and Karen was a cowgirl, so she kicked right back. "Not unless you carry me the whole way," she laughed.

"Heck, I'd do that," he confessed. "But it would have to be a short trail! I'm not as young as I used to be!"

They both chuckled. But, if Karen were having any trepidations about how David was going to react to her injury, his comments set her mind perfectly at ease, on the matter. She knew he would not joke about it, if it bothered him.

They drove south, from Reno, through Carson City, then joined Highway-50 to the lake. Since David had once lived in the area, he was quite familiar with the route. Once they reached the lake, and turned north on the Nevada side, they stopped at several scenic overviews, and talked all along the way.

David had hoped to take her to see the old Ponderosa Ranch, where the television show Bonanza was filmed, but the place had been closed for several years, so he just told her about it, along the drive.

Lake Tahoe seemed to cast a magical spell on the couple, and they took a great number of pictures. David was sure to include Karen in every shot he took. And Karen had such a glow about her that, if it had been dark outside, she could have served as a lighthouse beacon!

After they left the lakeshore, and drove toward Mount Rose, they stopped at a tavern for a late-lunch and a drink. The route was a big circle, actually, and after leaving Mt. Rose, they would continue eastward, joining the highway just south of Reno, then back to the hotel. It was an absolutely perfect trip.

As they sipped their drinks, they reflected on the beauty and wonder of Lake Tahoe. Karen admitted that she had always dreamed of having her wedding at the lake, although she quickly made it clear, she wasn't suggesting that she and David get married… not yet, anyway.

"Well, if we do get married, this would be the perfect place," David offered. "My family could come up from Vegas, and get out of the desert heat, and your family could come down from Chico."

Then, they let the subject slip away, and their talk turned to other things. Karen's glow intensified! He found out later, that at that very moment, she had started planning a Tahoe wedding!

126

Since it was late-August, the days were about 14-hours long, and sunset was fairly late. By the time they returned to the hotel, the sun was just dropping behind the mountains, in a glorious sunset.

He parked the Armada on the roof of the parking garage, and he and Karen watched the beauty unfold before them, as they sat on the hood of the car. David had gently lifted her onto the car, first, then he leaned her cane against the bumper. "Well, I guess it's time we go get checked into our rooms," David said finally, as he slipped off the car.

Karen hesitated.

"About that…" she stammered shyly. "I don't want you to get the wrong idea about me, but, uhmmm…"

David stepped in front of her, as she was still sitting on the hood of the car, and placed himself between her legs. She put her arms around his neck, and pulled herself very close. He leaned in, for their very first romantic kiss. And she responded to the deeply passionate kiss, as a soft moan escaped her lips, when they pulled apart slightly.

"Now, what was it you were saying?" he asked gently.

"Well, I didn't actually make a reservation," she confessed. "You didn't?"

"No," she said nervously. "But, I called them and asked about their occupancy this weekend, and they said it should be no trouble just walking up and getting a room… they had plenty of vacancies."

"So, what are you saying, then?"

David felt a slight stirring in his jeans, and he knew that the Little Outlaw was awake and paying close attention!

"Well, when I went to the bell-desk to drop of my suitcase, I was sure to confirm that they still had rooms left, and they did…"

David was still just a bit confused, but he liked where this seemed to be heading.

"So, you didn't make a reservation, but they have a room for you, whenever you want. I get it. Why'd you do it that way?"

"Well, you know," she stammered. "When we first met… if we didn't feel anything, no physical attraction, I thought I'd just go down, then, and get that room for myself." "But if we did?" David asked.

"Well," again she became very coy, eyes downcast and looking just a tiny bit fearful. "Well… in that case… you know, I just… well, I didn't think we'd need two rooms."

She looked up at him with hopeful eyes.

"But, I wasn't sure how you would feel about that… about me?"

David leaned in and gave her another long, passionate kiss, and held her even tighter than before. As the kiss ended, he continued the hug, and slid her gracefully off the hood of the car, setting her down beside her cane. "So, why don't we go get checked in to our room," he said with a devilish smile.

Karen patted the Wrangler-patch on his back pocket, and said, "Why not?"

David pulled away, so he could open the rear-hatch of the Armada and grab his duffle bag. Afterwards, he looped his other arm around Karen's waist and they headed for the front desk. By holding her tightly, she could just lean on him for support, without need of the cane, so she just carried it. The heat of the moment quickly passed, and David asked her if she still wanted to freshen up, and go get something to eat?

"We didn't eat lunch until almost three o'clock," she pointed out. "I'm really not hungry."

"You're right," David agreed. "I'm still full. That mushroom burger was huge!"

"This is a twenty-four-seven town," she offered. "If we get hungry later, we can just go grab something…"

"Or, order room-service," David added.

"Right now," she said. "I might go for a whiskey and water, though. I've got to tell you, my stomach is turning flip-flops! A drink might just calm me down a bit."

"It just so happens, I brought a bottle of Pendleton," David said. "They'll have glasses in the rooms, and an ice bucket… that's all we'll need."

Karen just smiled.

"Sounds good to me."

Once they got to their room, they decided to take turns in the shower, just because they hadn't actually seen each other naked, yet. It seemed like the polite way to handle it.

"I'll see if I can find a Country music channel on the television, while you scrape off a layer of dirt," David said with a smile.

Karen came over and gave him a quick kiss.

"David, I want you to know..." she said hesitantly. "I have never done anything like this before, ever! I've never even slept with a man on the first date, before."

"Then why me, why now?" he asked sincerely.

"I don't know," she answered truthfully. "It just feels right."

With another peck on the cheek, she turned and headed toward the bathroom. David watched her go, not even noticing her limp!

"There is nothing like a gal, with a cute butt, wearing tight jeans, to get a cowboy's full attention," he said to himself, smiling as she closed the bathroom door. "Or the Little Outlaw's either."

While she was taking a shower, and getting freshened-up, he looked at the television offerings from the hotel, as he had promised. There were no "music-only" stations, but he settled on CMT, Country Music Television, which featured a lot of terrific music videos, and there were even some "cowboy-crooners," like Chris LeDoux, David's favorite Country artist.

The bathroom was fairly large, and Karen had brought only a single suitcase, although it was big, and it felt completely stuffed, when David lifted it onto the suitcase stand, provided by the hotel. He had moved the stand into the bathroom, at Karen's request, so he knew she had her full travel wardrobe available.

He also figured the weight of the bag was due to things like a makeup kit, hair dryer, curling iron, evening wear, casual wear, and "lounging around" wear, like a pair of sweat pants and an over-sized tee shirt, which is what he expected her to be in, when she came out. He had also calculated that, since this was supposed to be just a weekend between two friends, that Karen would not have brought any lingerie. He was wrong on that count!

When she finally emerged from the bathroom, David was sitting on the bed, watching the music videos on television. The room itself was dimly lighted by a single desk lamp, making it easier for old eyes to see the television. Directly outside of the bathroom, however, was a vanity, and a closet, and the small area was brightly illuminated. Karen peered around the corner, nervously, the lights from the vanity much like a spotlight on her. David completely forgot that the television was even turned on. "Well, what do you think?" she asked nervously, as she stepped into full view.

"Oh, my," was all he could say… but he said it several times!

She was wearing a soft-pink teddy, with a built-in push up bra. With her petite figure, the bra actually gave her a hint of cleavage, which was a delight. The bottom was a G-string, and when she pirouetted on her good leg, David got the full view of her lingerie. He couldn't wait to see the rest of her, once the lingerie was piled on the floor.

He was off the bed in an instant, and wrapped her in a warm embrace, while his hands cupped her bare bottom for just a moment. She pulled away, pinching her nose playfully.

"Well, one of us is cleaned up, anyway!" she teased. "Shall we go for two?"

David gave her a quick peck on her forehead, grabbed his duffle, and headed for the bathroom.

"I'll be out in a jiffy," he said.

"That's because you don't have much hair to dry," she laughed.

She limped over to the bed, and took David's place, watching music videos. He had made them both drinks, and he raced back to the dresser, where he had placed hers, and handed it to her.

"Thank you, Hon," she said taking a gulp of the drink.

David carried his into the bathroom and closed the door. He took a quick shave and shower, and emerged from the bathroom in less than 15 minutes. He stuck his head around the corner, keeping himself mostly hidden from her view, as she sat on the bed.

"Oh," he said. "I meant to ask you, before I went in… boxers?"

He held a pair of boxer shorts out so she could see them, in his left hand.

"Or briefs?" he asked.

The briefs were in his right hand, and to show them to her, he stepped into the light, just as she had done. He was holding the briefs in one hand, boxers in the other, and he was completely naked.

"Well, well. What's wrong with what you're wearing?" she asked. "I think you'd better saddle-up, Cowboy…"

He dropped both pairs of underwear, and raced to the bed. They did not come out of the room for the rest of the night. It was one of the most romantic, and wild, sexual adventures either of them had experienced, in a very long time.

The next morning, at the crack of 9 a.m., David felt a stirring beside him. For a moment, he didn't even know where he was at, then it all came back to him. His eyes opened just as Karen was getting out of the bed, heading to the bathroom. She was still naked, and a smile crossed his lips, as the bathroom door closed.

David figured she would be in there for a while. He was guessing that she would emerge, dressed for the day, and ready to go eat breakfast. He wished that he had been able to get in there before she started dressing and fussing with her hair. His bladder was quite full.

"Oh, well," he thought. "I guess I'll just have to 'cowboy-up' and wait."

But the door opened a few seconds later, and she was still naked, hobbling back to her side of the bed. He rolled out the other side.

"My turn," he announced, as he raced to the toilet.

Karen giggled playfully. It was chilly in the room, and she climbed back under those warm blankets as fast as she could.

"I left the light on, for you."

Like Karen, David was a bit chilled, after leaving the bathroom, so he raced to the bed, and very quickly ducked under the covers, to get warm. They snuggled together, like two spoons in a drawer. Their passions ignited again, and their cold chill soon turned to heat.

The hotel's check-out time was normally at 11 a.m., but the front desk approved them to stay in the room until 1 p.m. So after they took a shower together, they dressed and went down to partake in the Sunday Brunch, at the hotel's buffet. They also had a great deal to discuss, such as their future together, and when they would next meet.

"Well, I have surgery on my hip, in just over a month," Karen reminded him. "And I don't think either one of us can afford a plane ticket, between now and then…"

"Yeah," David admitted. "Retirement is great, but those once-a-month paychecks take some getting used to. I get paid on the 1st, although, if the 1st falls on a weekend, I get paid the Friday before."

"Today is the 1st of September," she observed.

"Exactly. Which is why I had the money for gas to get here!"

"Well, my surgery is the first week of next month, then it'll be at least six-weeks before I can have sex again…" She suddenly realized what she had just said, and looked around to see if anyone might have overheard.

David chuckled at her embarrassment.

"Well, we have plenty of time to talk about all that stuff," he said looking at his watch. "We'd better be going."

"You're right," she agreed. We still have to repack everything, and clear out of the room."

Later, he walked her to her truck, carrying her bags, and his. They had a final embrace, and a very long kiss, while she warmed up her truck. Finally, she pulled away, and he headed back to the elevator, so he could get to his Armada on the top level.

"There is absolutely no doubt in my mind," he said to himself. "Karen…is the one."

Chapter 15

"For better or for worst, in sickness and in health!"

"Absolutely not," Karen said firmly, into the phone.

"But Karen, it makes perfect sense," David said, trying to convince her.

"I don't care what you say," she argued. "I am not going to let you come up here, and see me, right after my surgery!"

"I told you, I am not coming for a 'conjugal visit,' I want to come help you, during your recovery, that's all."

"My daughter can do that, just fine…"

"Karen, she lives fifteen miles away, and, she has her own husband and little boy to take care of. How is she going to be there every time you need a drink of water, or to help you getting to the bathroom?"

After the Reno-trip, David and Karen spoke every day, at least once a day. And after a few weeks, as her hip-replacement surgery drew near, it was their main topic of discussion.

"I told you, I am going to stay with Bonnie and her family for the first week, after I get out of the hospital." Karen was adamant. "The doctor said I can get out of bed, after that, and start walking."

"Yes, but he also said, just short walks…"

"Like to the bathroom, or to get a glass of water," she interrupted. "It'll be good for me to get up and walk."

"Bullshit," David snapped back. "What if you fall?"

"I won't."

"You don't know that, and what if you go to the bathroom, and you can't stand up? Your doc said that might happen, you know."

"I'll be fine," she said. "I don't want you to see me like that... like a helpless invalid."

"Oh, put your vanity aside," David countered. "What if we were already married?"

"Well that would be different," she admitted.

"For better or for worse, in sickness and in health. Do you recognize those words?"

"Marriage vows, so what?"

"So I take those vows very seriously..."

"But we're not married, David," she objected. "We've never said those vows."

"Not yet, but we intend to, right?" he said. "What better way for you to see just how serious I am about that. Think of it as a test run."

"We spent one night together," she pointed-out. "What makes you think we're ready for a test-run?"

"Okay, if you didn't need any surgery, and we'd had an incredible night together, as we did... would you invite me up there now? Just to meet your family, and your horse?"

"But I DO need the surgery..."

"Karen, you said you loved me. And, I love you. Let me prove to you just how much I love you."

Karen didn't interrupt. She was listening.

"Look, it's all a part of the deal... our deal," David continued. "We're not getting any younger, and well, let's face it, we are both going to get sick, and need surgeries, perhaps. Who knows? And part of our deal is to be there for each other, so we won't be a burden to our children... your daughter." "Yes, of course," she agreed.

"Let me prove to you that those are not just words, to me. Let me prove to you… no, let me show you, just how much I love you. Next month, when you really do need someone to be there with you. Let it be me."

"I don't know…" she said weakly.

"Karen, by the time you have your surgery, I'll have another paycheck, and I'd be planning to come see you anyway…"

"I told you, I can't have sex for at least three weeks, after the surgery."

"What the Hell? Who said anything about sex? I am talking about love, not sex."

"Well, just so you know…"

"Karen, I would love to be there to hold your hand before you go in," he said sincerely. "And to be the first face you see when you wake up, after."

"No. Absolutely out of the question," she said with firm resolve. "I told you, I have already made arrangements to stay with Bonnie and Bill, for a week after…"

"And Tyler!" David interrupted. "Don't forget you have a two-year old grandson running wild in that place, too. How restful do you think that will be?"

"He is a handful, I agree… but Bonnie will keep him under control."

"Good luck with that! They don't call them the 'terrible-twos' for nothing."

"Well, I can't argue with that," she chuckled.

"Okay, alright, how about this?" David offered. "When Bonnie takes you home… after a week… how about, I'll be waiting for you, there? At your house."

David was encouraged by the long hesitation.

"How long will you stay?"

"As long as it takes. Two, three weeks, a month. How long before the doc says you can go back to work?"

"A month after surgery," she replied.

"So, a week at your daughter's, and three weeks with me. Once you're strong enough to go back to work, you won't need me anymore, so, I'll take off."

"Ah, but by then… well, you know, that's when I'll want you the most," she said with a coy smile.

"I'll come back, I promise! I want that, too… but not on this trip!" David said eagerly. "So, can I come help you get back on your feet?

There was a long hesitation.

"Okay," she finally said, softly.

The next morning at coffee, with Chance, David caught him up on the newest development, in his new relationship with Karen. Chance was somewhat supportive, but more cautious.

"Don't you think you guys are just going a little too fast?"

"What're you talking about?" David asked. "You guys had one night together…" "One magic night," David corrected.

"Okay, one magic night," Chance repeated, sarcastically, "And now you're gonna drive all the way to California…Northern California… to play nursemaid to a lady you've known a few weeks?" "Almost a month…"

"Oooh, a month! That changes everything." Chance retorted.

"Look, Chance, she needs me…"

"Bullshit. She had that surgery scheduled before you ever met her, and she'd have gotten by just fine, even if she'd never met you."

"But, I love her, and I don't want her to have it rough," David defended. "I'd do the same thing for you."

"Well, I appreciate that, and I know you would. But, we go way back…been friends a lot of years. Think back, to when we had just met. What if I had needed a live-in nurse back then?"

"I see your point," David replied.

"And, I live here. Do you think for one minute you'd have traveled 600 miles to do it?"

"Chance, I understand what you're saying, but this is a lot different."

"Why? Because you had sex one night?"

"No, because I see a future with her. People can say shit all day long about how much they care for someone, or love someone, but it's just words. Me going up there is more than just words. It's actually showing her that there is iron, in my promises."[2] Chance sat back in his chair and sipped his coffee, as if he was barely paying attention. He knew that his friend had made up his mind, and there was no use talking sense to him.

"Besides," David concluded. "We'll be together 24/7 for three weeks. What better way to find out if we can live as husband and wife, than spending three weeks together?"

Chance took another sip of coffee, then looked over at David.

"Do you think Garrett should have pulled Romo last night?"

David shook his head for a moment, trying to figure out what he was talking about. Jason Garrett was the coach of the Dallas Cowboys, and both David and Chance were big fans of the team.

"You think Kitna could have done any better?" David asked.

"He damn sure wouldn't have thrown three interceptions…"

The conversation turned purely to football, after that. Chance had said his piece, and there was no sense "beating a dead horse," he thought. So, subject closed. Chance knew that David might well be heading for disaster, but he also knew the man was as hard-headed as a mule, and there was nothing left for him to do, except be there to pick up the pieces, when it was all over.

A few weeks later, David was pulling into a nice little "family" trailer park, on the outskirts of Chico. There were shade trees and fruit trees, yards were clean and well kept, and as he searched for the correct space, he passed a playground, with several children enjoying the warm autumn day.

"Well, if we're gonna be 'trailer-trash,' this looks like a nice enough place to do it," he said to himself.

He saw the tiny, single-wide mobile home, where Karen lived, and directly in front of it was a small parking lot, designated for "guests,"

---

[2] "Iron in my promises" is an American Indian saying that means true to his word.

exactly as she had told him. The trailer had an awning, and a covered redwood porch on one side, and a carport on the other. He recognized Karen's truck, and knew he was in the right place. But, they had spoken a few minutes earlier, and Bonnie and Karen were still on their way from Bonnie's house.

David got out, to stretch his legs. It had taken 12-hours to get there, from Vegas, but he was so excited about seeing Karen again, he hardly noticed the tired muscles. A few minutes later, a compact, silver SUV pulled up behind the truck, in Karen's driveway. David raced to open the door for Karen.

Karen was smiling, but her face still showed the pain, as she swiveled her legs around. David was surprised to see that she did not have a cast. Bonnie jumped out and ran around to help, just as David leaned in for a hug and a kiss.

"Get a room," Bonnie quipped uncomfortably.

David stood quickly, and turned to Karen's daughter, who reached out her hand, with a pleasant smile.

"Hi, you must be David," she said, as they shook hands. "I'm Bonnie."

She was very direct, and looked him over suspiciously. After all, this is the man who was dating her mother! David removed his hat, as was the cowboy-custom when meeting a lady.

"I'm pleased to meet you, Bonnie," he said. "I've heard a lot about you, and some of it was actually good!"

Bonnie laughed, and the ice was broken.

"They gave me a walker," Karen said, nodding toward the back seat.

Bonnie quickly grabbed it, and unfolded it for Karen, as David gently helped her to her feet.

"I've been walking, for about five minutes at a time, as often as I could," Karen said, adjusting herself to the walker. "For the past couple of days, anyway."

"She's been doing really well," Bonnie admitted. "But make sure she uses that walker for at least five more days."

As they approached the three steps leading up to the back door, Karen stopped.

"Oops," she said. "I guess I should have practiced climbing a few steps, too. I'm not sure how I can do this…"

"Easy," David remarked. "I'll carry you."

"Wait… let me unlock the door," Bonnie said, as she went around them to the back door.

"And go open some windows… and the front door," Karen told Bonnie, in a very motherly tone. "It's got a screen door," she said to David. "Yes, mother," Bonnie answered, stepping into the house.

"She never calls me 'mother,' unless I piss her off," Karen said softly to David. "Now, how do you want to do this?"

David stepped up beside her, and looped his arm around her waist. Karen let go of the walker and wrapped her arms around his neck. He was careful to stand on her "good" side, so the injury would not be pushing against his ribs, when he lifted her. "You let me know if this hurts at all," he said gently.

"Oh, if it hurts, you'll hear me scream," she chuckled. "But, I'll just 'cowgirl-up.'"

David slowly, and gently, swept her into his arms, and she clung to him like a new bride, kissing him softly on the cheek.

"I really am glad you're here," she whispered, as they slowly climbed the steps. "My bedroom is to the right, bathroom straight ahead, and the kitchen and living room are to the left…"

"So, where do you want to go?"

"Living room…put me on the couch."

"Windows and doors are open," Bonnie announced, standing just inside the door. "If you are going to lay on the sofa, I'll grab some pillows."

Bonnie darted toward the bedroom. David hesitated before stepping inside.

"Wow," he said, looking deep into Karen's eyes. "I guess it is totally appropriate that I carry my young bride across the threshold!"

"Not without kissing me first," Karen said, moving her lips toward his.

It was a deep and passionate kiss, and by the time they pulled apart, Bonnie had passed them, with the pillows.

"Oh, my God, Mom!" Bonnie admonished. "You know what the doctor said!"

"It's just a kiss," she replied innocently. "He said no sex, that's all."

Bonnie groaned, then chuckled as she quickly walked toward the sofa, with the pillows. David followed her in. Karen was pointing out the features of the small, but cozy little home, to David as he carried her into the living room.

From the hallway, it actually opened into a single large room. The kitchen had linoleum flooring, and where the carpet began, so did the living room. Karen had furnished it with quaint antiques, or copies of antiques, with a lovely high-backed chair and sofa to match.

David gently set her down on the sofa, and Bonnie fussed with her, making sure she was comfortable.

"Bonnie, I'm fine," she said gently, but firmly. "You better get back to Bill… you know he loses patience with that baby, when he's left alone for too long!"

"Where's your purse?" Bonnie asked.

"In the car?" Karen asked, unsure.

"I'll go get it. Geez, Mom, it's got your keys, your wallet, everything…"

"I know, I know." She replied. "But I knew you'd never let me forget it!"

"She is always leaving that thing somewhere," Bonnie said to David. "If you go anywhere, keep your eyes on it!" "I will…" David promised.

"Where do you think we're gonna go?" Karen asked innocently.

"Mom, I know you… you haven't seen Pistol in over a week. And he's just right over there," Bonnie pointed. "David, it's all gravel walkways, so promise me you won't let her talk you into going to see her

horse, until after she stops using the walker?"

"Bonnie!" Karen said, raising her voice slightly.

"I wasn't talking to you, Mother," she replied, while still looking at David.

"I promise," David said. "It's only going to be, what, five more days, you said?"

"Yes. Oh, that reminds me," Bonnie quipped as she headed to the car. "The hospital gave me a list of post-operative care instructions. I'll grab it, and go over it with you, before I leave." "Oh, that'd be great," David responded.

David looked at his watch, and saw that it was nearly six o'clock.

"Are you getting hungry?" David asked Karen.

"Oh, yes! Famished… Bill hates to have supper before seven o'clock. He's weird like that."

"Do you want me to run into town and grab something? A pizza, hamburgers?"

"No, I really want you to stay here with me…" she said. "I've missed you."

David sat down on the coffee table beside her, and leaned over for a quick kiss.

"I'm pretty sure there's hamburger in the freezer, and some spaghetti sauce in the pantry," she said pointing to it. "I'll take a look," he said, standing.

"After we go over these instructions," Bonnie said, having heard just the last part of the conversation.

"Just leave them on the table," Karen told her. "I can go over everything with David. I'm not in a coma, you know."

"Aw, Mom,"

"Bonnie, seriously, we can handle everything. You'd better get home and cook that man of yours his supper. David and I will be just fine," Karen finished.

"You sure?" she said hesitantly, as she set the purse and several pages of instructions on the table.

"Get!! Go on…" Karen said forcefully.

"We'll be fine," David said sweetly to Bonnie. "I'm going to cook us supper, and if I run into any problems, your mom has your number."

"You sure?"

"Yes. I can take it from here."

Reluctantly, Bonnie gave her mother a kiss, and she had a hug for David, before she headed out. David followed her to the door. Bonnie stepped down onto the porch, and leaned close to David, so her mother wouldn't hear.

"David, thank you," she said quietly. "You're a godsend… I don't know how I could've done this without some help."

David leaned down and kissed the top of her head.

"You're a good daughter," he said. "And, I am very, very happy to be here, where I am truly needed. I really love your mother, and she's in good hands. You'll see."

Bonnie smiled and started toward her car.

"You know… honestly… I was worried you might be some whacko, or serial killer, or something. But not anymore. I think Mom is very lucky to have found you, even if it was on the internet." "No," David replied seriously. "It's me, who is the lucky one."

He watched until Bonnie had started backing out of the driveway, then closed the door and locked it. He strolled into the kitchen, as Karen watched him, with a sweet smile on her face.

"So, what say I rustle us up some grub," David said, pulling open the pantry door.

Chapter 16

"The umbilical cord is still attached!"

The first five days David spent at Karen's, he stayed true to his word to Bonnie, and basically held Karen hostage in the house, or on the front porch. They actually spent quite a bit of time on the front porch, each day, once the morning began to warm. David sat in a large redwood beach chair, that was as almost as comfortable as an old wooden rocker – but, that's where Karen sat!

Karen scooted all over the little place, with her walker, but often, she just pushed it in front of her, rather than leaning on it. She was progressing very well, and healing quickly.

David quickly learned his way around the area, bought groceries, and a "u-bake-it" pizza, which they washed down with a beer. Karen was still on antibiotics, so her doctor told her, no more than one beer per day. But that was enough for her. They talked for hours on end, planning a future together, and they were intoxicated, just by each other's presence.

David cleaned the house, from top to bottom, although Karen was usually such a meticulous housekeeper, it wasn't hard for him to wipe off a little dust, here and there. He also doted over Karen, making certain she followed the post-op instructions, to the letter. But, the kitchen became his favorite place.

He had always loved to cook, and did all the family cooking while he was married. But, since his children had all moved away from home, he seldom had the opportunity, or need, to cook. At the grocery store, he loaded up on fresh vegetables, peppers and spices, and he couldn't wait to surprise Karen with his next creation, whatever it might be.

David noted that, Bonnie called, or texted her mother, at least five times, or more, per day. She would often call with, what he thought were ordinary child-rearing problems – her two-year old was giving her fits. What two-year-old didn't?

He knew that his own daughters had gone through similar difficulties with his grandsons, and they had called their mother occasionally (unless it was a cooking issue, in which case Dad took the call). But, Dana didn't dwell over them, so, eventually, their girls learned how to handle it on their own. David was very proud of the mothers, his baby girls had become.

"You know," David had told Karen, "...at some point, you are going to have to let go of your little girl."

"What do you mean?"

"I mean, like last night," he explained. "She called to say that Tyler was coughing, and it was keeping him, and them, awake."

"Yes, wasn't that awful?"

"Well, yeah," David admitted. "But, who taught you to give your daughter a teaspoon of cough syrup, when Bonnie was a baby?"

"Well, no one," she admitted. "I had to figure all that stuff out by myself."

"Exactly, me, too. Life is a journey," he explained. "And, once our babies leave home and start their own families, we have to let them learn those little lessons on their own, too. They have to realize they are competent, capable adults, and they can make their own choices. Children's RobiCough might have been the medicine that worked best for you, but they might have even better stuff today."

"So, what're you saying?"

"You should have just told her, 'Go get some cough syrup,' and been done with it. She'd have read the labels, and figured it out."

Karen nodded her head, but five minutes later, the phone buzzed again, with another text from Bonnie. And Karen instantly started tapping out a response, this time to tell Bonnie that, 'when you bake a cake, you have to turn it out to cool, on a wire rack, before you frost it.'

David just grabbed the laundry basket, with all of their dirty clothes in it, and told Karen that he was going to the park's laundromat. Karen never looked up, and never heard a word, as she was still typing her response to Bonnie. When she hit "send," she looked up at David.

"Oh, are you going to do laundry?" she asked.

"Yes… I just told you that," he said, a trace of annoyance in his voice.

"Oh, I'm sorry, I guess I didn't hear you…"

"I know," he replied. "Bonnie needed your advice on something. Again. I'll be back soon."

David made a note, literally, in his notebook, that they would have to work out a better way for Karen to handle Bonnie's constant texts and calls. David really didn't mind Karen answering every one, although he felt that Karen should just tell her daughter to figure out some of the smaller things, on her own. But, when that custom ringtone for Bonnie went off, text or call, Karen instantly turned her full and undivided attention to her cell phone.

David felt, that was just rude. He had always been taught that, the person in front of you is whom you should pay attention to first. If he really needed to respond to the phone, he was taught to say something like, "Excuse me for a moment, I need to take this call." He would never just immediately answer, or start reading an incoming text, while someone was talking to him.

But, except for the "communications" issue, everything else between them was going marvelously. David and Karen, had talked earlier, about his three-week visit being a good time for them to spot any potential issues that might cause them grief, somewhere down the road. They had both agreed to keep a notepad handy, so they could write these things down. And, before he left, they would have a chance to talk about them, and come up with solutions.

Both of them knew that their relationship was moving forward at lightening-speed, and all their friends and family warned each of them, to pull back… take more time to get to know each other better, first. But, neither of them felt there was a single problem they could not overcome… they were totally in love, and didn't love conquer all?

By the fifth day, Karen was totally ready to pitch her walker into the dumpster. She was walking well, with just the cane, and had an almost imperceptible limp. And, that was only due to the soreness of the hip, which was still healing, so it, too, would soon be gone forever. David helped her change the dressing on the incision-site, for the first day or so, but the stitches had already been removed, and it was quickly healed over.

"Do you want to go meet Pistol?" she asked, when David finally agreed that she could put the walker away, for good. "I'd love it if you'd take him out for a ride. I haven't been able to ride him, in like, forever."

"Well, that's not good," David said. "Has anyone been riding him?"

"No," she admitted. "I can't afford to pay a trainer, right now, so I've just got him turned out in a big corral."

"Trainer?" David thought to himself. All the cowboys and cowgirls, he knew, trained their own horses.

David realized that the horse would be feeling like a colt again, the first time he was saddled, after so long.

"Well, let's go meet him," David said. "I'll check his feet, see if he's got any sores, and such… and, if all looks good, I'll take him for a ride tomorrow."

Karen bubbled like a school girl who just got asked to the prom!

"Yea!" she beamed. "My doctor says I can start riding again, maybe in December… but probably in January."

By "rodeo-cowboy-standards," that was way too long! He'd known cowboys who had broken their pelvis, and they were back riding bucking horses, a month after the cast came off. He told her as much.

"I could show you some tricks," he said, "…to shorten that up quite a bit. We might get you back in the saddle by Thanksgiving, if you'll let me get you on a training regimen."

"Oh, no," she said. "I promised my doctor that I would follow every one of his instructions, to the letter."

"Hey, it's up to you," he said. "But if you really want to start riding again, I'm just saying, I can show you some good techniques to get you back in shape. And, of course, we'll let your doctor check you out, before you actually get on Pistol. We'd get the Doc's okay, first."

"Thank you," she said resolutely. "But no, I promised my doctor I wouldn't do anything foolish."

David let the issue drop, but he was puzzled. That didn't sound like the ranch cowgirl she had painted herself up to be, in their many phone conversations. That sounded more like a "California-cowgirl" answer, he thought. But, it was not a big deal to him, if she wanted to wait, it was her choice, and he would respect it.

Pistol was a beautiful Palomino Paint horse, about 15 hands tall, well-muscled, and eager for the treats Karen had stashed in her pocket. David looked at Pistol's feet, and he was barefoot, but recently trimmed, so he was ready to ride.

"Well, Pistol, old boy," David said patting him on the neck, "Tomorrow, we gonna get better acquainted, and see just how much 'fresh' you've got in you."

"Fresh horses," always had a little buck in them. But, usually, after a few minutes under saddle, with an experienced rider, they settled down and behaved themselves. David knew he was going to have his work cut out for him, but he was also a little excited about it. It had been a while, since he'd been on bucking horses, but he felt this might just take him for a trip down memory-lane.

The next day, with Karen beside him, they led Pistol into the saddling area, inside the main stables. It was a very fancy facility, and nearly every horse was a "high-dollar" show horse, of some kind, and Western saddles were seldom seen.

David nodded politely to the other riders, in their cute little English suits and helmets. He understood the joy of equestrian competition, but the "show-horse" stuff was just not for him, that's all. Most of the show-people were rich, and kind of snobs.

The "saddling area" had several individual stalls, with rings on either side of the opening, for cross-ties, so the horse could only move his head a foot, or so, in either direction. David had never used them.

Cowboys just tied their horses to a rail, or the side of a horse trailer, and saddled up.

"Go ahead and put Pistol in the cross-ties," Karen said, as she walked slowly toward the "locker room," using her cane.

The tack room featured dozens of individual "closets," with locking doors, to keep the rider's saddles and tack. Karen proceeded into the room, to unlock her little locker. David just looped Pistol's lead rope through one of the cross-tie rings, and followed her in.

When Karen opened the door to her locker, she had a beautifully ornate Western saddle, with matching bridle and reins. It looked awfully feminine to David, but after all, it was a lady's horse. It also looked, to David, very "Californian."

David thoroughly enjoyed the ride. And while Pistol had been hard-headed and stubborn at first, he never even offered to buck, or get crazy. The cowboy soon had him behaving well, and responding to all his cues. Karen watched them, with a huge smile on her face.

"I'll ride him every day while I am here." David promised.

"He really needs that," she acknowledged. "He's such a blockhead sometimes."

David dismounted, loosened the cinch, and they began to slowly walk back from the covered arena, to the barn. "By the time I leave, I'll have him gentle as a kitten," David said. "Are you sure you don't want me to show you how to shorten up your recovery-time, so you can start riding him yourself, by Thanksgiving?" Karen gave him a dutiful smile. "Thank you, but like I said…"

"I know, I know… you'll stick with the doctor's plan," he said shaking his head.

"Isn't this place beautiful?" Karen asked, quickly changing the subject.

"You know, it really is," David agreed. "A little too 'showy' for me, but I love the facilities…indoor arena, covered arena, round corral… it's got everything a cowboy needs. Well, except for other cowboys."

148

It was a little dig directed at all the show-people. Karen chuckled at the comment.

"I know," she said. "But Bonnie found this place… that's her horse over there."

Karen pointed it out. It was in one of the more expensive indoor stalls, with a small paddock attached. David instantly pictured Bonnie in one of those silly English riding get-ups, and the image fit her well.

"Nice," was all he could say, politely.

"And, when I found the vacancy at the mobile-home park next door, I moved Pistol right over." "I see," David said.

He was thinking that the umbilical cord was still attached between those two women. He hoped that his coming between mother and daughter, would not result in his being strangled by it.

"I wish I could find my own place, where I could keep Pistol at home, but we get a lot of rain here, and having a covered arena, is the only way to go."

"So, have you looked for something like that?"

"Oh, places with covered arenas go for, like, three-grand a month," she said. "Or more."

He just nodded his head, as they reached the saddling area. David dropped the reins, and started unstrapping the saddle.

"Shouldn't you, at least tie him up first?" Karen asked, reaching for the reins. "I usually put him in cross ties…"

David held up his hand to her, to just leave the reins hanging. "I guess you didn't know it, but your horse has been trained to stand ground-hitched," he said. "I checked that out, when we were in the arena. Besides, he's way too tired now, to fuss."

"Ground-hitching" is when a horse stands still, with the reins hanging in front of him, like in the old Western movies.

"Really?"

"Yes. Really," he said, as he slid the saddle off, and set it on the floor. "My trainer here didn't even know that," she said.

"I'll tie him, once I get a halter on him. Why don't you go get him one of those treats, he's so fond of?"

As she walked away, David realized that the Oregon cowgirl she had once been, was just a stack of memories for her now. After 20years of living in California, she had turned into a true "California Cowgirl." Even though she still talked of the "old days" fondly, and she truly believed she was still that same rough-n-tumble ranch cowgirl, she was completely "Californicated."

David knew that not every cowgirl who was from, or lived in, California was a "California-Cowgirl." There were a bunch of sure-enough cowgirls, from the Golden State. But "California-Cowgirls" were those who thought of their horses as "accessories," to make the girl look good, with expensive, matching bridles and tack. Those girls didn't much care how much "heart" the animal had, so long as it was the right color and height, to make the rider look her very best.

Cowgirls, on the other hand, didn't give a hoot about color, or height, it was all about the intelligence and heart, of the animal. And they never, ever used a trainer. Most real cowgirls he knew, just like the cowboys, felt that if they wanted a horse trained right, they'd do it themselves. And David had met a lot of these real cowgirls, Californians, on the rodeo circuit.

But, as far as David was concerned, Karen's transition to a California-Cowgirl was certainly no "deal-breaker," for their romance. It just meant he'd have to work at it a little harder. He might even have to learn a little of the culture, himself, so he could understand better, her perspective on things equestrian.

It would take some getting used-to, but a small bump in the road, is all that it was. He didn't even bother to put it in his notebook.

Later that evening, after David cooked roast chicken for supper, they sat on the porch and talked. It was cool enough that they both put on jackets. But the sunset had been beautiful.

"You know, we should check 'Gregslist' for local horse-properties… just to see what's out there, and what the rental prices are," David said.

"You mean, for us to rent together?" she asked, taking his hand, with a loving smile.

"Yeah. If you don't think it's too soon for us to get our own place?"

"Oh, I'd love to get a place together," she cooed. "I just think it will be way too expensive to get a horse property, right now."

"Who knows, until we look?" he stated. "If we can find something for, like $1,200, even as high as $1,500 if we had to, we could probably make that work."

"I think it'll be at least twice that," she replied. "But… it's worth a look, I guess. Gregslist is a great idea. I'll see what I can find on my computer, tomorrow."

David patted her gently on the knee, as he stood up.

"I'm going for another beer," he said. "Would you like something?"

She was still slowly sipping her daily allocation - one beer per day.

"No, I'm fine," she said with a smile. "I think I might like to take a bath, though."

"Well, then, I'll get the bathwater running, while I'm up," he said with a smile.

Helping her in and out of the tub was one of his favorite duties! They might not be able to have sex, just yet, but she still looked amazing to him, when she was naked!

After he had helped Karen into the tub, and she was soaking in exotic, healing oils and salts that Bonnie had found, David walked into the kitchen to do the dishes. Karen's phone rang, with Bonnie's special ring.

"David," he heard Karen call out. "Would you answer that, it's Bonnie!"

"I know," he said with a sigh, as he answered the phone.

The battery had been very low, so before she got in the tub, Karen had plugged it in to charge. The charger was in the kitchen, and David talked to Bonnie for a moment, then hung it up.

"Tell her I'll get right back to her," Karen shouted.

David walked around the corner, into the bathroom. Karen was draining the tub already anyway, and about to get up. It had been a short bath, but David knew her sense of urgency was all about getting 'right back' to Bonnie.

"I've already handled it," he said.

"You what?" she snapped.

"Relax, Karen," David said, trying to soothe her. "It was a cooking question. She's baking lasagna, and wanted to know whether to use ricotta or cottage cheese." "What'd you tell her?" she asked, as David helped her to stand up, and handed her a towel. "Well, ricotta, of course," David replied.

Karen hastily rubbed the towel over her hair and arms, then quickly wrapped it around herself.

"Oh, my God," she stammered. "I always use cottage cheese... I'll have to text her right now, so she doesn't screw it up!"

"Karen, both types of cheese taste great in lasagna, so what difference does it make?"

"Bonnie loves my lasagna," Karen explained, as she eased down the hallway as quickly as she could, without her cane, dripping water all the way. "She wanted to know how I make it, not you..."

David's jaw nearly hit the floor. He followed Karen into the kitchen, and she already had the phone in her hand, and she was texting furiously. "Seriously?" he said to her. "Ricotta is how the Italians make it. Cottage cheese is an American short-cut..."

But it was too late. He could tell that Karen did not hear a word he was saying.

"David was wrong, it's cottage cheese..." she was telling her daughter, via text message.

David just shook his head. Then, he had a passing thought. Standing just two feet away from her, David continued speaking. Karen was not talking on the phone, just typing and reading responses.

"In fact, in Italy, they passed a law," David said, in a normal speaking voice, "... that anyone using any cheese, other than ricotta, would be flogged in the town square. And usually, the crowd watching, became so incensed that they would stone the poor woman to death. That punishment continued right up until last year, when a spaceship landed in Rome, and the little Martians came out, demanding that the Italians start using cottage cheese, in their lasagna Believe it or not, the

Romans started throwing rocks at the little buggers. Then, the Martians grabbed some kind of laser cannon, and levelled the whole city. Millions of Italians died…"

Karen finally finished her "chat," laid the phone back on the counter, and turned to David.

"I'm sorry, what did you say?" She said sweetly.

David realized then, that this little communications issue might be a slightly bigger problem than he had imagined. But, he was still confident that they could come up with a solution.

Chapter 17

"This is it! This is right where we belong!"

At night, they slept together, with her in pajamas, of course, and him in his boxers, but they cuddled like spoons. Karen had to sleep on her side, to keep the replaced-hip elevated, and 'spooning' was just a natural position for them both.

However, between the torn rotator cuffs, and the pinched nerve in his neck, David could only cuddle for a little while, before he had to roll onto his back to sleep. But, it was still a comfort to them both just to be touching bodies, to feel the warmth of someone you love beside you.

That same night, after David had ridden Pistol for the first time, he helped Karen into bed. Then, he went into the bathroom to brush his teeth, and get ready, himself. While he was in there, he heard the bedroom television come on. He'd noticed the remote on her nightstand, but they had never watched it, at all, during his visit.

David knew that some people enjoyed watching television before they fell off to sleep, but not him. He was such a light sleeper, that, any noise at all kept him awake.

When he had traveled with different cowboys, during his rodeo years, if he wound up sharing a motel room with one of these "TV-people," he would wait until the other guy had drifted off to sleep. Then, he could turn the machine off, and fall asleep.

When it comes to television programming, again, it seemed, everyone had their own favorites... some liked reality shows, some science-fiction – zombies, werewolves, space aliens – but David preferred sitcoms, especially at night, if he had to watch anything at all. He figured, after the stress of the day, he just wanted to laugh a little. But the stack of DVD's beside Karen's television was mostly science-fiction, with a few historical dramas, like a show about Vikings. Nothing "comedy" about any of it.

By the time he came into the room, he found Karen laying on her side, watching one of her favorite shows. David had never even heard of it.

"You ever watch this show? She asked hopefully.

It was about zombies taking over the world. David turned to watch for a moment.

"No," he replied. "I don't watch much TV."

"Oh, I love this show," she said eagerly. "It's almost over. Do you mind if I finish this episode?"

"Of course not," he said, sitting on the edge of the bed. "I always wondered, though. If zombies are already dead, why do they need to eat humans? Or, anything at all, for that matter?"

"To make the show more frightening, I guess," she chuckled.

"And, once they take over the world, and turn everyone into zombies, will they all starve to death?"

"You think too much," she replied, holding up her hand. "Now, shush!"

He continued sitting on the bed, and tried to follow the show, but it all just seemed too bizarre. In both, books and television, he preferred characters and settings that could be real, such as the great classics, Moby Dick or The Iliad and the Odyssey – certainly not something like World of the Living Dead.

Finally, the credits began to roll, and Karen turned it off with the remote. David went back out and turned off the house-lights, checked the doors, and came back to the bedroom, wearing just his boxers. He slid in, beside Karen, and snuggled up beside her.

"Hey!" he said surprised. "Where's your pajama bottoms?"

"Oh, it's just too warm in here, tonight," she said innocently. "So, I took them off. You don't mind, do you?"

"Well, no, but, you know," he stammered. "You're supposed to wait another week yet, before we have sex…"

"My doctor said he didn't want me to try extending my hips until then," she said informatively. "But, cuddled up like this, with you behind me? I thought, well, hoped, we might give it a try?"

As she finished the sentence, her hand slipped inside David's boxers. That was all it took!

David was very gentle, but their passion burned like fire.

"Damn," he thought to himself later. "If watching zombies, before bed, always gets her like this, it just became my favorite show!"

But, it wasn't the zombies, that had sparked her fire, David was pleased to learn. And the "cuddle-sex" became a nightly routine… for the next week anyway, until she could resume "normal sexual activity" according to her doctor's instructions.

During the next few days, Karen's recovery continued at a rapid pace. They went to the stables each day, and Pistol was soon smooth gaited, responsive, and easy to handle. But, Karen hadn't had much success finding horse-properties, on the computer, in their price-range anyway.

"I told you, they're hard to find, and pricey, if you do," Karen said in exasperation.

"How big of a range are you looking? I mean, what areas?" "Well, it's the Chico page, on Gregslist," she responded.

"Maybe you should try some of the surrounding areas, like maybe as far north as Red Bluff," he suggested. "And, I don't know, Marysville to the south, maybe?"

"Not a bad idea," she said typing into the computer. "One of my best friends lives in Red Bluff. We might even look in Oroville… it's just 15 miles south of here, and has a beautiful lake. They have a recreation area, with horse-trails, too. And some great fishing."

David sat down beside her, on the sofa. She had her laptop on the coffee table, and they spent hours looking over the listings, in surrounding communities. They also had to consider that, once Karen was healed, she'd be going back to work—and her job was in Chico; so commute-distances were a big factor.

They were having little luck, and their hopes were slowly fading. They had found nothing affordable to the north, and had similarly struck-out in Marysville. They were down to a final area, Oroville. While she loaded that page on Gregslist, David went to refill his coffee cup.

"Hey… wait a minute," Karen gasped, looking through the Oroville listings. "Here's something on the north shore of Lake Oroville."

David quickly joined her, as the listing loaded.

"There's got to be some kind of mistake," David remarked.

"Holy crap!" Karen exclaimed, reading the property description.

The listing showed the place to be 28-acres of mountain wilderness, eight of which were irrigated bottomland pasture, fenced and cross-fenced. It had a huge, 100-year-old barn, a year-round creek that flowed the length of the property, passing 100 feet from a 2,000 sq. ft., 3 bedroom, 3-bath, ranch house. It also had an old "caretaker's cottage," which was actually the original old farm house, a swimming pool, a 20-tree, mature, fruit orchard, chicken coop, two tack rooms, and a five-stall horse stable.

"Oh, my God!" Karen gasped. "It's got a covered arena!"

David just whistled. And the price was listed at just $1,650 per month.

"That just can't be right," David said.

"I wonder what the heck the 'catch' is," Karen agreed.

"Well, it's a little over our budget," David admitted, "But I think we could handle it. That's almost exactly how much my retirement check is."

"And, I make enough to cover utilities, groceries and gas," Karen calculated, smiling.

"How far to Chico?" David asked, knowing Karen would have to drive it every day to work.

"Well… it looks like, around 40 miles," she said. "But, for a place like this, I'd drive twice that, if I had to!"

"There has got to be something wrong with it," David said suspiciously. "But, I think we ought to go take a look. Who knows?" Karen was already dialing her phone.

"You're only going to be here another week," she said, as the phone began to ring. "If it is still available, it won't be for long!"

"Boy, you've got that right!"

Karen spoke to one of the co-owners, a man named Dale. He told Karen that the place was, indeed, still available, but there was a young couple, with two children, coming to look at it that afternoon.

"We've had quite a few people come look," he said. "But, it's just too far for most of them to commute. Heck, gas is over four-bucks a gallon now."

Karen admitted that it was, indeed, a long drive, but that she had already considered it, and that it would not be a problem for her. She also explained about David, and that this was going to be their first home, together. She also told him that David was still residing in Nevada, and would only be in California for a few more days, this trip.

Dale was very nice, and said they could arrange a tour for the couple the following day.

"The folks who are renting it now," Dale explained, "…are there until the end of November, anyway. So we're not in a hurry to rent it out to the first people who come along. We're pretty fussy about our renters."

Dale told her that, he and his "partner" were only renting it out for another eight-years, until the mortgage was paid off. Then, they intended to move into it, and they could both retire from their County jobs. Karen wrote down all the information she needed, for them to find the place. She thanked Dale, and promised that she and David would see them the next day. "I think it's a couple of gay-guys," she said, hanging up the phone. "Who gives a shit?" David scoffed. "For that price, I'd rent it from the Devil, himself!"

Karen playfully punched his arm.

"Stop it," she scolded. "Dale sounds really nice. But, at least, now we know why it's still available."

"Yeah, too far away for most folks to commute," David said. "And, we've got two gas-guzzlers. We might have to trade one for something more economical."

"And, they are very particular about who they rent it to," she further explained. "So, they are just taking applications from anyone who is interested, and they'll decide later."

"Well, after we take a look, we'll get on that list, too," David promised. "We've got some time before I can afford to rent a moving truck, anyway."

Karen looped her arms around his neck, and kissed him on the forehead.

"Are you sure that we're ready for this?" she asked, genuinely concerned. "I mean, everybody keeps telling us that we need to slow down, you know."

"Look, ready or not, this place is a dream-come-true," David said. "It won't be available for long, and if we're lucky enough to get it, we'd better just say, 'Damn the torpedoes, full speed ahead.'"

Karen smiled, and kissed his cheek. David turned, and pulled her in for a real kiss.

"And, I don't know about you," he said, pulling back slightly, "...but me? I am darn-sure ready. Screw what those 'other people' say!"

"Me, too," she said, as she leaned in for a long, deep kiss.

The next day, they climbed into the Armada, and turned south toward Oroville. As the crow flies, it was only about 15 miles to the property. But, with the mountainous terrain, the only way to get to it, was to drive through Oroville, south of the lake, then all the way along the east-shore, to a point about a mile north of Lake Oroville.

After leaving Oroville, the scenery turned breathtaking. The winding, two-lane highway, that ran along the eastern shore of the lake, was mostly contained within the state recreation area, or the national wildlife refuge. There were two bridges along the route, and one of them looked like a smaller replica of the Golden Gate Bridge. It just added to the allure of the area.

After crossing the second bridge, David began to slow the truck down. Dale had told Karen that the ranch was the first property past the second bridge, about a mile away from it. He also mentioned that the ranch was also adjacent to the State Recreation Area, and that the creek, which ran through the place, emptied directly into the lake, after passing the ranch.

"Oh, my," Karen gasped. "This whole area is gorgeous."

David agreed enthusiastically. On their right, they could see a creek, and through the trees, what appeared to be green pasture, from the creek rising rapidly up an escarpment. Where the fence ended, the mountain wilderness began.

"I think this is all part of it," David pointed. "Yup, there's the mailbox, and the driveway."

Karen was just speechless, staring out the window at the magnificent spread. As they turned onto the asphalt driveway, they could see the huge old barn, and the ranch house. And, within a hundred feet of the highway, there was a steel gate, then a bridge passing over the creek. The gate was standing open, but the couple would soon learn that it worked from a garage-door opener... so there would be no unexpected visitors – salesmen, or the like.

Just across the bridge, to the left, and slightly up the hill, was the "caretaker's cottage," the original old farmhouse. To their right was the barn, and a level, gravel parking area, in front of the three-car garage. The parking area was large enough for at least four vehicles.

"This will be perfect for me to park my horse trailer," Karen said looking at the lot.

A blue, compact SUV was parked on the gravel lot, and a youthful looking, but silver-haired man was walking from the barn, toward the Armada. He was smiling, and waved as he approached.

Kathy waved back, as David pulled in beside the SUV, and shut the truck down.

"That must be Dale," Karen said, as she opened her door, and pulled her cane from behind the seat.

"Hello…" Dale said approaching. "My partner, Roy is up in the orchard, checking the watering system," he explained, as he offered his hand first to Karen, since she was closest to him.

"Wait a minute… seriously?" David said, as he offered his hand to Dale. "Roy and Dale?"

Dale rolled his eyes, and flipped his left wrist, leaving no doubt that he was gay.

"Yes, just like Roy Rogers and Dale Evans," he said with a smile. "We get that all the time. Trust me," he added, as he looked at David's hat, boots and jeans, "You are the only cowboy around here. The only thing I know about horses is, their manure makes great fertilizer!"

The trio chuckled, as Dale began the very extensive tour, of the large ranch and buildings. With Karen still having difficulty walking, and needing frequent rests, it took a lot longer than it should have. But Dale was understanding and patient. And, they saw it all.

David and Karen found the ranch to be exactly as the Gregslist ad had described it, and then some. It was more than just amazing.

The house had an intricate stone fireplace in the master bedroom, as well as another in the living room, which also featured granite floor tiles. There was a sliding glass door, from the master bedroom, out to a covered patio, just 15 feet from the swimming pool. And, directly outside the doors, under the patio cover, was a hot tub.

The look on both David and Karen's faces was the same as a small child, when they visit Disneyland, for the first time! For them, this was, indeed, a magic kingdom.

Looking out across the pool, the three fenced pastures, without any livestock to graze upon them, had thick, green grass that was at least a foot tall. To their left was the stables, and the covered arena. To their right, just beyond the barn, the creek splashed noisily, on its journey to the lake. As Dale continued the explaining all the details and features, the stream provided a quiet background noise to the dialogue.

And, as they looked out across the pastures, a group of wild turkeys could be seen feeding on grubs and bugs.

"Oh, my gosh," David exclaimed, pointing. "Are those wild turkeys?"

"Oh, yes," Dale said, with a cluck. "They can be real pests, sometimes. I think there's about fifteen or twenty of them that live here. Plus, all kinds of hawks, a few owls, and on the other side of the bridge is an

Osprey nesting site…very rare."

He went on to explain that there were also a number of deer, which came down from the mountain, through the pasture, to water in the creek, each evening. Also, there were occasional visits by black bears, elk, bobcats and, very rarely, a cougar.

"That's because the property adjoins the state recreation area, which is part of a 16-million-acre national wildlife refuge," he finished.

Both David and Karen were astonished. In their wildest dreams, neither of them had ever envisioned anything so amazing, especially for just $1,650 per month!

"This is it!" David gasped, looking at Karen. "This is right where we belong!"

"Oh, my, yes," she agreed. "Can we fill out an application?" Dale smiled graciously at them both.

"Absolutely," he replied, heading for the pool-gate, which was the most direct route to their vehicles. "I have some in the car."

David and Karen held hands, as they followed Dale. Karen was so giddy, she hardly used her cane at all. Earlier, when they had toured the orchard, which featured a variety of apple trees, peach trees, plum trees, and many other succulent fruits, Roy was nowhere to be seen.

Dale mentioned that "He could be anywhere!" Of the two, Roy was the real farmer, he'd explained. And Dale was the farmer's wife, David thought.

As they approached the car, Roy emerged from the barn. David thought he looked more like a real farmer than Dale, and not at all "gay-looking." He met them at the car, and introduced himself with a firm handshake.

As Dale sorted through his briefcase for the necessary paperwork, Karen engaged Roy in conversation.

"So, what happened with the young couple who came out yesterday," she asked.

"Well…" Roy stammered uncomfortably.

Dale had overheard the question, as he returned with the applications. He immediately came to Roy's aid, and answered for him.

"At first, they loved the place," Dale responded, shuffling his feet nervously. "But when I introduced them to Roy, as my 'partner,' the woman grabbed her children and started pushing them into their car. And the husband actually said, 'Oh my God! We can't rent from gay people."

Karen gave them a sad, sympathetic look. But David slapped his cheeks, feigning a look a look of shock and surprise.

"Wait a minute," David gasped. "You guys are GAY?"

Both Roy and Dale looked at each other in disbelief, frozen by his reaction…until David dropped the pretense, and a big smile crossed his face. Roy laughed, and lightly punched David in the arm. Dale took a moment longer to realize that the comment had been in jest.

"So, that's that famous, cowboy sense of humor, we've all heard about," Roy said, still smiling.

Dale gave an embarrassed smile, and Karen's mouth was still hanging open.

"Boy, you sure had me going there, for a minute," Dale admitted.

"I can't believe you said that," Karen added truthfully.

"Well, I've learned that, most folks just don't know how to handle a cowboy's sense of humor," David explained. "So rather than telling them about it, I find it much easier just to hit over the head with it, like a two-by-four."

Oddly enough, both Roy and Dale instantly relaxed. Gone was the "businessman" in Dale, and both began to laugh and joke, as they explained the application process. David could tell, they had just made two new friends.

After filling out the applications, and giving the completed forms to Dale, they began to head for the Armada, David and Dale beside them.

"Well, I can't speak for us both," Dale began, as he looked at Roy. "But if the credit report, and everything else checks out, I think you two will have a new place to live."

"We don't usually make this kind of decision so quickly," Roy agreed enthusiastically. "But I feel the same way Dale does."

Karen hugged them both, before climbing into the car, and David clapped each on the shoulder, in a rugged cowboy-manner, as he shook hands with them. There were smiling faces, all around.

As the Armada crossed the bridge heading back to the highway, Karen still had a look of shock on her face.

"I just can't believe it… can't believe this place," she muttered, as she was pulling out her cell phone.

"Well, get used to it, Honey… we've found a new home!"

Karen never heard his last comment, of course, because she was already texting Bonnie, all about the new place. David's smile quickly vanished.

"Yup, we gonna have to talk about you and that cell phone," David said out loud.

Karen never even looked up.

A few days later, Dale called and told them that the application had checked out perfectly. David had warned them that he had the corporate bankruptcy on there, but they just waved it off.

"That's just business," Dale said. "We're more worried about people who skip out on their personal bills."

Karen told them that David was going to be driving home in a few days, so Dale asked if they wanted to come sign the lease, before he left.

"The current tenants won't be out until the end of next month," he said. "And Roy and I will need a week, to clean, repaint, and get it ready for you guys. We want your new 'love-nest' to be perfect, when you move in. So, we can set the move-in date at… December 6th?"

Karen covered the mouthpiece, and relayed the information to David. He nodded his head, enthusiastically.

"That sounds fantastic," she concurred.

So, the next evening, they all met at a small family diner, in Oroville, and signed the papers. The boys offered to buy dinner, and David bought wine for everyone, so they could share a toast. The issue of them paying deposits, and their first month's rent was covered, when Roy mentioned that, so long as the money was paid before move-in, all was good.

The following day was David's last, before he drove back to Las Vegas. Karen was walking about the house now, without the cane, and showing no signs of even a slight limp. But, she still used it for longer walks, or anytime they went somewhere with rough footing, such as the stables.

At supper that night, the subject of their "problem lists," came up, and Karen said she hadn't written down a single thing. And, while David had only written down one item, he felt it was a major-discussion item. So, they retired to the front porch, to drink a beer and talk about their "communications issue."

David explained to Karen how she instantly responded to every text from Bonnie, completely ignoring whatever real conversation she was involved with, at the time. He didn't mention that the girl needed to start handling more of her own little problems. He just said that, if Karen were just more considerate, and finished the current conversation, before responding to the text, it wouldn't be a problem.

"Oh, my God," she gasped. "David, I am so sorry! I've just been living alone for so long, I guess it just became a habit."

David could understand that, he supposed. So, they talked of better ways to handle it, such as her not even looking at the phone, until at least a break in their dialogue. She agreed, apologized again, then slipped onto David's lap, hugging him around the neck.

"I am going to apologize to you, tonight, in a very special way," she cooed in his ear. "But first, I'm going to go jump in the shower."

"Don't jump!" he said playfully. "You're not quite ready for that, just yet."

She tousled his hair playfully, before kissing him lightly on the forehead. Then, she got up and headed inside, but not before he slapped her bottom lightly. The air was beginning to cool rapidly, since the sun had gone down, so she closed the main door gently, while David continued to enjoy the evening sky.

"Well, that wasn't so tough," he said aloud. "Boom! Problem solved."

Chapter 18

"California Here I Come!"

"You are out of your frickin' mind," Chance said earnestly. "Ain't you learnt nothin', boy?"

He was mimicking Walter Brennen's voice, as best he could, feigning an angry parent. But there was no humor in his assessment. David had just finished the very long story about his lengthy visit to California, culminating with the part about signing the lease for the mountain-ranch.

"What?" David was genuinely surprised at his reaction.

"You're blinded by love, fool. What do you think you're doing, dropping everything and rushing off to live with someone you've only known a few months?"

"Look," David defended, "I'm gonna find an eviction notice taped to my garage any day now. The foreclosure is happening, and happening fast. So I need to find a new place to live anyway."

"You're the one s'posed to have the college education," Chance continued flogging him. "But, you're acting like some high school kid. You ain't using your brain, here."

"Look, I'm retired, and that place is exactly the kind of place, I want to spend the rest of my life in. Karen, too. So, why not start now?"

"It ain't yours," Chance pointed-out. "So what happens when the fags throw you out, even if Karen don't?"

"Hey, wait, what?"

"Look, you do business with queers, you're gonna get screwed in the ass, old man. I guarantee…"

"Well, by then, Karen and me will be ready to buy our own place. No big deal…"

"And that's 'the rest of the story.' You and Karen? It sounds very shaky, at best. You guys still got a lot of issues to work out…"

"What? What're you talking about? I told you, the only real problem is that damn kid of hers, and her constant texting. And, she's aware of it, and we'll fix it. No big deal. We lived together for three weeks, for crying out loud. We gave it a test run, and all was good!"
"Bullshit."

"Okay, Wiseguy," David said sitting back in his chair, with his arms crossed. "What 'issues' do you see?"

"Okay, okay," Chance began. "Get out your notebook and write this shit down… if, for no other reason, you can look back later and say, 'Damn, I should've listened to that old Injun.'"

David hesitated, but Chance said not a word, until David had, reluctantly, opened his notepad. Then, the fusillade began in earnest.

Chance's list began with the fact that David had "fallen in love" with the "Oregon ranch cowgirl" that Karen had once been, and not the "California-cowgirl" she had become. He pointed-out that, while David knew and understood 'real' cowgirls, he would have no idea how 'Karen, the California-cowgirl' was going to react, in the same situations.

"And that, my man, should have been the first thing on your little list of possible problems."

"Aw, heck, that's not a deal-breaker," David defended. "So, she likes to look pretty on her horse, so what?"

"Don't interrupt," Chance scolded. "I got way more…keep writing."

David shook his head, but picked his pen back up.

"You're gonna think this is nuts, but try to follow me on this, College-Boy."

Chance brought up their completely different tastes in television programming and movies. He pointed out that, in his own experiences with women, if they didn't like the same types of shows, it was just the tip of the iceberg.

"They've done studies on this shit," he explained. "It has to do with differences in personalities, different levels of expectations, educations, and even differences in the creative thought process. What're you gonna do? Watch TV in two different rooms? What happened to cuddling up on the couch, and spending quality time, doing something you both enjoy?"

"Well, we can still…"

Chance held up his hand, and glared at David.

"I ain't done yet…"

Chance further explained that, beyond the simple program issues, and each of them enjoying different types of movies, there was the separate issue of watching television in bed. Chance pointed out that David had never even had a television set in his bedroom…ever. And, since Karen did, and she seemed to enjoy watching it before drifting off to sleep, Chance predicted the viewing times and programming would, indeed, become an issue. A major issue.

The same logic also applied to music, but since they both enjoyed Country Music, Chance indicated they had scored well, on that count. However, even on that point, there were slight differences.

David's favorite music was classic Western tunes, such as The Sons of the Pioneer's rendition of Tumblin' Tumbleweeds; or rodeo songs, such as almost anything performed by Chris LeDoux. While Karen was a "Modern Country" listener.

"Shit, they've even got Country-Rap now," Chance said wrinkling his nose. "And, Karen probably likes all that new crap."

David nodded his head that, indeed she did. The new music was often called "Hick-Hop," and David loathed it.

Chance pointed out that picking a radio station might not be so tough, but what about CD's or digital MP3's?

"What if she put a Colt Ford, or Boondox, CD into the player," he inquired. Then, he answered his own question. "You'd throw that CD player across the room, is what!" "You've got that right," David agreed.

"And another thing," Chance spun the conversation in a new direction. "You have always been an 'early to bed, early to rise' kind of guy… just like me. Sounds to me like she's going to be watching TV in your room, and staying up until she gets sleepy? How's that dog gonna hunt?"

"Oh, I'm sure it won't be like that," David responded. "After all, she has to get up and drive 40-miles to work, you know? So, she'll be early to bed, at least five-days a week, anyhow."

Chance just nodded his head condescendingly.

"And that leads me to the last item on my list," Chance said with his arms crossed menacingly.

He actually had no list, that David saw anyway. He had been just going right off the top of his head, so David knew the man had put a lot of thought into these observations. But still…

"And that is?"

"How in the Hell are you gonna pay for this move? I mean, you're about to lose this beautiful house, you're living from paycheck to paycheck, like the rest of us slobs. And what you make now is a quarter of what it used to be. All your little charge cards are maxed-out, and you couldn't borrow a dime at the bank, if you used a quarter for collateral."

David sighed deeply. Chance had hit the biggest nail of all, right on the head.

"And, I know you," Chance continued. "Once you get up there, you're gonna need new power tools, like a chainsaw for firewood, shit like that. And if you've got a covered arena, you'll need a drag-rake, and a tractor to pull it with…that dirt'll be like concrete, otherwise."

"I think I can make a 250 Quad work, to pull the drag in the arena," David offered.

"Oh? And, you got one of those?"

"No," David admitted. "But it'll cost a heckuva a lot less than a tractor…"

"You ain't got it, and you ain't got the money to buy one, either. And just how are you gonna pay for the rental truck, to get there?"

"Well, I haven't quite figured all that out just yet…" "Oh, I see," Chance said, nailing David's coffin lid down tight. "So you just decided that this was a great time to go ahead and sign a lease on a ranch in California? You can't even make the rent payments for that, by yourself. What happens if Karen walks out on you?" "Oh, that's not gonna happen," David replied confidently.

"Yeah, yeah, you're in love,"

"Well, we are!'"

"David, I love you, man. But, you are headed for a train wreck, I just know it. And, Buddy, I hate to see it happen."

"Thanks, Chance. And I know you think that, and you make some good points. But, me and Karen? We really work well together. This is going to be a dream-come-true, for us both. You'll see."

"I hope you're right, my friend. But the way I see it, your dream is about to turn into a nightmare," Chance said, as he stood up. "I just hope I'm wrong. But, I've got to get going."

David stood up, and the men hugged, in genuine caring. Chance patted David on the shoulder.

"And, one other thing, my man," Chance added, as he headed for the door. "Are you sure this whole deal isn't just the 'Little Head' talkin'?"

He didn't wait for an answer. David sat back down, and looked at his notepad. He sighed deeply, tapping on the paper with his pen.

"Boy, Chance is so far off on this one! Well, except for the money thing." David said to himself. "TV shows and movies, a deal breaker, or something? That's just crazy! Next thing you know, he'll say, 'If she didn't cry during Old Yeller, she's not worth having!' What a concept!"

Then, he turned his attention to the work at hand. He tore off the sheet with the notes from Chance's "lecture," wadded them up and tossed them into the trash. Then, he stared at the blank pad for a few moments, before finally writing, "How to pay for the move," across the top.

"Man, I sure do have a lot of figuring to do," he said to himself. "How in the heck am I gonna pay for all this shit?"

Indeed, it was a perplexing problem for him. He considered borrowing money from relatives, but he was in his fifties! His kids used to call him, for loans… until he filed bankruptcy. And, he didn't think his mother or siblings would be keen on sending him money, to move in with a gal he had only known for a few months.

"This one, I'm gonna have to figure out on my own," he sighed.

David went out to the garage, and looked at the storage racks against the wall. He saw a few boxes that hadn't even been opened in 20-years. Plus, he had quite a bit of photography equipment—old cameras, strobes, backdrops, that sort of thing. Suddenly, an idea began to take shape.

"Hey, hey," he said hopefully. "There just might be gold, in these here boxes of crap!"

David was smart enough to know, a garage sale would never raise the kind of funds he needed. But, if he found the right market for certain things, like the photography equipment, it just might work.

"Gregslist," he thought.

There were a wide variety of categories, including one specifically for photography equipment. And, as the idea began to gel in his mind, he realized that, Karen and himself would have many of the same things.

They certainly didn't need two refrigerators, for instance. And he had three of them… one old ice-box he kept in the garage, just for beer and soda, but he had a great 24 cubic foot, side-by-side, in the house, and a nice, but smaller, used reefer he had kept in his studio… and it, too, was now just taking up space, gathering dust in the garage.

And, the ranch house came with a washer and drier, a little older, but serviceable. He had a nearly new, front-loading set he had gotten from Sears, for more than $2,000, just last year.

"Heck, anything I can sell, is one less thing I need to take with me," he also figured.

Plus, his house was about to go into foreclosure… but it was still his, now. And, everything he had bought, and added to it, like the expensive chandeliers, and those gorgeous built-in appliances, could all be sold today, legally. If he waited until after the foreclosure, it would be grand theft.

He took his pad, and started making a list. Later, when he talked to Karen on the phone, he didn't mention to her about the expensive lighting fixtures, or the built-in appliances. But, he convinced her that, selling off their duplicate items, or those, like the washer and drier set, which came with the ranch house, just might produce enough money to pay for the rental truck, and the deposits, for the ranch. "You think it will really work?" She asked.

"Even if it doesn't quite get us there," he said. "It'll be a good start. Besides, if I sell it, I don't have to fit it into the truck. And whatever I can't sell on Gregslist, I'll sell at a garage sale."

"What the heck," she agreed. "It's worth a shot, anyway."

So, they went over everything she would be bringing to the new place, and they figured out where it would go. If David had something similar, that would then, be an "extra," and would go on Gregslist, or be offered at his garage sale.

"Man, this is a great idea," he said to himself, after they had said their "good-bye's."

The next morning, at coffee, even Chance thought the idea might have some merit.

"Besides, if you have a garage sale," he added, "…I can bring some of my stuff over, too. I have a ton of crap just collecting dust. Let's do it."

By the time all was said and done, and a large dent made in the amount of "junk" stored in the garage, there was a lot less to pack in the rental truck. But, the garage-sale hadn't produced nearly enough money. It wasn't even enough to pay for the truck itself.

After adding the "high-ticket" items, such as the camera equipment and washer and drier, there would be enough for the truck, but not nearly enough for the deposits on the new ranch. Plus, there were still things that they would need to buy, like the quad and the chainsaw.

David was demoralized, to say the very least. He grabbed his list of "assets," and stared long and hard, at the very last remaining item. He circled it, with his pen.

"Naw, I can't..." he whispered aloud, "...I won't. But, I guess I ought to, at least, see what I can get for it. Just for the sake of argument."

So, he climbed into his prized possession, his sole-remaining valuable asset—the Armada—and drove it to a dealership. The large national chain advertised that it would "buy your used car, even if you don't buy one of ours."

David had paid $52,000 for the vehicle, new... much more after adding finance charges... and he had only made his final payment on it, a few months previously. He'd checked online, and found the "retail value" to be just over $20,000.

The car dealership offered him $11,000. He was sorely disappointed, and told them that they were "nuts," before he stormed out of the showroom.

Then, he found himself, once again, looking at his list of assets, with the circle around the word "Armada." He absolutely adored that rig. It had served his every purpose flawlessly, and luxuriously, and he came to think of it as his "friend." He even named the 13-foot monster, "Big Red."

"Eleven-thousand," he said in disgust. "That's absurd! Barely half what they'd sell it for. That's bullshit."

But, time was racing by. The lease was to begin on December 6th, and already, it was nearly Thanksgiving. He knew he could get more if he sold the Armada himself, but would he have time? It was exactly two-weeks away. And that didn't include a day or two loading the truck, and another day driving it, more than 700 miles to get there.

With the Holidays approaching quickly, and the television filled with Christmas shopping commercials, he knew that very few people would have the "extra" cash, or want to use it, for buying a new vehicle...even Big Red.

"There's no way I'm giving it to those creeps, for a measly eleven grand," he said to himself. "But, I might as well just see, just how far the money would go."

He had already tallied-up the cash he had raised, thus far, by selling his other items, so he wrote that number at the top of a new page. He then added the "cash-offer" from the car dealer, and scribbled "$15,000" at the top-right of the paper.

On the left side, he started a list, beginning with "Rental Truck," and continued down. David wrote in the deposits, and the first month's rent for the ranch—totaling $3,300. Then, he listed items, such as the quad, chainsaw, and other "ranch necessities."

He used actual rate-quotes, or cost, when he knew them, or just used a generous estimate for the rest. This, he reasoned, would give him a good budget to use, when it came time to buy.

The last, and final, item on the list, was buying an economical car, for Karen to use in her daily commute. He would need to replace the Armada anyway, and with what money the little car saved them in gas, it would pay for itself in a year or two, he reasoned. He left that amount blank.

After David totaled all the remaining items, including gas for the rental truck, and food he would consume during the 14-hour drive. Whatever was left, would be the amount they would have in their "budget" to buy the economy car.

"Hey, that's not too bad," he said, surprised.

The remaining balance, their budget for the economy car, would be about $4,000. David knew that, for that amount, they could get a reasonably dependable vehicle for the daily commute. He also knew that they would still have Karen's big truck, to pull the horse trailer, get hay, or any other things around the ranch, that only a truck could do. Plus, they could wait to buy the economy car together, in Oroville, so he wouldn't have to rent a car-dolly for the move.

He was still very disgusted at the low-ball offer he'd gotten for the Armada. But, he realized, it was a viable solution to his problem. Thus far, it was also the only solution.

The next morning at coffee, Chance ripped David up one side, and down the other, for even considering the idea of selling Big Red. Especially for even considering such a terribly low price.

"You got a better idea?" David asked sincerely. "Seriously, any idea at all? I hate this, absolutely hate it. But, I can't think of a single way, except this, that would even be feasible...not in two-weeks."

Chance admitted that, he also, could see no other way. However, he also pointed-out that this very problem, is the reason he and Karen should have taken their time. If they had proceeded slowly, and cautiously, in building their relationship, David would not be in the bind he was in.

David pointed-out that it was a little late to close the barn doors, now. The horses had not only left the barn, but they were racing over the hill already, headed for California. Chance just clenched his jaw, and nodded his head slowly.

"That 'little head' of yours, sure gets you into big trouble, Kimosabe," Chance said quietly.

A week later, David handed over the keys, and title, to Big Red, and said his final farewell to his "old friend." Chance drove him to the place where David had reserved the rental truck, and two days later, it was stuffed tighter than their bellies had been, after eating Thanksgiving dinner. Yet, there was still much remaining in the garage.

David told Chance to just take it all to Goodwill, or sell it at his next garage sale...or keep it himself, if anything was worth keeping. Chance agreed to clean up the remaining items for him, so David gave him the keys to the nearly empty house.

Together, they walked through it one last time. Then, after they walked out the door, Chance locked it, and promised to be back in the next few days, to finish. The foreclosure had still not produced an eviction notice, although David knew it would be taped to the garage door any day, now.

"Well, Amigo," Chance said clapping him on the shoulder. "We'll go over to my place, so you can get a good night's sleep, before you head out in the morning."

"Yeah, I'd like to be on the road by 4 a.m. at the latest. It'll take me at least 14-hours to get there."

Then, he climbed into the truck, and slowly drove away from what had been his home, for the past 25-years. It was a very somber drive to Chance's place.

"California, here I come," he said meekly, still sad about leaving his house, and losing Big Red.

The next morning, his sadness was replaced by excitement. He was beginning a new life, in a great place, with the woman he loved, and those thoughts, reminded him of the reasons he had begun this adventure, in the first place. He plugged an old Kenny Rogers CD into the player, and as the song "Ruby" began, he sang along…but he made up his own words.

Instead of, "You've painted up your lips, and rolled and curled your tinted hair," he sang: "You've loaded up you truck, and now you're driving down the road," he sang, in harmony to the music. "Just think about the pretty woman, you have waiting for you there…"

Chapter 19

"We'll take the spaceship I found in the barn..."

Karen had been at the ranch house for most of the day, getting her own things moved in, organizing the kitchen shelves, and so forth. Bill had come along earlier, to help lift the dresser, sofa and bed—the only items Karen and Bonnie could not get on their own. The rest of her stuff fit easily into her pickup truck, and by noon, it was all inside the house, ready to be unpacked. Bonnie left shortly after that, to go take care of her own family.

David arrived at the ranch, in the early evening, just before sundown, and he was exhausted. Karen had stopped in town earlier, where she picked-up a u-bake-it pizza, and a 12-pack of beer. David just parked the truck, grabbed a beer, and sat down by the pool, to watch as the turkeys and deer meandered about the pastures nearby. He knew the truck would still be there in the morning, and he actually had two days left, before he had to turn it in, so there was no rush to start unloading. Karen came out and sat in his lap, kissing his forehead.

"I still can't believe this is home, now," she said, gazing in wonder at the beauty and the wildlife.

"What's even better," David said romantically. "We're together, forever, starting a wonderful new life, in this amazing place. How perfect is this?"

"The pizza will be ready in ten minutes," Karen said, as she stood up. "I'll go throw together a salad…"

"Awesome, Babe. I'll be in shortly to wash up."

A few minutes later, after washing his face and hands, he went into the "great-room," the living room, dining room and kitchen, all beneath a tall, vaulted ceiling, with exposed beams. The furniture for these rooms was all still in the truck, as Karen's bed, her little sofa and the stuffed-chair, were put into the large guest room, as they had agreed. He had a huge bedroom suite, with a California-King sized, 4-post bed, mirrored-dresser, armoire, night-stands and lamps, for their bedroom.

Karen was leaning against the kitchen counter, talking to Bonnie.

David heard the timer buzzing, as he entered the room. He wasn't sure how long it had been going off, but Karen did not even seem to notice. He went quickly to the oven, and pulled out the pizza, just as one edge was starting to get black. He tossed it on top of the stove, using a hand towel for a pot-holder. Then, he turned the oven off, and grabbed another beer out of the fridge.

"Oh, shit," Karen exclaimed, as she looked at the slightly burned pizza. "Bonnie called to let me know she got home okay, and I totally forgot why I came in here! Glad you grabbed it!"

"We talked about this before, Karen. When Bonnie calls, you go into your own little world, sometimes. That timer must have been going off for five-minutes! Talk all you want, but you have to pay attention to what's going on around you, too..."

He concluded his "speech" with a warm hug.

"This whole day has been crazy," Karen said with a sigh. "I'm just glad you're finally here!"

David grabbed a couple of paper plates from the counter, and served them each a slice of pizza. They would have to stand, to eat at the counter, as there were no stools unpacked yet. He had already looked into the "guest room," where Karen's furniture was already setup. She also had a half a dozen smaller, packed boxes, and a few empty ones.

"I'm gonna wait until morning to unload the truck," he told Karen. "I was thinking, maybe we'd just watch the sun set, relax, and go to bed early… if you know what I mean?"

"I was hoping you'd say that," she said, kissing his nose. "I didn't have to drive all day, like you did, but boy, I am worn out, too! Dale told me they just had the hot tub cleaned and serviced, so we might just give that a whirl!"

David noticed that her eyes were twinkling again. He loved it when she twinkled! He took another bite of pizza.

"I love hot tubs," he replied. "I had one in Vegas… for the past ten-years, every morning, I wake up, then climb into the hot tub! After riding bucking horses for 17 years, my old body takes a while to get fully awake! So, a hot dip first-thing gets everything warmed-up and ready to go!"

When he looked up, he saw Karen again texting. He knew she hadn't heard a word. He just shook his head, and waited for her to set the phone down. "You're doing it again," he said pointing to the phone.

"Oh, yes, Bonnie asked if we'd watch Mae West next week…"

"Mae West?" David asked.

"Yes, their little dog… she is so cute!" Karen explained brightly. "We just call her Mae-Mae. Anyway, they're going to San Francisco next week, for business, and they're going to stay an extra day and visit his brother. I told her that Mae-Mae could stay here. Is it okay?"

"Oh, sure…Lord knows, we have plenty of room for her," David responded. "But about the phone, we need to…"

He stopped talking when he saw that Karen was already texting the news to Bonnie. So he waited. When she had laid the phone back down, he resumed his conversation.

"Karen, did you see what just happened?"

She looked at him quizzically.

"This is exactly what we talked about, before I went back to Vegas last time. Remember?"

She still looked confused. So, he elaborated.

"You almost burned our supper, because you were talking on the phone… and just now, I was telling you something, and you just went away, into your little world, where only you and Bonnie seem to exist."

"That's a little harsh, don't you think?" she replied.

"Harsh? No, not really. It's a problem we need to fix, that's all. And if I don't remind you, whenever you 'go away,' how are you ever going to change the behavior? You don't even know you're doing it, unless someone points it out to you."

She took a deep breath, followed by a long pull on her beer.

"Sorry," she said finally. David gave her a hug.

"Hey, we'll get past this," he said gently. "But, put yourself in my shoes… I'm talking along, and then I notice, you're not hearing a single word! How do you think that makes me feel?"

"I'll work on it, I promise," she said. "Now, I think I'm going to go find my bathing suit…"

"What the heck you need that for?" David asked in an amused way.

"I thought we were getting in the hot tub?" David laughed.

"Karen, we are 15 miles from the nearest town, we have a thick wall of trees between us and the highway, the gate over the bridge is closed and locked; and nobody, I mean nobody, can see us naked!"

Karen looked a little surprised.

"I've just never, I mean… well, maybe in the hot tub…"

"Karen, we can ride our horses in the arena, while we're naked, if we want to!"

"Now, that might get a little rough on the behind," she said smiling, as she rubbed her fanny.

"I'm just saying, we could if we wanted to! Besides, it'll be dark in another half an hour, anyway. But even in broad daylight, bathing suits in the hot tub? Never. And bathing suits are completely optional in the pool," he added.

Karen let it all sink in.

"I think I am going to like living in the country, again!" she said with a coy smile.

"Me, too," he said, patting her on the behind.

After David grabbed a few things from the truck, including two terrycloth robes, and they finally climbed into the hot tub, it was fully dark outside. But the moon was full, and there was plenty of light for the two lovers, as the hot water worked its magic on their tired, sore muscles. And, their naked bodies worked its magic on their libidos! After the hot tub, they moved their "party" into the shower, and then into the guest room, where Karen's furniture was already set up… including her television. But they never turned it on, that first night. And, much to David's relief, Bonnie didn't call or text, again, that night.

In the morning, David was up way before Karen's alarm went off… it was back to work, for her. But, David already had half of the truck unloaded. Since they had a three-car garage, he was just pulling everything out of the truck, and setting it in the garage. He'd get it into the correct room, later.

While Karen was still in the bathroom putting on makeup, and such, David cooked her some bacon and eggs, since she had already unpacked all her kitchen wares, pot & pans and a toaster. When Karen came out of the bedroom, finally, she saw the plate of food he had been keeping warm for her.

"Oh… I don't usually eat breakfast, on work-days," she said apologetically. "But since you already have it made…"

She grabbed the fork off the plate David was offering her, and she gobbled down the eggs, and a slice of bacon. She took the toast and made a "bacon sandwich" out of the rest of the bacon, wrapped it in a paper towel, and headed for her truck.

David made a note to himself, not to cook her breakfast without checking first, to see if she wanted any. He walked her out to her truck, and gave her a kiss, once she was buckled-in.

"Now, don't forget, I have to take the rental truck back this afternoon… to Oroville," he reminded her. "So call me when you are leaving the office, and I'll just meet you at the truck place." "Where's it at, again?" she asked.

"I'll text you the address, but it's right there on Lincoln, by Oro-Dam Blvd."

"Oh, that's right. I wish I could take another day off to help you unload…"

"With the surgery, you've had all the time off you can afford, for now," he replied. "I'll get it all done, shoot, maybe before lunch, the way it's going!"

Karen smiled, put the truck in reverse, and waved as she backed out of the parking space.

David knew that she got off work at 5:00, and it would take her a half an hour to get to Oroville. It would only take him 20 minutes to get there, but he also had to take a few minutes for paperwork, so he left the ranch at 5:00, also.

He had texted Karen the address earlier, and followed up with another saying "See you at the truck place in half an hour," as he pulled out onto the highway in front of the ranch. He knew that she had a tendency to be a little forgetful, so he didn't want to risk being left at the truck dealership, waiting for a ride. But, it all went without a hitch.

The next morning, David was again up before dawn, but this time, he sat in the hot tub for 20 minutes, to awaken and stretch sore muscles, before he began going through stuff in the garage, to bring it in, as he started putting it all away.

This time, he asked Karen if she wanted breakfast, and she declined. "Well, I'm going to make a pot roast for supper." He told her. "Since it cooks in the crock-pot, all I have to do is carve the meat, and put the veggies in a bowl. That'll take like 20 minutes… so why don't you text me, when you get to Oroville tonight, and by the time you get home, I'll have a nice candlelight supper waiting when you walk in!"

She smiled pleasantly. "Okay… I'll text you when I get there."

They said their good-bye's and David went back to work, unpacking, and putting things away. His first choice to unpack, and set up, was the master bedroom. He even put his 32" television in the master suite. Even though he had never had a TV in his bedroom before, he knew Karen would appreciate it.

And, of course, he remembered to get the roast in the crock pot, so they could have that candlelight dinner! He had picked up fresh bell peppers, carrots, mushrooms, potatoes, sweet onions and a whole clove of garlic, to add to the stock, as the roast cooked. By early afternoon, the entire house was filled with the tantalizing aroma of the meat.

At around 5:30, Karen sent David a text, letting him know she was in Oroville, or about 20-minutes away. He already had the tablecloth spread, with a candelabra and half a dozen elegant tapers. The fancy china was still in boxes, but he found some matching kitchen plates, and the table looked quite romantic, indeed.

David took the roast out of the crock pot and carved it into slices, on a serving platter. Then, he strained the vegetables, mushrooms and peppers into a large serving bowl, and placed it beside the roast, on the table. The final touch was a bottle of merlot wine, which he was just opening, as David heard the truck pull into the driveway.

Karen walked through the front door, and David swept up the two glasses of wine, to greet her, as she approached. Oddly, she walked right past the dining room, with hardly a glance at the elegant and romantic setting David had created.

"Would you like a glass of wine?" David asked, as he handed her a glass.

Karen walked past him, ignoring the glass of wine he held out to her. She opened the refrigerator.

"Nah, I don't care much for wine," she said as she pulled out a bottle of beer. 'I'm just gonna have a beer, and go take a look at the stables, before it gets too dark. We're going to get Pistol this weekend, and I want to see if there is a stall ready for him."

David was nearly dumbfounded. Still holding two glasses of wine, he just watched, as Karen totally ignored his romantic gesture, and the lovely meal he had prepared.

"I already did that… the stall is ready, the front pasture is cleared, and all the gates are set…"

She acted as if she hadn't heard a word. Karen walked past the table, and glanced at the food.

"Looks good," she said flatly. "I guess I'm just not hungry right now. You go ahead… I'll warm something up later…"

"Wait, what?" David was beginning to feel the bile rise in the back of his throat. "I spent hours putting this together, for you…for us. Our first romantic dinner…"

"I'll eat some later… just not hungry now."

Karen pulled out her cell phone, as she slid open the sliding doors from the dining room, out to the back yard… and the stables and arena beyond.

"Then, why didn't you say something about that when you texted me from Oroville? You knew I was going to be setting up dinner…I could've waited on all this. That's just rude."

Karen never heard a word he said, as her head was down composing a text message. David just watched her walk away.

"What the Hell?" was all he could say.

David blew out the candles, poured the wine back into the bottle, recorked it, then covered all the food, before putting it into the refrigerator, uneaten. He pulled out a beer, and walked back to the pool, his favorite place to sit and watch the nature around him.

But, this evening, his eyes were locked on Karen, as she sat on the loading dock of the feed-room, near the stables, her feet dangling down. She sipped her beer, with a scowl on her face, looking everywhere, except at David.

What had he done? Why was she being so rude? He wondered. He could think of nothing.

Karen stood up, and walked through the backyard. She re-entered through the dining room door, avoiding the pool area altogether, even though it was the shortest route back to the house. David watched, then waited, to see where she would go next. He was too angry still to follow her into the kitchen.

Karen poked her head out of the back door, off the bedroom, where David was sitting by the hot tub. She had a fresh beer in her hand.

"You put everything away?" she asked, unemotionally.

"Well, you didn't want any…"

"Yeah, I'm just not hungry tonight."

"Well, you could have at least told me that, when you texted me from Oroville," he reiterated. "You knew I was going to start setting up dinner when you texted."

"Hey, I did exactly what you told me to do… I texted you from Oroville, just like you said."

David started to say something else, but Karen's phone beeped with Bonnie's ring-tone. "I'm gonna go take a shower," Karen said as she walked away, reading the incoming text.

"Well, that's the last romantic dinner I'll ever cook," David said out loud.

Since all of Karen's personal belongings, and household furniture, were still in the guest room, it was easier for her to shower, and change, in there. Besides, she hadn't even noticed that the master bedroom was completely set up, too. David busied himself by lighting the fire, in the living room fireplace.

The fire had been planned as his "grand-finale" to his romantic evening. He already had everything prepared to light, so, it only took putting a match to the paper, and a roaring fire was soon blazing. They were supposed to be sitting here together, finishing off a bottle of wine, after a delicious and romantic supper, cuddled by the fire.

Instead, he sat alone, drinking a beer.

Finally, Karen emerged from the guest bedroom, wearing a terrycloth robe, and flannel pajamas underneath… complete with fluffy slippers. She walked, again, to the 'fridge and grabbed a beer. After opening it, she leaned on the kitchen counter.

David was hoping for an apology from her, or at least an acknowledgment that she realized he had gone to a lot of trouble, for nothing, it seemed. But, she started talking about her day at the office, as if nothing had happened. David was still angry, but he let it pass.

"I saw you got the bed set up in the master bedroom," she said, finally turning the subject away from her day at work.

"I even hooked-up the TV for you," he said unemotionally. "But, the DVD player is still in the guest room."

"I saw that. Well, we don't have a satellite dish hooked up yet, anyway, so the DVD's will have to do for now, anyway."

"They'll be here on Friday, to hook up the satellite and a phone line, so we can get WiFi, too."

"So, what do you have planned for tomorrow?" she asked politely. "I'm going to unpack a few more boxes… maybe get the 'office' set up. But mainly, I am going to check out the aquifer, and see about getting some irrigation going to these front pastures."

"Oh, that'll be nice."

"Are we going to talk about this?" He asked, changing the subject quickly.

"About what?" she asked, genuinely confused.

"About what happened here tonight?" he responded.

Karen still looked as if she had no idea what he was talking about.

"I made us a very romantic, candlelight dinner, and you just blew it off…" David stared absently into the fire.

"Oh, that," she said. "Yeah, like I said, I just wasn't hungry, I guess. You should've asked me about it first…"

"We talked about it last night," David said, his frustration, and voice, rising slightly. "I told you to text me from Oroville, and I'd have everything ready, by the time you got here… and I did."

"You told me to text you from Oroville, so I did," she defended. "I didn't know what you were doing."

"Yes, you did… we talked about it. I told you exactly what I was doing."

"I guess I'm just not used to having someone around to do the cooking," was all she could say.

David stared into the fire for a few seconds, composing himself.

"Don't forget, tomorrow, I am stopping by Bonnie's on my way home from work," Karen began, taking a sip of her beer. "To get Mae-Mae."

"Look, Karen," David said finally. "We're supposed to be a team here. I figured, as long as you are having to drive to work every day, and I am stuck at home, I might as well do the cooking and the cleaning, to even out the load, you know?"

He looked up, and Karen was tapping away at her cell phone.

"What do you think?" he said loudly, trying to get her attention.

"About what?" she said, glancing up for a moment. She had just hit "send."

"What I just said, about us being a team?"

"That sounds great. What'd you have in mind?" she asked as her phone beeped with a reply to her text.

"Oh, I don't know, I thought we'd take that spaceship I found out in the barn, and see if I could get it running…

"Uh, huh," she said nodding her head, as if she were listening, "I had it out this morning, and all it did was smoke and sputter. But, I think I can get it running, if I tune it up a little…" "Oh, that'll be nice," she said, still lost in her texting. David just gave up.

"How can I be with someone I can't even talk to?"

"Uh, huh…"

He gathered his beer and headed for his chair out by the pool. David figured if he had to have a conversation alone, he might as well enjoy the view. Even after dark, the sounds were entertaining!

A little while later, Karen came out, her cell phone in hand, but apparently, she was through texting, for the moment. "I wondered where you went," she said with a smile.

"Well, if you'd turn off that frickin' cell phone, once in a while, you wouldn't have to wonder."

"Oh, please, you're not on that again, are you?" she asked, genuinely surprised. "I was listening to every word…"

"Oh? So, were you going to help me fix the spaceship?"

"Spaceship? What spaceship?"

"I thought you were listening to every word?"

"Well, not when you're talking crazy."

They sat in silence for a few minutes, just listening to the creek, and the night-birds.

"I'm going in to see my doctor again next week," she began, finally. "He still says I'm not ready to ride yet…"

"You'd have been riding two months ago, if you listened to me," he said flatly.

"He said it might be February…"

"What day? I mean, what day are you going to see him?"

"Tuesday, at ten, why?"

"Well, I think I'll see if I can have him look at this rotator cuff," David explained. "With the move, and lifting all the furniture and boxes, it is really giving me fits."

"Oh, he's the best," she said enthusiastically. "You can just drop me off at work, after we're done with the doctor…but you'll have to come pick me up when I get off."

"If you'd like, I can come inside to meet the folks you work with…"

"Oh, not Tuesday," she objected. "Since I'm taking the morning off, to see the doctor, by the time I get there, it'll be crazy. Maybe you can keep the truck one day, and you can come take me out to lunch? Something like that, might be nice."

"Okay, sure," David relented. "Just let me know…in the meantime, we need to get car-shopping this weekend, too. I've still got $4,000 to buy a small economy car for you to drive to work every day." "I hate driving cars," she said wrinkling up her nose. "But, it really is the most sensible thing for us to do. And if we get something this weekend, we can just meet-up at the doctor's office next week, and you won't have to come back and get me." "Now, we're talking," David said.

He was not looking forward to driving to Chico twice in one day, so his own wheels would be nice. Besides, with Pistol coming to the ranch on Saturday, he'd probably need the truck for a load of hay and grain, anyway. Karen got up and sat in David's lap.

"If you get that surgery done on your shoulder, it'll be my turn to be the nurse, and you the patient! Then, I can pay you back for how well you took care of me!"

"Hey, we're just here to take care of each other," he said. "That's what teamwork is all about."

They kissed lightly, then a little more deeply.

"How about we sleep in the master bedroom, tonight?" he said invitingly. "It's a king-sized bed…"

"I've already got my jammies on," she pouted. "And, nothing sexy about these…"

Her robe had come open before she sat on his lap, but the flannel pajamas more than adequately covered her up. David reached up slowly, and began unbuttoning the top. Karen just watched, a smile growing slowly across her face.

"Now what, Romeo?" she teased, as the shirt came open.

He slipped his hand onto her shoulder, and lifted the robe and the pajama top away, pulling them down her arm. A moment later, the robe and top were tossed onto the cover of the hot tub. David stood up, holding Karen, but he let her legs down, as they kissed. Then, he stepped back just a bit, and pulled the bottoms down in one motion. Karen stepped out of them.

"So, now, whatcha gonna do, Cowboy?"

He swept her up in his arms and carried her in to the bed. Sex has a way of making people forget the dissention and arguments, at least for a little while.

Later, David felt Karen get out of bed. He assumed she was just going to the bathroom, and she'd be back for snuggling in a few minutes. He was confused about her leaving the room, until he realized that all of her belongings were still in the guest room and bath. So, he decided to get up and use the master bathroom, himself.

The guest room and master bedroom were back-to-back, and their bathrooms also matched up. So while he was in one, he could hear her in the other... and she was talking on the phone. He couldn't hear the words, just the voice, and he knew. A few seconds later, he heard the toilet flush, and a few seconds after that, he heard the television come on in the guest bedroom.

"Well, so much for cuddling," he said to himself, as he headed back to bed.

The "little communications issue," he had uncovered in his first visit, was not only not solved, but it seemed to be getting worse.

"And now, every time I try to be romantic, or cook her a meal, she totally ignores my gesture," he thought to himself, as he tried to fall asleep. "Boy, I just can't figure this one out... one minute she's the most-rude person I ever met, and the next minute we're naked and swinging from the chandelier!"

"One day at a time," he concluded, as he finally drifted away to slumberland.

Chapter 20
"The Nurse from Hell!!"

True to her word, Karen brought Mae-Mae home from work with her the next night. She was a delightful little dog, part pug, part Lhasa Apso, and so ugly, it was actually cute. David did not cook supper, but he had a package of hamburger-meat thawed in the refrigerator, and a box of Hamburger Helper ready to go.

During the day, David played with Mae-Mae a little, but most often, the dog was found outside exploring the large fenced-in portion of the back yard. In the afternoon, the weather had reached a perfect 75 degrees, so David just slid open the sliding glass door, and Mae-Mae could come and go as she pleased.

When Karen got home, she rushed inside to see Mae-Mae. The dog was outside, however, and did not hear Karen's initial calls...

"MAE-MAE!" she yelled, as she raced through the kitchen. David pointed to the open sliding glass door, just as the dog came rushing in.

Karen grabbed the dog, and smothered her with kisses and scratches. David laughed.

"Well, so, how'd it go with Mae-Mae?" she asked, her eyes twinkling.

"Oh, she was a peach," David responded truthfully. "No trouble at all. And once it got warmer outside, I just left the door open, and she came and went, all day."

Karen was smiling, and happy holding the little dog, who seemed to be enjoying the attention as much as Karen was enjoying giving it to her! Then, suddenly, as if a painful memory had come over her, Karen's face went totally blank, and her eyes became cloudy.

"Karen?" David asked cautiously. "Are you okay?" "Uh-huh," came her flat response.

David had noticed that, lately, even when he knew that she had "gone to another place," she started responding to him with nods, grunts and the occasional, "That's nice." It was her way of saying "I was listening," without actually listening. And, David could tell, that Karen had definitely gone away.

"Well, like I was saying, Mae-Mae was a really good dog today," "Good dog," Karen repeated softly as she rubbed Mae-Mae's chin. "She spent most of her time outside. But it was really weird," David continued.

"Uh-huh…"

"Right after lunch, when I let her in, she was covered in green paint."

"That's nice," Karen said, scratching Mae-Mae's head.

"No seriously, green paint. It looked like she had fallen into a barrel of it. Then, the worst part…"

"I see…"

"She came running into the house, dripping paint like a brush, and she jumped right up onto the leather couch!!"

"Oh? Uh-huh…"

"There was green paint everywhere! It took me nearly four-hours to clean it all up! I just finished, right before you came home."

"That's so nice."

"Karen," David said, gently placing his hand on her shoulder. "You didn't hear a word I said, did you?

She shook her head, and her eyes again got bright.

"I did so…"

"Then, what'd I say?"

"You said, right after lunch, you let Mae-Mae in," Karen began in a flat monotone.

It sounded to David like a tape recorder! Her eyes were again flat, her face without expression.

"You said she was covered in green paint, and she…" Karen blinked, then blinked again. "Wait a minute? Green paint? Where did she get into green paint?"

"THAT is the reaction I was expecting ten minutes ago, when I first told you the story…"

"So, there's no green paint?"

"No. And even though you obviously heard the words as I spoke them, the first time you actually heard what I was saying, was when you played back your little mind-recorder."

She set the dog on the floor, and headed outside to go see her horse. David began supper.

The following few weeks could best be described, by David, as a period of adjustment—and, it was all up to him to make the adjustments! He gave up on the entire notion of trying to be romantic, even though it killed him to do so. He felt that, being spontaneous and romantic was half the fun of being in a relationship. But, for some reason, when he did anything romantic, it always made Karen rude, angry and cranky.

Karen never moved-out of the guest bedroom and bath. She explained to David that, he tossed and turned way too much for her to endure. And, while he didn't snore every night, on those nights that he did, she had to leave the room anyway. Plus, she still enjoyed watching her favorite television shows, while lying in bed at night, and she knew how much that bothered David.

David didn't bother to mention that he was relieved, not to be forced into watching what he considered to be "Garbage-TV." It also allowed him to keep to his own, "early-to-bed, early-to-rise" schedule, without waking Karen.

"Boy, if Chance could see how this whole 'television' thing worked out between me and Karen, I would never hear the end of it!"

David said to himself one night, after reflecting on Chance's words of warning.

And, as far as their sex-life was concerned, well, David just figured most married couples only actually have it once or twice a month, anyway. So, they were just like a real married couple, in that regard. But, when they did have sex, it was in the barn, or the stables, or in the pool or hot tub… plus the occasional liaison across the dining room table, or on the sofa. Or, when they really felt kinky, they'd use the bed!

"It's quality, not quantity," David said to himself with a smile.

He also stopped cooking or making lunches for Karen, even though he loved to cook. When he could stand it no more, he finally would beg her to let him cook dinner! He learned to cook things like spaghetti or casseroles, which could be kept warm, for just that precise moment Karen decided she was ready to eat. She was never hungry when the meal was first ready. Ever. Unless she was the cook, of course.

David spent his $4,000 on a 10-year-old Ford Mustang, but one with a V-6 engine, to get good gas mileage. It was also a lot of fun to drive on the twisting mountain roads near the ranch. Most days, Karen took the Mustang to work, and David kept the truck, in case he needed to run to town, for ranch supplies.

His whole "dream-relationship" was lying tattered and in ruins – no romance, no cuddling in bed, no spontaneity, he was still sleeping alone, and he had no one to give his love to. But, at least he lived on the most beautiful ranch he'd ever seen. It was his only comfort.

"So, it's no dream-come-true," he said to himself. "We'll take care of each other, when we need to, and it'll get better here… it has to!"

With David having already been scheduled for surgery, then canceling it, he brought with him recent MRI's and surgeon's notes. He was quickly scheduled for surgery, to repair the severed rotator cuff in his right shoulder. The surgery was scheduled for a Thursday in early January. The day before his surgery, he had an appointment to go into the doctor's office, for a "pre-surgery check-up," to make certain he didn't have any infections, or viruses, that might jeopardize the surgery.

Earlier in the week, while he and Karen sat outside watching the stars, he mentioned to her that he was going in for his pre-op physical on Wednesday, at 11. He mentioned that he could come by afterwards, and take her out to lunch.

"You know, like I had planned to do before? And maybe this time, I can actually meet those guys you work with. You talk about them all the time, and I feel like I know them, but I wouldn't recognize any one of them." "Oh, yes," she began enthusiastically, then turning sour. "Oh, wait. Wednesday? I told Joyce I would go to lunch with her, on Wednesday…"

"Joyce? The gal you work with, Joyce?"

"Uh, huh. See, on Wednesdays, we like to go eat at the food court, in the mall… and we can window shop while we eat!" Karen explained. "It's really fun, and it would break her heart if I had to cancel." "What about MY heart?" he was thinking. But, what he said was: "Oh, I see. Well, I wouldn't want to mess that up for you."

He didn't know if she was embarrassed of him, or of them, but she certainly seemed to be going out of her way to make certain that he never met anyone she worked with. That was just odd, he thought.

"Let me get this right," he said in exasperation. "You're blowing me off, because you don't think Joyce…a girl you see and work with every single day…Joyce, wouldn't understand if you told her that you had to cancel with her, because your boyfriend is coming into Chico, for once, and is taking you out to lunch?" "When you put it like that, it sounds awful…" "You don't think it is?" he defended.

"You're just being silly. She really looks forward to our once-a-week lunches. Poor girl, I think that's the most exciting part of her whole life! It would just kill her, if I canceled!"

David made another "adjustment" to his "dream-relationship:" "No more offering to take her out to lunch, or offering to meet people she works with."

His "dream" was slowly turning into a nightmare.

On the appointed day, David went in to the surgery center at 7:00 a.m. with Karen by his side. He was amazed at complex surgery, such as his, being done, and the patient being discharged, all in one day. But by the time the sun began to fade behind the Western mountains, David was staggering slowly out to Karen's truck.

David's right shoulder was heavily bandaged, and he had a sling, with a fat, foam spacer across his belly, to keep the joint in the exact correct spot for healing. He thought it made him look pregnant. Karen was on his left side, easing him along by his elbow. He had tucked a small bag, containing medication, antibiotics and antiseptic cream, into his sling. As they approached the truck, Karen rushed ahead, and opened the door.

Her truck had an "off-road" package, and sat quite high off the ground. With only one arm, it took him a few seconds to get into the best position to try to lift himself into the seat. Apparently, it was taking longer than Karen had anticipated, so she "helped" him get up, by grabbing his right elbow and lifting. Never mind the sling, or the bandages, or the fact that six hours ago, that shoulder was laid open like a codfish in the market…Karen just grabbed the arm, and pushed him up into the truck.

David screamed in agony.

"GEEZ!" Karen said, in disgust. "I was just trying to help you get in…"

She walked around and got in the driver's seat. David reached into his bag, and gulped another morphine pill.

"My God, Karen," David said finally. "I just had surgery on that shoulder."

"Well, I didn't grab your shoulder," she explained. "You're just a big baby."

"Just take me home… please?"

The drive home was in silence. When they pulled into the garage, Karen shut the truck off, then walked over to the kitchen door and held it open for him. Of course, David was still in the truck, struggling with the door handle. It finally popped open, and he rolled out, fortunately, and landed on his feet. He wobbled unsteadily, took a deep breath, and started slowly toward Karen.

"I just want to go to bed," he murmured.

From the garage, they entered the kitchen, with David still slowly staggering toward his bedroom.

"The doctor said you should eat," Karen remarked. "I'm going to have a salad. You want me to make you anything?"

He looked at her hopefully… "Chicken soup?"

"Oh, geez," she rolled her eyes. "All we have is that Campbell's Condensed. I can't stand that stuff."

"It's fine," he mumbled, as he continued walking toward his room.

It took him a while to use the bathroom, but upon successful completion, he was proud.

"I never realized how tough it is to pee, using just one hand," he had said. "But if I can do this, I can do anything!"

He laughed at his own joke. Morphine will do that to you! Just as he lay his hand upon the bed, to turn his covers down, Karen called out from the kitchen.

"It's ready! Do you want me to bring it in there, or do you want to come out here to eat?"

He took a deep breath.

"In here," he hollered.

Before they had left, David set up a TV tray beside his bed, so he could sit on the bed and take his meals. He was struggling to move it into position beside his bed…between the drugs, and only having his left arm to use, it was yet another challenge for him to overcome in his recovery. Karen saw that the tray was not yet in the right place, and he was not yet seated on the bed to eat. So, she set the bowl of soup on his dresser.

"There's your soup, Hon," she said, pointing to it, as she headed back out the door.

David got the tray in the right place, he moved his soup onto the tray, then finally, crawled into bed. He didn't want to move, but he knew he had to eat, so he rolled around, getting his feet over the side, and sat up.

"Umm, ummm, good!" he said softly. "I love Campbell's Condensed chicken soup!"

Karen did not have any vacation days left, so she had to go in to work the next day, leaving David alone all day, to care for himself. And he was actually happy about that! He had asked her, the previous night, if she could get him some Pepto-Bismol… and she brought him Pepcid AC. Both useful pharmaceuticals, but hardy interchangeable!

He had started calling her, the "nurse from Hell." But, it was about to get worse…

After a week, the doctor told him, he could remove the pad from the sling, so he didn't look like a pregnant seal any longer. They had him scheduled, initially, to come to the office and have his stitches removed on that same day, but David canceled, and just pulled the stitches out himself.

"They're nuts if they think I'm driving 80-miles, round trip, just to have them take five-minutes and clip a few stitches," he had said to Karen.

"I can't watch," Karen said, rushing into the next room. "It's not yucky, it just gives me the creeps," she finished.

When he was done, he turned on the hot water in the shower.

That's what he was really excited about! His first shower in a week, and he couldn't wait!! The guest bathroom had a shower stall, but no bathtub… so it was much easier, and safer, getting into, and out of, than the tub-shower. Hearing the water run, Karen returned.

David was just stepping out of his boxers, so Karen opened the shower door. As David smiled, and stepped toward the shower, Karen again grabbed him by the right elbow, and "helped" lift him into the shower.

"DAMMIT, KAREN," he yelped. "What're you thinking?"

"I'm just trying to help," she burbled as she ran from the room.

David climbed into the shower, grateful that she was gone. He luxuriated in the hot water for nearly half an hour, before he reached out and grabbed his towel. After getting dried off, David stepped out and opened the door, to allow the steam to escape. From the guest bath, he could see into the dining room and kitchen, and Karen was standing by the kitchen counter looking at her phone.

"Reading texts…" David thought. "Wait a minute…"

He looked again. It was not her phone, but his! He had plugged it in there to charge, before heading into the shower. He quickly donned his robe, and hobbled into the living room.

"What, in God's name, are you doing?" He demanded.

"Who the Hell is Tammy?" she demanded, even more lividly than David. "She says she 'loves you very much."

"What are you doing reading my text messages. That stuff is private… none of your business. What gives you the right to…

"We're in an exclusive relationship," Karen spat. "THAT gives me every right to make sure you are not cheating on me."

"Nothing gives you the right to go through my personal messages…"

"So, who is this Tammy? One of your Rancher's Only girls?"

"She's my niece," David spit back. "My brother's kid. I went to her graduation last spring… suma cum laude graduate from USC, for God's sake. Tammy is my niece," David finished, as he snatched the phone out of Karen's hands.

Karen had nothing to say. What could she say? She stormed into her room, and David did not see her for the rest of the night. He also quickly set a password for his phone, so she could not read his messages any time she wanted. He had absolutely nothing to hide, but it was terribly wrong for her to assume she had a right, to read his personal mail, he thought.

A month after his surgery, Karen wanted to drive up to Red Bluff to visit her oldest and dearest friend, Kylie. Kylie and her husband had a large ranch, northwest of town, and they had a lot of hunters passing through… for a fee, of course. It was nearly two hours each way, and after a tour of the ranch, and a very pleasant visit, David and Karen headed home.

Since it was only 4:00 in the afternoon, and they hadn't been invited to stay for supper, David asked Kathy if she had any ideas for their evening meal? After a bit of discussion, David suggested they just stop in Oroville for a pizza, to take home with them.

"Oh, that sounds wonderful," Karen said. "We'll get a vegetarian delight."

For the next 15 minutes, they talked of small things, then just listened to the radio. After a bit, David noticed Karen's lips moving.

"Whatcha doing?" he asked. "Oh, just going through what we have in the refrigerator, trying to figure out something for dinner."

"What's wrong with pizza?"

"Oh, pizza sounds great!" she exclaimed. "I'm glad you thought of that…

"WE thought of that," David corrected. "15-minutes ago… we had a conversation? We talked about dinner? You said you wanted a vegetarian-delight."

"Oh, I just wasn't sure you still wanted that," she replied with a smile. David was really confused. She wasn't even on the phone. "This might be a lot more serious than we first thought," he said to himself, remembering the green paint.

After they ate pizza, and washed it down with a beer, David insisted they sit and talk for a few minutes.

"Look, Karen, this little 'communications issue' we have is not getting better… it's getting worse."

"I haven't talked to Bonnie since we left, this morning," Karen defended.

"It isn't just about the cell phone, anymore," David stated. "What about the pizza thing tonight?"

"So, I forgot we talked about it," she snapped, her temper rising.

"What's the big deal? We all forget stuff when we get over sixty…"

"Karen, there is a lot of times, you ask me a question, I tell you the answer, then, twenty-minutes later, you ask me the same exact question again. I think it just might be a medical issue…"

"What? Like, you think I'm crazy?"

"Absolutely not," David tried to calm her. "People of our age, some forty per-cent, suffer at least mild cases of dementia, or even early on-set Alzheimer's, who knows? But, if it's a medical issue, there are treatments we can use…"

"I'm not crazy," she said, still doing a slow burn.

"Look, all I am saying is, that we can't fix it ourselves, if it is a medical issue. I think we should get you tested, just so we can eliminate it as the cause, if you're so sure it isn't medical. That's all I'm saying." Karen was glaring at him, and she stood slowly.

"Every time we have this problem, you bring up my Alzheimer's.

I am NOT CRAZY," she said rushing into the guest room—her room— and slamming the door.

David just watched her in shock. She continued yelling, "I am not crazy," repeatedly, from her room.

"MY Alzheimer's" he said to himself. "I never said she had Alzheimer's. But she did… I think she not only has it, but she knows she has it, and she is in total denial."

He knew there was no use continuing the discussion this evening, so he just filed away the information, for later. "Did she think I would leave her, if I found out she had it?" he wondered. "That's crazy… I'm in this deal for better or for worse… but I have to know what I'm dealing with! If she's got it, we need to treat it!"

A few nights later, they again attempted to discuss the issue. This time, Karen kept her temper under control, for the most part. David again stated that, all he wanted to do was have her tested, so they could isolate the problem, and correct it.

"Well, I'm not going to do it!" Karen stated resolutely. "There is nothing wrong with me, nothing at all."

"Then, what harm could it do to just have the test?"

"I'm not crazy, David. I told you that. And I will not let myself be tested like some lab rat. I am fine… take me or leave me, just the way I am."

"Look, Karen… we are both in this relationship to get married, eventually. But I can't marry someone I can't even talk to. Your wife is supposed to be your best-friend, someone you can talk to about anything… anything at all."

"Well, you can talk to me about anything…"

"Karen, every time I do, 20 minutes later, you've forgotten the whole conversation! What's the point in that? Why waste my time?"

"That's not fair."

"Fair or not, I honestly do not think it is wrong to want to have a nice conversation with your wife, without having to repeat it every 20 minutes!"

Karen stewed silently for a few seconds. David tried to give her a hug, but she pushed him away.

"Well, the only reason I am here, is to get married. And, if we're not going to get married, then I need to get out of here…"

"Look, Karen, you are being totally unreasonable about this. One simple test, is all I ask. Why is that so difficult?"

"I told you, I am not crazy…"

It was a vicious circle, and David knew the battle would not be won that evening.

"Look, we still have four months left on the lease… a lease we both signed. So, let's not do anything hasty. We'll just talk about it more, on another day."

Karen wanted it to end, right then and there, but she finally relented, and agreed to resume the discussion in another day or so.

Chapter 21

"If I don't have a chicken, I don't need a pan to cook it in!"

A few days later, on a calm clear night in late February, David and Karen sat out back by the pool. They had eaten supper, and were on their second beer.

"Karen, I just don't understand why you won't go get tested for, at least, mild dementia. It's just a medical test…"

"I told you," she snarled. "I am not crazy, and I won't be tested, like some kind of rat!"

"But, Karen," David tried to reason with her. "If you don't get tested, how can we know what it is, or what it isn't, that we're up against." "This is just how I am," she stated flatly. "And, I am not getting tested."

"Karen, I don't see any other way for us to finally be able to communicate, honestly and openly, the way a couple is supposed to. It's just a simple little test, that's all."

"So, if I don't get it, you're not going to marry me?"

"How can I marry someone I can't talk to?" Karen shifted uncomfortably in her seat. "Well, then, I guess we're done."

"What do you mean, 'done?' You would rather break up with me, then go have a simple medical test?"

"That's right!" she said proudly. "I told you, I am not crazy…"
"THAT'S the craziest thing I have ever heard, right there!" David stammered incredulously.

"Well, you were right, before, when you said we have a few months left on the lease… and we both signed it."

"The rest of this month, then three more months. The end of May…"

"Right," she said, keeping with her rhythm. "And we are basically just roommates now."

"Well, except for the occasional…benefits," he remarked with a smile.

"You've had your last 'benefits,' from this girl," she said authoritatively. "I don't see why we can't just be roommates, until the lease is up?"

"Well, I, yeah," David stammered. "I hadn't really considered that as an option. I wasn't ready to pull my wrap just yet, but if we're not going to solve this problem, I guess that's a good way to do it."

"Fine," she said, standing. "I'm going to watch some television."
"Hey, wait," David blurted out, before she closed the door behind her.

"Yes?"

"What about our financial arrangements?"

"What about them?"

"Well, we are not exactly splitting things 50-50, around here. I pay the $1,650 in rent, and it takes every dime of my retirement check. When I am done paying rent, I have exactly $2 left in my account."

"I know, but I pay for everything else," she said, surprised he would even bring it up.

"Well, I know," he said hesitantly. "But I've been doing some figuring, and even when the power bill is really high, the most you have ever paid out, for utilities, groceries, feed for your horse, and gas for the two vehicles… the most, you ever paid out was $1,200, in one month."

"Where'd you get that number?" she asked.

"I totaled up the utility bills, and looked at the receipts… we keep them all in that little basket by the phone."

"I know where the receipts are," she snapped. "But, I don't put them ALL in there. Let's just talk about this later, shall we?"

He didn't have a chance to respond, as she closed the door, and went to watch television.

The way they had set up their finances, early on, was fine, when they were a couple, David thought to himself. But, it was grossly unfair, if they were to be just roommates. So, David intended to make sure they reached a fair and equitable arrangement, for their remaining months together.

A few days later, on the first of March, a Sunday, he insisted that he and Karen discuss the breakdown of costs and expenses, and come up with an arrangement that would result in a 50-50 split. She was reluctant. "Like, I didn't pay all the power bill, last month," she explained. "But, I paid off one of my credit cards, and I intend to get the power bill caught up, this month."

"And, our pantry is getting pretty low on everything," David observed. "Well, I don't get paid until Friday, so I'll pick up some groceries then."

"Okay… tell you what," he said thoughtfully. "We'll keep things just the way they are, for now. But you put ALL the receipts in the basket…anything you spend on groceries, gas, what have you."

"I don't always remember to get a receipt…"

"Then, just use your bank statement… you use your debit card for most purchases, right?" he responded. "Just write down the item and the amount, on a small piece of paper, and put it in the basket. I'll write it all down, and we can see, at the end of the month, just where we stand."

"Okay, and that will give me a chance to get all the bills caught up, so you and me can finish April and May with a new deal? Is that right?"

"Yes, 50-50, just like roommates everywhere," David said pleasantly. "Who knows, we might just decide to stay another six-months like that?"

"Well," she said hesitantly, "…that seems fair enough."

"Hey, I'm not trying to be mean. I just want us to have a deal that is fair to both of us," he finished.

"Alright, then," she clarified. "This month, we'll keep to our original deal…"

"I pay rent, and you pay everything else, including you getting caught up on anything you are behind on, like the power bill."

"Right," she continued. "And then, next month, we split everything right down the middle… a new arrangement." "You hit it right on the head," David agreed.

"Okay, so tomorrow, you're going to pay the rent…"

"Leaving me with only $2 left to my name," he added.

"And, on Friday, I'll get groceries, and get gas," Karen concluded. "And next payday, I'll get caught up on the bills I am behind on? Then, next month, the new deal?"

David put out his hand, and they shook on it.

"I think we are both on the same page!" David said.

Karen smiled, then mentioned that she was going to go out and visit with Pistol. So, David decided to go split some firewood, for the rest of the afternoon.

During the month, Karen needed a few reminders to put receipts in the basket, but she did a pretty good job overall. David was not pleased, however, with the paltry amount of groceries she brought home. Her explanation was, that she needed the extra money to get caught up on the bills, and that once everything was paid up, whatever was left would go toward restocking the nearly empty pantry and freezer.

The first of April fell on a Monday, and Sunday evening, David and Karen sat down to discuss the "new" financial arrangement. The pantry was still not replenished, and groceries were slim, but Karen said she had all the other bills caught up, so it was going well.

"Okay, tomorrow, the rent is due," David began. "That's $825 each…"

"I don't have that much," she objected. "My last paycheck went to the power company—almost the whole thing. I don't get paid again until Friday…"

"So, how much will you have on Friday?" "I can probably pay half of my share," she said rationally. "And I can make up the rest the following payday."

"Okay," David said flatly. "I'll pay the rent tomorrow… but that's only going to leave me with $2. When you get paid on Friday, you can give me $400, and I'll get some groceries… seriously, there is nothing here to eat or drink."

"Sorry… I'm doing the best I can."

"No worries," David reassured her. "But, I am nervous going down to just $2, when I still have bills to pay, and groceries to buy, also. They're threatening to turn off my phone, if I don't pay them soon!"

"Well, I'll give you the $400 on Friday, and you can relax a little, anyway."

"Yes, I think that will do it…" David agreed. "Meanwhile, there is literally nothing here for supper. I might be able to throw something together for tonight, with that leftover pork, some rice and some veggies we have left. But, by tomorrow… nothing."

"I have about $40 left, so I'll grab something from the store, on my way home from work tomorrow. It's not much, but it'll have to do." David agreed to provide her with a "$40 shopping list," so he could stretch the food as far as possible, until Friday, when she got paid again. It wasn't working out the way they had planned, but it was "heading in the right direction," David thought.

The next day, David paid the rent, in full. He watched in dismay as the balance dropped to $2.56, in his account. He was really nervous, but he calmed himself by remembering that Karen was going to give him $400 on Friday.

Or, so he thought.

On Friday morning, David was awakened by the sound of truck tires on their gravel parking lot. When he looked out the window, Karen was backing her truck up to the horse trailer. He also saw Bonnie's car parked just inside the compound, near the bridge, and Jim's truck beside it.

"What the Hell?" David said aloud, as he pulled on pants and shoes.

By the time David got outside, Karen was lowering the trailer onto the hitch. She glanced up at him with a strained smile.

"What's going on, Karen? You going to take Pistol to work with you today?"

"Don't be silly," she laughed. "I took the day off, so I could move."

"What? You, what?" David was flabbergasted.

"Oh, don't worry, Jim is here to help with the heavy stuff… and I only have those few things in my bedroom. So, we won't bother you, at all."

"What do you mean, move? You said you were going to stay here until the lease was up?"

"I really can't afford it," she explained. "Bonnie found a place for me for just $500 a month… an apartment over a barn. He threw in a stall for Pistol for free…"

"Wait, what about the money you were going to pay me today? I paid your share of the rent already. There's no groceries, and I have two-bucks to my name."

"Oh, yeah… sorry about that," she pretended. "It took my whole paycheck to pay the first month's rent and the deposits, so I won't be able to help you out there."

"What in the Hell am I going to do for food?" he asked incredulously. "And the Mustang is almost out of gas… you've been using that to go to work every day."

She shrugged her shoulders, and said nothing. A loud clanging, from the back of the horse trailer was the only answer he would get. Bonnie was loading the horse into the trailer, as Jim pushed a cart with the animal's hay and grain. Their discussion was over, apparently, as Karen walked back to join the others.

David slowly walked back toward the house. He was in shock. He went out by the pool and sat in his favorite chair, trying not to listen to the noises from within the house, as Karen packed her bedroom away.

212

"She's been lying to me, all along," he realized.

David just didn't understand. It had never been in his nature to lie to people, not intentionally, and certainly not when it would cause someone else extreme financial difficulties. He didn't know how anyone could do that.

Finally, about an hour later, the trucks started up, and the caravan left his life forever. David took a deep breath, and walked in to assess the damage.

In addition to her bedroom, and assorted furniture, Karen also owned most of the cooking utensils, pots, pans, crock pot, cookie sheets, pizza pan. The kitchen was nearly bare, and the pantry was empty.

"Well, if I don't have a chicken, I don't need a pan to cook it in, I suppose," he said to himself, as the house phone began to ring.

He glanced at the caller-ID, and saw that it was the power company. After exchanging brief pleasantries, the agent explained that when she had last spoken to Karen, she promised that a payment on the account would be made today.

"Wait… she told me that her last paycheck went to pay off the power company," David explained.

"When was that, do you recall?"

"Two weeks ago," David replied.

"Yes, that's when we last spoke with her," the agent explained. "But she didn't make any payments… she said she would pay it in full today. I told her, if she didn't keep that promise, we would have to shut off the power on Monday…"

"Holy crap," David gasped. "So how much do we owe?" "Twenty-two hundred and fifteen dollars," the agent said.

"Whoa, wait, how…" David was in shock again! "That's way more than a month or two…"

"Yes, sir. You see, because of your solar energy, we send out statements… but normally, it doesn't get this far behind."

"So how far behind is it?"

"Well, you opened your account in December… and there have been no payments at all." David gasped.

"None?"

"No, sir. That's why I told your wife…"

"NOT my wife… she was just a roommate."

"Well, that's why I told…your roommate, that if it wasn't paid today, the power will be shut off on Monday."

"I don't have the $2,000," he said. "Shoot, I don't even the fifteen dollars! Is there any way, since Karen obviously lied to both of us, and she doesn't live here anymore…"

"Sir, I'm sorry. We have been trying to get a payment on this account for three months now, and you making a payment today, was our last and final offer."

There was nothing left to say, so David thanked her, and hung up. Quickly, he dug through the "basket" beside the phone, and pulled out the other bills… cable, internet, garbage, phone…all were past due. And all were scheduled for shut-off within two weeks.

"Oh, well," David said with a deep breath. "None of those things works without electricity anyway, and after Monday… that will be gone. I guess I'd better get to work splitting more firewood… a lot more firewood," he finished.

His biggest concern, once he lost power, would be the lack of refrigeration. What little food he had, would need to be eaten in one sitting, because there was no way to preserve the leftovers, or milk, or even make a beer cold. Then, an idea hit him.

The "caretakers' cottage," which was only 150 feet away from his garage, had a separate power meter, and it was in the landlord's name. The "guys" kept a few antiques there, and had timers on the lights, to make it seem as if someone were living in it. David also knew that the well pump, which supplied water to both houses, was also on the separate meter, so he wouldn't lose water.

"I saw a couple of long extension cords, hanging up in the barn," he recalled.

He hooked both cords together, and plugged the long-cord in to the cottage's single outside-receptacle. David stretched it through the shrubbery, where it could be hidden from view; then he routed the cord to the back of his garage, then into the back door.

His old "beer-box" refrigerator was in the garage, and still worked like a champ. There was just barely enough cord to reach it, but when he plugged it in, the motor began to hum, reassuringly.

"Cowboy-ingenuity," David said proudly to himself.

David was also able to plug his phone charger into the extension cord, so he could charge it at night. The ranch had no cell signal, and they had been using only WiFi, up until the power was cut. But David found that, if he climbed to the top of the hill behind the house, he could get a signal, and make calls when he needed to.

A few days later, David went into town and bought $150 worth of groceries. He picked-out a few inexpensive cuts of meat, chicken, pork and lots of hamburger, along with 10 lbs. of potatoes, rice, flour, noodles, sugar and shortening. He paid for it all with a hot-check, knowing he would not be coming back there until after the 1st… still three weeks away… and he had to eat.

While he was sorting through his storage boxes, after Karen had moved out, he had found some "camping" cookware, including a cast-iron skillet, a bowl and a plate, and a few other useful "kitchen" items. He added those to a set of three, aluminum "roasting pans," he bought at the grocery store. The roasting pans were made for turkeys, but useful to bake just about anything.

"Thank God the stove and water heater are gas!" David had exclaimed, when the power was first disconnected.

David had also found, in storage boxes, a number of candles, and two oil lamps. Since there was no power, he unpacked, and positioned these throughout the house. David was delighted that the oil lamps were almost as bright as a ceiling light, so he took to reading again, in the evenings!

David had split several cords of firewood, and he used the two fireplaces for heat. The temperatures then, generally fell only into the upper 40's at night, warming to the upper 60's during the day. David was grateful for the moderate weather.

In his search, for more "gold in them boxes," David realized that nearly everything of value had already been sold. After the sale of his Armada, he had purchased a used 250cc Quad, to use as a tractor, which he had paid nearly $1,000 for. However, three weeks after he got it to California, it just stopped running. David was not much of a mechanic, and he soon gave up trying to fix it. So, the machine sat where it had broken down, ever since.

"Tough to get a good price on something that doesn't run," he deduced. "Well, maybe I can get enough to buy some food, anyway."

At the end of his first week, of "roughing it," David had a nice routine worked-out. He was staying warm at night, he had a stove, and hot water, for showers and cleaning. He also enjoyed catching up on his reading at night, and he had a cozy, warm bed to sleep in.

Most of the time, he used a wood fire in the smoker, to "barbecue" meat, what little he had; but, the bulk of each meal was fried, or baked, potatoes, pasta or rice. It wasn't fancy, but it filled his belly.

Also purchased from the proceeds of the Armada, was a hunting rifle and scope. David had only paid $100 for the old Marlin 30-30, and since his meat was almost gone, and there was no money, he reluctantly loaded the rifle.

"Those turkeys are like my pets," he thought. "I sure hate to shoot one, but I have got to eat! I'm sure Tom will understand. He'll still have a dozen hens to fool around with!"

Because the wild turkeys were used to David's presence, he had no trouble walking up to within 20-feet of the grazing flock, the next day. He was more concerned about getting caught "poaching." Hunting game out of season was not a crime to be taken lightly, but David knew it wasn't about sport, it was about staying alive. So, he picked out a good-sized hen, one without any youngsters, and pulled the trigger. The other hens didn't even seem to notice, and Tom was nowhere to be seen. The hen he had killed, would feed David for a week!

After he cleaned the bird, and got it into the oven to roast, he reluctantly picked up his cell phone and headed out to climb the hill.

David had found any reason he could, to put off making the call, but he knew it was time.

"Hello, Dale?" David said, once he had found a good spot on the hilltop.

David told his landlord about Karen moving out, and about the financial crisis she had created for him. He didn't mention having to kill one of the wild turkeys, but he did tell Dale that he had hooked up his garage refrigerator to the extension cord, running from the cottage.

"I'm glad you thought of that," Dale said sympathetically. "Well, Roy is out working in the garden, so I'll talk to him about it, and get back to you."

"Oooh, that might be tough," David explained. "I have to climb the hill behind the house to get a signal... but you can leave a voicemail, and I'll get it next time I come up here."

Late that afternoon, David sat out by the pool, watching the turkeys and deer, when he heard the main gate opening. Puzzled, he got up and looked across toward the bridge... as Dale and Roy drove across, and into the parking lot.

David walked out to greet them, as Roy popped-open the back of the hatchback sedan. Dale got out and greeted David with a warm smile. "Instead of calling, we thought we'd just drop by," Dale explained.

"And, I brought you some things from the garden..." Roy added, bringing out a soda-case box of fresh tomatoes. "Where do you want them?"

"Oh, thank you, so much," David said reaching for the box. "I'll just take these..."

"Oh... there's a lot more," Roy said grabbing another box. "There's seven different varieties of tomatoes in that box... four kinds of bell peppers here, two kinds of squash, as well as jalapenos, green beans, raspberries, sweet peas..."

"My Lord!" David exclaimed looking at the number of large boxes in the back of the car. "You didn't have to give me all this! But, God knows, I need it. Thank you."

David was already smelling the savory turkey soup he would be making with all the peppers and fresh vegetables.

"Oh, this is just the extras," Dale said, with a smile. "We feed most of it to our pigs."

They unloaded all the fresh fruits and vegetables, then had a seat at the dining room table.

"All I can offer you is water," David apologized.

Roy's face lit up.

"Oh, I almost forgot…" he rushed out to their car, and came back in with three bottles of homemade peach "hooch." It was like wine, but much, much stronger. "They're still kind of cold," Roy said setting them on the table.

"No worries," David said standing up. "I have ice in the freezer, in the garage."

David grabbed three glasses, and headed out to the garage.

As they sipped the delicious liquor, they talked about the lease, and what David intended to do…what he could afford to do? It was finally decided that the landlords would let David out of the lease, but they would keep all the deposit money. The "last month's rent" was paid upon move-in, so David still had another full month remaining, without having to come up with rent money. David promised to move out, at the end of the following month, and he'd leave the place exactly the same as when he had moved in.

After the landlords left, David sat down heavily and sighed.

"Well, I won't starve… so I'll survive until the end of next month," he said to himself. "But then what?"

He drained his glass of hooch, and sighed again.

"Man, this dating dream has really turned into an internet nightmare."

Chapter 22

"Back in the saddle again..."

"So, you all settled in to your new 'love-nest,' Cowboy?" Chance asked humorously.

"Bite me, Chief," David responded over the telephone. "There's not much to settle, really. I've got a twin bed, my desk, a chest of drawers and my computer... that's about it."

"From Shangri-la to Shit-hole, in just six-easy payments!" Chance chuckled.

"And if you can't make the payments, just sell everything it took you a lifetime to accumulate!" David added.

It wasn't exactly the same as having coffee on the patio, and they didn't talk as often, but David and Chance still stayed in touch via telephone. During the last two weeks of March, with little else to do, David climbed the hill behind the ranch-house, so he could make a few phone calls, and Chance was usually on the list.

David found a room in town, advertised as an "efficiency apartment," which was actually a garage, that had been converted into an apartment. There was a small bathroom, with a shower stall, sink and medicine cabinet. Just outside of that was a "kitchenette," a short counter with a small stove and oven, built-in, and a short refrigerator also

"under-counter." He had a deep kitchen sink, but it was just a "one-holer," and he had arrayed his coffee-maker, microwave and a toaster on top of the counter, to the left of the sink, and a dish drainer to the right.

"It's hard to believe that, a year ago, I was living in a 2,500-squarefoot mini-mansion, with fountains, a hot tub, a library, even a gym… and today, I am grateful to be living in this 120 square-foot dump."

"You know, they haven't done one single thing to that house, since the foreclosure. Not even a 'for-sale' sign."

"Really? Well, it's probably because it needs a lot of work, before they can offer it for sale."

"It's just sad… all your fruit trees are dead, and one or two of the pine trees aren't going to make it."

"Damn. You know Dana and I planted those pine trees… they were Christmas trees."

"I know, I've heard the story… bought them in a bucket, and after the Holidays, you planted them in the backyard!" "That first one is over twenty-five feet tall, now," David reflected. "No… not anymore," Chance corrected. "They were afraid it might fall on the neighbor's house, so they cut it down. It's just a two-foot stump now."

"Damn. Losing a house is no big deal, but the memories that the house gave birth to… that's the hard part to walk away from."

"You think a house is tough to lose…and all those memories? Imagine how I felt after Donna died…" Chance said sadly.

"I can't beat the 'dead-wife' card, Amigo. But thanks for putting things in perspective," David said. "At least I have full-time cell service here, and free WiFi for my computer."

"Ah, the silver lining to your dark cloud," Chance surmised.

In the few days since David had moved into the garage apartment, he had spent quite a bit of time on the phone with his buddy, Chance. David explained that the rent was $450 per month, and included all utilities, plus the landlord gave David the password to his home WiFi, so David could log on for free. All he had had to pay was his first and last month's rent, and it was his to move-into.

On the first of April, David rented a truck, and a storage unit, in town. After taking a few items to the new apartment, the rest went into storage. He paid his cell phone bill, and car insurance, and he threw all of the other bills into the fireplace and burned them. It was more of an act of frustration, rather than one of defiance.

He knew he would have to pay all those bills, eventually, but all of the creditors would have to calculate their "final bills," and send him the new grand total. Then, David would send a small amount to each one, every month, until paid.

During the past two weeks, Chance had taken every opportunity to say, "I told you so," to David, about his nightmare with Karen. David often tried to defend himself, but Chance had been totally correct on all counts. The differences in their favorite television programming, and watching TV in bed, or not, was the reason David and Karen never shared a bedroom, Chance pointed out. And, they had never once sat down to watch a movie, or listen to music, together.

And, the fact that Karen still thought she was a tough Oregon-cowgirl, even though she had become 100% Californicated, was also an issue, simply because David just didn't understand how a horse and tack could be considered part of "a woman's accessories." The problem was, since Karen truly believed that she was still the same cowgirl she had been in her younger days, David never saw it coming. But, Chance did...

There, also, was Chance's prediction of financial chaos, since David had had to sell his most prized possessions, just to move to California. When Karen left him without food, power or cash, David became keenly aware of just what this impulsive move had cost him, over the past six-months. "Well, at least you got something for the quad," Chance remarked. "Yeah, my neighbor wanted it for parts," David recalled. "And when I ran into him, I had my 30-30 with me. He offered me $200 for the quad, but he bumped it up to $500, if I'd throw in the rifle. Man, I hated parting with that..."

"But at least you got something to help with the move," Chance noted.

"Yeah, I spent $1,300 for those two items, used them both a couple of times, and sold them six-months later for $500. What a bargain!"

But, in all fairness, the single largest issue was Karen's Alzheimer's, which neither of them saw coming. Karen refused to admit she had it, and she refused to deal with it, on any level.

"The bad part of that is, I think the reason she was in denial about it," David explained, "…is that, I think, she thought, I would leave her if she told me the truth about it. Ironically, I never would have left her, if she had only been honest about it."

"Yeah, so instead of her running you off, she just ran away herself," Chance observed. "That don't make no sense at all!"

David agreed, and as much as he was feeling sympathy for her medical condition, he pointed out to Chance that, even Alzheimer's was not a good excuse for leaving a man hungry, broke and with no power, or other utilities.

"I can never forgive her for that," David said. "Although… the fact that I lived there for almost a month, with no food or electricity, and I made it almost comfortable… well, that was a boost to my ego!" "You planning to move back to Vegas?" Chance asked.

"Well, I miss my kids and grandkids," David said sincerely. "But, even if I had the money to move back, where would I go? My house is gone…"

"You could live here for a while…"

"Thanks, but that would just be a temporary fix. Besides, I like this area… Northern California, and even on up into Oregon… it's a terrific place for my little hobby-ranch. So, if I move back there, I might just be turning around and moving back again, if I meet a gal from around here."

"So, you ready to mount up again?" Chance asked with a sly smile.

"I've already renewed my RanchersOnly membership," David replied matter-of-factly. "I am back in the saddle again, my friend."

"Well, that's the 'cowboy-way,' I guess."

"It's a little different this time…"

"I hope so, Dumbass," Chance quipped. "You have a lot more things to put on your list of rules…"

"Well, yeah," David admitted. "But I was talking about, the situation has changed. My finances have changed…"

"Yeah, to dead-broke," Chance slammed. "Maybe you can find a gal with a big ranch, and you can just move in with her?"

"Don't laugh," David remarked. "Of course, I'm not looking for a 'sugar-mama,' but it would be nice if the next gal is financially stable."

"One of ya needs to be, and it dang-sure ain't you!"

"Kiss my ass."

"I'm just sayin'," Chance said with a smile. "So, have you booked any 'coffee-dates,' yet?"

"Well, I've only been on there a couple of days," David explained. "But I increased my search parameters to 250 miles…"

"That's kind of a long drive for coffee, ain't it?"

"Well, yeah, but in the big picture, it lets me look into the central valley, in California, as well as most of Oregon… heck, I am only 90 miles from the Oregon border. And any of these places would work for my little ranch."

"So, you having any luck?"

"Well, I had one gal respond yesterday… from Visalia, about 300 miles south."

"Nice area," Chance commented. "Close to the mountains…"

"Yeah, and she has a small place, several horses… we look good on paper."

"But?"

"But, her pictures… she looks a little heavy, and I am just not thinking there is going to be any 'magic,' you know?"

"Well, there's only one way to find out…"

So, a few days later, David spent six-hours driving to Visalia, to meet this gal at a coffee shop. They visited for two hours, traded recipes for jams and sweet bread, and had a delightful conversation. But there was no magic, just as David had predicted, and he drove six-hours back home.

Meanwhile, he had a response from another lady in Madras, Oregon, which was a little more than 400 miles away. But, David had been to many rodeos in that area – Sisters, Prineville, Redmond – all had huge professional rodeos, and the whole area was full of ranches, cows, horses, cowboys, and of course, cowgirls.

"Surely you are not going to drive 400 miles, have coffee, and drive home again… all in one trip?" Chance asked incredulously.

"Back in my rodeo days, that would be nothing," David replied. "But, I am too old for that shit nowadays. No, actually, she is a singer in a band… she says she does a terrific 'Patsy Cline,' and a pretty strong 'Reba.'"

"Well, that's pretty cool… so what's the plan?"

"Well, she's off on Sunday, so we're going to meet at a little restaurant and bar in Madras. The place has a band, and Jolene wants to check them out."

"So, it's a working date for her, eh?"

"I suppose," David said. "But, we'll have supper, and maybe get in a little dancing."

"So, not your usual 'coffee-date…'"

"I actually suggested coffee, and she came up with this idea," David explained. "And, I told her, due to the distance, I was going to get a cheap motel room, grab a few hours of sleep, and head home in the morning."

"How'd she take that? She didn't offer you a couch, at least?" David laughed.

"Yeah…no," he said. "I knew she'd just say, 'We're not there, yet,' so I didn't even ask. But, man, oh, man, I have a good feeling about this one. She is so cute!"

"Well, cute don't catch the catfish," Chance observed.

"I know, but it sure is nice to come home to!"

A few days later, David found himself, once again, heading out on a long road-trip. He was glad the Mustang got good gas mileage, as he had a very tight budget. But, he knew it would all work out.

When David arrived in Madras, due to his early start, he had time to check into his motel, grab a quick nap and a shower, before heading over to the "Do Drop Inn." He had already spoken with Jolene, and she was also nearly ready. David figured if he got there early, it would give him time to have a drink of Pendleton whiskey – to calm his jittery nerves.

The place was set up like a typical sports-bar, with televisions around the house, all tuned to a variety of sporting events… it was Sunday, after all. David grabbed a Pendleton on ice, while he checked the place out.

It had a huge patio, with a dozen tables outside, and while there was plenty of room indoors, David noticed that they were setting up a stage, out on the patio, for a band. The inside tables were used primarily for people eating supper, or for kids, while mom and dad sat at the bar drinking a beer.

David grabbed a table, close to the patio-door, but where he could still see the main entrance. The cocktail waitress came by, and he ordered a beer, since the whiskey was too expensive to drink all night!

The girl explained that, in an hour, the restaurant would be hosting an "all-you-can-eat" spaghetti dinner, to benefit the Vietnam Veterans Foundation. That was a charity that was very dear to David, so he told the gal that he would probably take two of the $10 tickets, once his "date" arrived, and they had a chance to talk about it.

When Jolene walked into the bar, David had absolutely no doubt who it was! She had shoulder-length blonde hair, gorgeous green eyes, and a petite figure that was astounding for a woman over-fifty. She recognized David immediately, also, primarily due to the black, felt cowboy hat he wore.

She rushed over to him, and gave him a big hug, as if they were old friends. Of course, they had spent hours talking, almost every evening, for the past week; and they both felt like "old-friends," even though this was their first meeting. Before she let go of David, in that first hug, he knew instantly that the "magic" was definitely there, at least for him. "Sorry I am a little late," she gushed, as David pulled out

225

her chair for her to sit. "But I had to look perfect! And this darned hair was giving me fits."

David looked at it, and it was amazing. But, he knew that entertainers had a whole different standard, when it comes to "looking good," so he just commented that she looked "incredible." The waitress came by, and Jolene asked for a mug of draft beer. While the waitress went to fetch the beer, David told Jolene about the "all-you-can-eat" supper, to benefit Vietnam Veterans.

"Well, how awesome is that?" She replied with a smile.

So, when the waitress returned, he bought two dinner tickets, and gave the waitress his credit card, to run a tab. The restaurant was already setting up the steam tables, and bringing food out, so David knew they would not have much longer to wait. "I'm famished," he told Jolene.

"Me, too…" she agreed, but she was more interested in checking out the band-members, as they were setting up and tuning instruments, out on the patio.

"I think I know that guy," she said pointing to a guitar player. "If it's the guy I think it is, he is really good. He sings just like Garth!"

"Well, it's almost six," David said, looking at his watch. "The spaghetti dinner starts at six, and the band starts at seven."

"So, maybe we can stay for a couple of sets, once the band gets going?" she asked hopefully.

"We can stay for their whole show, if you like," David offered generously.

Jolene smiled brightly, and suggested that they might even get in some two-stepping! David admitted that he would really enjoy that. So they did.

They finished eating, hardly slowing down their conversation long enough to chew and swallow, but it was a very good first-meeting. When the band started playing, they moved out onto the patio, near the dance floor, and enjoyed the music. Occasionally, when a good song came on, they would dance. It was pure magic for them both.

David was partial to two-steps and cowboy waltzes, but when a distinctly slow song began, Jolene grabbed his hand and pulled him out onto the dance floor. Fortunately, the floor was crowded, so they easily got lost in a very romantic dance. In fact, it was hardly a dance at all, more of a "lover's embrace," as it were. At the end of the music, David leaned in for a short "first-kiss."

He intended it to be just a quick peck, but as he leaned in, Jolene placed her hand on the back of his head and pulled him in for a long, deep kiss. They were totally oblivious to anyone else, until they pulled back, and the crowd applauded them!

Despite the moment of embarrassment, David could tell that Jolene was feeling the magic, too, and he was delighted! After they returned to the table, the band took a break, and Jolene started talking of her music, and the way her band performed some of the different songs they had heard.

"Wow, I really wish I could hear you sing," he said. "Maybe next trip?"

"Yes, I would love that..." she began. "Hey, wait a minute... I've got a CD out in my car. It's just a short demo, four songs, but maybe, when we leave?"

"Are you kidding," David responded enthusiastically. "I would love to hear that!"

"Well," she began tentatively. "It is getting late... and the band just finished their second set..."

"So, why don't we finish these beers, and go listen to you sing?" David finished.

Jolene laughed, then emptied her half-full glass in a single gulp. David's beer was nearly gone, so he gulped his, too, and they stood to leave. The waitress brought him the check, and he told her to just run it on the card. Once she brought it back, they walked out to the parking lot.

"It's this one," she pointed to a small Volvo sedan.

She unlocked David's door, and as he slid into the seat, he reached across and unlocked her door. It had a bench seat, so when David slid back, he stayed closer to the center of the seat. Jolene got in, and started digging through her CD's, until she found the right one. As she slipped it into the deck, she slid over close to David, so he put his arm around her shoulders, and they waited for the music to begin.

She was, indeed, a remarkable singer, David told her, halfway through the first song. She thanked him with a quick kiss… which lingered for a few moments. Then, she threw her left leg across his lap, and pulled him in for a very deep, passionate kiss. That kiss lasted for two more songs!

By the time all four songs were finished playing twice, Jolene had to re-button several of her blouse buttons… however, she did so reluctantly. Both of them were being swept away by the passion of the moment.

"I hate to stop this," she whispered. "Boy, you're a good kisser!"

"No, you're right. We both agreed to move slowly, before we see where this is going, so I'd better head out… for a cold shower!"

They kissed again, more controlled this time, and David got out. "I'll call you before I leave in the morning," David said, while holding open the car door. "Maybe we can get together for breakfast, or something?"

"Dang… bad day for that. I have an appointment with the vet, to get my dog's shots updated."

"Well, no worries," David responded lightly. "We'll just talk for a bit, and then, I'll start my journey homeward-bound."

He leaned in for a last kiss, and they parted company. David was singing, as he got into the Mustang and fired it up.

"Hot damn," he said, as he watched Jolene pull out onto the boulevard. "I got to second base on the first date… and it was all her idea!"

David was trying to be on his best behavior, and he vowed to keep the Little Outlaw locked away. He didn't want to make a mistake with this lady, especially on their first date. But when she threw her leg across his lap, in the car, her hand quickly followed to his crotch. And since she had initiated that "first contact," he decided to let the Outlaw play, just a little.

The next day, before he got on the highway back to Oroville, he went for a drive around some of the local farm communities, and picked up local newspapers, so he could get an idea of the market prices. He had learned his lesson from the Karen-Nightmare, that he did not want to rush into anything, but it was a good idea to start looking, he thought. "Besides, I can just get my own place," he said to himself, "…and Jolene can move in, whenever she is ready!"

That was his idea, anyway, however, a few days later, when he mentioned that he was looking for a place near her, Jolene objected.

"Wait, David, you're looking for a place around here?" Jolene asked.

"Well, yeah," David replied. "I'm not a big fan of long-distance relationships."

"David, if you want to move someplace around here, because you were already planning to, then fine. But, if you're moving here, just to be in a relationship with me, then please don't."

"I'm not sure I like what you're saying," David responded.

"I'm just saying, people don't move someplace just to be close to someone they had a fun date with…"

"Well, yeah, it was a fun date," David reasoned. "But, if we are going to move forward with this relationship…and I hope we are… then we need to live a little closer, that's all…"

"OH, MY GOD!" She screamed into the phone. "You're looking for a WIFE, aren't you?"

Jolene snarled the word "wife" like it was a sailor's choice cussword.

"Well, yeah," David replied in a daze. "I thought, that was the whole idea behind these dating sites?"

"I'm just looking for a boyfriend," she said, still irate, but calmer. "Someone I can go out with, and have a few laughs, once in a while."

"But, Jolene, we talked about…"

"Don't ever call me again," she snapped, then she disconnected the phone.

David stared at his cell phone, still wondering what had just happened.

"Son-of-a-bitch," he swore. "It's usually the men who are the 'commitment-phobes.' But not this time, no sirree. This is just weird.

"Well, dust yourself off, Cowboy...they're loading another one into the chutes! And, it's almost time to nod your head!"

Chapter 23

"Aw, shucks, ma'am. It's only 600 miles!"

"What the Hell?" Chance remarked. "I thought that was the whole point of these dating web sites?"

"That's exactly what I told Jolene," David said. "That's when she hung up on me!"

Although they were talking on the phone, David could picture Chance sitting back with a big smile, enjoying every minute of David's misery.

"Well, at least we had a fun date… 400 miles just for a cup of coffee, would have been much worse!"

"So, you're not having fun driving that much further? Is it doing you any good?" Chance asked, referring to David expanding his search parameters to 250 miles, instead of 50.

"Doing me any good? That's hard to say. I mean, I'm no closer to finding 'a wife,'" David snarled the "wife" part, mimicking Jolene. "But, I actually like the driving…seeing country I had forgotten about."

"Ah, that wonderful silver-lining!" Chance observed.

"Yeah, I honestly never really looked, at that part of Oregon, before."

"I thought you said you used to ride rodeos there all the time?"

"Oh, yeah, I was there," David explained. "But, I never saw it…I never pictured myself living there. Now, that whole Redmond-Bend-

Prineville area of Oregon… it feels like a lady trying to seduce me—calling me in."

"Hey, you wanna be alone for a while?" "Screw you," David laughed.

"Naw, I know what you mean," Chance let him off the hook. "So, you're still looking for local girls, right? I mean, even as much as you enjoy those 400-mile cups of coffee?"

"Yeah. I met one gal here in Oroville, for coffee. But there was no spark… nothing. And I have another one lives up in Grass Valley…"

"Where the heck is that?"

"It's really close to Donner Pass. Anyway, it's only 45 minutes from my place, so I'm looking forward to meeting that one… just to save some gas!"

"Well, now, that's a little better deal,"

"That's what I was thinking, too," David agreed. "But I still have a couple of other gals, who're scattered about, and I'm not sure if I want to drive that far again, just for coffee…"

"Aw, come on, man," Chance implored. "If you're not driving eight-hours for a cup of coffee, what the heck are we gonna laugh about in the morning?"

"Oh, you might be laughing, but not me. I'm doing serious research! Besides, I have my limit set to 250 miles… anything outside of that, is girls who are picking me, not the other way around."

"Yes, Kimosabe, but that's why you have your list of rules…and your checklist."

"I know, I know… but dang, some of them are really cute! I hate deleting them just because they live a little further away than I like."

"You're thinking with the wrong head, again," Chance reprimanded.

David clicked a few buttons on his phone, and sent a picture to Chance.

"Take a look at this one," David said, hitting the 'send' button.

The picture was one David had downloaded off the RanchersOnly web site just the night before. The lady was in her early 50's, but her pictures all looked like she was 10-years younger.

"Damn!" Chance whistled. "That is one gorgeous woman."

"I know, right? And she has a body to match! Seriously… she still wears a bikini!"

"Hey, we've both been down that road…me with Darlene and you with Tina…"

"Hey, first thing I did was get her to send me a new selfie…"

"So, you've actually started talking with her? How far away does she live?"

"About 600 miles. Place called Kelso, Washington… it's like 50 miles south of Tacoma."

"Holy shit," Chance exclaimed. "You're going for a new world record in distance-drove for a cup of coffee!"

"Hey, I haven't even decided if I am going to do it, yet," David said. "We're chatting, getting to be friends, but I told her that she lived a lot further away than I cared for…"

"You'll go," Chance predicted. "Once you start thinking with that little head…" "Hey, I've been keeping 'Junior' locked up, pretty well, lately.
But, Kendra is just too cute to delete."

"Kendra, huh?" Chance quipped. "You'll go…"
Later that evening, David was talking with his "Kelso-connection."

"So, have you given any more thought to whether you might come visit me, or not?" she asked, innocently.

They had already talked about the great distance, and David had mentioned that they might consider meeting somewhere in-between. But, Kendra said that she often ran her grandkids to school, or afterschool events, and it would be difficult for her to get away, she claimed.

During the initial phase of communication, especially with people who meet online, through a dating web site, the conversation bounces

233

around frequently. A lot of subjects get discussed lightly, but if it comes up again, it can be discussed in more detail.

One of the items they had previously discussed was tattoos and body piercings. David told her that he didn't care much for either, on a woman, but he was weakening. He said he didn't mind the little tattoo women get in the small of their backs.

"I find that very sexy, when a gal bends over, and her tattoo shows…especially when she's wearing thong-panties!"

"All I wear is thongs, but, I don't have any tattoos," Kendra said, "However… I do have a pierced naval?"

"Ah, well those are not bad… sometimes, with a long, dangly earring, they can be pretty hot, actually," David admitted.

"I'll have to send you a picture of mine, sometime…"
"Be careful," David warned her. "I just really might like that!"

"Well, I don't have any pictures, but I can always snap one for you, with my phone."

"Shit-howdy, ma'am, that'd be plumb awesome," David said eagerly. "I just don't like the facial piercings… and I'm not really a fan of pierced nipples, or anything else!"

"Oh, I agree," she said. "With the face piercings… but things that a lady keeps covered by her bra and panties, well, I don't mind that… it's her business, I think."

"So, what do you have pierced?" David asked, as he felt the Outlaw beginning to stir.

"Well, I don't have my nipples pierced…" Kendra said hesitantly. "And, let's just leave it at that, for now."

"If it ever comes to that point, I am sure I'll love whatever you have," he relented. "If you love it, I'll love it!"

They talked for a few more minutes, then Kendra said she needed to get some errands run, and she had a few chores to do.

"But, when we hang up, I'll send you a picture of my naval ring… just to see if you like it."

"Oh, I'm sure I will… and I can't wait to see the picture!" David said trying not to sound too excited!

"Who knows? You might just decide to come up here, and buy me that cup of coffee," she teased.

About ten-minutes later, his phone beeped with an incoming text. He quickly opened up the text-app, and watched the photo download. On his phone, larger pictures opened from the top, slowly revealing the remainder of the photo, as you watch.

"Holy shit," David exclaimed, as he watched the photo opening.

As the top quarter of the image opened, he figured out that the picture began just below her breasts, and she was, apparently, lifting her blouse or shirt, to expose her belly. It was a nice, flat belly, he observed… and as the photo continued slowly unveiling the image, he saw a very cute belly ring! And the photo kept unveiling, lower…

"Oh, my GOD!" he exclaimed when the image was fully opened!

"She's not pulling up her blouse… she's lifting up her SKIRT!"

The image showed her torso, from her bust-line all the way to her knees! She was seated, legs spread slightly, her back arched, to flatten the tummy, and she was wearing a pair of royal blue panties. But, they were very sheer, and left little to the imagination.

"Wow," David was still in shock. "She is completely shaved! And what is this?"

He expanded the photo out, for a closer look, and very clearly, he could see she had a small ring in her labia, right at the very top.

"Now, that looks like a real tongue-pleaser," he said to himself, with a huge smile!

He hit "reply" to the text, and sent her a message that said: "Aw, shucks, ma'am. It's only 600 miles! When do you want to meet for coffee?"

When David told Chance about his decision to drive to Kelso, the next time they spoke on the phone, the old Indian rocked back and laughed out loud!

"David, you idiot," He said finally, trying to catch his breath. "Ain't you learned nothing?"

"I know, I know… but Chance, you should SEE this picture she sent me!"

"You're thinking with your little-head again, Pal," Chance objected seriously. "I don't care how good she looks, 600 miles for a cup of coffee is insane! You're frickin' crazy, if you drive that far just to meet her…"

Click, click, "send." David blasted the photo through cyberspace, to Chance's phone. David waited a few seconds, for the image to load on Chance's phone.

"Holy shit," he said. "You're right, my friend… 600 miles is nothing! Oh, man, is that… has she got a ring… down there?"

"Yes… quite a tongue-tickler, right?"

"Holy shit," he said again. "So, when are you going?"

"Next Tuesday," David responded flatly. "It's going to take every last nickel in my bank account, to get gas, a motel room…"

"And coffee," Chance interrupted. "Can't forget to put that in your budget!"

"Yeah, right," David laughed. "And, if coffee goes well, I might just stay another day or two…"

"I get that. But, seriously," Chance offered. "If you run a little short, I can put a hundred in your account, if you need it."

"Well…." David considered the offer. "I honestly might have to take you up on that, if you've got it to spare?"

David and Chance banked at the same national chain of banks, and they had long ago traded account numbers. If either of them got in a jam, the other one could just get cash out, and deposit it into the other's account.

"Tell you what," Chance said. "I'll go down on Monday and deposit a C-note for ya, and if you don't need it, you can give it back right

away… otherwise, I can wait until payday."

"Hey, you're the best, Amigo."

"Oh, yeah, but it's going to cost you…" Chance said, his humor returning. "If you get any more sexy pictures of that gal, you'd best be for sharing them!!"

"Count on it," David assured him.

After they disconnected, David just shook his head.

"So, not only am I driving 600 miles, each way, for a cup of coffee… but I'm having to borrow money from my friends to do it!" He looked down into his lap. "You better be right about this girl, Little Outlaw, or I am never going to put you in charge again!"

When Tuesday finally arrived, David raced down the highway with a song in his heart. He kept bringing up Kendra's photos, from his phone, especially the sexy one, and glanced at them, all along the way. When he stopped for gas, near Portland, he decided upon his favorite picture of Kendra, one that he had downloaded from RanchersOnly. He set it for the background on his phone.

"Now, I don't have to flip through the pictures, I can look at her beautiful face, any time I want, by just glancing at my phone!"

David also figured, he might make a few points with Kendra, when he showed it to her. But, that all depended on how well their first coffee-date went, he knew.

When they had first begun planning this trip, Kendra told David about a motel, near where she lived, that was adjacent to a shopping center, which had a national chain coffee-shop in the parking lot. He wouldn't even need to drive!

Their plan was, once David got checked into his hotel, they would meet for coffee. He told her that he expected to be in Kelso by 3 p.m., so by having coffee first, they could decide if they then wanted to meet for dinner.

David and Kendra both just assumed they would, so she was going to pick out a nice restaurant. After coffee, he could go take a short nap, then get ready for supper, and she could go home and get ready, at her leisure. That was the plan…

They were texting frequently, by the time David pulled into the motel parking lot. He parked, got checked-in to the motel, then he just walked directly to the coffee shop. Kendra had texted him that she was "on the way," and would arrive within ten minutes. David was exhausted from the 10-hour drive, but the walk across the parking lot, and glancing at Kendra's sexy picture, one last time, soon had his tail wagging like a puppy.

Kendra said she drove a big, red Chevy Suburban, and as David approached, he saw nothing like that in the parking lot. So, he just went in and ordered a small coffee, then picked out a table. Kendra arrived shortly after, and David greeted her at the door. They hugged, like old friends, and he escorted her to the table, before he went to get her a cup of coffee.

"Man," David said to himself. "She's even more gorgeous, in person! I just hope she likes me, too."

They sat and talked for nearly two hours! They each got refills on their coffees, and they talked about their families, mostly, but also about hobbies, hopes and dreams. David felt that it had been a marvelous visit, especially when she smiled, or laughed. But, as it began growing dark outside, he ventured the "big question."

"So," he said, looking her in the eyes. "Are we ready for a second date? A nice dinner?"

Kendra kept smiling, but David could tell, she was forcing it. His stomach began to tumble.

"David… I have really enjoyed our visit," she said sincerely. "You know? You remind me so much of my dad!"

"Well, that's a good thing, right? I mean, you said you admire and respect him…"

"Yes, I do," Kendra offered. "But, I certainly don't want to sleep with him!"

If a bomb had exploded, at that very moment, David would not have noticed it.

"Well, it looks like we're done here," David said, when he was able to breath normally again. "Can I see you to your car?"

A few minutes later, David was walking across the parking lot, back to the hotel, and he glanced at his phone. When he saw her picture on his wallpaper, he stopped immediately, and deleted it.

"Five hours," he said. "That is the shortest time I ever had a girl's picture on my wallpaper!"

After a quick shower, David collapsed on the bed, and slept until just after midnight. He got up, brushed his teeth, and was soon watching Kelso disappear in his rearview mirror.

"No sense waiting until morning," he said to himself.

David arrived back in Oroville at around 10 a.m. Then, he slept for about five hours. When he couldn't fall back asleep, he got up and started working on his RanchersOnly page.

He called Chance, later that evening. Chance had been sending him repeated texts, wanting to know how it was going with Kendra. So, David called him, and told him the whole story!

"She really said that?" Chance asked, still laughing.

"Yeah, she really did!" David had to chuckle himself.

"Yup, 1,600 miles, round trip, just for a cup of coffee, that's gotta be a record!" Chance laughed harder. "David, my man, you're only three hours from Reno. It would be faster and cheaper, just to go to one of them brothels. At least then, you'd get what you pay for!"

"Yuck it up, Ass Wipe," David retorted, but humorously.

"So, you ready to get back on that horse?"

"Oh, yeah, right," David responded sarcastically. "I got online a while ago, and I had a flirt from a girl who lives in Portland…screw that!"

"You were just in Portland, weren't you?" Chance was still poking fun.

"Yeah, that's what I told her," David finished. "I told her I was just there, at like, 4 a.m., passing through. And it's going to be a good, long while until I go back!"

"Did you tell her how much you enjoyed going to Kelso?"

"Asshole…" David said sourly. "I've only got a few days left on that site, and honest to God, I am not renewing, this time…"

"What? The internet dating God is going to take a break?"

"For a while, anyway. I can't afford these long-distance cups of coffee anymore!"

Later that night, David got a response from the girl from Portland. She told him that she understood about his reluctance to get involved with someone so far away. But, she had only been trying online dating for a few weeks, and was not having much luck with it. For some reason, she said, she felt that David was a gentleman, and could be trusted… and she asked if he would help her make her dating profile more appealing.

This kind of plea, always brought out David's shining armor suit…he could not resist a damsel in distress! So he brought up her profile, and began to assess the plusses and minuses.

On careful examination of her profile, something he had not done when she first made contact, he learned that she was a widow, but there was no further information about her deceased husband. She stated that, she had only been married once, for more than 20 years, and that she was brand new to online dating. There was no mention of recent boyfriends, or any other implications of her dating anyone, since her husband's passing.

David assumed from this, that her husband must have died within the past year or two, and she was just coming out of her mourning period, to start rebuilding her life, with someone new. He thought that was quite noble.

The Portland-girl also described herself as, "a good Christian woman," and in her self-description, she indicated that she felt sex should wait until after marriage. While that was an honorable thing for young Christian ladies, David felt that, at her age, it was probably not something she should list, right up front.

"Sex is something you discuss, after you get to know someone,"
David wrote in his notes, which he was going to pass on to "Portland."
David felt a slight stirring in his heart, not in his pants. It wasn't pity, he was feeling, but admiration. In his mind, he pictured a happily married woman, who had raised a family, and had a devoted husband. Then, when the husband died suddenly, after a proper period of mourning, she decided to get back out, and start a new life, with a new man. He also assumed, from her "Christian woman" comments, and her desire to wait until after marriage to have sex again, that she had probably been a virgin when she got married, and quite possibly, her husband was the only man she had ever had sex with! So, depending

upon how long ago her husband had died, David felt, she probably hadn't had sex since his passing.

David was touched, and very interested in finding out more about this struggling widow; but he had already "blown-her-off," when he told her that he wasn't coming back to Portland "any time soon."

"It's probably best this way," he said to himself. "I can help her get into the modern-age of online dating, and I'll go back to looking for someone who lives a little closer. But not online! I'm tired of all this online dating crap, myself."

Finally, after reviewing all of her "RanchersOnly" information, he wrote her a message, sent through the RanchersOnly mail system. He told her that her profile looked fine, except for a few minor changes, which he spelled-out for her, including that she should remove the information about "waiting" for sex, until after marriage.

David told her that he admired her for having the desire to wait, but it was something that she needed to tell someone, in person. He said, once they became close enough to be able to talk about sex, honestly and openly…that is when that subject should be brought up. It's not something you "advertise" ahead of time.

But, the big problem, he felt, were her photos.

"Most of them make you look like an old librarian," he told her in the RanchersOnly message. "But the one where you are holding the dog? That one is sexy as Hell! You have a beautiful smile, your eyes are twinkling, and the first time I saw it, since you had on a beige summer shorts combo, I thought you were naked, and using the dog to cover up the important stuff! Wowee, it really caught my eye."

David waited for two days, and still had not received a response from his Portland damsel. So, on the third day, he sent her a new message explaining that his "RanchersOnly" membership was going to expire the following day. He gave her his cell-phone number and email address, and told her that, if she wanted to talk further, about her profile, or anything else, she would have to call or email. He would not have access his RanchersOnly mail, after midnight.

The next day, he had still not received a response from "Portland." But, for the first time in two-years, David was off all dating web sites. So, he decided to go fishing!

"Well, I hope that sweet, Portland-widow, follows my advice, especially about her pictures," he said to himself, as he loaded his fishing gear into the Mustang.

He didn't have a boat, but his idea of a perfect day of fishing was, a cooler full of beer, a nice tree to provide a shady place to sit, and then, a whole day of just watching his bobber! He didn't even care if he caught anything, he just wanted some "alone-time."

After he got a line in the water, popped-open a beer and got a comfortable seat under a tree, he pulled out his cell phone, to see if he had missed any calls or messages. He hadn't, but he saw that he only had one-bar of service...

"Weak signal," he said. "But I didn't come to the lake so I could chat on the phone!"

He smiled, took a drink of beer, and leaned back against the tree. After an hour, David actually caught a 2-pound catfish. Once he had the fish in the cooler, he re-baited his hook and tossed his line out again. Then, he opened another beer, and glanced back at his phone.

It had been silent, since he got to the lake. But, it showed a missed call, and a new voicemail message.

"Damn, weak signal," he said as he punched in the number to listen to his voicemail.

"Hello, David, this is Evie, from RanchersOnly?" the voice was sweet, but difficult to hear, through the static of the poor connection.

"Evie?" David said to himself. "That has to be the Portland widow."

Evie mumbled something, that David could not make out, or, he thought, it almost sounded like she was sobbing. He could hear her breathing, but she said nothing for another few long seconds. "Please help me..." she whispered, finally.

David was certain that she was crying. But, after "help me," the connection was lost.

Evie sounded as if she was continuing to say more, but the recording simply stopped. David frantically looked at his phone, to try to call her back – however, his call log, and the voicemail ID both said the same thing – "Number Blocked by Caller."

"How? What? Shit!" he yelled in frustration. "I've got no way to call her back!"

And, the only method he had ever used to communicate with her, was through the RanchersOnly messages. Since he was no longer a member… he couldn't use that option either.

"I don't know what the Hell I am going to do," he said as he reeled in his fishing line. "But whatever it is, I won't be doing it here. There's a lady out there who needs my help!!"

He quickly stowed all his fishing gear in the car, being very careful not to get any water on his shiny suit of armor! Soon, he was racing back to his room, and an idea came to him. All he would need to do, is renew his RanchersOnly membership, and then, send her another message!

"Okay, so I have to pay for another month," he rationalized. "But, at least I went a whole 18-hours without belonging to a dating web site!"

An hour later, after David renewed his membership for yet another month, he went to his RanchersOnly mailbox. Evie had responded to his previous message, but her message had come in after his page was closed, so he'd never seen it.

"PLEASE HELP ME!!! I recently received a request for a meet and greet with a gentleman, well maybe a gentleman, who is from Eugene. I am quite nervous. Guess that is to be expected. This may sound crazy because I don't know you but I want your advice. I'd feel comfortable talking to you, if you'd like to call me." Then it listed her full name, phone number and email address.

David was quite disappointed, to say the least. He realized that she had probably left the same message on his voicemail… and perhaps he had over-reacted just a tiny bit? It had cost him nearly $30, just to help a stranger, get prepared for a date, with a guy, he didn't even know!

Since he was already in the RanchersOnly mail program, he composed a note to Evie, explaining that her number had been blocked, her voice-mail message got cut-off, and the only way he could communicate with her was to renew his membership on RanchersOnly!

He also said he intended to call her, later that evening, and asked her if she preferred any specific time? She replied to his message within 15 minutes, and said that "seven would be perfect," and that she was looking forward to talking to him.

After he closed down his computer, he grabbed his phone and entered all of Evie's information into his phone's address book. He realized that she was only looking for help in finding someone else to date, and that she had not expressed an interest in David. But, he continued to reflect on her profile information, in his head, and he kept looking back at the picture of her with her little dog. He was completely intrigued by this little widow-woman.

"Evie Abaddon, huh?" he said thoughtfully. "You don't know it yet, Evie, but, I just might be going back to Portland, a whole lot sooner than I thought!"

When David called her, later that evening, she began by asking for help with the fellow from Eugene, whom she had mentioned wanted to meet her. Evie told David that the man claimed to be a big rancher, in the Eugene area, and he invited her to come down to his ranch for a weekend.

"I told him, sex was absolutely out," she finished. "But, he said, he was too much of a gentleman to even consider such a thing. He said he had a complete guest bedroom and bath, and I would have total privacy, any time I needed. It was just about two people getting to know each other, and having a nice weekend on the ranch."

"No, absolutely not," David said. "That is simply way too far, too fast, and you are way too 'at-risk' being stuck on his place, like that. Do you know the kinds of date-rape drugs they have out there, these days?

"No. You have to, at least, meet the guy first," David continued. "Once you see if there is any spark between you, then you can start planning weekend adventures, sex or no sex."

"I'm glad you said that," Evie responded. "I thought it sounded a little off-base, too. But, I figured maybe that's how it's done on dating web sites?"

David laughed. "And, what kind of a gentleman, asks a lady to drive three-hours, to meet him?"

"Yeah, I thought that sounded a little odd, too."

"If you really want to meet this guy... I mean, if you like his profile, and think he is nice looking, then suggest to him that you meet halfway... like a coffee shop in Salem. That's about halfway in-between Portland and Eugene."

"I don't know anything about Salem, or finding a coffee shop," she replied timidly.

"Just put 'Salem coffee shops' into your computer's search engine, it will bring up a map, with all the coffee shops pinpointed. Pick one right off the freeway...it'll give you the exact address, and their hours of operation!"

David told her how he used to set up a nice, safe "coffee date," with girls he met online. He told her about the "escape clause," and, he added that, even when he drove as far away as Kelso, he still left a way for them each to get out quickly and safely.

But, once he brought up Kelso, he had to tell her the whole Kelso incident, leaving out the sexy photo, of course. But since Evie had contacted him on the very same day he had driven home from Kelso, she knew a little bit about the incident, already.

"Oh, my Gosh," Evie exclaimed. "So, just like that, date-over, and you drove home?"

"Yup," David said. "Just like that. Well, I slept a few hours first! But, at least I had the option of leaving right away...because of the coffee date. Even though, we were both expecting a little more romantic weekend. When there was no spark, no magic, it was time to just give it up, and go home!"

"Boy, I'm glad you called me," she confided. "I am going to write this all down, and make sure I do it just this way!"

"So, do you really want to go meet this guy?" David asked solemnly.

"I don't know…maybe. He's not bad looking… but I'm just not drawn to him, you know?" Evie said softly, then added, "The way I was to you."

"Really?" David responded eagerly.

"Well, I understand about why you don't want to do the 'long-distance' thing, and all, but…"

"Evie," David interrupted. "I was a fool for saying that…for even thinking that."

"Really?"

"Are you kidding? I drove 600 miles, each way, to have coffee with that gal in Kelso," David explained. "Driving only 500 miles to have coffee with you? That would be a snap!"

"Well, when you put it that way, it doesn't sound so far," she chuckled.

"Nothing to it."

Chapter 24

"The beginning of a dream-come-true!"

"So, you were off the dating sites, for 18-hours, huh?" Chance said, with a grin. "Well, that's about 17 hours more than I figured!"

"It was weird… that little 'help me' message is all I got on my voicemail," David clarified.

"And you figured, a lady in need?

"More like 'damsel in distress,'" David offered. "And me with a shiny new suit of armor! I just couldn't resist…"

"Okay, so you got back on Ranchers, just so you could get a message to this gal."

"Evie," David interjected.

"Just so you could get a message to Evie?" Chance asked.

"Yeah, there wasn't any other way to do it."

"So, you sent her the message, but let me ask you this…" Chance continued. "While you were on there…did you load a 'member-search,' just to see what new 'talent' might be out there? I know you…"

"Maybe you don't know me as well as you think," David responded. "I didn't, and I haven't, done any new searches… not since I talked to Evie."

"Not even one flirt?" Chance was surprised.

"Nope… Chance, I know I have said it before… but there is something about this little widow-woman, that makes me feel like a high school kid all over again."

"There it is," he laughed. "You popped a yard-on, a hard long! She's got you by the balls!"

"Absolutely not," David countered. "She is a good Christian lady. She won't even have sex again, unless—and until—she gets married."

"That could spell trouble," Chance cautioned. "Them 'Christians' use the Bible like a cowboy uses a whip and spurs. The Bible is a great excuse for those 'Holy Rollers,' whenever it talks about something they don't want to do; but they set the Good Book aside, when it conflicts with things they like to do."

"Well, I kind of like it," David admitted. "You know, I'm not much into religion, but I figure, if a gal is a good church-goin' woman, there's a lot less likelihood that she's gonna run me through Hell! She knows that I am not big on religion, especially not 'fear-based' theologies. We've talked about it…a little."

"I'm writing this one down, for our 'I told you so,' conversation, after you and Evie crash and burn!"

"Eat shit, Chief."

"Mark my words," Chance said solemnly, "'Christians' are the most judgmental and hypocritical bunch of people out there. She won't let up on you, until you are standing right next to her in church, thumping your Bible as hard as she thumps hers."

"Well, that ain't going to happen. We talked about our differences in religion…"

"Like, you don't have any?" Chance retorted.

"Hey, I believe in God…it's organized religions I hate. God didn't create any church… Man created them all. And, not to serve God either, but to sell God and 'eternal salvation'… as well as exercising complete mind control over their church members. Them churches are all about making money… and about power, and about getting absolute, unquestioning, obedience from their 'flock.'"

"And Evie is okay with you feeling that way?"

"Well, she doesn't like it. She probably figures she'll convert me, but we both agreed that religious differences can be lived-with, by simply showing a little respect for how the other person feels, even if we disagree with them."

"Mutual respect," Chance said. "I like that."

"Yeah, that's exactly it."

"Okay," Chance observed. "So, you don't think the religion will be an issue... but what about waiting until you're married, to have sex?"

"Hey, when Dana and I first split up, I went over a year without having sex," David explained. "It can be done!"

"Yeah, but that's only because you weren't dating anyone... how are you gonna be when you love this woman, you're making out, and your hand starts to roam... and then, she says 'No, no, no?'"

"I've thought about it... sure," David replied earnestly. "And I told her I didn't think waiting was a good idea...BUT, I figure if I respect her religious convictions, by abstaining, maybe she'll see that I am a man of honor, even if I don't go to church. And maybe, she'll show me the same kind of respect for my beliefs."

"Fat chance," Chance replied sourly. "Them Christians must get bonus points toward getting into Heaven, for every soul they convert! It ain't in their nature to just live and let live."

"Sure seems that way, don't it?" David laughed.

"Okay, so have you started talking about your coffee date, yet? Your first meeting..."

"Well, yeah, we talked about it... still are," David said.

"So, no date yet?"

"Well, she knows about the 'Kelso Incident,' since she contacted me the day I got home from there!" David explained. "And I told her, then, I had to borrow money from you, just to get home." "You told her that?" Chance was surprised.

"Well, yeah, I don't want her to think I am some rich guy," David said, stepping into the pulpit. "The best relationship is built on a foundation of honesty and trust. We both agreed on that... and agreed to be totally honest with each other, even if it was a little painful, sometimes."

"So, where'd you leave it?" Chance asked.

"Well, I told her I don't get paid again until the first…"

"So, the first weekend of next month?" Chance interrupted with a smile. "That's only a couple of weeks."

"Well, I suggested that, but she says that the following week, she's got a three-day weekend."

"So, the weekend after, then?"

"Well, maybe… I'm trying to talk her into going away somewhere, on her long weekend. But, before we plan something like that, we have to meet first, make sure there is magic, you know?"

"Yeah, yeah, so?"

"So, I'm thinking I might drive up there on the first weekend of the month…we can have coffee, and see if there's magic. If not, we're done. If we feel the connection, and, I'm sure we will, we can plan a romantic getaway for the following weekend…"

"See? I told you that you'd never be able to wait until after you were married, for sex!"

"Bite me, Asswipe," David retorted. "No, I offered to pay for a separate room for her, wherever it is we decide to go, IF we decide we even want to go, after we meet."

"So, how'd she take that idea?" Chance asked.

"Well, I'd have to say, she was receptive to it. But, since I had told her how broke I was, she was afraid of how much money I might be spending… so, we're going to talk about it more this evening, when we talk again. She said she wanted to think about it, a little."

"Not bad, Amigo," Chance replied. "So, you going to need another loan?"

"Naw, I'll make it work. The gas, round-trip, is just about $100, maybe $120? And, I can get a room at a cheap motel for like $35 a night…"

"How many nights?" Chance asked humorously.

"Well, one night for sure," David replied earnestly. "And, if coffee goes well, maybe two nights. But she has to be back to work on Monday. So, I should be able to pull off the 'coffee-date' weekend for about $200."

"Well, let me know how she answers you..." Chance finished.

"I've gotta get running."

They said their good-byes, and disconnected. While it was still fresh on his mind, David started writing out all the bills he needed to pay, from his next check, and creating a "travel budget," to go meet Evie.

"Okay, here's what I've come up with," he explained to her, later that evening. "When I get paid, on June 1st, and pay all my bills, I'll have about $600 left over..."

"Well, that's not too bad," Evie said, but she was not convinced. "But, if I help..."

"Wait, let me finish," he implored. "I figure, it'll take around $200 for me to come up that first weekend for a 'coffee-date,' and if everything goes well, we can plan a trip somewhere, maybe up to the mountains? For the following weekend? I'll have close to $400 left over for that."

"Well, how about we do it this way?" Evie began. "How about, you drive up here, after the first, for a couple of days...we'll do coffee, as you suggested, but you can meet some of my family? And maybe, on Saturday we can drive up to Mount Hood and do some hiking, or something? "Well, that sounds terrific," David said.

"But, since you are paying for all the gas, and I'm not paying for anything, I'm going to pay for your motel..."

"Oh, you don't have to do that," David objected. "I told you... "Wait, let me finish," Evie interrupted. "You even said yourself that you usually try to meet at a point halfway in between, for coffee, right?"

"Well, yeah, but halfway for us would be somewhere around Grants Pass... that's like 250 miles for you. No, that's not a good idea."

"You're right," she agreed. "But, since I'm not driving, the least I can do is chip in for the expense. I can get you a room at a place in Gresham for $29 per night. Even if you stay three nights, I'd still be paying less than $100, and you said it would be just a little more than that for gas."

"You know, Evie, I really don't feel right making you pay for my room," he began. "But, if you have the money, three nights would be better than two, and, it will leave us $500 for the following weekend… assuming we still want to move forward with our relationship, after the first weekend."

"Yep, that's what I was thinking," Evie said. "And, I've given some thought to the following weekend, too…"

"Oh, you have?"

"Well, I know you love the Bend area…" Evie said.

"Boy, do I? That rodeo at Sisters is one of my favorites," David responded.

"Have you ever heard of Eagle Crest Resort?" Evie asked.

"No, I can't say that I have."

"Well, it's close to the Sisters ski area, outside of Redmond," she began. "But this time of year, it's really just a huge golf resort… they have three or four different courses."

"Sounds fun, but I'm not much of a golfer…"

"No, but my son is… his girlfriend, too. Besides, they have horseback riding, ATV trails, there's all kinds of things for people to do besides golf…"

"Wait? Your son?"

"You'll meet him, when you come to Portland," she said matter-of-factly. "Anyway, Brandon's birthday is on the 10th, and I have been trying to figure out what to get him." "Okay," David said skeptically.

"So, I have some old friends that live in Redmond, and one of them works at Eagle Crest. She said, I can book a 'golf-package' vacation, which includes a room for two nights, and four rounds of golf…"

"I might be able to do one round, but four?"

"Not for you, Silly. For Brandon and Chrissie," Evie continued. "If I give them the golf package for his birthday present, they'll have to drive me down there…so no long drive, alone. Then, Brandon and

Chrissie will be out on the golf course for two days, while we get to spend time together."

"Well, I like the sound of us spending time together," David countered. "But how much is all this going to cost? I already promised to get you a separate room…"

"Well, the kid's room is going to be included in the golf-package, so I'll just book an extra room, for myself, and add to it. It's only $125 per night…"

"Well, that's $250 per room, for the weekend," he was calculating in his head. "Times two rooms, is $500. I can cover that, but there won't be a dime leftover for doing anything else."

"Well, since I'm going to make it about Brandon's birthday, I figured I would cover the cost of my room, too…"

"Now, wait a minute, Evie," David objected. "I already promised to pay for your room…"

"So, where do you have in mind to go? If we don't do Eagle Crest?"

David was stumped. "Well, I dunno…"

"This is a good place, it'll be a lot of fun, and we'll have chaperones, even if they are out golfing every day. If you let me pay for our rooms, you'll have enough left over, well, for other stuff. You'll just have to get there, and pay for your own room."

"Okay, I'll consider it, but we're getting a little ahead of ourselves here," David said. "We still have to meet, and see if we like each other well-enough to even have a second-date, let alone spending a wonderful, romantic weekend together."

"You're right. But, my girlfriend told me that this is their slow season, at Eagle Crest, so I can wait until after we meet, to book the rooms, and the golf package."

"It's hard to believe that we haven't even met, in person, yet," David observed. "I feel like I've known you all my life!" "I know, me too," Evie agreed.

"So, why am I getting a room in Gresham? I thought you lived in Portland?"

When they had first started talking, David had told her about the garage-apartment he was renting. Evie laughed, because she, too, was renting a room… a basement apartment, in Portland. In her case, she was renting the basement from her brother and sister-in-law, both to help them out financially, and because it was only a few miles to her work, in southeast Portland.

"Well, Brandon and Chrissie live in Gresham," Evie explained. "I've made arrangements with them, so I can stay in their spare bedroom for the weekend, and you'll be right around the corner."

"And that's better than where you live?"

"Well, yeah!" Evie said. "My brother thinks I am nuts to be meeting someone I met online, anyway. And, it's so small… at Brandon's I can cook you supper, and we can just watch TV or listen to music. We don't have to be 'out' and spending money for entertainment."

"Well, I like the sound of that," David admitted. "Especially about you cooking supper!"

"Oh, the kids love it when I cook for them, too! It'll be fun," Evie continued. "Plus, Brandon and Chrissie each have a child from a previous relationship… I just consider them all, my grandchildren… and Melissa, we call her Missy, will be there for the weekend, so we may end up babysitting, a little."

"Oh, that doesn't bother me at all," David said enthusiastically. "I love spending time with my grandchildren… so I know I will love spending time with yours, too."

"And Chrissie works at the golf course… a bartender… and they have a terrific Sunday Brunch. We'll all go."

"Wow, that sounds really good," David admitted.

"And, Saturday night, at the golf course bar, they have Karaoke Night. I love singing karaoke, so we can have some fun, maybe even dance a little!"

"Okay, okay," David laughed. "I'm convinced! Honey, you came up with a wonderful plan, and I can't tell you how excited I am to get up there."

"Me, too," she said warmly. "I mean, I'm excited for you, to get up here!"

"You know what?" David asked. "I'll bet you, the first time we meet, we'll be finishing each other's sentences before I leave!" "I know, we think so much alike, it is frightening sometimes!"

They talked for another hour, then finally called it a night. David was so excited, he couldn't sleep a wink. As he lay in bed, his thoughts carried him back, to the start of this whole "internet dating" ordeal. He laughed at his own naiveté, and some of the foolish mistakes he had made along the way. And, even when he thought he had it right, with Karen, it turned out to be so wrong!

But this time…it was different. They had already covered watching television in the bedroom, of which, neither was a big fan. They enjoyed the same types of television programs, and when they began to list their favorite movies, most of them were on both of the lists!

They also discovered that, while they both loved Country music, they also shared a love of the 60's and 70's oldies... the stuff they grew up on. Evie sent David a link for a music video, "Always and Forever," by Heatwave. She said that, when she heard it, all she could think of was David. He sent her back a link for Kenny Rogers' "Lady," and soon, they were exchanging music videos almost daily. Music was always going to be special for them, David felt.

"Hey… hey…" David said to himself, as the idea came to him. "I'm going to take all those music videos, and put them on a DVD… like a "love tape."

Of course, once he got the idea, he gave up on sleep. He grabbed a beer out of the 'fridge, and fired up his computer.

"Dang," he said with surprise. "There's twenty-six songs here!"

David couldn't figure it out a way to download music videos from YouTube… it baffled him. So, he had another idea.

In order to make the video DVD, he had to first go to YouTube and bring up each song individually. Then, he set his computer program to "record the screen" and he would play each song, in real time. Once it was played and saved, he put the video into a folder.

He did that for each and every song, over the next few days. When he finally had them all saved, he strung them together into a two-hour "movie." The file was so large, he had to break it in half, and use two

DVD's for the whole "mix-tape."

When he was finally ready to begin his drive to Gresham, a few weeks later, he had the whole DVD saved to his laptop, so they could just play it from there, while he was in Oregon. He also burned a pair of DVD's, so he could leave a copy with Evie, after he left.

As he turned the Mustang north on the freeway, he was lost in thought about this intriguing little widow-woman he was fast falling in love with.

"This is the beginning of a dream-come-true," he said to himself. "I just know it! This time, I got it right!

Chapter 25

"Caught-up in a whirlwind of Romance!"

As David crossed into the city streets of Gresham, Oregon, he spotted a modern, national-chain, grocery store on the corner. It was the kind of place that had a bank located inside, as well as a deli, a pharmacy, a liquor store, a bakery…

"…and a flower shop," David said aloud, as he read one of the many signs posted outside of the store. "Bingo!"

He pulled in and parked the car. After he had made his purchase at the flower shop, he went into the liquor store and bought a bottle of Pendleton whiskey. He had mentioned bringing a bottle of wine, earlier, to Evie. She told him that they were not big wine-drinkers. So, he asked if he could get beer, or anything?

"Brandon is bringing home some beer, so we should be fine. But there's no hard liquor in the house. If you want something like whiskey, you'll have to bring it. They're just out of everything," Evie explained. "I even had to run to the store to get toilet paper! They were down to using paper towels!"

"Yikes," David.

"I think that they only invite me over here, because I cook for them, and I clean everywhere I go! I can't stand a dirty house!"
"I know what you mean!" David replied. "How about a bottle of Pendleton whiskey?"

"Oh, that would be lovely," she had said.

"Special events deserve a special drink," he said.

Earlier, when she had mentioned her staying at Brandon's, she told David that, on the weekends they had a babysitter, Brandon usually took Chrissie to work, and stayed there, "having a few beers with the boys."

And, after Missy went to bed, they would have time alone. That's when David intended to break out the Pendleton, and his new "love tape," which he would play from his laptop.

After turning back onto the main road, David looked at his phone's navigation system. It showed that he was ten-minutes to his destination.

"Ten-minutes to my destination," he said aloud, savoring each word. "My destination…finally meeting the woman I have dreamed about being in love with, since I was a very young man. My destination, literally, is the woman of my dreams."

When David was still racing up I-5, toward Portland, Evie had sent him a text, letting him know that she had already checked him into his motel, and that she had the key. David responded by telling her that he would be getting into Gresham at around 5:00 p.m., and that he would go straight to Brandon's house.

"Good," Evie said. "Brandon gets off work at five, and Chrissie doesn't have to be at work until seven…"

"I thought you said she works days?"

"Not on weekends. It's better tips working Friday and Saturday night," Evie continued. "But, we'll have a couple of hours together, as a family, before she leaves for work. So, we can all eat supper together, and visit for a while. I'm making ham and scalloped potatoes." "That would be terrific," David responded.

"And, Missy is here, helping Grandma cook supper, huh, Honey," she said to her little helper.

That had been an hour ago, and now, David was parked out in front of the conservative little house, in an older, but nice, neighborhood. He sent Evie a text, just before he climbed out of the car.

"I'm here…"

He got out, and walked up the driveway. David was holding a single yellow rose, in a slender glass vase, in front of him. He climbed the steps onto the front porch, but before he could knock, the door came open.

Evie stood there, framed in the light of the big-screen television, which was on in the living room behind her. David thought she looked like an angel.

"Evie?" he asked, extending the rose toward her. Her eyes lit up like fireworks on the 4th of July!

"David!" she exclaimed, as she threw her arms around his neck.

They hugged for a very long time. Just standing there, holding each other, felt so good to them both.

"Get a room," a man's voice startled the newly introduced couple.

Brandon was walking up the driveway. He was in his late twenties, and stood about six-feet tall. He had the broad shoulders and chest of a construction worker, but also the start to a nice beer-belly, too. But, that just made him look more intimidating, David thought.

Neither David nor Evie had even heard the truck, when he had arrived. The young man was quickly on the porch, sticking out his hand. "Brandon," he said, smiling. "David," he responded, switching the rose to his left hand, so he could shake hands with Brandon.

Evie took the rose from David, as Brandon swept past them, into the house. He had a 30-pack of beer under his arm.

"I'm going to get this stuff into the 'fridge," he announced.

Evie gestured for David to follow him inside, where he found a shy Missy peeking around the kitchen door at him.

"Well, who is this? Are you, grandma's little helper?"

The little girl smiled brightly, and nodded her head. Evie closed the front door, then leaned over and tussled Missy's hair.

"She sure is," Evie added.

"Where's Chrissie?" Brandon asked, from the kitchen.

"She took a shower, and now she's getting dressed," Evie responded.

Brandon excused himself, and headed for the master bedroom. Evie placed the rose in the center of the kitchen window sill.

"It'll get late afternoon sun, this way," Evie explained. "I love it…a total surprise… but why a single yellow rose?"

"I'm glad you asked," David answered. "The yellow rose always stands for joy and happiness, and it means friendship. And, in this case, it is also from, your Yellow Rose of Texas."

"Now, that is very, very appropriate," she said, giving him another hug. "A yellow rose from my yellow rose."

He leaned in for their first kiss. David planned to make it short, and sweet… more "friendly" than romantic. Somehow, one of them got the signal wrong, and it turned very romantic, very fast. David pulled back, and Evie looked around. She saw Missy watching a children's show on television, oblivious to her grandmother and her boyfriend.

"Thank goodness," Evie chuckled. "I kept expecting her to tug on my shirt at any moment, and ask what we were doing?"

David laughed. "I know, right?"

Evie gave him another quick kiss, then spun around to check on the scalloped potatoes, which were baking in the oven.

"You know," David began. "There's a bit more to that yellow-rose story."

Seeing that the food was doing well, she turned back to David. He hugged her around the waist, and she rested her hands on his shoulders. "Well?" she asked.

"The legend of the yellow rose, is this," he began in earnest. "If a Texas cowboy gives his lady, a yellow rose… if there is true love between them, the yellow rose will turn into a red rose, overnight. Otherwise, they'll just be friends forever."

Evie smoothed his hair, and looked into his eyes.

"Well, you know what, Cowboy?" Evie said. "I already feel like we've been friends forever, and we always will be…"

"No matter what," David added, finishing her sentence. It was something they had said many times. "Well, just don't forget to check on it, in the morning…"

"Oh, I won't forget!"

"I have never seen it work, not even once, but who knows? This might be the right time!"

Evie pulled away, to go check on Missy, who seemed to be having a problem with the television remote. As Evie passed behind David, she patted him gently on his Wrangler patch.

"I know I've got the right Cowboy," she said seductively. "And, I don't need a rose to change colors, to tell me that!"

While Evie helped Missy find a new program, Brandon and Chrissie came out of the bedroom. Chrissie was already wearing her bartender "uniform," a bright red satin top, with a stretchy neckline, so it could be worn off-shoulder, or on. She had it pulled up conservatively, at this point, but even at that, a generous amount of cleavage was exposed. She was also wearing black panty hose, and a short black skirt. She was gorgeous, and sexy as Hell.

"There's no doubt why she makes good tips, in that outfit," David thought.

"Hey, Cowboy," Brandon began, as they approached. "This is Chrissie."

They hugged, like family, which made David feel even more like he was at home with his own family.

"I've heard so much about you," she said smiling.

"Well, mostly good stuff, I hope?" David said.

"All good," she said with a chuckle.

Brandon went into the kitchen, and returned with a beer for everyone.

Later, when they sat down dinner that evening, a beer-toast was made to, "David, Evie's newfound friend." And David toasted back, "To my new family." They all smiled, and nodded their heads in agreement.

Missy tugged on Evie's arm, to pull her grandmother down, for a secret. Evie burst out laughing.

"Well, I don't know Missy, why don't you ask David, and find out what he thinks about it?"

Missy tried hiding behind Evie's arm, but she peeked around and said, softly: "Can I call you 'grandpa?'"

David got up, and walked quickly to her chair, to give her a big hug.

"Of course you can, Sweetheart. But do you know what own grandchildren call me?"

"What?" Missy asked.

"They call me 'Papa.'"

"Can I call you Papa?"

"I would love that," he said kissing her forehead. She smiled and giggled.

"Well, it's official now," Chrissie sighed. "Missy seldom takes to strangers…almost never. And if she's going to call you 'Papa,' then I guess we're all family now."

David raised his glass. "Cheers," he said proudly.

After supper, David helped Evie clear the table. Even in early June, the nights were quite chilly, so Chrissie was putting on her jacket, getting ready to leave for work. Brandon was playing with Missy in the living room.

"Brandon, do we have any Fireball left?" Chrissie asked.

"No, we finished the bottle last night," Brandon replied.

"Shoot, I could use a shot, before I go to work…" "What's Fireball?" David asked.

"It's a cinnamon whiskey," Chrissie answered. "And, man, it packs a punch! A shot before work, really settles my nerves."

"Well, I don't have any of that, but I have a bottle of Pendleton whiskey, out in the car?"

"That would work!" she said smiling.

David walked out to his car to get the bottle of whiskey, but quickly donned one of his long, rodeo jackets, due to the chill. He also brought his laptop computer back with him.

Once inside, David handed the bottle to Brandon, who went into the kitchen to get a shot-glass for Chrissie, who was "fixing her makeup" in the hall mirror. David set his computer down by the door.

"Is that your laptop?" Evie asked, as she walked over to give David another embrace.

"Yeah… I brought you another little surprise," David said, finishing his sentence with a kiss for Evie. "What is it?" She asked excitedly. "You'll see," David said. "It's for later…"

She smiled, then went into the kitchen, to finish cleaning up. David removed his jacket, and hung it over a dining room chair. Brandon and Chrissie each had a shot of Pendleton, at the door, before they left. Brandon also made it clear that he would not be back for a while.

"I'm taking Chrissie to work," he announced. "So, I might just as well stay there with her, until she gets off, so I don't have to make two trips!"

"Geez, Brandon," Evie said with a motherly tone. "They don't close until two. You'd better take it easy on the drinking…"

"Oh, Mom," he responded like an errant schoolboy.

After they left, Evie asked David again, about her surprise. So, he reached into his computer case, and pulled out the two DVD's.

"Here," he said handing them to her. "You know how we're always sending music videos to each other?"

"Yes."

"Well, I put them all on these two DVDs." He explained.

"OOOO! Can we listen now?"

"Those are for you to take home… but I have the whole thing on a single file, on my laptop, so we won't have to change disks. But, maybe we should wait for Missy to go to bed first?"

"That's an even better idea!" Evie said as she tucked the DVDs into her purse.

"And, after she's in bed, I was going to break out the Pendleton," he said lifting the bottle. "Or, what's left of it!"

The "shot" Brandon and Chrissie had, at the door, was apparently not their first. The bottle was down about a third of the way… still plenty left, but he was surprised at how much, and how quickly, it was drunk.

"Yeah, Brandon loves that stuff… he even gave a shot to me!"
"Well, then I don't mind so much!" David smiled, pulling her in for a kiss.

"How come this feels so comfortable?" she said, embracing David.

"Because it's right," David replied, this time not with a little kiss, but with a deeply romantic, and sensual kiss.

"Missy!" she called out, when they came up for air. "You about ready for bed?"

"Grandma, it's only seven-thirty," Missy objected.

"Oh, I guess it is," Evie responded with surprise. "Okay, you've got another hour playing video games. Then, it's bedtime, and I don't want no trouble." "Okay, Grandma."

During the next hour, Evie spent a lot of time with Missy, playing games on the home computer. They had it hooked-up to the big-screen television in the living room. David watched them from the kitchen.

Evie and Chrissie had cleared all the supper dishes away, which were now in the sink, soaking, but nothing had been washed yet. So, David started washing them, while Evie was playing with Missy.

David recalled Brandon mentioning to Evie that their dishwasher had broken, and he'd need to call the landlord to get it fixed. So, David used the empty machine as a drying rack for the dishes he washed.

During the course of the "games," David had to take a break from dishes, to play "winner," once or twice. The three of them just laughed, and enjoyed the time together. Whenever Evie and Missy played, David returned to the dishes.

Soon, the kitchen was spotless, and David turned out the main florescent light. He turned-on the stove light, softening the mood considerably, since kitchen, living room, and dining room were essentially just one big room.

"Oh, that's nice," Evie remarked, as the florescent light was extinguished. "Well, Princess, it looks like it's about time for bed…"

"Oh, grandma! One more game," Missy whined. "Just one more game, then I'll go to bed."

"Promise?"

"Yes, I promise!"

"Okay, one more game," Evie said shrugging her shoulders to David. He laughed.

Finally, it was time for them to head off to Missy's bedroom. "Give Papa a kiss good-night," Evie told Missy, as they headed toward the hallway.

Missy ran over to David, who squatted down to wrap the little girl in a huge bear hug. Then, he stood, and whirled her around in circles, while Missy laughed delightedly.

When he set her on the floor, again, she reached for another hug, so David stooped over, hugged her, and kissed her forehead. She wrapped her arms around his neck, and said:

"I love you, Papa."

David was so touched by that simple act, those few words, he got choked with emotion.

"I love you, too, Missy," he said softly, before letting her go. "Now, be a good girl, and get to bed!"

"Okay, Papa, I will!"

"I'm going to have to read her a bedtime story," Evie told David.

"YEAAAHH!" Missy yelled, grabbing her grandmother by the hand, and dragging her toward the bedroom.

"Take your time," David replied to Evie. "I'll set up my laptop on the coffee table."

"That'll be perfect!" Evie replied, as she was pulled into Missy's bedroom.

David laughed, then walked over to where his jacket was hanging on the dining room chair. He reached into the inside pocket, and pulled something out, then he went back into the kitchen, for a few minutes. Digging through the glasses, in the cabinet, he could find nothing that looked like a "highball" glass, so he grabbed two "Cinderella" plastic children's cups. He filled them with ice, and mixed them both a drink… about half water, and half whiskey.

When he finished in the kitchen, he grabbed the computer and started setting it up, as well as finding a place to plug it in. When he was finished, Evie was still reading Missy a story, so David picked up the big-screen's remote, and did some channel-surfing, trying to find a music station. He stopped on the local news instead.

"What the heck, we have my laptop for music…"

Looking around, David realized that the big-screen, and the stove light, made for a perfect romantic ambiance, in the living room. When Evie came out of the bedroom, he simply muted the television. Then, he turned-off the dining room light, and grabbed their drinks from the kitchen. She had changed into an "Oregon Ducks" tee-shirt, and a pair of flannel pajama bottoms.

"I went ahead and put on my pajamas, just to be more comfortable," she explained.

"Nice."

"Cinderella cups?" Evie laughed, as he handed her the drink.

"It was either that, or a shot glass."

"Yeah, they do have a lot of shot-glasses, don't they?"

Evie and David sat beside each other, on the sofa, directly in front of the computer screen. While David got the laptop warmed up, and the "love-mix" video loaded, Evie pulled up her legs, and curled up to watch.

Finally, David adjusted the volume, and pressed "play." The first song on the recording was the first song he had sent to her, Kenny Rogers version of Lady.

"I tried to keep them in order," David explained, as he sat back on the sofa, and the music began to play.

The way Evie was seated, legs pulled up onto the sofa, it was very difficult for David to snuggle up closer to Evie, so he just sat beside her, and rested his hand on her knee. Evie leaned forward, to take a drink, and when she did, her feet went back on the floor. When she sat back again, David wrapped his arm around her waist, and held on tightly. "That's better," he said with a smile.

"Much better," Evie admitted. "Could we just cuddle, while we listen?"

David thought that was what they were already doing. He was wrong.

Evie stood up, and told David to lay on the couch, on his side. Then she lay in front of him, and, like a pair of spoons, they fit together.

"Just remember, we're not having sex…"

"Until after we're married," David finished. "I get it, I got it, and I've agreed to it. I know it is important to your religious beliefs, that you not have sex outside of wedlock. I may disagree, but I love the strength of your convictions!"

"It just feels so good, to cuddle," she said, turning her head, to give him a kiss. "Listen, about this 'wait until we're married' stuff?" David began. "I used my computer to do some research on it, and in every instance sex is mentioned in the Bible, it calls it "intercourse." And intercourse is defined as, 'the insertion of the penis into the vagina.'"

Evie rolled flat on her back, so she could look David in the eyes.

"Okay, so, what are you getting at?"

"Well, if we're abstaining from having sex, because of your religious beliefs—all I am saying is that the only thing forbidden by the Bible is when the penis is inserted into the vagina. Everything else seems to be okay…"

Evie's eyes were twinkling.

"Yes, but 'everything else' covers an awful lot! And, once you get started down that road, I don't know about you, but I get so carried away, I sometimes can't stop myself."

"Look, I know you don't know me well enough, for me to ask you to trust me, but, trust me!" David responded solemnly. "Even if you lose control, I won't. I gave you my word… and my penis will not enter your vagina, until after we get married. That's my promise, and I always keep my promises."

Evie's reply was pulling him down for what would be a very long, romantic kiss. That kiss would be the start of a "high-school make out session," which lasted for three-hours. But, through it all, David kept his promise—even though, he felt, there were a few passionate moments that he could have easily broken that promise. He also knew that, even if he had, neither one of them would have cared, at that moment! But, later, there might have been regrets, so, David kept his promise.

An hour after they had dressed, or re-dressed, Evie was in her pajamas and robe, folding the blanket they had cuddled under. David put, what-remained of, the Pendleton Whiskey, on top of the refrigerator,

"out of the hands of children." He noticed that there still remained about a third of a bottle.

A few minutes later, David was standing beside the door, about to leave. Evie walked him out onto the porch, so their voices wouldn't wake up Missy.

"Well, I've just got one question for you, Cowboy," she said softly, as they embraced in the clear, cool evening air.

"Yes, I still respect you," he said solemnly.

"It's not that," she said, with a giggle.

"Shoot! Then, ask away, whatever it is…"

"Do you think… I mean, after all of this…" she struggled to find the words, but pointed through the open door, toward the sofa.

"You mean, us having sex…but without actually having intercourse?" He offered.

"I wouldn't have used those words," she said.

"Of course not," he agreed. "But, I know what you'd have said, and my mama taught me not to use language like that, around a lady!" She punched him playfully in the arm.

"Well, you know, we've gotten to know each other pretty well," Evie stated.

"Almost as well as Adam 'knew' Eve?" "We
didn't go that far…" she objected.

"That's why I said 'almost.'"

"Anyway," she continued, after rolling her eyes. "Do you think we could…how do I put this?"

"If I knew the answer to that, you wouldn't be struggling. Just spit it out!" he teased.

"Well, I was just thinking how expensive next weekend is going to be, for us both," Evie explained. "But if we were to share a room..." "We could even get twin beds, if you like," David offered. "Have you lost your mind?" she laughed, pushing him away playfully.

"No, seriously," David said calmly. "You're asking if I could keep my promise to you, under those conditions, right?"

"Exactly."

"Without any hesitation, I can say, we will absolutely, positively, not have sexual intercourse!"

"Well, if it's okay with you, I'll call Eagle Crest, in the morning and make the reservations?" Evie asked.

"Okay? It would be awesome!! But, I am going to pay for our room..."

"...and the rest of the charges will be for the golf package – my birthday present to Brandon," Evie finished.

"I told you we would be finishing each other's sentences, before I left here," David said, pulling her tightly to him. "I just didn't think it would be on the first night!"

"So...Do you want to come over in the morning, for breakfast? I'm just making pancakes from a box mix...that's all Chrissie has."

"Pancakes sound great, but I'm not a big breakfast person, and since it's already after midnight, how about we call it brunch? Tenish?"

"I was thinking the exact same thing!"

"Then, I'll see you around ten," David said leaning in for a goodnight kiss.

She pulled her face away from his.

"Wait! You'd better call first, just in case Brandon and Chrissie are not up yet."

"Well, whichever one of us wakes up first, send a text to the other..."

"That's a good idea," she said, as she pulled him in for one final, passionate kiss. "And send me a text when you get to the motel... I don't want you to get lost."

"Make a right turn here, left at the stop-sign, right at the signal," he began.

"…and the motel will be halfway down the block, on your right," she finished.

They both chuckled. After one last, quick, kiss, David headed to the car. Evie stood on the porch until after he had driven away.

"I hope she doesn't turn the kitchen light on, until the morning," he said to himself, with concern. "But if she does, she'll text me…or, call me, right away."

He was still smiling when he pulled into the "Oasis Motel." Since he was already checked-in, he looked for room numbers, and parked right outside his door. He reached over the seat and grabbed his overnight bag, then headed inside to let Evie know he was safely in his room.

"I'm in my room," he texted. "Going to bed, and I'll see you in the morning. Love ya."

"Ten o'clock," she texted back. "I love you, too."

Ordinarily, when David went to bed, he turned his phone off, and plugged it into the charger. He was always in a sour mood when someone woke him up, so by turning it off, he had a more peaceful world!

But, not tonight!

As David lay down to sleep, his phone was charging on the nightstand. It was still turned-on, and the ringer was up to full volume. If Evie called or texted him during the night, he didn't want to miss the call!

Chapter 26

"Trouble in Paradise?"

David "slept-in" until eight o'clock, which was very unusual for him. Normally, he was up between 4 and 5 a.m. There were no messages from Evie, so he sent a text to her, "Y'up yet?" There was no reply.

"Good, she's still sleeping," he said to himself. "And, apparently, she didn't go into the kitchen last night."

After a quick shower and shave, he called his buddy, Chance, to update him on the situation. But since it was all good news, "like something out of a fairy-tale," David told him, it didn't take long.

"All I can say is this," Chance offered. "Look for the not-so-obvious."

"What the heck does that mean?"

"Every train wreck you've had, there was plenty of warning signs, but you just didn't see them."

"I know, and you're right," David admitted. "But, so far, I am just not seeing a thing in the world wrong with this lady."

"That's exactly what I am telling you," Chance explained. "You never saw the signs before, either. Look for them, the warning signs, that's all I am saying." An incoming text from Evie beeped on David's phone, so he bid Chance a hasty farewell.

"Well, it looks like Evie is awake, so I'll talk to you later, my friend."

"Be careful out there," Chance warned, just before he hung up.

David looked at Evie's text.

"Kid's are still asleep, Missy is eating breakfast, and I'm making a pot of coffee."

"Coffee sounds good," he replied. "I was going to run down to the 7/11, on the corner, for a cup."

"Why don't you just come over here? We have plenty."

"I'll see you in 15 minutes," he answered.

As he walked up the driveway, a few minutes later, he could see the rose he gave to Evie, still framed by the kitchen window, exactly where she had placed it. He smiled.

David knocked very softly, so he wouldn't wake Brandon or Chrissie, and Evie was quickly at the door, letting him in. She was still in her pajamas, and Missy was playing with a "My Little Pony" doll at the dining room table. There was a half-eaten bowl of cereal beside it.

When David walked in, Missy jumped down from her chair, and rushed over to give him a hug… but she had to wait for her grandmother to let go of him, first! "Papa!" she exclaimed excitedly.

"Very quietly, Missy," Evie admonished the child. "Mommy and Brandon are still sleeping."

David swept the little girl into his arms, and gave her a big kiss on the cheek.

"How's my little sweetheart, this morning?"

"Fine," she replied shyly.

David took her back to the table, and set her on her chair.

"Well, little girls need to finish eating their breakfast, so they'll grow up to be big girls! You want to be a big girl, right, Missy?" Missy nodded her head enthusiastically.

"How do you take your coffee?" Evie asked walking into the kitchen. "She usually only eats about half a bowl, anyway."

"Black," David replied. "I take my coffee black."

He walked into the kitchen, as she poured coffee for them both. David leaned against the kitchen sink, with the window directly behind him. He chose this position carefully, and intentionally. Evie turned back from the coffee pot, and handed him his cup.

David took the coffee from her, but as she handed it to him, she glanced over his shoulder, toward the window. Her eyes widened, and her mouth dropped open. "Oh, my God," she whispered.

"What?" David responded, brushing at his shoulders. "Is there something on me? A spider?"

Evie could say nothing, she just stepped to the side, and reached for the rose, on the window sill… the red rose.

"It's red," she said softly, showing it to David.

David pretended to be surprised.

"Oh, my God!" he exclaimed. "I've never seen it change colors, before!"

"What? How? When?" Evie was still stunned.

"You know what this means, don't you?" he asked.

Evie was still just staring at the rose, dumbfounded.

"It means," David answered his own question. "That you have found your true-love."

Evie set the rose on the counter, then threw her arms around his neck. He leaned in for a deep, passionate kiss.

"Now, that's what I like waking up to!" he said, as they finished the kiss.

"Me, too," she agreed. "But how did you…" David placed his finger on her lips.

"It's magic… the magic of love." "I love you, so much," she whispered.

"And, I love you more," he replied.

She kissed him again, just before Missy called for "Papa" to come see her empty cereal bowl. Evie and David walked into the dining room, and Evie placed the red-rose in the center of the dining room table. David picked a few dead leaves off of it, but when he went in the kitchen, to throw them away, he noticed the empty bottle of Pendleton whiskey on the top of the rubbish.

David held up the empty bottle, so Evie could see.

"Did you know they drank this?" he asked quietly. "At least, I assume it was them?"

Evie rushed to him, so they could whisper.

"Yes. The kids came home drunk last night, and having a fight," Evie explained. "Well, we were out of beer, and Brandon wanted to drive to the store to get some…and Chrissie and I both knew he was too drunk to drive. So, I told him, if he'd promise not to drive to the store, he could have some of the whiskey. I didn't think he was going to drink it all, though!"

David gave her a hug. "I'd have probably done the same thing…" he said, forgivingly.

"Grandma, can I go play now?" Missy asked.

"You sure can, Sweetheart," Evie answered. "But, we need to go get you dressed, first."

Missy ran straight to David, for another hug. David told her what a good girl she was, for finishing her breakfast.

"Her dad is coming to pick her up, in a little while," Evie explained. "I'm going to get her dressed, and ready."

Evie put her hand out, and Missy clutched it tightly. Then, they went down the hall, and into the bedroom. David took the empty bowl into the kitchen, and put it into the sink. Then, very quietly, he slipped out the front door, and headed for his car.

A few minutes later, he was in the kitchen, pouring himself another cup of coffee, when someone knocked at the door. David started to answer it, but Brandon, wearing just his pajama bottoms, came down the hallway.

"It'll get it," he announced. "It's Keith…Mom? Is Missy about ready?"

"I'm just pulling her hair back for a ponytail," Evie hollered from the bedroom.

A few minutes later, Missy was heading out, with her real father, Brandon was in the kitchen, pouring coffee, and David was standing by the dining room table. Evie closed the front door, and walked toward David. Behind him, on the dining room table, she saw a dozen red roses, in a beautiful cut-glass vase, with a single yellow rose positioned in the center of the arrangement.

Evie stopped mid-stride, her mouth opened, and she just stared at the bouquet. Slowly, a smile came upon her face, and she went to David for a hug and a kiss.

"David, this is the most amazing thing," she began. "I've never had anyone do anything like this, for me…"

"Bullshit, Mom, a lot of guys have given you flowers," Brandon interjected from the kitchen, as he poured himself some coffee. "A lot of guys?" David was thinking.

"Yes, Brandon, but not like this… I'll tell you the whole story, later," Evie replied. "Is Chrissie up yet?"

"Yeah, she was brushing her teeth when I came out," Brandon said, as he was heading for the garage door. "I'm going to grab a smoke."

Brandon had set up a small table and a few chairs, into what he termed his "smoker's lounge," out in the garage.

"Well, I need to get come clothes on, then I'll start breakfast," Evie replied.

She gave David a quick kiss, looked again at her roses, then darted off toward her bedroom. David went out to the garage to talk with Brandon.

"Hey, Brandon, can we talk for a minute?" David asked as he walked from the kitchen into the garage.

"Sure," Brandon replied cheerfully. "What's up?"

"Well, in the cowboy world…" David began, as he pulled up a chair. "…it is customary for a fellow to speak with a young lady's father, to get permission to court her."

"Uh, huh," Brandon replied, with a slightly confused look on his face.

"Well, since Evie's father, your grandfather, died many years ago, I felt it was appropriate to have that talk with you, about my courting your mother. You're the man of the family."

"Seriously? You want to ask me if it's okay, for you to date my mom?"

"Yes, family is very important to me… and you guys have made me feel as if, I am already a member of the family… but I just want you to know that, my intentions with your mother are quite honorable…and will hopefully, result in marriage."

"That's awesome, man," Brandon replied, slapping a hand on David's shoulder. "Look, if I didn't approve, you wouldn't be in my house, right now."

"I also want you to know that it's not my intention to ever try to replace your father. Evie is always telling me what a great guy he was. I just think it's time Evie moved on with her life, and has a chance to find happiness, again."

"Well, thank you, David. That means a lot… and we do, already, feel like you are a part of the family. I think you will be very good for her."

They then talked about the motorcycles, and parts of motorcycles, that were scattered about the garage. Fixing up dirt-bikes was a hobby for Brandon, as well as snow-boarding and alpine skiing, and the equipment for those was also hanging in the garage.

"You haven't met my son yet," Brandon said pointing to a miniature dirt-bike. "that's his. Josh loves riding… and he loves helping Dad work on the bigger bikes, too."

"I can't wait to meet him," David said sincerely.

"He's at his mother's this weekend, but he'll be back Sunday night."

"Well, next trip, for sure. I have to leave Sunday morning."

"No worries, he's usually always here, except one weekend a month. This just happened to be that weekend, is all."

After a while, Evie opened the door, and called them to breakfast. She was wearing blue jeans, a pink top, and a blue-jean jacket.

As "the boys" entered from the garage, they saw the table had been set for breakfast, and the roses were in the center of it. Chrissie was bringing out glasses of juice, while Evie was flipping hot-cakes in the skillet.

"Nice flowers, David," Chrissie said. "Mom told me the whole story…how romantic!"

"Well, as soon as we finish eating, I want to take a few pictures of Evie holding them," David replied. "And I want a shot of you guys, as well, for my scrapbook!"

"No way," Evie objected. "I hate having my picture taken!"

"Oh, Mom," Brandon admonished. "David spent a lot of money buying them roses, least you can do is let him take your picture!" He winked at David.

"I think so, too," Chrissie added. "We don't have hardly any pictures of you, and this would be a good one." "I'll be sure I get you a copy of it," David offered Chrissie.
"Wait, wait," Evie objected. "Well… okay, but after breakfast, so
I can brush my teeth and do something with this hair first."
"Then, let's do breakfast," David said sitting down at the table.

A little while later, after breakfast, while they were waiting for Evie, David asked Brandon and Chrissie to pose, first, so he'd have a remembrance of his first visit to Gresham. They said they were glad to accommodate, as soon as Brandon got dressed.

"It'll only take me a minute," Brandon said, walking toward his bedroom. "We'll be waiting on Mom for an hour."

Brandon was back in just a few minutes, and David took a dozen pictures, of him and Chrissie. When Evie was ready, she came out into the living room, and Chrissie handed her the bouquet of roses. Brandon excused himself, to go back out to the garage, and smoke.

David noted that he never saw women so radiant, and naturally charming, as when they are when holding roses. And, David also felt, that the smiles those women wore, were always sincere and genuine. Evie was to be no exception.

As David trained his camera on Evie, he saw the beautiful, radiant smile, her eyes sparkling like fireworks in the night sky, and that warm glow of the passion, that burned within her. He took several photos, with his digital SLR camera, and when he stopped to see what he had shot, Chrissie looked, too.

"Oh, my God, Mom," Chrissie exclaimed. "These are the best pictures I have ever seen, of you!"

Evie set the flowers down on the coffee table, and rushed over to look.

"I think that's the first picture I have ever seen of you, where you were showing your teeth. This is exactly the smile I wanted!" David said proudly.

"Oh, I've sent you pictures where I was smiling like this," she said looking at the photos. "Wow, these are pretty good though."

David was "thumbing" through his phone's photo gallery, while the girls tried to decide which photo they liked best.

"Nope… not one," David reported. "A lot of closed-mouth smiles, but no teeth. I could understand that, if you had rotten teeth, but you have a beautiful smile."

"I don't know why? But, I just don't think they're all that nice…my teeth," Evie told David. "I could have sworn I sent some to you."

"Just one, when you were holding a toddler," David replied. "The baby is blocking half your face, but the smile looks great!"

"No, no…" Evie said, as she pushed buttons on her phone. "Here, didn't I send you this one?"

David's phone binged, with an incoming message, and he quickly downloaded the photo. It was a picture of Evie, smiling beautifully, while sitting on the lap of a cowboy. The cowboy appeared to be about ten-years older than Evie, with grey hair and mustache. It was taken in a tavern, with a bunch of drinkers in the background. Both Evie, and the cowboy, held pool cues, and Evie had her arm around the neck of the cowboy, who was looking at her, the same way a bulldog eyes a hambone.

"Wow," David said, genuinely surprised. "You're right, it's a beautiful smile… I only wish that I was the one, who had made you smile like that!"

"You just did," she said, showing David his own photo of her.

"That's true, I did, didn't I?" David said pleasantly, however, the smiles were not the same. "But who is this guy…whose lap you are sitting in?"

"That guy? Oh, that's Johnny. I told you about him…"

"I don't think so,"

"Yes, I did. He's my best friend. I talk about him all the time."

"Oh, I'm sure you did. It just might not have registered," he said,

But, he was certain he would have remembered. What he saw in the image was a picture of two people, in-love. The look on both of their faces, is what struck him. So, he was relieved to find out that they were just friends.

Chrissie came and looked at David's phone.

"You're right, Mom. This is a good picture. Johnny looks pretty handsome, too," Chrissie remarked. "You guys were still living together, when this was taken right?"

Whatever image David had created, in his own mind, about his "sweet, virginal, widow woman," and thinking that he, David, was her first boyfriend, since her husband had died, lay shattered.

"Yeah," Evie answered Chrissie. "That was about a year ago, so we were still together then."

But, Evie hadn't lied to him about it, David rationalized. He had simply never asked her. He was afraid she might not be ready to talk about her dead husband… but it never occurred to him that she might have had other boyfriends, since his passing. But, he rationalized, he had never volunteered any information about his little internet romances, either, although he did talk about Karen, and the financial mess she left him with.

Later, when they were alone, David returned to the topic of "post-husband-boyfriends."

"How long ago did Bob… you know, pass away?" David asked gently.

Evie looked up, as if calculating a trigonometry equation.

"Let's see," she said. "It'll be ten years in April."

"Wow. I had no idea."

"What do you mean?" Evie asked in puzzlement.

"Well, the way it appeared to me, from your Ranchers Only profile," David explained. "You know, it showed your marital status as 'widow,' and you indicated that you were brand new to online dating… I just assumed that Bob had passed away just a year or two ago, and you were finally ready to get back out there." "I never said that," she replied tersely.

"No, no, no, Honey," David softly. "I never said you did…in fact you didn't do anything wrong at all. I told you, I'm the one who made the assumption. I should've asked, that's all."

"Honestly, I thought we had talked about Bob… and Johnny," she replied calmly.

"Well, I have to admit, it kind of put me in shock to learn about an ex-boyfriend from your daughter, and not from you."

"I'm sorry about that," she chuckled. "I seriously thought you knew about Johnny. But there's nothing to worry about… like I told you, we are best friends, now, and that's all."

"So, how long have you two been split up? David asked.

"Oh, hmmm," she calculated again. "About six months. Yeah, that's right. About the time we split up, my sister-in-law got laid off from work, and they thought they might lose the house. So I moved into their little basement bedroom six months ago." "I see," David remarked.

"She got back to work a month later, and they really don't need me there any more… but it's only a few miles to work, and I have my own separate entrance and everything, so it's cozy, and nice."

"So, how long did you live with Johnny?"

"Well, we dated for about two years," she replied. "Then we lived together for three-years."

"Holy cow," David exclaimed softly. "I had no idea you were in such a committed relationship, after Bob died… and for five-years?"

Now David understood why the hair was still standing up on the back of his neck. It was all about that look in their eyes, in that picture.

The comment he had made, when he first saw it, still echoed in his mind – "I only wish that I was the one, who had made you smile like that!"

"That's it," he realized, to himself. "We've been saying 'I love you,' to each other for two weeks now, and I have never seen that look on her face, not once, not ever."

"Does that make a difference?" she asked, snapping him out of his musing.

"Oh, no, not at all," he responded truthfully. "I fell in love with you, today, who you are now. The past doesn't matter. It's just…"

"Just what?"

"It's just that I had created this picture of you, in my mind…" he began. "But, you did nothing wrong, it's just something new, to me, about your past, that I have to put away, in my mind, that's all. With Johnny… when you say that you lived together, was it like man and wife? I mean, in the Biblical sense?"

"Yes, of course. But, I wasn't real close with Jesus then," she explained. "Like I am now."

"Were there any others, before Johnny, I mean?"

"Oh, I dated a few guys... but the only other one I lived with was my insurance agent." "Your insurance agent?" he reacted in surprise.

"I rented a room from him, Silly," she laughed. "We weren't sleeping together!"

"Whew!" David sighed loudly.

"What kind of a slut did you think I was, Butthead?" she playfully punched him in the arm.

"No, no, nothing like that," he said. "This is all just kind of new to me, that's all. So, why did you and Johnny split up?

"Well, after living together for three years," she explained. "I asked him where we were headed, you know? Like, is marriage still in the cards?"

"I can understand that. So, what'd he say?"

"He said he had already been married four-times, and he wasn't going to do it, again. Ever. So, I told him that I couldn't be in a relationship with a man, if it wasn't heading for marriage." "I've heard that before," David replied, thinking of Karen.

"So, about that time, my sister-in-law got laid off, so I rented a room from them…and that's where I am now. Johnny and I, well, we just decided to remain friends. And now he's my best friend… well, next to you, of course. You and me, we'll be best friends forever, right?"

"Yes, of course… but do you think you can handle two best-friends at once?"

Evie just laughed, and didn't actually answer the question.

"You got nothing to be jealous about," Evie said, wrapping his neck with her arm, so she could look him directly in the eye. "You're the man I am coming home to…"

"So, what have you told him about me?" David asked sincerely.

"Nothing… nothing at all," she replied truthfully.

"You mean he doesn't know that you have a new boyfriend?"

"Oh, he knows I'm seeing someone, but he told me that he just doesn't want to know about my new love-interest, so I don't talk about you."

"I get that," David admitted. "So, how often do you guys see each other, I mean, as friends?"

"Oh, we usually get together once or twice a month, to watch movies at his house, eat popcorn, you know? It's fun. I have a girlfriend that I do that with, too."

"I see," David told her. "Well, I don't have any problem with you being best friends with your ex-boyfriend, but, he's going to have to take us both in, as friends…because, we're a team now, you and I. If he doesn't want to meet me, it's because he has other ideas in mind for you."

"You mean, like us getting back together? Don't be ridiculous," she scoffed. "We talked about it, and we just laugh. No, us getting back together? Not gonna happen…"

Then, she kissed him, passionately. And that was the end of their conversation.

Chapter 27
"She's just using you, to get back together with her EX!"

"A 30-pack of beer, and a fifth of Pendleton whiskey?" Chance asked, over the phone. "That's a lot of booze, for four people, in one night."

"I know, right?" David replied. "I think Brandon might be an alcoholic. But, when I told Evie what I thought, she said Chrissie drinks more than he does."

"So, both of them might need help from AA, huh?"

"Evie drinks a lot, too," David admitted. "She calls herself a "functional alcoholic.""

"What the heck is that?"

"I never heard of it either. Evie says the difference is, she doesn't drink at work, or before work, so she's a dependable employee, keeps her bills paid, takes care of her house. Like a normal person, but she likes to drink a lot more, that's all."

"I thought that 'No alcoholics,' was on your deal-breaker list?"

"Well, yeah!" David replied. "And I told Evie that, too. Nobody can live with an alcoholic! They are beyond reasoning with…no sense applying logic to an argument, an alcoholic will be right, every time, and you'll be wrong…no matter what the issue."

"Amen to that. So what're you going to do about Evie's drinking?"

"Well, she says that her being a 'functional alcoholic' is totally different, and that I have nothing to worry about. So, I'm just going to go along, for now, and see if she's right."

"Giving her the benefit of the doubt. I hope that works for you."

"I'm actually more concerned about her best-friend Johnny, than I am her drinking."

"I think they are both 'red-flags,'" Chance replied. "Remember those 'warning signs' I was telling you about? But, why are you so concerned about Johnny?"

"It's just something about that picture, of her and him," David replied hesitantly. "I should have asked her, right in the beginning, about how long ago her husband had died. If I had known that it was ten years ago, I would have asked her about other guys she dated, since his passing."

"But you thought you were the first guy, after he died?"

"Exactly. But she's had a relationship with this guy, Johnny, for the past five-years, and they've only been split-up for the past few months."

"You think, she's just using you, to get back together with her ex?"
"It's possible…quite possible," David surmised. "I mean, according to Evie, the only reason they broke up, was because he said he never wanted to get married again. She never said they stopped loving each other, just that they were going to different places, I guess." "So, what if he changes his mind?" Chance asked.

"Exactly," David said. "That's what I'm worried about. Evie says she is much happier with me than she was with him. She says, even if he changes his mind, she won't change hers…"

"Yeah, right."

"That's what I say, too."

"And, she was having sex with Johnny? But not you?"

"Yeah," David sighed heavily. "Evie says that, Johnny came before her newfound 'relationship with Jesus.' And that God was punishing her for having sex with him, by taking him away from her.

And, she doesn't want to risk ruining our relationship, by having sex outside of wedlock."

"Okay, here's a thought," Chance said. "Now, this is really out there, but suppose… just suppose for a minute, that she is still in-love with Johnny, and she wants to make him jealous, just to make him change his mind about marriage?"

"I've thought about that," David said.

"And just suppose that, because she's still in-love him, she doesn't want to 'cheat' on him. So, she gives you this whole load of manure about 'Jesus,' just so she can be able to tell Johnny that you guys never had sex?"

"I've thought about that, too," David said earnestly. "And, frankly, that makes a whole lot more practical sense, than her whole, 'I don't want Jesus to punish me again,' story. It's just not fair that she slept with all those other guys, but with me, the man she supposedly loves, I get none? That just ain't right."

"I warned you about them Holy-Rollers, didn't I?" Chance interjected. "So, what're you gonna do about it?"

"I don't know," David replied. "Nothing, I guess."

"What do you mean, 'nothing?'"

"I'm just going to keep an eye on things, and do my best to get her to introduce me to Johnny. If they are truly best friends, I would think he'd want to meet me."

"Damn right," Chance agreed. "It's what best friends do… look out for each other. Any time I am interested in a girl, first thing I want to do is introduce her to my friends, so they can tell me what they think of her…"

"Exactly." David agreed. "So, if Johnny doesn't want to meet me—he doesn't even want to know about me, according to Evie—then, that means there is more going on, than what she is telling me. Maybe not with her, but certainly with him."

"So, you figure that the three of you can be buddies, or what else?"
"I don't know what else? I'm just saying, if Evie is telling me the whole truth about this guy, and they are truly just friends, then he should have

no trouble being my friend, too. All I've got to do is to meet him. And, Evie says she thinks it would be a good idea for us all to meet…"

"Really?" Chance asked. "She's okay with that?"

"Sure, but she says she needs to wait, until Johnny is ready, before we meet."

"She's sure being awfully considerate of that guy," Chance observed.

"I know, right?" David responded. "C'mon, they were in a relationship for like, five-years. Surely they still have feelings for each other, but if they are 'just friends,' then why isn't he interested in knowing anything about me?"

"Well, like I told you before," Chance stated. "Keep an eye out for those warning signs…"

"I know, I know…and I am," David said. "I just don't know what to do about them, once I see them…"

"Such as, her ex-boyfriend, Johnny?"

"Yes, and her heavy drinking," David added.

"And, don't forget that 'Holy-Roller' warning sign, too. Suppose Jesus tells her to go back to Johnny, or something like that?" "Well, I can't argue with Jesus, I suppose," David sighed.

"So, is she preaching to you, yet? Trying to convert your lost soul?"

"Oh, a little. We have the same taste in music…"

"I remember, you told me you trade YouTube videos, right?" "Yeah. Well, every once in a while she slips in a Christian song. But the music is good, so I just ignore the words, and listen to the tune."

"I told you, she won't stop, until you're thumping on that Bible, same as she does."

"Well, she does quote scripture to me once or twice a day."

"And is she receptive to listening to you, talk about your own spirituality?"

"Oh, no," David replied quickly. "She talks for ten-minutes about the Bible, then, when I try to tell her what think, she pulls out the, 'We're not supposed to talk religion,' card, and stops me cold."

"You've got to let her know," Chance said sincerely, "...that it is not a one-way street."

"That's exactly what I told her... if she wants to talk Bible to me, she needs to hear what I believe in, as well."

"How does she take that?"

"I told you, she stops the conversation, and says we can bring this up another time," David admitted. "So, we always just put it off. But, she's right, that is what we agreed to."

"Just so long as she gets her preaching in, first, right?"

"Well, I'm hoping that, someday, she'll at least be curious enough about my beliefs, that she will ask me about them. I'm certainly not interested in 'converting' her, I just think, if we are to live with religious differences, we need to know exactly what those differences really are."

"Well said. And I totally agree. But, I also have to tell you that, she will never ask you about your beliefs. Them Christians all figure that, they alone know the Divine Truth, and everyone else is working for the Devil..."

"I know, and you're right. And, except for the religion-thing, we think so much alike, that it's frightening, sometimes. You know, we already finish each other's sentences!"

"That's all fine and good, my friend," Chance responded. "But it seems to me, you have several red-flags to keep an eye on."

"One day at a time, we'll just have to see how it unfolds."

"I don't know, Partner," Chance said. "But, something about this whole thing just don't feel right."

"I know. I have the same feeling... but when I am with her? Man, I feel like I am exactly where I am supposed to be."

"Well, maybe she is just using you to get back together with Johnny, but maybe she'll realize that you are offering her a whole lot more, than him..."

"That's what I am hoping... that she'll give up on Johnny, and just be glad she found me!"

"Good luck with that," Chance offered. "So, what's on-tap today, for you guys?"

"I'm heading over there in a bit, so we can go to the golf course for their Sunday Brunch… all four of us. Then, I'll be homeward bound…back to Oroville."

Sunday brunch was quite enjoyable. The subject of Johnny was not brought up again, on this trip. But, David made a mental note, that Evie and the kids, had had three or four rounds of Mimosas, which he felt was a bit excessive, before noon. David was drinking straight orange juice, since he still had a very long drive ahead of him.

A few days later, David and Evie were talking on the phone. David said he was getting tired of living in Oroville, alone, and it was time he made some positive changes to his life-situation. Evie came to the same conclusion, about her situation, renting a basement room from her brother.

"So, basically, we are both ready to move," David concluded. "We just don't know where, or how?"

"Or, with whom?" Evie added.

"You know, we could just rent a place together," David offered.

"Oh, David, I don't think I'm quite ready for that, yet. We're still just getting to know one another."

"True, but we both need a place to live, and we've already determined that we are best friends forever, so why not just be roommates?" Evie pondered her answer for a few seconds.
"I'm not saying yes, and I am not saying no," she began, finally.
"How about, let's talk about this next weekend?"

"That sounds like a good plan."

The following weekend, the four of them—Evie, David, Brandon and Chrissie—met just outside of Redmond, Oregon at the Eagle Crest Resort. It was a beautiful resort, with thousands of acres of wilderness, with lakes, ponds and streams, as well as four championship golf courses, and a modern, but rustic-looking hotel. Since it was still early in the afternoon, the kids raced up to the club house, to squeeze in a round of golf. David and Evie opted to go to their room and take a nap.

When they had first begun planning the trip, David asked Evie if she could get Friday or Monday off work, so they could spend an extra day together. But Evie explained that she had already used all of her vacation time, and accrued sick-leave.

"The only way I can take off now is, thanks to the new Oregon State family sick-leave act. Of course, you don't get paid, but the employer cannot refuse, and the employee cannot be penalized. And with seven siblings, there's always somebody in my family who is sick!"

"Well, that's all fine and good, but we really need to be saving up your leave, so we can take a real vacation together…you know, like scuba diving in Tahiti!"

"Well, I'm not so sure about Tahiti, but I agree. Now that I have a man in my life, I need to save up my leave-time, and my money!"

"We both need to do that," David agreed. "The money part, I mean. Even if we get a place in Portland, it's going to take time and money to get me moved up there."

Evie agreed, and soon their conversation turned to their hopes and dreams, catching a moonbeam, or a falling star, just to let it go again. They were like two lovesick Mourning Doves.

David and Evie so enjoyed each other's company, they almost forgot about Brandon and Chrissie having a room right down the hall. But, they had good cell-service, at Eagle Crest, and stayed in touch via text messages.

Once David and Evie had freshened up, after their nap, they walked the hotel grounds. There was a small strip mall located right next to the hotel, which had a restaurant and night club, and they would be featuring a band, later that night. Next to the door, the club had a menu of Italian food posted, at fairly reasonable prices. "Hey, this looks like a good place to have supper," David said. "And the band starts at eight," Evie responded, looking at a poster placed in the window. "So, we can come around seven, to eat," David began.

"And go listen to the band for an hour, after we're done," Evie finished.

"Maybe two hours, if they're any good."

"Maybe. Or, maybe we could just head back up to our room, and crack open that new bottle of Pendleton, you brought."

"That's even better," David suggested. "But, I don't want the kids to know I have the bottle of whiskey…not after last weekend."

Evie winced. "Again, my fault. Sorry."

"No, not at all. Brandon should have known better than to finish off a third of a bottle of someone else's expensive whiskey. He knows what that stuff costs…"

"I know, but they were drunk…"

"That's really not an excuse. If being drunk were a legal defense, our prisons would be empty." "I'm not excusing, just explaining," Evie stated flatly.

They let the subject drop, and resumed their tour of the grounds, winding up on a paved "wilderness trail," that wound through the lake and ponds, and ended right back at the hotel. They held hands, or walked arm-in-arm together the whole time, just two people in-love.

By the time they got back to the hotel, Brandon and Chrissie had already returned. Evie got a text message saying that, they were going to clean up and change clothes…and would be ready to eat supper in half an hour.

Evie texted back the name and location of the Italian restaurant, featuring live-music in their lounge.

"We'll get a table, and wait for you there," Evie concluded.

"So, we going to just head over there?" David asked.

"Brandon said they'd be at least a half an hour, so we're not in a hurry, Evie replied. "We probably have time for a drink, before we go."

"Well, we are on vacation," David agreed, as he broke the seal on the Pendleton.

The Italian food was fabulous, and the band was pretty good. After watching two sets, dancing to quite a few songs, and running up a good-sized bar-tab, David and Evie parted company with Brandon and Chrissie, who stayed in the lounge. They had promised to get together for breakfast, in the hotel's coffee shop, in the morning.

After another night of their "love-making, without making love," David was convinced that Evie truly did love him, and he felt his concerns, about Johnny, were all just way off base. So, he put away the negative thoughts, and he vowed to show Evie more love than ever, so, he might just win her affections away from Johnny.

"All I can do is hope she finds more in me, than she found in Johnny," he said to himself. "And, maybe someday, she'll love me as much, or more, than she does him." It was all he could hope for.

The next morning, after an early breakfast, the kids ran off to play more golf, and David and Evie took their coffee down by the lakeshore, to enjoy the crisp, cool spring morning.

"It is so beautiful out here, isn't it?"

"I'm glad you think so," David said. "This area… Redmond, Bend, Prineville… this is where I want to build my last ranch – just a little hobby-ranch, maybe 50 or 100 acres, a few cows, a few horses…"

"And chickens! We have to get chickens," Evie added enthusiastically. "We had chickens when I was a little girl, and they are so funny to watch!"

"So, you wouldn't mind living around here?"

"I'd love it," she said. "The problem is, I have two more years before I am even eligible to retire. How would we pay for it?"

"You've gotta have faith, Kiddo, you've gotta have faith," David responded. "Isn't that a popular saying among the Christians?"

"Yes, it is, but they're talking about faith in God, not getting money."

"It's all the same. Faith, I mean. If we believe hard enough, God will show us a way."

"It's odd hearing you talk about God," she said. "I thought you didn't believe in any of that stuff."

"You've never asked me what I believe in," he defended. "I believe in God…the same God as you. I just don't believe in organized religions. They package and sell God, and salvation, to the highest bidder." "Oh, stop," she said jokingly. "Of course, my church isn't like that."

"Of course not," he smiled and let it drop. "Maybe we should go to the lobby and pick up a local newspaper… you know, maybe check out the real estate market?"

"That's a great idea!" she said.

"Well, it may be a few years until we can move here," David said. "But, if we can find some raw land, it's only three-hours from here to Portland, we can just park a camper on it, and come out every weekend to build the barn, house and outbuildings."

"Oh, my gosh," Evie exclaimed. "That would be wonderful!"

From the first time they had begun talking, Evie had told David how much she hated living in the city. Like him, she really wanted to find a small country home, where the elk and deer are more common than people.

By early afternoon, they had actually met with a local agent, and viewed one property. It was a nice double-wide mobile home, with a small barn and woodshop. But, both David and Evie felt it was just too close to town, and had far too many neighbors. So, they thanked the realtor for his time, and he promised to keep an eye out for more rural properties, or raw land packages.

"Brandon said they just finished 18-holes, and they are heading to another course, to play another round," Evie said, reading her text messages.

"Well, that'll give us like two or three hours before supper," David speculated. "Wanna go take a nap?"

"You read my mind!" She chirped, giving David a kiss on the cheek.

After they awoke from their nap, they decided to just get dressed, and ready for supper, and then wait for the kids, in the cocktail lounge. It would give them time to talk.

"So, have you given any thought to the whole, 'Let's be roommates' scenario?" David asked, setting two cold beers on their table.

"I have, actually… a lot," Evie replied tenuously. "David, this is moving scary-fast, don't you think?"

"Absolutely," David agreed. "But I love a fast horse, and a wild ride!"

"I just don't want to get bucked-off!" Evie added.

"Nothing to worry about," David offered. "Do you still want to move out of your brother's place?"

"Well, yes," she replied. "I feel like I have overstayed my welcome…"

"And I am going nuts living alone in Oroville. I don't know a soul down there. At least no one that Karen didn't introduce me too…"

"But, moving in together? Do you think we're ready for that?"

"Ready or not, I think we should consider it, simply for the reason that, if we don't work out, as a couple, we can always move into separate rooms, and just be roommates."

"And, we would split everything 50-50?" Evie asked. "Rent, groceries, utilities…"

"Absolutely. It would be just like finding a roommate on Gregslist, or something like that. Except, we're not strangers, and we already know we are going to be lifelong friends."

"And, I could tell my family, that we are just roommates, then maybe they'll get off my back about us moving too fast," Evie stated, warming up to the idea.

"Well, if you think that's best. So far as I'm concerned, I'm ready right now, to spend the rest of my life with you, and I don't care who I tell that to! That's how much I love you!"

She leaned in for a kiss. "And I love you, too!"

"You know, since I live 400 miles away, looking for a place is going to fall squarely into your lap. Do you think you can handle it?"

"I may not be a cowboy, but I can git 'er done," Evie said, smiling. "I'll send you links for the listings I find, and we can decide, together, which ones I'll go look at."

"That sounds like a workable plan. Especially since you were born and raised in that area…"

"Oh, yeah, I know some great little communities, that are more country than city," she agreed. "But, they're still within commuting distance of Portland." "So, any word from the kids?" David asked, noticing their beers were nearly empty.

"Chrissie texted me a few minutes ago…Brandon is in the shower. They'll be down in half an hour."

"Then, I'll go get us another beer," David said, getting up from the table.

While he was waiting at the bar, David noticed that Evie was still sending out, and receiving several text messages. She was smiling genuinely, and had a twinkle in her eye. He assumed it was from the kids, telling her a funny story about their golfing escapades; but when he brought the drinks back to the table, Evie straightened him out.

"I just got a text from Johnny," she began, "…asking me if I remembered about Monday?"

"Monday? What about Monday?" David asked.

"Oh, I'm sure I told you about it," Evie started in, hastily. "Johnny asked me about it two-months ago. Before you and me even started talking."

"About what?" "He is having a medical procedure on Monday," she explained. "It's day-surgery, so he really needs someone to drive him home, after the operation."

"Oh, well, that's not a big deal, to pick him up after work, right? So, what's the problem?"

"Well, I'm planning to take him, to the surgery-center, and just wait until he is done, so I can bring him home."

"What about work? I thought you were out of leave time?"

"Well, I am. But I told my supervisor that Johnny was my brother, so they had to give me the day off, for family sick-leave."

"So, she won't even consider taking a day off to be with her new boyfriend, but she will take a day off for Johnny?" David thought to himself. "Winning her love away from Johnny, might be more of a battle than I thought"

"So, you're going to lose a day's pay?"

"Well, yes… but he has done so much for me… loaned me his truck, whatever I need, he's always there for me," she explained. "So it's nice to be able to repay some of the favors."

"I understand that," David said, sincerely. "A good friendship has to have as much give, as take."

"Precisely," she agreed. "Well, again, I didn't even know you when I agreed to this, but, he's my best friend, and I can't let him down. I hope you'll understand…"

"What're you talking about?"

"Well, after I get home tomorrow, I am going to drive to his place and spend the night."

"You what?" David asked in surprise.

"Well, he has to be at the hospital at six in the morning," she responded. "So, even if I sleep on his couch, we'll have to get up at four a.m. to be there on time. If I don't stay at his house, I have to drive 25 miles to get there, and 30 miles back, to get to the hospital, so I'd have to get up at, like, 2:30."

"So, you're telling me, that you are going over to spend the night with your ex-boyfriend? Now why on earth, would that bother me?" David sarcastically.

"I knew you'd be upset!"

"You know, I just read a statistic in a magazine that said that 55% of divorced couples have sex together, after the divorce. It's just convenient and comfortable…"

"I wasn't married to Steve."

"No, but you've had a relationship with him for five years, and the last three years, you were living as husband and wife. I'm just saying, the odds are…"

"It takes two to tango," she said. "And even if he had something in mind, which he doesn't, I am in an exclusive relationship with you! And, I won't allow it. Don't you trust me?"

"Yes," he admitted. "Yes, I do. It's just him, I am concerned about. I still expect him to drop down on one knee and ask you to marry him, rather than losing you to me."

"Oh, you're being silly."

"Oh, yeah? Well suppose he does just that? Drops down on one knee, and asked you to marry him? What would you say?"

"He won't. That will never happen," she said, completely skirting the question. "Look, if you don't want me to do it, I can call and tell him I can't make it."

"No, no… that would be wrong… you gave him your word, and he is expecting you," David relented. "I'm not happy about it, but yes, I do trust you. So, well, do what you need to do."

"I love you," she purred.

They kissed softly, just as Brandon and Chrissie joined them at the bar.

"Hey, save that stuff for your room, Mom," Brandon said approaching the table.

The rest of the night was enjoying the food and entertainment offered at Eagle Crest, and they all had a blast. When the evening was over, David reminded Evie that they still had a half a bottle of Pendleton whiskey in the room.

"Ooo, then why are we sitting here paying five-bucks for a drink?" Evie responded, with a sensual kiss.

Later in the evening, Evie gave him a special "thank you," for giving his "blessing" to her plan to spend the night with her ex-boyfriend. David and Evie still did not have intercourse, but what she did for him that night, was just as good!

But somehow, it just didn't take away David's concern about Johnny.

Chapter 28

"We've found our little piece of Heaven,
right there in Sandy!"

A few days later, David and Chance talked on the phone. David told him all about the wonderful time he and Evie had had at Eagle Crest, and about their plans to become "roommates." He also told him about Evie spending the night with her ex-boyfriend.

"Turns out, the 'procedure' Johnny was going in for was a colonoscopy!" David explained. "If she had told me that, right up front, we wouldn't have even had to talk about it."

Both David and Chance had been through the procedure, and they both remembered drinking a half-gallon of laxative, the night before. It did not make for a pleasant evening.

"Shoot, the way I remember," Chance responded. "I couldn't get no more than ten feet from the toilet, at any time."

"Like a volcano erupting, with ten-seconds warning," David agreed. "So, I am certain, having sex was the very last thing on his mind."

"Could you imagine?" Chance laughed. "Don't move, Baby, I'll be right back!"

"Well, maybe I earned a few points with her, by showing her that I trusted her," David said.

"Maybe. So do you think you are ready for the big move to Portland?"

"Emotionally ready, but not financially ready."

"So, how are you going to pull it off... financially, I mean?" Chance asked.

"Heck, we haven't even found a place yet. Evie just started looking yesterday," David explained. "Once we find a place, then I'll have to put the pencil to the paper, and do some figuring. Right now, we don't know any of the specific amounts."

"But you have a good idea?"

"Oh, yeah. Most of my stuff is already in storage, here in Oroville," David explained. "And Evie has all of her household stuff in storage in Portland... from a three-bedroom house. Which is what we're looking for, to rent together."

"That's convenient," Chance agreed.

"Yeah, so I'll just leave my stuff here, and we'll move her stuff into the new place, we should be fine, until I can afford to make a run to Oroville, to get the stuff I have in storage here. Brandon already said that he'd be happy to ride shotgun on the trip, and help load and unload the truck. When I can afford to come get it."

"So? Ball park figure?"

"For the move? For me, two tanks of gas. All I have to do is drive up to Portland, with everything I can pack into the Mustang – basically, everything I have here in my little apartment – clothes, computer, printer, blankets. It's not much of a load."

"Well, that doesn't sound too bad," Chance admitted.

"And, we'll need to rent a truck in Portland, to move her stuff from storage to the new place. Day rates for trucks, local rental, and gas, should be around $100. The only wild-card is how much we're going to have to come up with, up front, for deposits and utility hook-ups, that kind of thing. So, until Evie finds us a place, I'm just in a holding pattern."

As he was talking, a text-message came in from Evie, so David stopped to read it: "I think I found our place!"

"Chance?" David said eagerly. "I gotta go... Evie thinks she found our place!"

"Well, keep me posted, Amigo."

After hanging up with Chance, he called Evie.

"Hi, Honey," Evie answered. "I'm still here with Marilyn, the owner. She is so sweet!" "So what's it look like?"

"It's the most charming little three-bedroom house I have ever seen. And, it's right on the edge of town – Sandy – which is the last town you hit, driving from Portland to Mount Hood. So, out our front door is nothing but the Mt. Hood Recreation area!"

David liked the sound of that! If he had to live close to a city, like Portland, at least he'd be as far away from the urban mess, as possible. "Is it within commuting distance to your job?" he asked.

"Yes… it's a bit of a drive, from what I am used to, but it's only around 22 miles, each way. I'll text you some pictures. Marilyn's mother used to live here, but when she passed away, Marilyn got it. Marilyn had just finished building a new house, right next door, but she couldn't bear to part with the place, so she turned it into a rental property."

As Evie was talking, photos started coming in, to David's phone, via text.

"Wow, that place looks amazing," he said honestly. "But what's it going to cost us?" "It's only $1,450 per month, on a six-month lease!" Evie exclaimed excitedly.

When David and Evie talked about the search for a new place, they determined that the most they wanted to pay was $1,600 per month. So, finding a place for less than their top figure, was a bonus.

"And, the deposits and utility hook-ups?"

"She's asking for first and last, and a $300 non-refundable cleaning fee." "Hey, that's not bad," David said enthusiastically. "When is it available?"

"June 1st."

"Damn! That's only two weeks from now. I mean, my half of that is $1,600… and come payday, that's about all I get. That would leave me nothing left over, even to drive the Mustang up there. Will she hold off a month, so we can save up a little more money?"

"No, she said she has several other interested people. But, I can cover most of it from my savings," she said. "And, you can just pay me back, when you can."

"Okay. So, what's the next step?"

"I have to give her a $500 deposit to hold the place," Evie began. "Then, she'll verify our application, and do a credit check…"

"Oops," David said. "You know I just had a foreclosure on my house, and I filed corporate bankruptcy last year. My credit ain't so good."

"Well, mine is," Evie said confidently. "And I already told Marilyn about your business problems, and losing your house. She said, so long as we disclose everything, she's not worried about it."

"Well, a federal retirement check is certainly dependable income, anyway," David agreed.

"I'll fill out an application, while I'm here, if you think we should get this place?"

"Sweetheart, I think we've found our little piece of Heaven, right there in Sandy! See, I could live anywhere, so long as it is with the woman I love! You bet, I want to get it… if you do?"

"I'm in love with this place, are you kidding?" Evie replied enthusiastically. "I'll give her a check, to hold the place. And, I'll leave her my application. Then, I will email a blank PDF copy to you." "Great. I can print that here, fill it out, and send it back." "You really think we're ready for this?" Evie asked.

"I don't know about you, but I am more than ready!"

"Me, too," she replied happily. "I'd better go take care of business with Marilyn. I'll call you when I get home. I love you!!"

"Sounds great!" David responded. "Yes, we'll talk later. I love you, too."

After they hung-up, David looked at the pictures of the little place, over and over again. He was so excited, he forwarded several of the pictures of the house to Chance, with a note that said: "Our little dream house."

Chance called him immediately. "Did you already get the place?" Chance asked right off the bat. "Evie put a deposit on it, and we still have to go through the application process," David replied. "But, if we get approved, we can take possession on June first."

"Holy shit, Man," Chance exclaimed. "Are you sure about this?"

"Yes, I'm sure it will be available on the first…" "That's not what I'm talking about, and you know it."

David laughed. "Look, we both need a new place to live, and if this whole relationship-thing doesn't work out, we agreed to just be roommates. We're splitting everything 50-50. She's not even telling her family, that we're a couple. She's going to tell them that we're just roommates, so she won't have them climbing on her back for going too quickly, with someone she just met. Brandon and Chrissie will know, of course."

"Her family is right, and I totally agree. I think you guys might be getting the cart before the horse! Maybe you should both listen to us?" Chance said. "There's still a lot of red-flag issues that you guys need to resolve… especially with her drinking."

"I know, I know, but me and Evie? We are so good together, I know we can work out any problem that comes up!"

"And, Johnny?"

"You know, Chance, the truth is, I don't even think Evie realizes that she is still in-love with him."

"Bullshit."

"No seriously. We've talked about him a lot, and about the three of us becoming friends. She said, if he didn't want to meet me, then she wouldn't see him anymore, even as a friend."

"Well, that sounds encouraging," Chance admitted. "If it's true…" "Once we get settled, she's going to invite him over to have supper with us, and maybe jump in the hot tub…"

"Hot tub?"

"Oh, I forgot to mention, this place has a hot tub out back. It's fantastic! I told you, this is our little dream-house."

"Well, if you're wrong about those red-flags, it may turn into a nightmare…"

"No worries, we have it all under control," David said confidently. "Heads-up, eyes open, and plowing forward at full throttle."

"I can see you are running at full-speed," Chance warned. "But, I'm not sure that you see the big wall, that's right in front of you?"

"Nothing to it," David laughed it off. "We'll adapt, adjust, and overcome. Isn't that what the Army Rangers say?"

"Yes, it is," Chance agreed. "But the last part of it is, 'Or die trying.'"

After they finished talking, David got out his paper and pencil, and started making notes, and scribbling numbers. By the time Evie called him back, he had finished his notes, and was waiting for a pot-pie to finish cooking in the microwave. "So, are you excited?" David asked.

"Very excited," Evie admitted. "But, also just a bit scared. What if it doesn't work out, between us?"

"Hey, it'll be fine, if you stop with the negative thoughts! You should be asking, 'What if it does work out?' The answer to that is, we'll be the happiest couple alive, that's what!"

"You are always so positive, about everything," Evie said cheerfully. "I love that about you!"

"So? You talked to Marilyn," David inquired. "How do our chances look, for getting it?"

"Well, we still have to get your application in, but she said, so long as we are honest, and tell her everything up front, it won't be a problem. We told her about your bankruptcy, so that won't be a problem. But, if you've ever been arrested for anything, be sure to put it down there."

"Well, I've never been arrested, for anything," David admitted. "Have you?"

"Unfortunately, I have," she confessed. "I had a DUI a couple of years ago…"

"Really?

"Yeah, the cop was a real jerk," she explained. "I didn't even have that much to drink."

"Well, what did Marilyn say?"

"She said it was not a big deal, since I told her about it, up front."

"Good. At this point, that's all that matters," David said. "Now, we just have to wait and see what she says."

"Well, I'm going to pray about it," Evie said.

"Well now, that's an excellent idea!" David agreed. "I am going to pray, too. If God wants us to be here, then, it will happen!"

They actually didn't have long to wait. Two days later, Marilyn called them with the news that they had a new home, in Sandy.

"Marilyn said that the current renters will not be out until the 31st," Evie explained, after getting the news. "And she wants four days to clean and touch up the paint."

"So, our move-in date is on the 5th?" David asked.

"Yes. Which actually works out well, because that's a Friday, so we'll have that whole weekend to move in. Of course, she'll pro-rate the first month's rent."

"That'll save us a couple hundred dollars on our move-in," David said cheerfully.

"So, let's talk dollars and cents," Evie stated, very businesslike. "With the first month's rent adjusted, and adding the cleaning deposit, we'll need to come up with $3,000, total, on move-in."

"Minus the $500 you already gave her, right?" David inquired.

"Right," Evie acknowledged, "So, another $2,500. How much of that can you cover?"

David glanced over his list of bills and expenses, and told Evie he could come up with $1,000, of the balance, on the first. She said that she could cover the remainder from her savings, and that David would just pay her back $500, whenever he could, to get his share up to 50%.

"Well, it looks like we've got our first home," David said to himself, after he hung up the phone. He looked around at his tiny apartment, and added, "Thank God!"

A few weeks later, David and Evie signed the lease together, at Marilyn's house, and she gave them each a set of keys. That made it official. It was now, their first home, and there was no turning back from the course they had chosen.

They got moved-in quickly, just unloading boxes and furniture into the house. It would take weeks, before it all got put away. But that was the joy of moving!

With Evie working in Portland, and heavy morning traffic, she had to be out the door by 6:00 a.m. David, an early riser by nature, was usually up around 4:00 a.m., so he made sure there was a fresh pot of coffee made, by the time he heard Evie's alarm clock sound.

She would go directly into the bathroom, to brush her teeth, shower and get ready for work. David would bring her coffee to her, and ask her if she wanted breakfast. He had learned that lesson from Karen – always ask, before preparing a meal. But, Evie was so very different from Karen, she welcomed David's attention. Evie normally ate only toast for breakfast, or a bowl of cereal, and she was always grateful when he made her a sack-lunch, to take to work.

David enjoyed writing her little love-notes, and hiding them in her lunch bag. She would find them later, and text David, "I love you!" Another thing he enjoyed was finding cute animal pictures on the internet, and sending them to Evie via text message. He knew those kinds of photos always brought a smile to Evie's face, even if she was having a bad day, on the job.

Both David and Evie loved to cook, and while Evie didn't mind David's help, getting her off to work on time, supper was another issue. She usually got home from work a little before 5:00 p.m., which was "plenty of time" for her to cook supper, she explained to David. With the sun staying up until after eight at night, they usually didn't eat supper until after seven, anyway. So, they worked out a schedule, and took turns. Or, if they were warming up leftovers, for example, they would cook together, with Evie making a fresh salad, and David possibly baking biscuits, or something.

When they were together, at home, they always had music playing.

Their standard radio station played "classic rock" tunes from the 60's and 70's. But, quite often, they would each load three CD's of their favorite artists, in Evie's 6-disk CD player, so the disks would switch from his to hers, and repeat. His choice was usually rodeo or Western music, from his rodeo-days, while hers was mostly classic rock, or "inspirational" Christian music.

Just as Chance had predicted in his "red-flag" speech, Evie took every opportunity to "preach" to David, about becoming a Christian. But, when he tried to explain to her about his own beliefs, she generally closed the conversation. She also kept her car-radio tuned to a Christian talk channel, which David found just totally boring. But, when they went somewhere in her car, he never complained. For the most-part, however, they respected each other's beliefs, and did not discuss religion. Usually.

Another of Chance's "red-flag" items was the consumption of alcohol. Before he moved to Oregon, David's beer drinking was limited to two or three, per day. Sometimes, he would have a fourth, but more often, he would only have one. Evie, on the other hand, would drink from four to seven beers, after she got home from work, and she would often add half a bottle of wine, to the mix. She drank twice that, on weekends, since she would often start drinking before lunch.

Because they were splitting the cost of groceries, which included the beer, David felt that he should drink at least three beers, out of every six-pack, since that is what he was paying for. So, he increased his own consumption accordingly, trying to keep even with Evie.

But, for the first three weeks they lived together, in Sandy, it was, according to David, "Like something out of a fairy-tale." Evie even told David, during that time that, as much as she hated her job, she didn't even mind going to work, so much, knowing that she had him to come home to. That made David feel even better, about their love affair.

In spite of their rather large appetite for beer, those first few weeks together often found David and Evie playfully patting each other on the bottom, or sitting naked together in the hot tub. They also would often push the coffee table out of the way, and the lovers would dance in the living room. David kept his promise not to have intercourse with Evie, so she could protect her promise to Jesus, about abstaining from sex until after they were married. But, as the alcohol consumption increased, so did their passion, during their "no-intercourse" sexual encounters.

One Saturday night, after they had already emptied a 12-pack of beer, they had a particularly rousing encounter in the hot tub. So intense was their "foreplay," that both Evie and David had to steel their resolve, to avoid having intercourse. When it almost became too much for them, they decided it was time to get out of the hot tub, and turn their attention to other matters.

"We should take a shower together," Evie suggested. "That's always fun."

David knew that it was not a god idea, as passionate as they had become in the hot tub, but he wasn't exactly thinking with his "big head," at the time. So, they took a shower together. Between the booze and the passion, their promise to wait until after marriage to have intercourse, flowed down the drain. But neither of them voiced any regrets. Their "first time," had been wildly erotic, and so passionate, that neither of them would ever forget it.

Later, David apologized to Evie for failing to stop the action, before they went "too far."

"You wouldn't have been able to stop me, even if you tried," she said sincerely.

They never discussed having intercourse, or abstaining from having intercourse, again. Once they had crossed that line, there was no holding back again.

During the next week, always bolstered by too much beer to drink, they made-love two more times. But unlike the first time, the booze had a significant impact on their desires, and neither of the subsequent sessions were very remarkable, or memorable. Alcohol can do that.

The following Saturday, David and Evie decided to spend the beautiful morning, sitting in the hot tub, sipping mimosa's. Evie mentioned that she was feeling remiss for not attending church more regularly, on Sundays. David told her that, if she felt that way about it, she should just go. Evie said she was planning to do exactly that, but she decided to use the opportunity to try to talk David into accompanying her.

"I told you, Evie," he explained. "I'll go with you to hold your hand, if you like, but I do not believe in organized religion. And you will not have any luck, trying to convert me. It's a waste of time."

"Now that sounds like the Devil talking, to me," she said lightly.

"You see? I don't even believe in the Devil."

"What are you talking about?" Evie gasped in shock. "How can you not believe in the Devil?"

"Look, Evie," David explained sincerely, seeing that she was growing very upset. "It isn't that I believe, or don't believe, in the Devil. I just refuse to give Him any power over me. And, I will not blame Him for my own mistakes."

"What are you talking about?"

"I think Christians invented the Devil to be their scapegoat. 'It wasn't me, that stole the money, it was the Devil!' Well, in my world, if I do something wrong, I admit it. Then, I do my best to right the wrong, apologize, and seek forgiveness, from the person I wronged. I don't blame the Devil for my own misdeeds."

Evie had a look of shock and disbelief on her face.

"I just can't imagine someone, who doesn't believe in the Devil…"

"What're you talking about, Evie?" David replied. "We both knew that we had different beliefs, going into this thing. And, we agreed, we could both live with those differences."

"Well, I just didn't realize that you didn't believe in the Devil…"

"So, you have a problem with the fact that I take full responsibility for my own actions, and don't look for someone, the Devil, to blame, for my own transgressions? How is that a bad thing?"

"I just don't think I can marry someone, who doesn't believe in the Devil," Evie stated flatly.

"We're not even engaged yet," David defended. "You're being totally unreasonable about this issue. How can this be a "deal-breaker?"

Evie climbed out of the hot tub, and began drying off.

"When I go to church tomorrow," she said, as she turned to enter the house. "I am going to pray for your soul." Then, she turned and slammed the door.

"You've got to be shitting me?" David said to himself. "This is just plain crazy!"

Chapter 29

"The Nightmare begins..."

David climbed out of the hot tub, dried off, then followed Evie into the house. He found her in the kitchen, standing beside the stove, looking out the window. He stepped up behind her, and wrapped his arms around her waist. Evie shuddered, as if he were made of ice.

"It's going to be alright," David said gently. "We'll make this work. We just have to talk it through."

Evie was warming, and she placed her arms over his.

"We're just going so fast, we hardly know each other, really," she responded softly. "I know it will be alright. It's just going to take some time for me to adjust, that's all."

"Attagirl!" David said with a smile. "There's nothing we can't do, if we do it together. And, we can get through this!"

Evie spun around, and David held her in his arms.

"Just give me some time, before we talk about this again, okay?"

"Of course," he replied, leaning in for a kiss.

Evie responded, but it was a "friendly" kind of kiss, with no passion or desire. David thought it was similar to when he would kiss his mother good-night. "But, at least she didn't scratch my eyes out," David thought. "Oh, don't forget, Brandon and Chrissie are coming over tonight for supper," Evie said, pulling out of the embrace, and walking toward the refrigerator. "They'll have Missy and Josh, too. I need to get the roast in the crock-pot. Would you mind running to the store? I need carrots and a few other things."

"Yeah, no problem," David responded. "Do you have a list?"

"Yes, right over by my purse, on the counter." David grabbed the list, and looked it over.

"Wine? We never drink wine."

"I thought it would be nice to get a bottle of inexpensive red wine, for dinner," Evie said. "And, you'd better get a 30-pack of beer." "Yes, dear," David sighed.

"At least we won't have any Fireball, or whiskey. That's just throwing alcohol on the flames!" David thought.

David knew how volatile Brandon and Chrissie could be, when they were drinking hard liquor. He hoped that by limiting their choices to just beer and wine, it might keep things more calm.

That notion went right out the window, later that evening, when Brandon and Chrissie arrived, with the children. Brandon was carrying a half-empty bottle of "Fireball" cinnamon whiskey.

"I knew you guys wouldn't have any 'Fireball,' so I brought enough for everybody," Brandon announced with a smile.

Chrissie and the children were close behind.

"You have any shot glasses, Mom?" Chrissie asked, as she ushered Josh and Missy into the house.

David had already tuned the television to a kid's channel, and Missy was drawn immediately to the cartoons. Josh was playing video games on his cell phone, and they both sat in the living room, in front of the big screen.

"No, but I have some juice glasses," Evie responded, pulling four small juice glasses down from the cupboard.

"Nice!" Brandon said, looking at the glasses. "Now, that's what I call a shot glass!"

"Brandon, you do not have to fill those glasses to the top," Evie admonished.

Brandon did anyway. And after all four glasses were full, there was just a tiny bit left, in the bottle, so Brandon downed the last of it.

"We need to make a toast, to you guys, and this great little house," Brandon said.

Chrissie began handing glasses out, so they could share a toast. Sensing that something was happening, the children wanted to be included, too.

"Can we have a toast, too?" Josh asked walking toward the kitchen.

"Dammit, Josh, go sit back down," Brandon said, raising his voice. "Brandon!" Evie admonished, as she rushed over to Josh and gave him a hug. "We have orange juice, the kids can join us, if they want." "Oh, Mom," Brandon sighed. "He's been a pain in the butt all day..."

"They just want to have a toast, too," Evie scolded. "Missy, do you want some juice, too?"

Yes, Grandma, and some toast, too," Missy replied.

Everyone laughed. While Evie grabbed two more glasses, for the youngster's juice, Chrissie explained to Missy what a "toast" really was.

David could sense, from the elevated voices so early in the evening, that Brandon and Chrissie had already had a shot or two of the Fireball. He was glad the bottle was now empty.

"That stuff just brings out the 'mean' in people," David thought, of the "Fireball."

Brandon and Chrissie made a heartfelt toast, welcoming their newest family-member, David, and the new life David and Evie were just beginning, in their new house. And everyone, including the children, emptied their glasses.

"We've still got an hour before dinner is ready," Evie announced. "Does anyone want to get in the hot tub?"

"Mom! Really?" Brandon addressed his mother. "That thing is way too hot for the kids."

"I already thought of that, Brandon," David interjected. "I turned it down to 95 degrees. Their bathwater is hotter." "Right on," Brandon said with a smile. "Cool." "And, I brought their bathing suits," Chrissie said.

While the girls took the children to the "guest room" to change clothes, David and Brandon, both with fresh beers, headed out back, to uncover the hot tub. Along the way, Brandon confessed that it had not been a peaceful day, at their house. He and Chrissie had been arguing, mostly about a guy who had been hitting on Chrissie, while she was at work the previous night.

"I was sitting right there," Brandon told David. "You know, and this guy is hitting on her. I was ready to go pound sand up his ass." "So, did Chrissie handle it?" David asked.

"Well, yeah, but not before he was asking her out."

"I gotta tell you, Brandon, she's working for tips," David explained. "Yeah, he's rude and drunk, but she flirts with him a little, and she gets twice the tip."

"Hey, I don't want my old lady flirting with other guys," he said firmly.

"Brandon, it's not about flirting, it's only about money," David continued. "The best way for you to handle it, is to drop her off outside, and you never go inside."

"Bullshit," he replied scornfully.

"No, seriously! Look, do you trust her?"

"Yeah, it's them I don't trust…"

"If things get out of hand, the owner… what's his name? Bill?"

"Yeah, Billy."

"Well, Billy, or that big Samoan bouncer, who works weekends, one of them will toss the guy out on his ear."

"I still think it's bullshit."

"Well, listen, Brandon," David began, putting his hand on Brandon's shoulder. "Let's have a peaceful evening tonight, okay? Your mom's been working on that roast all day long, and we really want to have a nice, pleasant 'family' supper."

"I get it," Brandon said extending his hand. David shook it.

"I'd like that, too," Brandon admitted. "But, you'd better talk to Chrissie, she's the one keeps wantin' to fight."

"I will," David promised, as the girls and the kids, stepped out the back door.

Chrissie and the children had swimsuits on.

"I'm going to get in with them," Chrissie said. "Anyone want to join me?"

The other adults declined the invitation.

"Brandon, would you get me another beer?" Chrissie asked as she stepped into the hot tub with the kids.

"Sure, Hon," he replied, draining his own. "I need another one anyway."

David still had ¾ of his beer left, and they had opened them at the same time. Evie didn't get in the tub, but orbited around it, taking pictures, and chatting with her grandchildren, and with Chrissie, as the children splashed about in the water.

A little while later, Evie excused herself, so she could go inside to check on the roast. Brandon and David were talking about construction, since they were both carpenters, but from two different generations. "Back when I swung a hammer," David pointed out. "We didn't have nail-guns or laser levels. We had to do it the old-fashioned way…"
"That's why it used to take two or three days to frame a house, back then," Brandon said. "Nowadays, my crew can do a whole house, in one day… just four of us!"

"Well, you've got a good point, there," David admitted.

"You ready for another beer?" Brandon asked, standing up.

"I am," Chrissie called out.

"Naw, I'm good," David said.

David was drinking his third beer already, and with the double shot of Fireball, he was beginning to feel the effects.

Brandon disappeared into the house, and a few minutes later, David could hear Brandon and Evie arguing about something. He couldn't make out the words, but the volume was getting louder and louder. David, the self-appointed "peace-keeper" decided to go see if he could throw some water on the fire, that seemed to have erupted in the kitchen.

As David entered the kitchen, through the back door, Brandon was coming out.

"Good luck with that one," Brandon said lightly, and with a smile.

"Hey, no hill for a climber," Dave responded with a smile.

As they passed, Brandon held his hand up for a "high-five." David slapped it.

"Right on," Brandon said lightly, as he headed over to give Chrissie her beer.

David walked in, and Evie was staring at the back door scowling at Brandon. David noticed a half-empty wine glass, on the counter by the sink. No one else was drinking wine. He walked over to give Evie a hug, and she pushed him away. "Don't touch me," she admonished.

"What the Hell did I do?" David asked, as he reached into the refrigerator for another beer.

"Nothing," she snapped. "I'm not mad at you…just don't touch me right now."

"Look, Sweetheart," David said, moving toward her, still hoping for a hug. "You've spent all day cooking and getting ready for a nice 'family dinner,' so can't we just make nice?"

"How could you take his side?" she said, as she took a sip of wine. "What?" David asked incredulously. "I don't even know what you guys were arguing about…"

"Oh, sure," she said accusingly. "I saw your 'high-five.' You wouldn't even back up the woman you love? I expect you to take my side, and to support me, when I am arguing with someone."

"I told you, I don't even know what you guys were arguing about," David defended. "I just came in for a beer…"

"Evolution. We were arguing about evolution," she explained. "And I expect 'my man' to back me up."

David knew that Evie's position on evolution, was straight out of the Bible. She believed that Adam and Eve were the first humans to inhabit the earth. And, by the most generous estimates, Adam and Eve had to have lived on earth, 15,000 years ago, or less.

"Look, Evie, we've talked about this before," David began. "I've got to tell you, when it comes to evolution, I agree with Brandon. I mean, how can you look at the fossilized remains of a human that is almost a million years old, and say, 'That doesn't exist?'"

"The Bible says God created man, in his own image. And Adam and Eve were the first humans," Evie's voice was rising.

Even though David was drinking far less, than the others, he was still feeling the effects. And the very large shot of 'Fireball" he'd drank, made his patience too thin for a rational argument. It was drunk against drunk, and with that combination, there was no winning possible, for either of them.

"How can you look at something, right in front of your face, and say you don't 'believe' in it. It exists, and we know every form of life on this planet has the ability to evolve, adapt and survive. Don't you see? That was God's greatest gift to all living things... the ability to evolve."

"That's just the Devil talking," Evie stated matter-of-factly. "Oh, that's right, you don't believe in the Devil, do you?"

"No, I don't. But I thought we agreed to talk about that, at a different time?"

"This is a different time..." she stated.

"I am not talking about religion, with a drunk," David said, as he walked back out the door.

When dinner was almost ready, Evie came out back. The women got the kids out of the hot tub, which was no easy task, as the children were having a blast playing in the water.

"Joshua Michael Abaddon!" Chrissie yelled. "You get out of that water right now!"

It worked. Josh had heard that angry voice before, and he knew to duck out of the way!

Dinner was delicious, but very quiet. It seemed that everyone was working hard not to start another argument, and the result was, no-conversation. David and Evie hadn't spoken a word, to each other, since their "conversation" about evolution. Not one word.

After Brandon, Chrissie and the kids had gone, Evie started putting away the leftovers. David went into their bedroom and got ready for bed. Once he had brushed his teeth and put on a pair of sweat pants, he came out of the bedroom. He noticed the wine bottle was now empty, and Evie still wore a stern, almost angry, look on her face.

"At least a six-pack of beer, and a whole bottle of wine," David thought. "This is a girl I want to avoid, tonight!"

"I'm sleeping in the guest room tonight," David announced. "Maybe, you'll cool down by the morning."

"I don't need to cool down," she spit the words out angrily. "You're the one with the problem."

"Me? You're the one who's been yelling at everyone, all night. Even your grandkids…"

"I did NOT yell at those children," Evie said, her voice rising.

"Bullshit! Joshua asked you to help him hook his iPad up to the television, so they could play games on it, and you bit his head off."

"I was trying to get the rolls in the oven, and I don't know a damn thing about that television."

"That's why I hooked it up for them… but you didn't have to yell at the poor kid."

"I DID NOT YELL AT HIM," she screamed.

"Yeah, right," David said softly. "I'm goin' to bed."

He walked down the hall to the guest room. Evie slammed the cupboard doors, and was cursing incoherently.

David had never seen this mean, angry side of Evie before. In the past, when she got drunk, she might argue with others, but she had never turned on David before. David realized it was mostly the beer, wine and Fireball she had been drinking, but he was fairly drunk himself, which just made it worse.

In the morning, Evie got dressed and went to church. She didn't ask David to accompany her, which suited him just fine. After she left, David called Chance, and filled him in on the events of the past few days. "She actually said that?" Chance asked.

"No shit," David repeated. "She said, 'I can't marry someone who doesn't believe in the Devil.' Just like that."

"Do you think she was serious?"

"I don't know," David admitted. "But, ever since we had that conversation, something has changed in her. She's just cold... mean."

"Well maybe church is a good thing for her then?"

"I sure hope so. Man, I do not like her, when she's like this." "So, what're you thinking?" Chance asked.

"I'm thinking that she's put up a big wall between us, with this religion-thing."

"What can you do about it?"

"The only thing I can do, is try to get her to understand that our beliefs really aren't that far apart," David explained. "If she would only let me tell her about it."

"Them Christians are the most close-minded, judgmental people, on earth," Chance quipped.

"I know, right? But, little by little, I might wear her down, and at least get her to listen to my theology."

"Good luck with that," Chance remarked.

"What other choice do I have?" David responded. "If we're going to get past this issue, we need to talk about it, identify the differences, and come up with a resolution. We have to figure out how we can live with it."

"Easier said than done, my man."

"Hey, I am not ready to throw this thing away, just like that," David explained. "Not over something as silly as 'I don't believe in the Devil.'"

"So when do you think you'll be able to talk about it?" "Hopefully sometime soon, when we're both cold-sober."

"I hear that," Chance remarked.

"I moved here to spend the rest of my life with this woman, and if we have to get through a few rocky roads, here in the beginning, it'll make for smooth sailing, for the rest of our lives."

"Well, look at the bright side," Chance began.

"There's a bright side?"

"Yeah, you haven't said a word about Johnny, so at least you only have one major issue to deal with, at a time."

"That's not exactly the 'silver-lining' I was looking for, Chief."

After they hung up, David got a text message from Evie, telling him that, when church was over, she was going to have lunch with her sister. David knew that particular sister was as much of an alcoholic as Evie was.

"So much for 'cold sober,'" David thought.

Later that afternoon, when Evie came home, she went straight to the refrigerator for a beer. David knew that it wasn't her first, so he grabbed one, to try to keep up. But at least they were being civil and polite with each other. "So, how was church?" David asked.

"It was good," she replied. "I did a lot of praying, and afterwards, I talked with my sister, too."

"I see," David said. "And, what was it you prayed, and talked to your sister, about?"

Evie shifted uncomfortably, and took a long pull on her beer. "Well, you know, we've been saying all along that, if things didn't work out between us, we could always just be roommates and friends, right?"

"We have talked about that, yes," David acknowledged. "But, I didn't move out here just to be roommates... shoot, we've only lived together a few weeks. We had one fight..."

"Well, I think maybe we just rushed into this, too quickly?" she explained. "And maybe we should just back up. Get to know each other better, you know, work on our friendship, before we start acting like husband and wife?"

"What exactly are you saying?"

"Well, I think, maybe, you should move into the other bedroom... just for now," she stated. "We can try just being roommates for a while, and see if we really want to go forward with our relationship."

David started to argue, but he realized that, if he were in the guest room, when she got to drinking too much, and she started getting mean, he could just go to his own room. And perhaps, it would be easier on them both emotionally.

"So, you just want to take a little step backwards?" David asked.

"We'll be roommates, but we're still dating, right?"

After the very first time they had met, they had both agreed to have a mutually exclusive relationship, and David wasn't sure if that agreement was still in place, or not?

"Well, yeah, we're dating," she said with a smile. "But since we're just friends, I suppose we could also see other people?"

"Yeah, right," David scoffed. "I don't know a soul here, and even if I did, you are the only woman I am interested in pursuing. Forget it."

"All I'm saying is, you could if you wanted."

"Well, I don't want," David said. "And, I hope you don't either."

"All I want, is for us to be friends, right now. I don't like the fighting and arguing, and I just think this will be a much more peaceful way for us to live, for now."

She didn't actually answer the question. As a result, David still considered them to be dating each other exclusively, while Evie seemed to have left the door open to seeing others. This misunderstanding would come back to haunt them later.

"Alright, then," David said reluctantly. "I don't have much stuff anyways, so I'll get moved over to the guest room today."

Oh, that'll be just fine," she said. "Chrissie wanted to go to the gym today…I can get her in free with my guest-pass, so I'm going over there in a little while, to pick her up."

David knew what that would mean… Fireball and beer. When she got home, he figured that would be a good time for him to be safely entombed in the guest room – his room, now.

"That's cool," David said. "Tell them I said 'hello.'"

"I will."

Once she changed, she was out the door quickly, so David went to work transferring his clothes and shaving kit, to the other bedroom and bath. It took less than an hour, so David decided to just take a nap. As he lay down, his thoughts were racing.

"Maybe this is a good thing?" he thought. "It'll take a lot of pressure off of us both, and maybe her family will get off her back, about this whacko-cowboy she met on the internet. And, maybe we can actually get to be friends?

"Yeah, this won't be so bad…" David thought, as he drifted off to sleep.

Chapter 30

"Evie's taken marriage off the table."

"Wait, I can't hear you. Where are you at?" David shouted into his phone.

It suddenly got quieter.

"There, how's that?" Evie said into the phone.

"Good," David replied.

"I'm in the ladies' room…at Chrissie's bar."

"What're you doing there? I've got dinner ready. When are you coming home?"

"Slow down, Cowboy," Evie laughed. "The girl who works this shift called in sick, so they asked Chrissie to cover. It's a seven-to-ten shift, only three-hours, so I told her I'd just wait here, maybe play some pool, while she works."

"You sound like you've been drinking?"

"Yup," she giggled. "That's why I am calling. I don't think it's a good idea for me to drive all the way back to Sandy. I have extra work clothes over at Brandon's house… so, I'm just going to give Chrissie a ride home tonight, and stay with them."

"Just promise you'll let Chrissie drive," David stated with concern.

"Oh, I'll be fine, it's only a mile…"

"Evie!"

"Oops! Gotta go! Bye!" David heard the line go dead.

"Well, it looks like I get one more night in the 'big-bed,' before I have to move to the guest room," David thought. "Not much of a silver lining, there."

When he awoke, it was still dark outside. He staggered into the bathroom and reached for his toothbrush…

"Whoops," David said aloud, remembering that he had moved all of his toiletries into the "guest bath."

He went to the other bathroom, and finished his ablutions. Afterwards, he grabbed a cup of coffee and his cell phone.

"Yeah, boom, just like that," David was saying enthusiastically into the phone. "Let's just be roommates."

"Damn, I'm sorry, Hoss," Chance sighed. "So, can you date other people?"

"Like I told her, who the Hell do I even know out here? Date other people? That's crazy."

"I don't know, it sounds to me like Evie might have other ideas about that," Chance advised.

"Why do you say that?"

"Well, last week you were all worried about having to compete with her past… her ex, Johnny. This week she comes up with some lunatic religious thing, and tells you she only wants to be friends? This ain't about religion, my friend, she just wants everyone to think it is."
"Where are you going with this, Chief? David asked, confused.

"Suppose her whole deal, getting a place with you, and all that, really was all about making Johnny jealous?"

"And, now she can go cry to him, about what a monster I am?" David picked up on Chance's line of thinking.

"What man can resist a woman in tears?"

"None," David said softly. "Dammit. You know, she told me she broke up with him, only because he didn't want to get married, ever again. If that's the case, he would have reconsidered marriage – the minute I showed up here, he'd have been down on one knee."

"So, what are you getting at?" Chance asked.

"Well, it seems to me there is a lot more going on, with that whole story between them, than just a simple commitment issue. I just don't know what it is…"

"It could be just about anything, Amigo," Chance acknowledged. "Well, if I am back in competition with Johnny, I'm screwed. When we were arguing, I was just as drunk as she was… I got just as ornery as she was… and, I turned into some kind of raging monster."

"And that 'white-knight' in Johnny's clothing, will have to come rescue the damsel in distress." Chance finished.

"Boy. You said it," David observed. "Well, I'm not out of it yet. I'm going to try to see if I still have a shot with her."

During the workday, in weeks previous, David and Evie exchanged text messages periodically. She wasn't allowed to have her cell phone at her work station, but on breaks and at lunch, they would catch up, via text.

He had sent her a text, at around 7:30 a.m., asking if she had made it in to work alright? She responded a few hours later: "Almost late, but I made it. I'm exhausted."

"Hungover?" he responded, and regretted it immediately. "Just kidding," he typed in quickly.

She didn't respond for the rest of the day. But, when she arrived at home, she was bright and cheerful, as if nothing bad had ever happened between them.

"Well, the bar closes at ten on Sunday's," Evie explained, about the night before. "So, I figured I'd be in bed by eleven, at the latest."

"And?"

"Well, Chrissie decided she wanted to talk," Evie continued. "You know, she never really knew her real mother?" "Why not," David asked.

"She was a drug addict. Got busted, and Chrissie was raised in a string of foster-homes." "Well, that's sad," David admitted.

"So when Brandon started dating her, I've always tried to be like a real mother to her. You know, give her advice, recipes, small talk, whatever."

"That's nice of you."

"Well, last night, she decided she needed a mother-daughter, heart-to-heart talk! We were up until nearly 1:00 a.m.! But I couldn't turn her down."

"I don't blame you," David replied sincerely.

"So, I'm looking forward to climbing into bed early, tonight."

"Well, we still have plenty of leftovers, roast and chili, so you can just throw something in the microwave, whenever you want." "Good! Early supper, early to bed," she sighed.

"Say, Evie?" David asked. "Since we are still... dating... how about we go out on a real date Friday night?"

"That sounds good," Evie responded excitedly. "Friday is catfish and hush-puppies night at the bar."

"I thought we might go out to dinner somewhere else, and maybe see a movie or something?" "Oh, no, David! You have got to try their catfish and hush-puppies. They are to die for!" Evie explained. "And Chrissie will be working, so we can just stay there and play pool until we want to come home..." "Yeah, well, okay, sure," David agreed. "So it's a date?"

"Yes, it is," Evie replied. "Oh, and Wednesday? I forgot to tell you this. Chrissie has a court appearance in Portland...has to be there at seven in the morning."

"Uh, huh?"

"So, after dinner tomorrow, I'm going to pack a few things, and spend the night with them. That way, we can get as much sleep as possible, before that alarm goes off!"

"So, another day without pay?"

"Well, yeah, but Chrissie is family, I can't turn her down."

"Did you ever think that, I could take her? I don't have a job to go to."

"Oh, I couldn't ask you to do that?"

"Why not? Everyone keeps saying I am part of the family... well, this is what family do for each other."

"Okay, but, I've already got it set up at work, so, maybe next time."

Something felt odd, or out of place, to David, but he just couldn't put his finger on it. Not yet.

"Yeah, sure. Next time," David said quietly.

Evie grabbed her phone, then went into her room to change clothes. David walked out the kitchen door, to the back yard. He loved watching the evening sky, as the brilliant sunset burned to an orange dusk. There was a bench, near the hot tub, which sat just outside a large window from the master bedroom. It was his favorite place to sit and enjoy the serenity.

"Ah, now, this is peaceful," David remarked, enjoying the hummingbirds which had gathered by the feeder.

Inside the bedroom, Evie was talking on the phone. David wasn't trying to eavesdrop, but in the calm evening air, Evie's voice carried very clearly, and he was drawn into the conversation.

"Did you get the tickets?" Evie said excitedly. "Oh, good! I can't wait to see how good he sounds, in person. Uh, huh. Well, I'll be at Brandon's by 6:30 tomorrow night, so I guess I'll see you then." David stood up, and walked back into the kitchen. Evie, wearing her sweat pants and pajama top, came out of the bedroom, smiling.

"Listen, Evie, I swear, I wasn't trying to eavesdrop," David began.

Evie's face went blank, then a weak smile.

"Did I hear you say something about getting tickets for tomorrow night? David asked.

"Oh, that? Well, that was, ah, my girlfriend, Judy," Evie said. "Yeah, her husband got them tickets to the Kenny G concert tomorrow night. He was called out of town on business, and can't make it, and she knows what a big fan I am… so she wants me to go with her." "I see," David said.

"And, since she lives in Gresham, too, I told her to just pick me up over there at Brandon's. We'll be home by eleven, so I'll get plenty of sleep before I have to take Chrissie to the courthouse, in the morning."

"I see," David said again.

Evie just turned and started digging through the refrigerator for leftovers. David grabbed a beer, and walked back out to the patio.

The next evening, Evie came home from work, and quickly ate supper. David had made spaghetti. Then, Evie went into her room and packed an overnight bag, and a makeup kit, and was soon heading for the door, on her way to Brandon and Chrissie's place.

"I'm going to get dressed for the concert over there," Evie explained, when David inquired as to why she was leaving so early. "I've got to do my hair, all that, and since I had all this stuff packed, it's just easier to take it all over there, to get ready."

"I see," David remarked.

Evie gave him a peck on the cheek, as she headed for her car. David waved as she drove away.

"She said she was going to the concert with her friend, Judy," David told Chance on the phone, the next morning. "But, if that's the case, then why did she wait until after I overheard her conversation, before she told me about it?"

"That is the $20,000 question my friend," Chance replied. "Do you think it could be, that she went with Johnny?"

"It's possible," David admitted. "I've never met any 'Judy'… but then, I haven't even met all her brothers and sisters yet, either."

"Or Johnny," Chance added. "Whatever happened to you guys inviting him over for dinner?"

"Johnny must not 'be ready,' I guess," David remarked. "Frankly, with all the Devil crap, I had put it out of my mind…guess I forgot."

"Well, maybe it's time you brought it up again?"

"Are you crazy?" David snapped. "I've got a date with her tomorrow night! I am not going to risk getting into a fight with her, for nothing. I want it to be a really good date, so I can show her what a great guy I can be."

"It's tough competing with her past," Chance remarked.

"Boy, you've got that right," David agreed. "I'd still like to find out what really happened between her and Johnny. I just know she's not telling me the whole story."

"So, you haven't talked about religion at all?" Chance asked.

"Nope, nary a word."

"But, that's why you guys are sleeping in separate rooms?"

"According to Evie, that's why," David answered. "Here, I'm trying to get us back on track, as a couple, and she's… well, I don't know what she's doing, but it sure seems like she has just totally written off our relationship, and she is much happier just being 'friends and roommates.' It's like, Evie's taken marriage, between us, off the table."

"Well, maybe you can find out what's really going on with her, when you guys go out tomorrow night."

"Maybe, we'll see."

A few hours later, in the late-morning, David got a call from Evie. She told him that, when they were driving in to the courthouse, Chrissie got a call from her lawyer that the "other side" had requested a continuance, and Chrissie would not be appearing in court until a month later.

"We just turned around, went back to the house, and went back to bed! I just woke up…"

"So, how was the concert?" David asked innocently enough.

"Oh, it was amazing. I know you probably don't like Kenny G, but he is such a talented musician!"

"Actually, I have a couple of his old records, I'd love to see him, sometime." David admitted. "So, what time did you get in?" "It was like one o'clock in the morning," she said.

"Wow, that was a long concert…"

"No, silly, when the concert got over, me and Judy went to a little bar for a drink. The traffic was horrendous, so we just waited an hour or two, in the bar. By the time we left, the traffic was all gone."

"Well, I guess it's a good thing you didn't need to go to work today."

"Right?" she said with a chuckle. "Chrissie wants to go grocery shopping, and Brandon has the truck. So I'm going to take her, before the kids get home from school. I'm thinking I'll be home about 4:00?" "Do you want me to make some dinner?" David asked.

"Oh, we still have plenty of leftovers, spaghetti and some roast, so no, we'll just warm something up." "Okay, Sweetheart, whatever you like."

After supper that night, Evie put on a Kenny G CD, and David and her danced in the living room, together. It was fun, for them both. They laughed, especially when they tripped over each other's feet, and fell to the floor in a heap. They had been drinking beer since Evie got home… at least, David had been drinking that long. Evie had started a little earlier, at Brandon's.

The alcohol had them both feeling a little romantic, but for Evie, it made her more tired, than frisky. It was still early, barely eight o'clock, when Evie announced that she was going into her room, to watch a little television, and go to sleep early.

Right after David had moved his things into the guest room, Evie had asked him if he wouldn't mind hooking up her small television in the master bedroom. They had never even discussed putting a television set in there, because they had both said that they didn't much care for watching TV in bed. But, apparently, Evie didn't mind it, occasionally. So, that was the last David saw of her, that night.

The next morning, Friday morning, David got up early and made coffee, taking a cup into her room, the way he used to do every day, when they were a "couple." He also made her a lunch, which he had gotten out of the habit of doing, when they changed to "roommates only." He even put a little note in the lunch: "See you tonight, on our date!"

David was going all-out, to make a very favorable impression on her, to win her affections back. He even sent her a couple of cute animal cartoons while she was at work, and she responded with little "smiley faces."

David was remembering how wonderful those first few weeks had been. They had been so in-love, and every minute was a delight. "How had it gone so wrong?" He wondered. But he really didn't care about the answer… he just wanted those days back, that feeling they shared, in the first weeks after he had come to Sandy.

When they went out to dinner that night, at the golf course lounge, the catfish and hush-puppies were as delicious, as advertised. Chrissie made sure that they had very generous portions, though neither could finish all that was offered.

The lounge had two pool tables, and being on a golf course, they were not often used. So, even on a Friday night. Both tables were open. David chose the table furthest away from the bar, in case anyone wanted to use the other table, they wouldn't bother David and Evie. Chrissie brought them fresh beers, as David racked the balls up.

The first few games saw the two acting like love-birds, kissing between shots, and patting each other on the bottoms! David was very pleased, as it seemed to be going so well. He was determined to show her that he was every bit as much fun as Johnny, with the difference that David was ready to get married, any time she wanted!

A short time later, David noticed a young man, perhaps in his mid-thirties, who had moved over to a table close to the pool tables. He was watching them play. David didn't much care for the way he leered, every time Evie bent over to take a shot. "Hey, can I play winner?" the fellow asked David.

"Listen," David said quietly, to the man. "My wife and I are just having some fun, and if you don't mind, we'd like to just keep it between us."

"Oh, sure, no problem, my man," the fellow said reaching out to shake David's hand. "I get it!"

Then, the man moved back over toward the bar. David was pleased. Evie was not...

"What the Hell do you mean, lying to that guy like that? I'm not your wife! How dare you tell someone we're married!"

"Evie, I just thought it was just you and me playing... he's right over there, if you'd rather, I can tell him he can play winner."

"No, I don't want to play with him, I want to play with you... I just don't want you telling people we're married, that's all."

"Why is that a problem?" David asked. "We're in a relationship...I thought, heading for marriage, so why not fudge a little, just to keep the peace?"

"We're dating, that's it," Evie corrected him.

"Well, okay, but at least I got rid of the guy," David said, pulling her in for a hug.

Evie leaned in for a kiss, and David responded passionately.

"Get a room," Chrissie said smiling, as she placed two more beers on their table. David let go of Evie, to take his shot, and the girls gabbed for a few minutes, until Chrissie got called back to work. David was still wondering why Evie was mad at him for calling her his "wife." Then, it hit him!

"This is her bar, her favorite watering-hole. She knows most of the regulars, and she has them all convinced that she is a single woman… she plays pool in here all the time. And me telling that guy she was married, might have just ruined her 'game.' She probably knows the guy. Heck, they've probably played together, one way or another." David thought. "That's the only thing it could be."

But, David didn't dwell too long on his theory, as Evie was acting very frisky toward him, like she used to do when he had first come to Sandy. Finally, they were getting back that loving feeling, they once shared.

"You know," Evie said rubbing David's butt. "We could go home and jump in the hot tub, naked."

David instantly put his hand in the air, to signal Chrissie. When she looked at him, he made a check-sign in the air with his hand. She understood, and brought them the tab.

David felt that he might have had too much to drink, but Evie had matched him beer-for-beer, plus, Chrissie had brought two shots of Fireball. David was afraid to drink the hard-stuff, because he knew he'd be driving later, so Evie downed them both. Between the two of them, David figured, he was the more-sober one, so he just got in the car and drove.

Evie teased him a lot, during the drive home—little kisses on his ear, rubbing his crotch, that kind of thing. At every stop sign or traffic light, they made out like teenagers, briefly. Fortunately, they did not encounter any police on the drive home, and soon David parked the car in their driveway. One last kiss, then they got out, and headed up the front steps.

When they got into the house, Evie reached in the refrigerator and grabbed them a couple of beers. Handing one to David, she pulled her phone out of her purse, and looked to see if she had missed any messages or calls.

"Shoot," she said. "My phone is almost dead…I'd better plug it in…"

"While you do that, I'll go get the hot tub ready" David said, heading out to uncover the hot tub.

While Evie was plugging in her phone, and David was still outside, her phone rang. Since it was already plugged in, beside her bed, she just sat on the bed, and answered the call.

A few minutes later, David came into her room, to see if she was ready to get into the hot tub. He found her laughing and chatting on her phone. He was perplexed. When Evie saw him, she stood up and waved David over. When he got close, she pulled him onto the bed next to her, and she held her finger to her lips. David had no idea what was going on, or with whom she was talking.

"Shhhhh," she said, as she put the phone on speaker.

"Well, little lady, when I saw your profile on Rancher's Only, I just had to get hold of you…I'm glad you gave me your phone number."

"Well, I'm glad you called," Evie said with a girlish giggle. "Me and my…friend…just got back from dinner."

"Well, Darlin' I'd sure like to take you out for dinner myself," David just shook his head, when he realized what was happening.

"Wait. What? Evie, I am not ready for this…" he began.

She quickly clicked the phone off speaker, and held her hand up for David to stop talking, so she could hear what her 'Rancher's Only love-interest' had to say. David felt the anger rise within himself.

"I am not ready to sit here and listen to you flirt with some guy you met on Rancher's Only," David said loudly.

Evie tried to cover the phone, so her new boyfriend wouldn't hear him ranting. And rant, he did. Evie angrily pointed to the back door, indicating that David should leave. So he walked back outside, then stood by the window shouting obscenities at her, for all the neighbors to hear.

Evie continued to talk to her "fella" for a full 20-minutes, before she finally hung up. Then, she was angry at David for getting mad and storming out! She promptly started yelling at him, for being rude to her new 'gentleman caller.' And David was drunk enough to yell right back at her.

"What are you so mad about?" she demanded. "We said we could date other people."

"No, you said you could date other people," David corrected. "I made it very clear that I was not interested in dating other people…couldn't even if I wanted to, because I don't know a soul around here. YOU are the only one who is looking to date other people!"

"Well, I thought you were looking, too."

"Bullshit. I made it very clear that I moved here just to be with you," David said. "…and, nobody else. If you want to date other guys…fine, but I am not ready to listen to it. I don't want to know about it, at all. I am not looking around, at all, and I don't want to hear anything about your new love interests."

He turned and walked away, heading for his room.

"So much for our romantic date," David thought to himself.

Chapter 31

"I fell in love with the wrong woman!"

Since it was Saturday, and they had been up late Friday night, drunk, they both stayed in bed longer than usual. David, who was normally up before six, slept until 8:30. Evie slept until after 10:00 a.m.

David decided to keep his distance from Evie, when she finally came out of her room, so he took his coffee and went outside to watch the morning sky. He was still very hurt from the phone call Evie had forced him to listen to.

"Why on earth would she think I'd want to sit there, and listen to her flirt with some guy on the phone?" David kept asking himself.

Realizing that he had left his phone in the kitchen, David went back inside to grab it. Evie was sitting on a stool, eating a bowl of cereal, on the kitchen counter. She had her phone beside the bowl, and she had it on speaker, so she could use both hands to eat, while talking.

"So, is Johnny still on the wagon?" David heard an unfamiliar female voice ask, as he stepped in from the back door.

Seeing David, Evie hastily grabbed her phone, took it off of speaker, and turned her head away.

"Yes, I think so," she replied softly.

David could tell he was making Evie very nervous, so he grabbed his phone, and went back out the door.

"Johnny, again," he mumbled under his breath. Then, he sat back down on his bench, and started trying to make sense of it all.

A little while later, Evie came outside, smiling and cheerful, as if nothing had happened. She could tell that David was not in a good mood.

"You still sore about last night?" she asked.

"Why did you do that to me?" David asked sincerely.

"Quit being a baby," she said. "I thought you'd get a kick out of listening in. That's what friends do, isn't it?"

"We're not exactly, just friends. And you're the only one looking for love, someplace else."

"Well, I thought you were out there looking, too."

"We were on a date last night," David replied, still confused about her behavior. "At the very least, you could have told the guy to call you back another time. You sat there for 20-minutes, flirting with this dude, while I was pissed, and ranting about it."

"Yes, you did over-react, quite a bit," she said.

"Over-react? Me?" David defended, his voice rising.

"When you moved into the other room," she explained sternly. "We became just roommates. We weren't in an exclusive relationship, anymore."

"No, you weren't in an exclusive relationship anymore," David said. "I'm still in an exclusive relationship, because you are the only love-interest in my life. But, I didn't realize until last night, that you had already started looking for someone else."

"Well, maybe you should start looking, too?"

"I didn't move all the way up here, to Sandy, to be just roommates with you. I moved here to be with the woman I love, and that I intended to be with, for the rest of my life."

"Well, I don't see how that is possible, with our religious differences," she responded. "You don't believe in Satan, and you will never accept Jesus as your savior."

"Jesus? You're going to talk about Jesus?" David was getting agitated. "It wasn't Jesus that took you to that concert the other night... that was Johnny."

Evie froze like a statue.

"How did you find out about that?" she demanded.

"I wasn't sure, until just now, when you told me…"

"Johnny and me are just friends, but I didn't think you'd understand," she defended.

"Yeah, especially about the three-hours you spent together, after the concert was over."

David turned and walked back into the house. A short time later, Evie left, saying that she was going to her sister's house, to visit. David was just glad to see her go.

David was still in love with her, even after all she had done to him, but at the same time, he hated her for it. His heart was a confused mess. He felt anger and hurt, but always, those first few weeks came back into his mind, and all he could think of, was how happy they had both been. But the questions kept running through his mind.

Had Evie been pretending to love him, all along? Was this really all about her trying to make Johnny jealous? And why, why did Evie and Johnny really split up? Did Evie have this whole "roommate thing" in mind from the very start? Was there even one minute, when she had seriously considered marrying David?

Surely this had nothing to do with religion, did it? They had never really talked about religion, just those times Evie got to jump up on her soapbox and preach to him. He never got to respond, and he never told her, even a small bit, about his own beliefs. All she really knew about it, is that he did not believe in the Devil, and he did support the scientific proof of evolution. Those two things were all Evie knew about his theology. And, apparently, those two things were very wicked and evil. "Where do I go from here?" he asked aloud.

Evie called later, from Brandon's house, she claimed. But after she had lied to him about going to the concert with "Judy," and it was really Johnny, David realized, he no longer believed anything she told him. His trust in her was completely gone.

"It's raining out here," she said. "…and Brandon has to stay home with the kids. So, I'm going to stay here and babysit, so he can go to the bar with Chrissie tonight."

"Yeah, whatever," David mumbled. "David, I know you are still upset, but I didn't do anything wrong. We were split up. We were not a couple anymore. You need to stop seeing us as a couple, and see us just as friends, and roommates. Like I do…"

"Yeah, I get that," David responded. "But you've had a couple of weeks to get used to it…I just found out about it last night."

"Well, that's your fault. We talked about it."

"Whatever," David said flatly. "So, I guess I'll see you tomorrow?"

"Yes, I should be home sometime after breakfast. I have to do my laundry. And my bedroom and bathroom are in bad need of cleaning. Are you okay?"

"Not really," David replied. "It was kind of a shock, last night. But, now that I know exactly where I stand, with you, it'll just take some getting used to."

"Best friends forever, right?" Evie echoed her favorite mantra.
"Yeah, right," David said sarcastically. "Maybe another night alone, is what I need to sort all this stuff out... I'll see you tomorrow."

Evie said her "good-bye," and they disconnected the call. David just stood staring at the phone, for a few seconds.

"Looks like I'd better just get used to the idea of being just roommates, with Evie," he thought. "We did agree that, if things didn't work out, we'd still remain roommates. And, things obviously didn't work out, so roommates, it is. The lease is up in five-months, and I will not renew it."

"You win, Evie," he said out loud. "You win. You've got your Johnny, and a roommate, too."

When Evie got home, David did his best to only think of her as a friend. But it was very hard for him. When she reached into the refrigerator, to get herself a beer, David grabbed one, also. They both worked at keeping the conversation on non-controversial topics, but it was difficult to do. And, David told her so.

"It's just really, really hard for me to look at you, and just see you as a friend," He confessed.

Evie stepped into his arms, for a hug.

336

"Look, neither one of us wanted it to end up this way," she said. "But it is, what it is, and we have to accept that."

"Well, you accepted it almost two weeks ago," he responded. "And, I just accepted it, the night before last. So, just give me a little time to get used to it, that's all."

"Of course," she said, pulling his head down, so she could kiss his forehead.

"Oh, and I thought about it, a lot," David said, "…I mean, a lot, today. And, since we're both on the lease, I'll stay here, as roommates, until the end of the lease…no more."

"And then you're leaving? I thought you loved this little place?"

"No, I loved sharing this little place, with the woman I intended to marry," he said firmly. "I told you, I came out here for one reason, and only one reason – to be with you, forever. And now that you've taken marriage between us, off the table, there's nothing to keep me here, except that lease. When it's done, well, so am I."

Evie pulled away, walking toward her bedroom, then she stopped and turned back to David.

"You know, that's really sweet of you to stay, I mean, if that's the way you feel," Evie said sincerely. "At least it will give me time to find a new roommate, or pay off a few of my bills, so I can afford this place, on my own."

"Glad to help," he said with a forced smile.

"I'm going to get my laundry started," she said, as she walked into her bedroom.

The next few days were cautious, at best, for David. His heart was still broken, and even though he knew that he should hate her, for all the mean things she had done to him, he still loved her. He could still not get over the joy they had shared those first few weeks…until she started listening to her family, he thought.

"Her family must really like Johnny," he thought. They were always talking about him, when they didn't know David could hear them. "Like that sister, Evie had on speaker-phone the other morning."

"What'd she say? 'Is Johnny still on the wagon?'" he said out loud, mimicking a woman's voice. Suddenly, he stopped, and the little lightbulb in his head flickered on, as the epiphany came to him. "Wait a minute! Wait, wait, wait a minute," his mind was racing. "That's it!!"

David had learned long ago that, when he was getting involved with a subject he didn't know, he would always consult with an expert in the field…except for internet dating, of course. So, he called his older sister, who was a professor of nursing at Baylor University, in Texas. "Hi, Annie-Fanny," he said into the phone.

"Hello, Brat. What kind of trouble are you into now?" she asked with a chuckle. "What is a 'functional alcoholic?'" he asked.

"No such thing," his sister responded. "An alcoholic, is an alcoholic, is an alcoholic. Period. A lot of alcoholics use the term 'functional' to differentiate between those who work, pay bills and maintain fairly normal lives, from those who are jobless, homeless, and on skid row. That's all. But they all have the same disease, and they all require the same treatment."

David and his sister talked for nearly an hour.

The next morning, after Evie had gone to work, David called his buddy, Chance.

"So, how are you, on this fine Thursday morning, my friend?" Chance said, when he heard David's voice.

After a few minutes of chit-chat, David began to fill Chance in on his hypothesis, about why Evie and Johnny had broken up, in the first place.

"So, you see, when Johnny decided to get treatment for his alcoholism, Evie would have either had to go in for treatment with him, or she would have had to move out. Part of the treatment regimen is to change the 'drinking environment,' and that includes the people you normally associate with. If one of them is also an alcoholic, the one being treated needs to stay away from them."

"They've got to remove the temptation, right?" Chance asked.

"Pretty much," David explained. "So, apparently, when Johnny got help, he told Evie that she would have to choose between him, or the booze."

"And, she picked the booze," Chance finished.

"That's right! So, when Evie told me that she left Johnny, because he didn't want to get married, she forgot to mention that, he didn't want to be married to an alcoholic, any more than I do. And, it was his choice to end their relationship, not hers."

"That throws a whole 'nuther light on it, don't it?" Chance remarked.

"My guess is that, Evie just figured to wait around, until he fell off the wagon," David explained. "My sister, Anne, says that, in more than half of the cases, the person seeking treatment fails, and goes back to drinking. So the odds were in Evie's favor."

"So, if Johnny were to fall off the wagon, him and Evie could just pick it up, right where they left-off!" Chance interjected.

"Exactly," David said. "But, when it looked like Johnny was actually going to make it through the program, Evie had to come up with another plan…"

"So, she goes online, and meets you?" Chance asked.

"I think so," David remarked. "I'm not sure if she intended it to go so far, with me, as it went, especially not having sex with me, three different times. At least in the beginning, she was just trying to make Johnny jealous. But, when he asked Evie not to talk about me, it spoiled her little plan. How could she make him jealous, if he won't let her talk about me? Right?

"So, she comes up with this, 'best-friends-forever' crap, talks me into moving out here, with her whole idea being that we were always going to be nothing but roommates, and 'best-friends-forever.' She knew that, before I ever moved out here."

"Let me get this straight," Chance said. "You think she never had any plans to marry you, not even in the beginning?"

"Nope. None. That's why she came up with that story, right in the beginning. When she told her family that we were just roommates. She wasn't lying to them…she was only lying to me!"

"Damn," Chance said. "That's cold-blooded."

"Oh, I might have swayed her there, for a few weeks," David admitted. "Those first few weeks I lived in Sandy, were magical, and she felt it, too. But her family was so much against me…" "Or, so much for Johnny?" Chance added.

"Right, either way. So, they are all telling her what a mistake her relationship with me is, and despite us having a warm, loving relationship, she started to believe them! And, that's why she suddenly got mean, at the dinner party, and started arguments with me."

"Whatever she was doing, to get Johnny back, wasn't working, so she had to turn up the heat?"

"Exactly. She picks a fight with me, and when I start hammering back, she goes to Johnny for sympathy."

"And her whole, 'saving myself until after marriage' thing?"

"Just a ploy, so she can tell Johnny, and her family, that 'We're not sleeping together, we're just roommates.' But, now she has to explain how we 'did the nasty' three separate times! It's all a part of her 'I'm a good, Christian-woman' act."

"It's all an act?"

"Oh, Hell yeah, it's all just an act," David explained. "Just because she can quote the Bible, and she listens to Christian talk-radio, that doesn't make her a Christian. To be a Christian, she would actually have to live the Bible, not just talk about it. She's an alcoholic, and the only God she truly worships, is alcohol. For Evie, all that Bible stuff is just a cover-story, anyway." "No shit?" Chance asked.

"Look, I don't believe in the Devil, but Evie does. And, as far as I am concerned, every time she takes a drink of beer, she is giving Satan another blow-job. She might say she loves Jesus, but it is Satan's cock she has in her mouth."

"So, what about the guy from Rancher's Only? How does he fit in?"

"I've got no idea…unless she wanted to keep someone handy, in case I got pissed and moved out?"

"That's possible, I guess," Chance agreed. "They call that a 'backup' guy."

"You know what?" David remarked. "That's exactly what Evie called him! I swear!! The night we were fighting about the phone call, she said she thought it was a good idea, to keep a 'back-up guy' around, in case things didn't work out, between us."

"Holy shit," Chance exclaimed. "Now, it is all making a whole lot more sense."

"Well, apparently her plan worked," David said. "Because Johnny took her to a concert last week…and Evie didn't get home until three hours after it was over!"

"So, what're you gonna do, about all this?" "Nothing,"
David responded.

"What do you mean by that?" Chance asked. "Just what I said…nothing. She beat me, she made Johnny jealous. I guess, after she turned me into a monster, and a raving lunatic, she had a lot to get sympathy for. Now, she's back on 'friendly' terms with her ex. And, I am stuck with a lease, I signed, that lasts for another five months. What else can I do?"

"You can pack up right now, and get the Hell out of there, is what. Screw the lease."

"That's what my sister said, too. But hey, I'm the one who fell for her line of bullshit, and I signed the lease."

"Yeah, but you didn't know that she was lying to you…" "Hell, Evie probably didn't even know she was lying to me," David remarked.

"How's that?" Chance asked, confused.

"My sis told me, alcoholics spin such an intricate web of lies, that they often forget the truth, and actually start to believe their own lies are true! Anne told me that, often-times, they can even pass a polygraph test."

"No shit?"

"No shit."

"Man, oh, man," Chance said. "What have you gone and gotten yourself into?"

"I asked myself the same question," David laughed. "But, hey, I'm a big boy. I made a mistake, and I fell in love with the wrong woman. Now, I've got to pay the price. It's just for another five months…"

"And, you're okay with that?"

"What choice do I have?" David replied. "Besides, it hasn't been so bad these past few days. We're just acting like 'friends,' and keeping it light."

"So, you're okay with that whole, 'friends' thing, now?"

"I'm still not ready to listen to her talk about her new 'love-interests,' but so long as we treat each other with respect, we'll be fine, for the next five months."

"Ah, what the Hell," Chance said humorously. "Knowing you, you'll be back on Rancher's Only in a few days, and you'll be making coffee-dates all over Portland!"

"I don't think so, my friend," David replied sincerely. "I intend to just sit here and lick my wounds for a while! Five more months, to be exact.

Chapter 32
You are nothing more than an alcoholic Bar-Slut, Evie."

When Evie got home from work that night, she brought with her a fresh 12-pack of beer. She and David each grabbed one, and then, later, another, as they talked of ordinary things – work, weather, family – things all friends speak of, when the conversation is light.

Then, the two "roommates" had a nice dinner, washed down with another beer. After eating, Evie decided to put some music on, so, she started loading music cd's into the changer.

"I want to dance," she said, as the "oldies" rock music began to play.

"Well, I'd offer to dance with you, but I'm not sure if friends are allowed to do that?" David asked sarcastically.

"Shut-up and get over here," Evie replied. "Of course, friends dance!"

David took her in his arms, and they danced to a slow song.

"I told you, this whole 'friends' thing is still a little awkward for me, but I'll get there," David said, as they danced. "It's getting easier, every day."

"Well, since we are just friends, I guess I can tell you what happened to me Saturday night, at Chrissie's bar…"

"Wait, I thought you were babysitting Saturday night, so Brandon could go to the bar?" David asked.

"Well, I offered to watch the kids. But, Brandon said they were broke, so, he was gonna have to stay home, anyway. Then, he asked if I wanted to go? So, what the heck? I went."

"Yeah, what the heck?" David agreed, half-heartedly. "So, what happened?"

The slow song ended, and a fast, upbeat song began. David didn't feel like dancing to it, so he sat on the sofa, and Evie kept dancing, alone. "Well, this guy…one of Chrissie's regulars, I guess," Evie began. "Anyway, Chrissie called me 'Mom,' and this guy heard, so he comes over, to where me and Chrissie were standing, and he asks if I am really her mom…"

"So, what'd you tell him?"

"I told him that I was, of course," Evie continued. "So, he tells us, since Chrissie was still standing there, how great Chrissie is, as a bartender, and since I'm her mom, he wants to buy me a beer."

"That was nice of him," David said, beginning to feel uncomfortable with the direction of the conversation.

"Well, yeah, that first one was nice. He was just being polite," she said. "But then, when that one was gone, he bought me another one."

"The bastard," David said sarcastically. "Were you sitting with him? I mean, did he join you?"

"No, he was still sitting at the bar, and I was playing pool," she explained. "That's why it was starting to piss me off."

"A guy is buying you drinks, and it pissed you off?" David asked, confused.

"Well, yeah. He's a friend of Chrissie's, not mine. I didn't even know the guy," Evie explained. "And, with him buying me beers, people might have thought we were together."

"Oh, I see," David said, remembering how furious she had gotten with him, when he had told that fellow, that Evie was his wife.

David also remembered how amorous Evie was, the night he played pool with her. The way they made-out, between shots, it was an effort to keep their clothes on!

"So, he was ruining your game?" David added.

"Yeah, that's it," Evie agreed, not even catching the double-meaning of the word "game." "So, when I finished the second beer, he bought me another one. Now, that really pissed me off."

"So, what did you do?"

"Well, I was going to go over there, and tell him off," Evie explained. "That's what I intended to do, anyway."

"So, what happened?"

"Well, I'm not real sure… I must have blacked out, or something, because I don't remember any of it. But, Chrissie told me that I went over and kissed the guy."

"You what?" David was stunned. "You mean, like a little peck, to thank him for the beers?"

"No, according to Chrissie, it was a pretty passionate kiss…and she said, I was kissing him right back, so it wasn't just him, I guess. Isn't that weird?"

David was still reeling. This is not the kind of conversation he had hoped to be having with Evie. He had told her, no, begged her, not to tell him about her new love-interests! And yet, here she was, telling him about a stranger she was making-out with, in a bar.

"Weird? That's not the word I would use," David said, trying to control his anger and frustration, but with four beers in him, he was losing control. "So, you blacked out? You don't remember kissing this stranger…but your daughter tells you, that it was a passionate kiss?" "That's what she said," Evie confirmed.

"So, during this passionate kiss, where were his hands? Where were your hands?"

"Oh, it wasn't like that," Evie defended. "We were sitting right at the bar…"

"Yeah, right. But you don't remember, for sure? You blacked-out. And trust me, I know first-hand how passionate your kisses can be." David asked. "But, I think the guy really screwed up." "How do you mean?" Evie was getting angry, as well.

"Well, he bought you a couple of beers, so you go make out with him…"

"We weren't making out," Evie interrupted.

"Hey, if you're sticking your tongue down a guy's throat, then, you're making out. Plain and simple."

Evie had stopped dancing, and stood angrily with her arms crossed, glaring at David.

"So, like I was saying, if the guy had been smart, he'd have bought you a couple of shots of Fireball, instead of the beer. Then, you'd have probably given him a blow-job in the back booth, and not just a kiss."

"FUCK YOU!" Evie screamed, as she headed for her room.

"You are nothing more than an alcoholic bar-slut, Evie," David called after her. "And, that's what bar-sluts do…the more booze you buy 'em, the more sex they give you, in return. I've had a few of those blow-jobs myself, in that back booth."

She slammed her bedroom door. They both continued yelling hurtful words, since they were both quite drunk. Then, it grew quiet, and David went to the 'fridge for another beer. The music was still blasting away, in the living room, so David turned the volume down, and sat on the sofa. He was still angry, and hurt.

"I begged you not to tell me about your new love-interests," he said out loud, hoping Evie might hear his angry words. "And, somehow, you figured, that must mean, I want to hear about your slutty behavior in a bar…in front of your daughter, no less. Boy, I bet Chrissie is as proud as heck of her good little Christian mother, eh? What do you think Jesus thought, when he watched you dry-humping a stranger in the bar?"

David finally ran dry, his anger released through his venting, and he sat quietly, stewing. A few minutes later, Evie's door opened and she came out of the bedroom pulling a large, rolling suitcase. She also had a smaller make-up bag over her shoulder.

"I don't want to stay here with you, anymore," she announced. "I'm going over to Brandon's to spend the night. I'll go to work from there…" "Looks like an awfully big suitcase for an overnight trip," David observed.

"When I get off work tomorrow, I'm going to spend the weekend out at the coast, with some friends…"

"Friends?"

"A couple I know, own a cabin on the shoreline. They invited me out to spend the weekend… we do this, every year. It's just a group of friends, that's all."

"Convenient. This 'friend-weekend' just so happens, when we're having a fight…"

"No, it's not that way," Evie defended. "We've been planning this for over a month. I just didn't tell you about it, until now."

"And, of course, your best friend, Johnny, will be there, right?"

"That's none of your business," Evie snapped.

"Wait a minute," David did the math. "A month? You've been planning this romantic weekend with Johnny for a month?"

"It's not a romantic weekend. Just a group of friends, getting together, that's all…"

"A month ago, we were still together," David observed. "You and me were still a couple when you started planning this weekend-getaway with Johnny.."

"No, wait, not a month," Evie scrambled, trying to cover her tracks. "Whenever we split up, that's when she called…it was after we split up…"

"Are you sure that's the story you want to go with?" David remarked, knowing she was lying.

Evie opened the door, and stepped out onto the front porch.

"Are you planning to tell Johnny, about your slutty behavior Saturday night?"

Evie just glared at him, then she started towards her car.

"Hey, if you do, to Johnny, what you did to me, you'll have him drinking again, before the weekend is through."

Evie stopped at the bottom of the steps and turned back to David.

"I hate you," she said with fire. "You're not even my friend any more. I wish you'd just go away and leave me alone. Just get out of my life!"

Evie reached for the back door, and threw her suitcase into the car. Then, she walked around to the driver's door and opened it.

"Oh yeah, you'll throw me out now," David said. "Now that you have Johnny back, you don't need me anymore."

Evie got in, started the car, then drove away…

"So, she's having a nice, romantic weekend with Johnny, out at the coast. Now isn't that special?"

David had another beer, then passed out on the sofa.

At 7:00 a.m., David's phone beeped him awake. Normally, he turned it off, when he slept, but it was still strapped to his hip, where he had slept on the sofa, fully-clothed.

"Lemme call ya back," he whispered hoarsely to Chance. "Coffee…"

Twenty minutes later, teeth brushed, coffee in hand, David called Chance back. His head was still sore, but he felt like a new man. David launched in, immediately, with the latest twist in "The Nightmare in Sandy."

"And, then she says, 'I wish you'd just go away and leave me alone. Just get out of my life!'"

"So, why are you still there, my man?" Chance asked. "Obviously, if she wants you out of her life, she is not too concerned with the lease…"

"How could it go from being 'that-good,' to being 'that-bad,' like, overnight?" David asked.

"Hoss, let me ask you a question," Chance offered. "Like Granny used to do. She'd say, 'Look inside your heart, and listen, to what it tells you.' What does your heart say, David?"

David placed both his hands over his heart, and just sat quietly, with his eyes closed. It was only for a few seconds, but it seemed like minutes had passed.

"I need to get the Hell out of here," David said, finally.

"Then, why are you still sitting there?" Chance asked.

"Well, you see, Amigo? That, there, is the real problem…"
"What's that?"

"I have exactly $14 left in my bank account, until the 1st," David admitted. "I can get all my stuff loaded in the Mustang, but I can't go 200 miles on the gas I've got."

"I'll deposit $300 in your account, this morning, as soon as the bank opens," Chance offered. "Will that be enough?"

"Heck, yes, it will, Chief!" David said with a smile. "When Evie gets back home, sometime next week, this cowboy will be long-gone – nothing but a memory!"

"You've got that right, Hoss."

"You know, I'm actually sad to be leaving so suddenly," David said. "Now, I might never find out how this little plot Evie pulled off, will end?"

"There's only two ways it can end," Chance observed. "Since she's back on good terms with Johnny, she is either going to cause him to fall off the wagon."

"And, then Evie can live happily-drunk ever after," David interjected.

"Or, he's not going to fall of the wagon, and he'll give her the boot, once he finds out what a bar-slut she really is," Chance finished.

"Or, there's one more scenario, my friend." "Yeah, what's that," Chance asked.

"Well," David began. "She could always wake up, and realize what her drinking has cost her, and continues to cost her! Two men who loved her, and one of them, she actually loved back. Maybe she'll finally go looking for the help Johnny got? She might even seek forgiveness from God? If she can get off the booze, she can marry Johnny, and maybe, she can become that sweet little Christian woman, she always pretended to be."

"Yes, sir," Chance commented. "That would, indeed be a happy ending for Evie. Me? I'm betting she has Johnny back on the sauce, before this weekend is over! And, I'll guaran-damn-tee you, she's not going to make Johnny wait, until after they're married, to have sex!"

"You might be right, my friend. You just might be right," David agreed. "But, you know, it's just not my problem anymore. Johnny can have her…"

Two hours later, David was turning the Mustang out onto the freeway, heading back to Las Vegas! The nightmare in Sandy was finally over!

Chapter 33

*"Look inside your heart, and
Listen, to what it tells you."*

The drive from Portland to Las Vegas would take nearly twenty hours; and that's a lot of time to think. David found himself lost in the recent-past, his entire "internet dating experience." Thus far, he wasn't impressed.

From the girls who used old photos, or photos that were just plain fakes; or the ones who lied about their age or marital status; to girls who were manipulative and devious, or who simply didn't know what kind of man, or relationship, they really sought. There were good times, and laughter, but an awful lot of heartache and tears, to back it up.

And then, there were those, like Karen and Evie, who had a sickness—a disease which is treatable, like Alzheimer's or alcoholism. But, to treat them, *the person first has to admit* that they have a problem, and seek help for it.

David felt that the very worst thing he had encountered, however, was the women who *lied*, without knowing, or realizing that they were. He reflected on his "romance" with Karen, and how she had truly believed she was still the same tough, ornery cowgirl she had once been, even though her years in California had changed her. It's hard to catch someone in a lie, when they don't even know they are telling one!

Women like Evie, on the other hand, weave such intricate webs of lies and deceit, that they begin to believe the lies are *true*. David didn't know which of these was more difficult to detect?

David went back over his "rules" and his "checklist," and he was actually proud of all he had learned and applied, as far as internet-dating was concerned. They say, "Every mistake is a lesson learned," and David had surely learned a lot of lessons! And the questions on his checklist were good – but only as useful as the *honesty* of the answers given.

"I'm asking all the right questions," David surmised, "But, how does anyone know, if the girl is answering honestly?"

You don't.

He understood why so many people just assume that, every statement anyone tells them, is a lie, until it is proven true. But, David remembered something his father had told him many years ago: "You can go through life trusting everyone, or trusting *no one*. If you trust everyone you meet, you will often be disappointed, and taken-advantage of. But if you trust no one, you will spend your entire life *alone*."

David chose to trust everyone, at least until they gave him a reason not to. It was in his nature, in his heart, to always think the *best* of people. Perhaps that's why he kept rushing so quickly into these silly romances? And, it's why each and every one of those women, who lied to him, so easily took advantage of him.

"*How do you have a positive 'internet dating experience?*'" David thought, as he reviewed his online-dating history, and he thought of the women he had "met" online.

"Charlene," the "Ghana-Girl," who wasn't even a girl, signed up for internet dating so she/he could make money off of love-sick American men. David had sent "her" $250… so for "Charlene" it had, indeed, been a *positive* dating experience!

Kim, the married lady from Texas, got on the internet to have wild sexual adventures, with someone *other than* her husband. And for her, it was certainly a positive dating experience!

Tina McNabb, who was using her daughter's picture to improve her own self-worth? She spent two weeks being courted, wooed, and feeling loved, and she got a new pink cell phone! Another positive experience!

Rachel got her loafing shed built for her horses, and her water pump rebuilt, for a pot of coffee and a tuna sandwich. Bingo! Another good dating experience!

And Evie, master manipulator, got a new place to live, and she got her ex-boyfriend back. She got _exactly what she was after_, when she signed up for her internet-dating experience.

David began to see a pattern! The people who were out there, with _"evil intentions,"_ were the ones having the most _positive_ internet dating experiences! Those dreaded people, who prey on the lonely, were having the _best luck,_ with online-dating!

There were others, of course, such as Kendra, up in Kelso, who was looking for a _younger_ man. She had to throw David back, and go looking again. And, Jolene, who only wanted to find a casual dating partner… for her to have a successful dating experience, she would only have to first _read_ the gentleman's profile.

Then, there was Jenny Kendall… Doctor Jennie Kendall, the air force doctor who got stationed in Afghanistan. David realized he was smiling, when he thought about her.

"Neither one of us had a good internet dating experience, there," he thought. "We never even got to meet in person, before the Air Force sent her halfway around the world. Boy, I sure wish she had stuck around!"

As David drove the Mustang toward Las Vegas, he thought also of the many conversations he had had with his old buddy, Chance. They had been through a lot together, but the words Chance had said to him most recently, kept echoing through his mind.

"Look inside your heart, and listen, _to what it tells you."_

David remembered Chance saying that his grandmother is the one who first spoke those words. She had been an Indian shaman, a "medicine-woman," and a holy seer. David had a lot of respect for the Indian beliefs, or theology, as it were. Unlike Christians or Jews, Indian beliefs were not "fear-based," and were founded on humans being in harmony with the universe, and having a love for mother earth, and father sun. And the American Indians knew that the heart, was the key to the soul.

Driving into the night, David grew quiet and calm, his thoughts of internet-dating having played themselves out. He placed a hand on his heart, and he felt the comfort of his own heartbeat. And, he *listened…*

"Love is all around you, in every living thing. Give your love to all you encounter, and your love will come back to you, bigger and stronger than that which you gave."

David's hand was still on his heart, and he was content just to feel the beat. When he heard, or felt, those words David understood what Granny meant by, *"Listen, to what it tells you."* His *heart* was speaking to him!

"But what about finding that perfect woman to grow old with? To build my little ranch?" David asked himself. Then, he answered his own questions, when he listened to his heart.

"You are going home, to your family, and closest friends. They all love you, and they need the wisdom of your years. Why look for a woman to love, when all the love you have, comes from your own family? The love of family is pure and unconditional love, there is no greater joy than that."

"God?" David was confused. Where were these answers coming from? It was probably just his own subconscious thoughts, his own repressed ideas, now given light. Or perhaps he had touched-lightly on his own alter-ego? There could have been a number of rational, and logical, explanations for the "voice" David heard. But David knew, it came from his heart.

"So, what will I do next? Where am I going? Is there a point to all these terrible internet dating experiences?" David asked. He thought. He waited. He *listened.*

"Seek to find your highest *purpose, in life. Once you find that, you will have no more questions to ask. How? Look where you have been, to find out where you are going. Often, to find the* highest *purpose, you must first experience the* lowest.*"*

"Well, I certainly have experienced the *lowest*, so far as internet dating goes, anyway!" David quipped.

"Look <u>beyond</u> the internet, look at <u>life</u>. *What you will see is the Yin and the Yang of eternal order. What is good, without bad? It is nothing*

at all. What is right, without wrong? It simply is. What is beauty, without ugliness? It is just a form. A thing, is nothing, until an opposite exists, by which to compare it. And to know one, you must first experience the other."

David dwelled for a moment, on his "goal," for the past year, while he was being roughed-up by online dating. But, it wasn't his *goal* he was searching for, it was his *purpose*.

"Well, simply stated, my *purpose* was to find a little ranch somewhere," David explained. "So I could live out my remaining years without being a burden on my family, and I could maintain my independence and dignity. And, I want to *share that ranch*, with a woman who loves me, as much as I love her."

"And what are you willing to give up, to live such a dream?" the voice asked.

"Give up? I've lost *everything* in this crazy quest. I've already given up *everything* it took me a lifetime to acquire… my house, my car, all my fancy appliances, everything. And, I am right back where I started, but flat-broke."

David's mind wandered, again, across the miles his journey had taken him, on this internet-quest. He remembered everything he had sold, to try to pay for a new life, in a new place. He had destroyed his old life, hoping to find a new one. Then, the idea hit him… a little at a time!

"Set aside your quest, for a <u>woman</u> to share *your dream, and think only of the dream,"* the Voice told him.

"It isn't the *woman*," he thought. "It's the life…*the ranch*…<u>that</u> should be my purpose."

And, once he realized that he should be looking for *a place*, and not a person, his mind began to race.

"How can you make it bigger? How can you fill it with love, for <u>all</u> living things?"

"You know, many, many times," David said aloud, "…over the years I spent in rodeo, I met old rodeo champions, heroes of mine, who were selling their trophy saddles and buckles, just to try to make ends meet. I always wished there was something more I could do for them… so sad, to see them wind-up that way.

"Instead of just building *my own* little retirement ranch, I can build one that's big enough to share with a lot of these old rodeo champs, who have fallen on hard times! That's it, a retirement home for old cowboys, and for old horses, too. That'll give the old-timers something to do, taking care of the old horses, and even old cow dogs.

"We can have an arena, and have some cows to throw ropes at. Yeah, a working cattle ranch, run by a bunch of old cowboys. We'll have a nice fire-pit, where we can pass around the guitar, or just tell old rodeo stories. And we'll need to build a chapel…"

David was never one to "think-small," and, as his imagination began to build a new dream, in his mind, it kept getting bigger, and better.

"And we'll need a big bunkhouse, with private rooms, and maybe a little motel, so when their families come visit, we can put them up. The families can go riding, roping, or just feed cows, pigs and chickens!"

David was amazed at the vision, *the new dream,* of a place for old cowboys, including himself, to live out their lives with dignity and purpose…and fun. But, he also knew, it wasn't just a place to *live*, it was also a place to die.

"With old people, there comes a time when they can no longer live, without assistance, where will you send them to die?" his heart asked. David's *vision* grew even larger, yet.

"Shoot, if we put in a medical facility, a nursing home and a hospice, that would cover it. But, what the heck do I know, about those things? I'd need a partner with a medical background to run that part of it. And even if I found someone, how would we pay for it? Those kinds of medical facilities will cost more than a cattle ranch can earn…"

As the sky began to brighten with the coming of dawn, David's thoughts went back to his new "purpose in life," and the retirement ranch. He knew that he could not build it, all at once, so he just decided to take it one step at a time.

In his mind, he began drawing up plans, for the grounds, the cross-fencing, the arena, the bunkhouse…everything a working ranch needs to be successful. He would start with the barn, and build out, from there. After the barn, the corrals and fencing would be next.

But, even those things cost money, *he no longer had*. He knew what he wanted, but he had no clue how to pay for it. Suddenly, the sun peeked over the Eastern mountains, and a single ray of sunshine filled the Mustang. Oddly, David did not even squint, as the sun warmed his face…and an idea leapt into his mind.

"That's it! A 501(c)3, non-profit organization! That's what we need!"

David knew that, if he founded a non-profit organization, he could take donations from individuals, and also from big corporate rodeo sponsors, like Justin, Wrangler and a variety of beer sponsors. They could hold fund-raising rodeos and gymkhanas, even fancy gala's or balls.

And, David thought, if they could interest the Professional Rodeo Cowboys Assn., it was possible they could even get enough money to fund the medical facilities. The PRCA was, in effect, just a labor union for cowboys, and most unions had a retirement plan, so why not the PRCA? And part of that plan would include funding for a home for the indigent, including assisted living and hospice care.

"What the heck do I know about building medical facilities?" David wondered. "But, 'we're not there, yet.' When it is *time* to start designing the medical portion of the ranch, that's when I'll worry about it. By then, I'll find a *partner* who has the knowledge, to get it done right!"

And, the best part, David thought, was that he was finally *done* with internet-dating! David had been thinking about his new dream, the retirement ranch, for more than an hour. He knew that, he had enough on his plate now, to keep him busy for years, without having to worry about finding a woman on-line to share it with. "I'll focus on building this ranch," David thought, cheerfully. "And, the *right woman* can find *me*!"

David was lost in his thoughts, incredibly overjoyed that he had found a new purpose in life, and he was, already, on the road to making it happen. He was already figuring out how to make it a "family" project, too. He'd enlist the help of his children and adult-grandchildren, to build web-sites, design marketing strategies, as well as coming up with a fund-raising plan.

The ringing of his cell phone startled him. David looked at the number on his caller ID. "Unknown caller – Austin, Texas," was all it said.

"Hello," David answered, curious about who the caller was.

"Hi…Darren?" a female voice inquired, with a slight Texas-drawl.

"No, this is David Remington. Who am I talking to?" The lady-caller laughed.

"Oh, my God, David, this is so funny! I was trying to call my brother, Darren, and I must have hit your number on the speed dial by mistake! They're right next to each other. This is Jenny…Jenny Kendall?"

"*Doctor* Jenny Kendall?" David asked incredulously. "Where are you?"

"I'm at Andrews…just got off a transport from Afghanistan. I'm going from here, back to Austin, for two-weeks leave with my family."

"Where will you go from there?" he asked, but somehow, he already knew the answer.

"Well, I've only got a year left until I retire, so the Air Force wants me to work in the Desert Warfare Center, teaching medical people how to establish and maintain mobile hospitals."

"Isn't the Desert Warfare Center located at Nellis?"

"That's right, I'll be coming back to Las Vegas in a few weeks," she said. "I know I should have just deleted your number, when I shipped out last year, but I couldn't bring myself to do it. Something made me keep it."

"I am awfully glad you did," David confessed.

"Well, surely, you are not still single?" she asked hopefully.

"Well, actually, I am," he replied.

"It's funny, how I always felt that there was something special about you, and yet, we've never even met in person!" Jenny said, smiling.

"I know, right?" David laughed. "I can't tell you how many times I imagined what *that night* would have been like, if we had been able to meet at the Peppermill…"

"Me, too," she said demurely. "Can I tell you something? No, it's silly."

"Please, go ahead, and tell me."

"This past year has been a living Hell for me," she said quietly. "Many times, at night, I just cried. But I always kept your picture, on my phone, and every time I looked at it, it made me smile, and made me think of things that might have been… or things that, *could be,* someday. You helped me survive out there."

"This past year has been Hell for me, too," David confessed. "As soon as you get back to Vegas, we're going to the Peppermill, and we're going to pick up, right where we left off! What do you think?" "You know," she said. "If this works out, between us, we'll be able to tell people that we met on an internet dating site, and that we knew each other for *more than a year,* before we actually met in person. Isn't that weird?"

"Not really," David chuckled. "Sometimes, God works in weird ways! And I'm sure that this was all a part of His big plan, don't you agree?"

"Yes I do," she replied honestly. "I really do…"

"How about that?" David said smiling, after they hung-up. "Maybe, just maybe? My Internet Dating Nightmare, will have a happy ending, yet?"

The End